UNDER
THE
MOON

UNDER THE MOON

JANE BUCHAN

WINTER BLOOMS
Vermont

Winter Blooms
56 Norway Road
Greensboro Bend
Vermont 05842

Cataloging-in-Publication data

Buchan, Jane, 1945-
Under the moon / Jane Buchan. – 30th anniversary ed.
p. ; cm.
ISBN 978-1-896760-03-2 (pbk. : alk. paper)
ISBN 978-1-896760-02-5 (ebook)

1. Older people – Toronto (Ont.) – Fiction. 2. Painters – Toronto (Ont.) – Fiction. 3. Long-term care facilities – Toronto (Ont.) – Fiction. I. Title.

Publishers Note on the 2013 Edition Text Changes: As I created an electronic copy of the 1983 edition of *Under the Moon*, I noticed a few stylistic errors begging to be changed. As weak verbs, leaden sentences, and ambiguous meanings presented themselves, I asked myself the big question: Do I honour every word I and my editor at M&S chose thirty years ago, or do I, with the benefit of three decades of writing practice, lend my younger self a hand and clean up the manuscript? I chose the latter. I love Edna and want to honour her original story, but if I were to sit down today to immerse myself in retirement-home and nursing-home issues, I have no doubt I would write a very different novel. In spite of my evolution in understanding, I didn't want to dishonor Edna by altering her story significantly. Instead of a complete rewrite, I chose to leave her story as I initially wrote it while doing my best to tidy her up for this, her second outing. It has been my intention to make these changes subtly, without distorting the themes, plot, and characters of the first edition. If I have failed in this endeavour, I have only myself to blame.

Jane Buchan/Winter Blooms
September 2013

For
Anne Woodall Durst,
mother, grandmother, great grandmother
and wizard

And . . .

For
women and men everywhere
who are doing their best to age authentically,
with power, love, creativity, and joy

Under the Moon, Thirtieth Anniversary Edition
Author's Introduction

I first began to "hear" and "see" Edna and Elizabeth when I was researching retirement and long-term care facilities for my great aunts shortly after I moved to Toronto in the summer of 1973. Their need for information and their desire to move to a retirement home coincided with my enrolment in the English Specialists' Faculty of Education course at the University of Toronto (FEUT). To meet the major-project requirements for this course, I opted for a creative treatment of educational issues affecting learners of reading and writing skills in non-academic high schools. At the end of this course work, I had my Specialist's Certificate for teaching senior English and something else as well – the germ of a novel that would, after many revisions, be published as *Under the Moon* by McClelland & Stewart some ten years later.

When I began my research into the worlds of similarly warehoused adolescents and seniors, I was a single, childless twenty-seven year-old, disaffected PhD student who had returned to teaching. When M&S published *Under the Moon* ten years later, my life was very different. I was married, mothering my two beautiful children, and most days writing and revising *Under the Moon* during early mornings, nap times, and evenings after my children's bedtime.

Under the Moon found readers at a time when scandal after scandal broke regarding long-term care abuses in Ontario. After a few changes to by-laws and supervision intended to address neglectful and unsafe conditions, public interest waned and the novel's readers dwindled until, in 1988, it went out of print. Had I followed that story with another "more marketable" tale (my publisher's suggestion), *Under the Moon* might have continued to garner readers through association with a more commercial story. This was not how things turned out. I was writing my second novel when life intervened and I resumed my teaching career.

Despite my shift in professions, I remained very aware of the conditions in nursing homes because I continued to spend time with my great aunts and the other women I was closest to – my grandmother, mother, and aunt. Seeing the world through my aging family members' eyes, I couldn't forget Edna, *Under the Moon*'s protagonist and driving force. Edna's ability to see the positive shifts that were possible in the worst situations, and her joy in helping others not only see these possibilities but manifest them, continued to reflect the very best of my relatives' approaches to life.

Fast forward from *Under the Moon*'s initial publication in the early eighties to present-day Vermont. During the spring semester of 2013, I became aware of a number of tragic situations in long-term care facilities while researching possible topics for students in the writing courses I was teaching at the Community College of Vermont. These contemporary news stories suggested that the same issues and procedures plaguing Ontario nursing homes and chronic-care hospitals back in the seventies and eighties continue to distress residents, families, and long-term care staff across North America today.

Neglect resulting from over-medicating clients—what I learned in my 1970's research is termed chemical restraint — continues in most facilities. The widespread use of convenient, over-processed food robs residents of the benefits of consciously prepared fresh foods as well as the joy of participating in food choices and food preparation. Rules to support facility routines such as early waking procedures continue to ignore the natural sleep cycles of those receiving care. Restrictive programs in hard-to-access buildings prevent older adults from participating in intergenerational relationships beyond institutional walls. Few facilities make Martin Buber's I-Thou relationships a priority.

Too often as we age we are expected to surrender our sense of agency because the lens through which we view aging is a disease-oriented one. This lens distorts reality because it assumes that once we reach a certain age we enter a period of steep and inevitable decline that prevents us from caring for ourselves and contributing to the life of our communities. In this view, as if a switch is flipped, we become unsafe, incompetent, and useless at some arbitrarily chosen age. This is the propaganda of an ageist culture. We are challenged to find alternatives to this negative view of aging, but they do exist.

Today, people involved in designing the best living arrangements for older people keep the twin desires for autonomy and engagement central to their vision. In stellar homes designed for living as well as dying, schedules honour individual rhythms of wakefulness and sleep. Kitchen practices honour the human need for unprocessed, real foods required to satisfy a diversity of tastes as well as the innate human desire to be intimately involved in choosing and preparing food. The most accommodating buildings let in light and fresh air, house diverse populations and pets, and are welcoming to a variety of visitors. The very best homes are so site and population specific that they form a natural part of the greater community. Daily life in such places is designed to meet our basic human needs for stimulation, reflection, and contemplation as well as physical wellness. Although such homes are rare, they do exist.

Many care facilities currently invite pets to visit. In some of the most progressive, residents are invited to foster animals on site. Music events, art classes, dramatic readings, dance classes, and other arts programs that nourish the spirit and enliven conversation to the last moment of life are chosen by residents and reflect a variety of tastes and interests. I'm sure some wonderfully creative group is, at the moment of this writing, considering how we might evolve a form of intentional intergenerational living on a large enough parcel of land to create community and build skills in a Permaculture environment that addresses poverty and sustainability while supporting positive human and non-human interactions regardless of age.

Edna and her best friend, Elizabeth, along with a few of the novel's other characters, taught and continue to teach me how important it is to imagine and manifest ways to live together and separately that nurture respectful and loving interdependence to our last breath. In spite of the novel's positive message about aging creatively and vibrantly, *Under the Moon*'s characters discover the joys of agency only after they endure the deep losses experienced by the old in a culture that devalues the aging process and hates old age. In the spirit of adolescent acting out, the novel's characters shoplift, swear, and break rules to express their outrage against the ageist culture that holds them captive. When I first met these characters, I understood their rage. After a day of teaching and visiting with my aunts, I would catch myself ranting about what was wrong with warehousing and institutionalizing the young and the old instead of doing something positive to help to transform the situations I knew could and should change.

In those days, as I was navigating my personal transition from late adolescence to adulthood, writing *Under the Moon* restored my sense of agency as effectively as painting portraits restores the fictional Edna's. Over time I learned that we cannot possibly address every problem that comes to our attention. What we can do is light our candles to dispel the darkness in one or two dark corners in our immediate vicinity. Doing what we can do, faithfully and with love, rewards us with a marvelous sense of peace.

The choice is ours. We may choose to make a positive contribution to the attitudes, beliefs, and practices that will affect us personally when we are older adults, or we may choose to self medicate with food, drugs, television, or other distractions while waiting for someone else to make the cultural changes we know need to be made. The second choice is a poor one because it inevitably leaves us feeling helpless, angry, and physically sick. The first choice brings joy, amazing vitality, and purpose to our lives.

There is no right way to grow old joyfully. In fact, there are as many ways to accomplish this feat in our current hostile-to-aging culture as there are inventive, creative, energetic, resourceful, and loving people who want to age well and help others do so also. Because of my birth date in 1945, I find myself on the cusp of what our culture calls Baby Boomers, a population demographic born in the mid-to-late forties, fifties and early sixties that is now aging into the fifth and sixth decades of life. Not surprisingly, boomers are thinking about aging issues a good deal of the time.

Generally speaking, boomers have had the opportunity – and responsibility – to participate in transforming attitudes to race, gender, nature, and peace by asking a fundamental question very early in life: Do we learn how to live in harmony with other humans and the natural world or do we dominate and exploit what we can as if there are no inherent interrelationships among people, other species, and our shared home that we are required to nurture and protect.

Today, some boomers (often those most visible in dominant-culture media) abdicate responsibility for answering this question, choosing instead to make participation in the consumer culture we helped to invent and continue to perfect a priority. Far more of us, however less visible, remain hopeful, engaged, and committed to nurturing the balance essential to sustainable, fulfilling experiences with people and the natural world at every stage of life.

In the eighties, at least in my part of the world, we weren't talking about shamanism, but we were talking about consciousness raising and its empowering effects as we learned to dismantle exclusive language and practice entrenching our patriarchal power system. Firemen became firefighters, policemen police officers, these new titles making it possible for little girls as well as little boys to see themselves as heroic people who might help others in distress. These may appear to be insignificant changes in language use and yet their effects are so profound that they were and are belittled by those determined to continue to exclude women, people of colour, and diverse minority groups from active roles in crafting democratic policies in government, education, religion, business, and the arts. When we are members of an elite group in an undemocratic system, we belittle what threatens to diminish our power. Despite past and present belittlement, these tiny and seemingly insignificant changes from exclusive to more inclusive language, along with computer advances that would eventually lead to cyberspace initiation and support of world-wide human rights and democratic movements, are the fruits of transformation, the shaman's work.

Edna doesn't call herself a shaman as she undergoes her personal transformation, recognizes her personal power, and embraces her opportunities to effect change. She calls herself a painter. I call myself a teacher and writer. You may call yourself a nurse, physician, server, parent, student, CEO, technician, or any of the myriad titles we give ourselves to make our interests and abilities clear to ourselves and others. Whatever skills we have, when we use them to effect changes that improve life for everyone, we are practicing the art of transformation, the work of the shaman, whether we use the term or not.

I hope reading about Edna's shamanic adventure will inspire readers to effect changes that contribute to vibrant, intergenerational communities of citizens all over the world. In 2006, the International Network for the Prevention of Elder Abuse (IPNEA) invited the world's citizens to participate in the first World Elder Abuse Awareness Day (WEAAD). Organizers inspired diverse communities to mark the day in their own way, and under this aegis many municipalities and private citizens formed WEAAD committees to bring awareness to specific aging issues. Some seven years later, communities continue to mark WEAAD with fundraisers, conferences, information sessions, and the like. I would like *Under the Moon* to be part of the growing movement to raise awareness regarding the indignities older adults suffer because of ignorance, greed, and fear of aging. My hope is that Edna's story will inspire readers to explore intergenerational ways of living together and separately that add to the general pool of wisdom about how to age vibrantly, creatively, and sustainably wherever we may live on this beautiful planet Earth.

At first blush, dismantling our mindsets in order to reinvent how we view aging may seem impossible but the impossible becomes possible when we remember that every journey begins with a single step. We can begin our journeys into transformational work with the care facilities in our individual neighbourhoods. Once we know what's out there, we can use the web to explore supports for empowered, participatory aging, including INPEA, founded in 1997 and located on the web at www.inpea.net. Canadians will find information specific to Canadian resources at the National Initiative on Care of the Elderly (NICE) at www.nicenet.ca. Americans and Canadians will find reliable sources of investigative journalism serving the public interest on a variety of subjects, including aging issues, at www.propublica.org. Individual communities often create watchdog groups such as I discovered in Toronto in my early days of research. A caution: wherever your first step may lead you, choose to place your attention on what might be rather than on the negative situations so prevalent today. See what's out there, do your grieving, and then, as Edna does, focus on the possible and howl for your pack. In an amazingly short time you will find your energies blending with the unstoppable transformational force that is manifesting positive living and dying circumstances for people all over the world.

Changing our cultural attitudes to aging is not something we can leave to others. It is our right, our responsibility, and our privilege to create stimulating, sustainable communities for ourselves and for people of every age. Every one of us, on some level, longs for our individual human life to serve some higher purpose. Participating in cultural transformation is that higher purpose. Effecting this kind of massive change is not as daunting as it may first appear once we summon the courage to begin and remember that we are not alone in this or any of the inevitable movements that come into being to serve life on this beautiful planet. And boomers, those with the most to give and to gain in the movement to transform our attitudes to aging and old age, are millions strong. We are energetic, well educated, resourceful, and inspired, especially when we catch the scent of injustice on the wind. Let us always remember, each of us alive today is invited to learn the shaman's art of transformation. Like Edna, let us accept this invitation with relish and set to work.

If you are moved to do so, please send along your personal experiences of positive agency to jane@winterblooms.net or post them on the Winter Blooms blog at www.winterblooms.net. Sharing our experiences of positive agency reminds us that every person's energy, imagination, and loving kindness is necessary for cultural transformation. Because we are in this work together, we cannot fail.

Jane Buchan
September 2013

At last they come to where Reflection sits, - that
strange old woman, who has always one elbow on
her knee, and her chin in her hand, and who steals
Light out of the past to shed on the future.

Olive Schreiner
Dreams: The Lost Joy

PART ONE

SUNSET LODGE

ONE

Diana Mallory walked into the hushed foyer of Sunset Lodge happy to begin what she hoped would prove a fertile assignment. On the foyer's sofa, four dainty women quietly chatted about the weather. Mesmerized by the unusual sight of a young woman in grey knickers and black riding boots in their retirement home, these women halted their conversations mid-sentence, the way birds do when startled by the sudden appearance of a cat. Receiving this attention with equanimity, Diana addressed the woman behind the information desk. "I'm looking for Edna Carver. What's her room number, please?"

The woman behind the desk answered, "Seven-o-one," in a peculiarly hollow tone of voice that conveyed nothing of her emotions. She wore grey-tinted lenses that obscured her eyes and further prevented Diana from discerning what the woman might be feeling about this unscheduled visit. "Would you like me to page her?" the woman asked in the same odd tone. "Is she expecting you?"

Diana braced against an unexpected chill. "That won't be necessary," she said, doing her best to match the woman's cold civility. She turned to find the elevator, but not before observing the fat white scar scrawled across the woman's neck and the green plastic nameplate above her left breast:

BERNICE WILSON, SUNSET LODGE MANAGER.

Inside the elevator, Diana took out her notebook and wrote the woman's name and title in confident script, then returned these tools of her trade to the outside pocket of her bag. As she completed this comforting routine, she felt a return to her usual equilibrium.

When the elevator doors wheezed open on the seventh floor, the young writer hesitated for a moment, surveying the long hallway before her. Edna Carver's door was the second from the elevator, directly opposite a large open room that permitted the afternoon sunshine to illuminate a small rectangle of the otherwise dusky hall. Edna's door was ajar. Diana rapped lightly a couple of times, inadvertently opening the door a few inches more.

Two women, one splayed across a rumpled bed, the other relaxed on the lap of a cane-backed rocker, broke off their conversation to look the young woman over. Diana made a similar assessment of them. The woman on the bed appeared to be quite tall, her dark-grey hair severely knotted at the top of her head creating a no-nonsense demeanor. Diana guessed she might be in her sixties or perhaps her seventies, she couldn't be sure. The woman in the rocker, smaller and plumper, with short, softly curled hair, looked older than her companion, and her too-large, maroon-coloured dress contrasted sharply with her pale face, blue eyes, and white hair. The tall woman's complexion, high by comparison and dominated by a pair of shrewd brown eyes, was an even match for the navy dress she wore.

Diana smiled. "Please excuse my intrusion. I'm Diana Mallory," she said. "I believe one of you is Edna Carver."

The woman on the bed stood quickly. "I'm Edna," she said and thrust out her hand. "You must be Marion's friend, the little writer who creates sympathy for lost dogs and recalcitrant children." She turned to the woman in the rocker, unconcerned with the sudden flash of irritation in the writer's eyes. "This should be fun, Lizzie. Shall I get out the sherry or will we have a little tea?"

"Tea, Edna," the smaller woman answered sharply, rising from the rocker in little jerks, and finally using the nearby bureau to pull herself fully upright. "I'll go across and plug in the kettle." At the doorway, she extended a delicate, cool hand to Diana. "I'm Elizabeth Schmidt," she said graciously. "I'm pleased you've come."

"I'm happy to meet you," Diana replied, allowing the hand to rest in her own for a moment and struck by the contrast of this flesh with the heat of the first handshake.

Feeling uncharacteristically awkward, Diana concentrated on Elizabeth Schmidt's walk across the hallway through the rectangle of sunlight before taking a breath and turning to Edna Carver where she stood in front of a large wall mirror tidying her hair. As she waited for the woman to finish, Diana noted the homogeneous blonde bedroom set, the serviceable gold carpet, and the matching curtains and quilt. Except for the rocker, a small needlepoint-covered footstool, and the intercom in the wall near the door of Edna's bed-sitting room, the place might have been a room at any mid-priced hotel. Diana imagined that the other rooms on the seventh floor would contain identical furnishings in identical arrangements, all presided over by the same faint odour of mothballs and a floral sachet. Lavender perfumed the air in Edna's room.

Edna caught Diana's assessment. "Not up to much, is it," she said, startling Diana into looking at her reflection in the big mirror. "These little cells are the repository of a hundred or so withered dreams of retirement bliss." She surprised Diana further when she laughed. "Did you expect a dignified Helen Hayes to greet you cordially and speak in hushed tones about the joys of playing cribbage endlessly?"

Diana opened her mouth, to apologize for her unspoken judgment or to chide Edna for her presumptuousness concerning what a stranger might be thinking, she wasn't sure which. Before she could answer, Edna went on.

"We'll have tea in the lounge across the hall," she said, still fiddling with her hair. "My damn windows won't open. It's fresher over there."

Tidied, Edna turned from the mirror, an intelligent force whose strength dominated the dreary room. Diana backed into the hallway, felt the sunshine on her shoulders, and let out the breath she unconsciously held. Edna walked past her into the lounge. Diana followed, surprised to discover she felt more like an obedient dog than a reporter. Once seated at one of two small, square tables in the communal kitchen and dining room designated "The Lounge," Diana attempted to restore her sense of balance by retrieving her notebook from her purse once more.

Edna looked at the little book. "That makes it official enough," she said. "Tell me, before we begin, just how is it you know my daughter? She's much older than you are."

The unmistakable edge in Edna Carver's voice unnerved the reporter. All at once she felt inadequately prepared for this interview. She thought briefly that she should have listened to her gynecologist's advice concerning a two-week convalescent period following her surgery. After all, she told herself, she'd been released from hospital only a few days earlier. She'd be justified in postponing this interview for another week. Aware that Edna was waiting for her answer, Diana searched for another smile before she began.

"Your daughter and my mother belong to the same club," she said at last. "They see one another fairly regularly, at book groups and lectures, I think."

"Do you always run around doing your mother's bidding? That doesn't seem very professional to me."

Diana surprised herself when she answered in an equally contentious tone. "A story's a story, Mrs. Carver. A good reporter doesn't much care where her leads take her, just so long as they point to something of interest to write about."

"Hear that, Lizzie? Our troubles are not in vain. This young thing can make a good living out of them."

Carrying two rattling cups and saucers, Elizabeth Schmidt walked carefully to the table. She set the delicate porcelain down and went back to the counter for a third cup and small tea pot. "Cream and sugar?" she asked Diana, ignoring Edna's performance.

"No, thank you," Diana answered, relieved this woman displayed no urge to attack her.

"Good," Elizabeth said. "We take our tea clear as well. There's less to fuss with." Joining Diana at the small table, she patted her hand.

Aware of growing tension in her neck, Diana slipped her hands under her heavy hair to rub her shoulders. As she did, she noticed Edna's sudden interest in the large copper earrings that had been hidden by her shoulder-length hair.

"Say," Edna said, pointing at the copper hoop closest to her. "I like those. Where did you get them?"

Diana touched the earrings, again off balance. "Oh, these," she said, fingering the rings of hammered copper. "A friend makes them. Would you like a pair?" She hoped the offer didn't sound like a bribe.

"I would. I'm sick of clip-ons. Fake diamonds, fake jet, and all the other insubstantial little nothings we decorate ourselves with. I flushed all my pearls down the toilet. But these are very smart." Edna reached over to swing both delicate hoops against Diana's neck. "Does your friend do business in the Eaton Centre?" she asked. "We get down there quite often."

"Hush, Edna," Elizabeth said, her urgent tone strangely out of place is this mundane conversation.

"Settle down, Lizzie," Edna said. "I'm not going to tell her." She returned to the point of Diana's visit. "So you think you can solve all my problems with a story," she said. She gave the writer's notebook a contemptuous glance.

Diana took a long breath before she answered, willing herself to remain in her chair and converse politely. "I'm not sure there's a story here, Mrs. Carver. Your daughter said you were unhappy with the lodge. She didn't go into any detail. I won't know until I hear what you have to say."

"Did she tell you I think they're trying to poison us?" Edna asked, knowing by Diana's instant blush that Marion had probably described her as a wretched old woman suffering from paranoid schizophrenia. "My daughter's such a fool. She takes everything I say literally," she said quickly, before Diana could deny the accusation. "Well, the food *is* shockingly bad, but it's only a small part of a much larger problem. The trouble is, we live here and we hate it."

"You hate it," interrupted Elizabeth. "Speak for yourself, Eddie."

"Oh, shut up," Edna said pleasantly. "You know damn well we all hate it, but hate, like love, comes in varying degrees. I hate it more than the rest of them. I complain. They suffer in silence."

"And what do you expect to accomplish through someone like me, Mrs. Carver?" Diana hoped her tone conveyed a business-like interest.

"Eddie's not happy unless everyone's stirred up," Elizabeth answered, delighted to explain her friend. "I'm surprised Marion spoke to you about her. She's been listening to Edna's malarkey ever since she moved to the lodge three years ago."

Edna glowered at Elizabeth. "Don't listen to her, Miss Mallory. This place is not just stultifying. There is something very sinister going on. Even if Marion doesn't take me seriously, someone like you should." She wagged a long index finger under Diana's nose as she spoke.

Diana sat back in her chair. "If there's no real problem with the food . . . ," she began. Edna's withering look made her stop.

"You'd be quick enough to write about us if we started to drop like flies, wouldn't you?" Edna asked, comfortable with her contempt. "What I complain about is metaphorical poisoning. You're a writer. You should know all about what that means."

Diana had to smile. "I can't very well write a piece condemning this place just because you're unhappy, Mrs. Carver."

"I'd like to know why not," Edna answered hotly. "It would pay your salary as well as anything else, wouldn't it?"

"No," Diana answered, her confidence growing. "It wouldn't. If this is for a magazine, there has to be some general human-interest aspect that merits public attention." She studied Edna's finely chiseled features for a moment, wondering how best to phrase her next thought. "Perhaps it's a social worker you should be speaking with, or a doctor, Mrs. Carver."

Edna stood abruptly. "To hell with you if you can't find anything of human interest here, and to hell with social workers and doctors. This place is already crawling with them. Yes, and RNs and psychologists. Those bloodsuckers live off institutions like this. Why would they promote any change? If we were happy, we wouldn't need them."

Despite Edna's outrage, Diana laughed, liking the way this woman got to the heart of the matter. "I'm sorry, Mrs. Carver," she said. "I feel blindsided, but I'll get over it. It never occurred to me that retirement homes might be anything less than their advertisements claim. It's time I remedied my ignorance. Do you think I could stay here, say for a week?"

Edna didn't appear to be surprised by Diana's change of heart. "You can have my room and I'll share with Lizzie. It's the best we can do. The doctor makes sure we're always full."

"Like ducks we'll share!" Elizabeth said. "You know Bernice won't let outsiders stay. Besides, Edna, I want my privacy."

Edna ignored her. "Can you talk your way in? Miss Wilson confuses her duties with that of a prison warden. You'll have to be very smooth."

Diana smiled despite a sudden sharp pain in her abdomen. "I think I can handle her," she said recollecting the large white scar and unusual voice. She hoped her words conveyed more than bravado. Standing she said, "I'll get your manager's permission, go home to pack, and be back in time for supper. What time do you people eat?"

Edna walked Diana to the door. "We people," she said gravely, "eat when we are told to eat, at five-thirty, whether we are hungry or not." Diana felt Edna's words as a punch to her stomach. Cradling her sore abdomen, she walked to the elevator alone.

"What do you think, Lizzie?" Edna asked as the elevator doors closed.

Elizabeth poured more tea. "I think we'll have a week of hypocrisy and then be free to have a good time again."

"No," said Edna. "I mean of her. I bet she's hoping Bernice will veto our little project. I think she was frightened of me."

"No wonder. You weren't exactly charming."

"Why should I be charming? You know damn well there's a good story here. Some reporter. She didn't seem to have any guts. Aren't they supposed to be curious?"

"Goodness, but you're hard to please, Eddie. The poor thing's doing what you want her to do. Let her alone. Be grateful."

"She was pale, too, a bit green around the gills if you ask me."

"Edna, really. You should have more charity."

Edna laughed pleasantly. "Lizzie, dear Lizzie," she sang. "You always confuse charity with blindness. I'm telling you, there was something not quite right about her."

"What do you care," Elizabeth snapped, thinking of the upheaval to come. "You're getting what you want. She'll probably write a nice little article on the monotony of a place like this. And maybe that will be the beginning of a change for the better."

"I hope so," said Edna. "If something isn't done soon, I'm going to do something no one can ignore."

"Oh, Eddie!" Elizabeth said, laughing. "No one can ignore you now. Blustering around like a bull in a china shop. Just wait until the rest of them hear what you've gone and done. That poor girl will be hearing about everybody's bowels and insomnia and grandchildren. She'll probably end the week by committing suicide just to make sure she doesn't end up in a place like this."

"See?" Edna cried, triumphant.

Elizabeth shook her head and squinted at the tiny watch on her wrist. "Say, Eddie. It's just four. Let's go over to the mall and lift some sherry before she comes back. We wouldn't want our little excursions to be written up in her article."

"I'm sick of sherry," Edna answered. "Why don't we pinch a nice ruby port? Or an apricot brandy?"

"I don't much care what it is, so long as it helps take the edge off." Elizabeth sat forward suddenly, rapping the table top with her knuckles. "And I don't much fancy sharing my room with you for a week. You've got some nerve, Edna."

"Nonsense, Lizzie, we'll have fun. You wouldn't want me to spend a week with any of the others, would you?"

Elizabeth thought about this. "I think you deserve to spend the week with Merle."

Edna tapped her friend's arm. "I'll never speak to you again if you suggest that to Wilson." Elizabeth offered her a coy smile. "I mean it," Edna threatened. "Our friendship will be over."

Satisfied with her small victory in the matter of putting Edna in her place, Elizabeth stacked their cups and saucers with care. "You'll have to be awfully nice to me," she said in a deliberately smarmy voice. "I expect very special treatment if I let you invade my privacy."

Edna nodded absent-mindedly. "Did you think the writer's face was swollen? What's it called when you retain fluid? Edema! Maybe she's got edema."

"What does it matter? She's going to write a story for you. Be grateful."

"God, I hate it when you're pious. You remind me of Mrs. Wallace."

Elizabeth winced. "Well, that was a low blow, even for you. I don't know if I want to go to the mall now."

"Come on," Edna growled. "I can't help it if you're blind. You just don't see things. And then you blame me when I point them out to you." She walked to the balcony doors and, with considerable effort, slid one open. "It's spring, Elizabeth. We mustn't argue. Come, look at the CN Tower."

"Why? It always looks the same."

"Take a deep breath. I'm sure I smell lilacs."

"No," Elizabeth said, joining her. "It's too early. The hyacinths aren't even up yet. That's sap you smell. The trees are coming to life again."

The two women leaned against the high, thick balcony railing arm in arm, absorbing the clear, bright afternoon. The sun ignited a few of the windows in the buildings around them, and the warm air reverberated with the cries of circling gulls.

All at once, a radiance illuminated Edna's features, and her eyes shone with a quickening memory. Elizabeth knew the look well and waited. Edna closed her eyes as she spoke.

> The trees to their innermost marrow
> Are touched by the sun;
> The robin is here and the sparrow:
> Spring has begun!
> The sleep and the silence are over:

The petals that rise
Are the eyelids of earth that uncover
Her numberless eyes.

"Lovely," murmured Elizabeth.

Edna opened her eyes, delighted to recall another bit of youthful memory work. "Sometimes I think nothing matters but this," she told the calm blue afternoon.

"You're right. Nothing does," said Elizabeth. "That's why it hurts to look at it. I'll be saying goodbye to it all far too soon."

"Stop that." Edna nudged her with her elbow. "I won't have any more of that morbid talk. You've been talking about dying for ten years now. You're not going to die."

"But I am, Edna. So are you."

"Well, not today."

"No, not today, but it might as well be today."

Edna grasped Elizabeth's hand. "Then let's get to the mall." She pulled Elizabeth from the balcony into the lounge. "It won't be much fun to shoplift alone, so we'd better lay in a supply."

As the pain of another unbearable cramp subsided, Diana feared she might retch. She felt so sick that, traveling slowly down in the airless elevator, she wanted to give in to an alluring swoon. Instead, she inhaled deeply several times, slumped against the imitation wood-grain wall, and willed her body to perform with its usually reliability. When the doors finally opened on the first floor, she was grateful to discover the restroom sign and its helpful arrow. Inside the windowless room, she locked herself into the first of three stalls and sat heavily. Gingerly, she leaned over to put her head between her knees.

After five minutes of drifting, she felt a little better. She sat up slowly to avoid a return of the nausea. After another minute, she stood. She left the stall to survey the damage in the mirror presiding over the industrially sanitized sink. She was as pale as Elizabeth Schmidt had been. With the same determined professionalism that prompted her to respond to Edna's desire to have someone pay attention to her concerns, she pulled a small compact from her purse and applied a little colour to her cheeks and lips. Satisfied to at least appear the picture of health, she fluffed her hair and peered at her image critically. Seeing the reflection of the familiar, healthy woman she wanted to be, she left the restroom in search of Bernice Wilson.

Diana found the manager standing next to the sofa, empty now, in the large, bright foyer, listening to a man she guessed to be a visitor because of his comparative youth. She heard the man's exasperated tone, if not his actual words, and noted the manager's quiet assurance in dealing with an obvious complaint. Watching them, she knew she would have to choose her words very carefully if she were to persuade this woman to agree to her presence for a week at the lodge. When the manager dismissed the man, she startled Diana when she abruptly turned to face her.

"Did you find Mrs. Carver?"

"Yes. Thank you," Diana answered, closing the distance between them and looking around the foyer. "This is such a lovely space." When the manager's features softened somewhat, the writer seized her moment. "I'm a freelance writer, Miss Wilson. I'd like very much to do an article on Sunset Lodge."

The manager made a hesitant gesture. "Please step into my office, Ms Mallory," she said, leading Diana around the information desk and through the small area behind it to a small dark space, crowded with desk, filing cabinet, and two chairs. This room contrasted so sharply with the cheerful foyer that Diana caught herself wondering if the cramped airless space was a metaphor for the manager's inner life. Unaware of the young writer's poetic musings, Bernice Wilson gestured to one of the chairs. Diana sat, crossed her legs, and leaned forward.

The manager removed her grey-tinted glasses and shocked Diana with her warm, welcoming smile. The writer blinked at the transformation. Earlier, she had placed the unfriendly woman somewhere in her late sixties, but this lovely creature looked decades younger. Her smile revealed beautiful teeth, straight though the smile was not. Diana sat back in her chair.

Despite her warm expression, the manager's odd voice remained coldly inquiring. "May I ask what your interest in our home has to do with Edna Carver, Miss Mallory?"

Looking into this younger, more engaging face, Diana suspected that the woman's odd voice – no doubt connected to the scar now hidden beneath a festive daffodil-yellow silk scarf – made her seem less approachable than she was. The younger woman returned the manager's smile as she answered, hoping her instincts in the matter were correct. "I'm here because Marion Andrews is quite worried about her mother." Diana paused to form her next comment carefully. "I'm sure you're aware of Mrs. Andrews' concern," she said, making sure her voice contained no hint of criticism.

"Oh, yes," the manager answered. "Mrs. Andrews and I have a very nice rapport. She's one of our most faithful visitors. That's why I feel so badly about our Edna. Her deterioration is so hard for Marion to bear."

"Deterioration?"

"Mrs. Carver was far less confused when she came to us three years ago. Dementia is always far harder on the members of the family than it is upon its host." She lowered her voice. "You thought she seemed fine," the manager queried with what might have been playfulness had her tone and the subject been different.

"No," Diana answered cautiously. "Not fine. Mrs. Carver appeared to be angry, overwhelmingly so. But she didn't seem senile."

Diana knew she'd been finessed when Bernice Wilson's smile broadened. "You have a great deal of experience with senility, then?" the manager asked.

The writer hated the blush that spread over her face and neck. "No, I have none at all. But I understand a senile person to be someone who . . . ." She searched for the words she wanted. "Isn't present," she said at last. "Mrs. Carver appeared to be very much in the here and now when I spoke with her."

"Oh, yes," the manager answered. "She's very much here. But her judgment about here is greatly impaired. Only last month, Mrs. Andrews and I spoke of finding a safer environment for our Edna, one where her judgment won't threaten her well being. In fact, Mrs. Andrews gave me the go ahead to arrange for a bed for her mother at Tranquil Time in the next few weeks, but if she's sending reporters to interview her, perhaps she's changed her mind."

Diana determined to avoid involvement in any conflict brewing between the manager of the lodge and Edna Carver's daughter. "Tranquil Time?" she asked, shifting in her chair.

"It's our nursing-home affiliate. Residents are moved from a retirement home such as Sunset Lodge to a nursing home when they require more hours of nursing care per day."

"How interesting," Diana remarked. "You've given me an idea for a series of articles exploring all the senior-citizen accommodation possibilities." She smiled gratefully. "I wonder if you'd permit me to stay here, say, for a week, so I could really catch the atmosphere of a retirement-home facility."

The manager sat back in her chair, her smile fading. "I have a responsibility to my residents," she said. "I am the guardian of their privacy, as I'm sure you understand, Miss Mallory. I'm responsible for their daily well being."

"I do understand, Miss Wilson," Diana said quickly. "And I wouldn't interrupt any routines. Let me assure you that all my questions would focus on exploring why they are here, such as why they chose to leave their homes, what they miss, what they have here that they wouldn't have living alone."

"Am I to understand that Mrs. Carver wouldn't figure in your piece?"

Diana hid her triumph with an earnest look. "She wouldn't necessarily be mentioned at all. You would have to be, of course, and I'd include the names of any people I quote directly."

"I'd want to see anything before . . . ."

"Of course," Diana said. "I'd be happy to show you what I write before I send it in." She resisted adding a smug *autographed*.

Bernice read the triumph in Diana's bright eyes. While she liked the idea of an article praising the lodge, she felt uneasy at the thought of a constant, alien presence underfoot. "We're so full," she began. "There's really no place at all for you to . . . ."

Diana jumped in eagerly. "Perhaps Mrs. Carver could share with Mrs. Schmidt," she offered. "They seem so close. Actually, Mrs. Carver brought up this possibility during my visit with them."

"Rollaways and extra sheets," the manager muttered. "And Mrs. Schmidt will find Mrs. Carver as endurable as a virulent case of shingles."

As the manager offered her half-hearted protest, Diana felt the woman's eagerness for recognition. She suspected that behind her façade of concern for residents, Bernice Wilson was imagining a story profiling her indispensable role as Sunset Lodge's tireless and efficient manager. The writer stood and extended her hand.

"I like to start a project on Mondays," she said, doing her best to radiate professionalism. "I'll go home to pack a bag and be back in time for dinner. Is that all right, or will my timing give your cook a problem?"

"Gracious, no," the manager said, glad to impart confidence in her staff. "The cook is always ready for guests. We encourage the lodgers to invite their family members anytime, just as long as we have sufficient notice."

"Is this sufficient notice?" Diana asked.

Bernice checked her watch. "I think so. It's just past four now. We serve at five-thirty. Does that give you time enough to get your things?"

"I'm in the west end just across the river," Diana said, pulling her purse strap over her shoulder.

"Well, then," said the manager. "It's settled."

As she opened the big glass doors to Bloor Street, Diana heard the elevator doors open. When she turned to see who might be visiting the lodge, she discovered Edna and Elizabeth stepping into the foyer. "Mrs. Carver," she called. Edna raised her long forefinger to her lips. Amused, the reporter waited, holding the door and then following the pair into the warm spring afternoon.

Outside, Edna turned on Diana so swiftly that the writer stepped back, tripping on the low step at the lodge entrance.

"Never say anything in front of that bitch," Edna hissed. "She's out to get me."

The enthusiasm Diana had for the project began to ebb at the same moment that another cramp began to build. "But Mrs. Carver," she said. "Miss Wilson agreed. I'm going to stay for the week."

Edna dismissed Diana's victory with a wave of her elegant hand. "I wonder if it will do any good," she said, taking hold of Elizabeth's arm. "Marion is such a dud. I'm a fool to trust a friend of hers."

Feeling betrayed by both her body and Edna's lack of faith in her, Diana did her best to regroup. Without saying a formal goodbye, Edna guided Elizabeth down the street to the light at the corner. Sore and angry, the writer stared after the women. She longed to forget about the lodge and go home to bed, but as she observed the pair, the tall, straight woman leaning over to talk rapidly to her smaller friend, she knew she would not. Edna's anger intrigued her. It was the most powerful force she'd felt inside Sunset Lodge.

Elizabeth clutched Edna's arm as they stepped off the curb. "Go slowly now. I want to die in my own bed and not out here under the wheels of a taxi."

"Oh, stop it," Edna said gaily. "Taxi drivers lose their licences when they run down old ladies. As for other threats, I've filled you full of precautions."

"If you're talking about that desiccated liver you stole last week, the only thing that's filled me with is gas. You aren't going to keep my body alive past its time, Edna."

"You're always so negative. I don't know what you'd do without me. *Psychology Today* says that the B vitamins can stop your hair from graying and falling out. Besides, we have to do something to resist, even if it's futile."

On the other side of the street, the women stopped so Elizabeth could catch her breath. Edna unbuttoned her navy spring coat and untied the scarf at her neck. "It's wonderful out here. I feel sure summer is going to make an enormous difference to the way you feel."

"You'll catch a cold, leaving your coat open like that, Eddie. Mother always kept us buttoned up until the twenty-fourth of May."

"Nonsense, Lizzie. This weather makes us feel good. Take off that stupid hat and let the sun give you a little Vitamin D."

Elizabeth clutched at the cranberry felt bowl on her head. "Don't touch it. I don't like to go out without my head covered. Your hair's a mess now. You should have worn yours."

"Don't be absurd," Edna said. "Let's think about what we're going to steal."

"Don't say steal, Eddie. Let's think of it as borrowing," Elizabeth said, making Edna laugh noisily.

The pair began to walk down the sloping pavement to the mall half a block from the lodge. It was an outing they tried to make daily since Edna convinced Elizabeth of the value of daily exercise and fresh air. Edna stopped to touch a tree trunk. "Look at that, Lizzie. There's a nest up there." She pointed high above their heads.

Elizabeth smiled as she looked up. "I bet the next time we come out we won't be able to see it for leaves. They're slow to start, but once the initial thrust is made, they seem to leaf overnight."

"Do you think they'll open the roof garden soon?"

"Not until the end of May. Wilson says the wind's too cold till then."

"What a stupid rule," Edna said. "It should be open all year. Even winter has its moments. It's a good place to sit and think about life when there isn't a crowd."

"The best time's at night," said Elizabeth. "I wish she didn't lock the doors at nine. When I have insomnia, I dream of perching up there like a pigeon, watching the sun rise."

Edna grew excited. "Let's steal the key. We can have a duplicate made at the hardware store before she misses it."

Elizabeth shook her head and laughed. "You're going to get yourself thrown out of there yet, Eddie."

"Nonsense, Lizzie. Bernice would be bored to death if she didn't have me to worry about."

"You're wrong. You're playing with fire where that one's concerned. I bet she almost had heart failure when she found out that young thing writes for magazines."

"I hope so. Maybe they'll be carrying her out when we get back."

"Edna!" Elizabeth said feigning shock and pulling on Edna's arm. "Not so fast. I need to catch my breath again." Edna slowed. "They should put benches along here for us. We could walk a few yards and then sit in the sun. Not that going down is as bad as coming up. One of these days, someone's going to have a stroke climbing up this hill." Elizabeth shook off Edna's arm and resumed walking. "I'm fine now. I have a fancy for dried apricots. Do you think we can get some from the supermarket?"

Edna thought for a moment. "I don't like going in there ever since that woman got caught stealing meat. What was her name, anyway? She was only with us for about three weeks. You know the one. She was a nice sort, real, unlike most of them."

"Real!" Elizabeth cried. "You mean she was as bad as you are. Imagine trying to walk out of Loblaw's with your coat stuffed with sausages. She was crazy!"

"I think they're suspicious of all of us now. Maybe we can get your apricots at the health-food store. It's still relatively safe territory, like the liquor store."

When the women reached the mall's parking lot, they stopped to rest again. From this point the level ground made walking much easier for Elizabeth. Before they began to walk again, Edna pulled at the collar of her dress to peer between her breasts. "Damn. I'm wearing my new corset, and the elastic isn't flexible yet. You'll have to steal the sherry today. I can't stuff anything in this one."

"I don't mind," said Elizabeth. "This old sack has room for half a dozen bottles."

"Hah! If we stole that many you'd look like Mae West and probably fall on your face. Shall we buy anything or do you think we should save our money for something more urgent?"

"Like Polident? No. Let's buy one bottle of something. It helps our cause when you fish out your money in front of that young man. He always looks at his feet. I never worry about anything sticking out."

"I suppose you're right. But I'm getting so I hate to pay for anything these days. I think we've paid enough."

The women wove their way around the parked cars until they came to the pedestrian walkway. The mall entrance was quite close now, and yet it took them another five minutes to get inside because of the curbs they had to negotiate carefully for Elizabeth's sake. Once through the automatic doors, they headed to their favourite bench.

"I like it here," Elizabeth said, settling in to study the milling shoppers. "I think it's because there's hair every colour of the rainbow to be seen. I'm sick of looking at grey hair."

"What about Merle's?" cried Edna. "Her hair is so red it glows. When I was a young girl, there was a name for that colour, but propriety prevents me from repeating it."

"Propriety! Since when do you observe propriety?"

Edna chuckled. "That's another good thing about being old. It is really so very invigorating to be able to ignore propriety."

"Speak for yourself, Eddie. There are still a few of us who care about at least looking respectable."

"Well, you don't have to care."

Recalling several of Edna's recent donnybrooks at the lodge, Elizabeth warned Edna. "You don't have the good sense to be frightened when you challenge her. I'm telling you, I think Bernice has had her fill."

"And what if she has? I'm not afraid of her. She's not God."

"She might as well be as far as we're concerned." Elizabeth rubbed her thighs before she stood. "Really, Edna, you should be more circumspect in front of other people. We can still have our fun, but privately."

"You're a coward, Elizabeth," Edna said, standing and taking her friend's arm.

"You're damn right," the little woman admitted happily. Chatting amiably, the two friends began their slow meander to the liquor store.

As soon as Bernice Wilson informed the cook that a guest was to be with the lodge for a week she returned to her office, went quickly to her desk, and pulled out a file of phone numbers. Marion Andrews' name was second from the top. The manager checked the time and decided to call immediately, dialing the number using the end of a ball-point pen. She tapped the pen impatiently until Edna's daughter answered.

"Mrs. Andrews? It's Miss Wilson," she said, though because of her unique voice identifying herself was mere formality. "The matter I want to discuss with you concerns Diana Mallory . . . ." She smiled as she listened to the woman's nervous response. "I'm sure you meant well, Mrs. Andrews. Please rest assured, I'll see no harm comes from this. In future, please speak with me before making any such arrangements. I have responsibility for a great many people here. Something like this can be upsetting, despite our good intentions . . . .Miss Mallory will be staying with us for a week, as it happens. I have nothing against the woman's presence here, but it's my duty to oversee all the activities at the lodge. Do I have your word that you will speak with me before sending anyone else over to talk with your mother?"

She smiled broadly now. "In any case, I'm afraid it is time to remind you of our Tranquil Time discussion. Every day I grow more convinced that our Edna is in need of a more protective community. She just wandered out with Mrs. Schmidt, and I must say, every time I see her leave, I get a little nervous. A person in her state of mind could get into trouble without any effort whatsoever . . . . Shall I call Tranquil Time again to see if I can hurry a bed along for her, or do you wish to make private arrangements?" She suppressed an indiscreet urge to laugh when she heard Marion Andrews' predictable response. "I thought not. No, it's no trouble at all. The head nurse is a dear friend of mine. She understands emergencies like these. I'll let you know when the arrangements have been finalized . . . . Oh, yes, she meets the requirements, and the hour and a half of nursing care she'll get each day should put your mind at rest . . . . No, Mrs. Andrews, there is not a thing for you to do except perhaps oversee the placement of your mother's few belongings. We share an ambulance service with Tranquil Time and this expense will be added to your mother's bill. Yes, Tranquil Time is more expensive, but please don't forget, it would cost twice as much if nursing homes had no government funding . . . . I understand, Mrs. Andrews. When someone we love becomes unbalanced, we don't want to believe it. We can only hope for a protective environment until the end comes. I assure you, her final days will be much safer at Tranquil Time. Her confusion will be contained and she'll have far more suitable company. . . . Oh, not at all. It's my great pleasure to be helpful . . . . You are so very welcome, Mrs. Andrews. Goodbye now."

The manager concluded the call with a look of smug satisfaction. With the same ball-point pen she dialed Tranquil Time's number and resumed her tapping until the receptionist answered. "I'd like to speak to Mrs. O'Shea," she said sharply, remembering her resentment at discovering their mutual budget did not include funds for a receptionist at the lodge.

At the liquor store, Edna and Elizabeth soon found the port they were after. It was nestling now between the tiny empty sacs that had once been Elizabeth Schmidt's full, suckling breasts. Edna carried a sherry bottle to the cash register, plunked it down ostentatiously, and then felt more deeply than she had to into her cleavage for the spending money she kept inside a small satin change purse fastened to her bra. As soon as she began this elaborate money-retrieval show, the young man at the cash register flushed and bent under the counter, pretending to straighten his cache of paper bags. Edna, as always, delighted in his reaction. She waited for her change and laughed outright when he locked his register and ran off to avoid watching her fumble in her bosom a second time.

"It gives me the greatest feeling of power," she whispered to Elizabeth. "What do you suppose would happen if I took my damn dress right off?"

"He'd probably die on the spot," Elizabeth observed sagely. They linked arms and walked slowly down the mall.

The health-food store had become one of Edna's favourite shopping places since she'd read about the salvation offered by vitamins advertised in *Psychology Today*. Despite her skepticism regarding the information, she enjoyed the tactile pleasure of fingering the small brown bottles that she had come to see as the modern world's icons of hope. It calmed her to shuffle through the pamphlets on this or that vitamin and to smell the various herbs on display in big glass jars. Sadly, most of the things in the store were impossible to steal since the shopkeeper could see all around the place from his seat behind the narrow counter to the right of the door. Despite this restriction, Edna loved to poke around.

The day she took the desiccated liver, the man had been busy with a group of students from the nearby high school. While he was showing them some new books on body building supplements, Edna casually reached over the counter to the shelf where the tablets sat. Fingering the bottle as though reading the label, she made sure everyone was otherwise absorbed before slipping it into the bodice of her dress.

"We won't have the same luck with the apricots as with the liver," she said to Elizabeth as they walked along. "Those bags are too damn noisy. Shall we break down and buy them?"

"Heaven forbid," said the smaller woman. "Our self-respect would be shot. Why don't you talk to him for a while? I'll pick up a bag and then we'll walk out absent-mindedly. Even if he notices, he won't think it's intentional."

"And to think you were horrified when we first started this business! Do you remember the sour candies at the market? I thought you were going to faint when you saw me tuck them in my dress."

"I almost did faint, Edna." Elizabeth was pensive for a moment. "The only thing I can say is that I've been ruined by bad company. I don't want to crowd the port, though, Eddie. You better see what you can do with the apricots." They walked into the health-food store and smiled at the proprietor.

Looking and sounding like tangible proof of the benefits of his products, the young man greeted them enthusiastically. "Hello, ladies," he said. "Isn't this a beautiful day!"

"It certainly is. Just what these old bones need," Edna answered with equal zest. He went back to his newspaper after they assured him they only wanted to look around.

Almost immediately, Edna found the apricots and grimaced at Elizabeth, pointing to the display of stiff plastic pouches on a stand at the end of the counter. Elizabeth shook her head decisively, hoping Edna would understand she was not to risk anything so dangerous. Edna answered with an imperious smile.

"Come over here, Lizzie," Edna said in her best stage voice. "Here's that book I was telling you about." She picked up a nutrition almanac and leafed through it, smirking when the man got off his chair to join them at the far side of the store.

"That's a fine reference book," he told them. "It lists every vitamin and mineral, what they do for the body, even what foods you can find them in. And it includes diseases caused by deficiencies of diet, something women your age should be concerned about."

Elizabeth smiled at the man. "Oh, my, yes," she said charmingly. "We practically live on tea and toast. When one gets to be our age, why bother?"

"But that's just when you should bother," he said, launching into a speech on the value of supplements. Edna wandered back to the counter, leaving the man to proselytize and Elizabeth to keep him busy by pretending to absorb his every word.

Edna took the apricots down very carefully, without squeezing the bag. When the proprietor glanced at her, she placed them on the counter, hoping it looked as though she had more shopping to do. She meandered to the cooler where yogurt and bottled juices chilled. There, next to the bottles of goat's milk and bags of nuts, were more apricots, these hand-wrapped in soft, silent sandwich bags. She turned to the man to make sure he still focused on Elizabeth. His back was to Edna as he spoke, and Edna could see Elizabeth nodding and smiling at his vast knowledge of the dietary benefits of Vitamin E. Quickly, Edna snatched up two bags, placing one over each of her breasts inside her corset's brassiere cups. She inhaled and looked down at herself, very pleased with both the breast enhancement and the adhesion of plastic to flesh. She sauntered back to the counter to finger the other apricots.

"Goodness," she heard Elizabeth say. "It's almost five. We have to be back by five-thirty. Thank you so much for all the information. When my pension cheque comes, I'll be back for the book." The man followed her, still beaming, to the counter.

"I don't know," Edna said as if thinking aloud. "They're awfully dear. What do you think, Lizzie? Will we splurge and buy these?"

"I didn't bring a cent with me, Eddie. If you want them, you'll have to pay."

"I barely have enough for this month's rent. I'd better not. Thank you, anyway," she said to the proprietor. "Would you like me to put these back?"

With boundless goodwill, the man took the apricots and said goodbye.

"I'm so glad you didn't risk it," Elizabeth said when they were outside the store. "Still, I would have loved a treat."

Edna said nothing as they walked along, determined not to smirk and give herself away.

Bernice Wilson tamped into alignment the edges of the admission applications on her desk, the phone cradled between her left ear and shoulder, before arranging the forms in a neat pile on the right-hand corner of the tidy surface. She opened the desk's wide, shallow middle drawer, and studied the contents critically to assure herself that every item – pencils, pens, erasers, memoranda pads, paper clips, elastics, and the folder containing emergency numbers – was in its proper place. Satisfied with the order there, she shut the drawer with a bang, picked up the one stray pen lying on the blotter, and resumed her tapping. Her controlled features were inscrutable when she finally spoke into the receiver.

"Mrs. O'Shea. That was a very long wait. In future, have that girl take a message to return my call. *I'm* a busy woman, too. I only waited because this is an emergency. I have a resident in need of a bed . . . . Yes, immediately. I spoke to you about her some *weeks* ago. I'll be frank. She's becoming something of a troublemaker . . . . No, she's not on Metaphin, but you can start her on it as soon as she arrives . . . . I'd like the bed this week if possible. Perhaps there's a favour I can do for you . . . ." She bristled at the woman's insulting tone. "We have a young writer here for a week. There's no reason she shouldn't do a story on Tranquil Time." She felt a little better when she heard the head nurse's speedy offer of a bed. "That's fine, Mrs. O'Shea. I'll expect an ambulance Friday afternoon." She hung up, glanced at her wristwatch, put the pen in the middle drawer with the others, stood, pushed the chair into place automatically, and then walked briskly to the foyer.

In pre-dinner clutches, several lodgers passed the time in discussions about the beautiful weather. Three women sat on the large sofa talking animatedly about someone's scheduled surgery and anxiously glancing at the large clock above the dining room French doors every few seconds. No one was allowed in the big room until precisely five-thirty, lodgers were constantly reminded, because the waitresses and the cook needed to prepare for dinner without distraction. Home from their walk, Edna and Elizabeth joined the people waiting in the foyer.

"Have you two been out gallivanting again?" A frail determined man approached Edna with his arms outstretched.

"Get away from me, you old fool," Edna muttered. "I swear I'll knock you sideways if you touch me again."

The old man laughed but put his arms down. "Can I take your coat?" he asked, hopeful. "You don't want to go upstairs with it. You'll be late."

"Mind your own business," Edna told him, secreting the brown liquor-store bag in the folds of her coat. She grabbed Elizabeth by the arm and steered her into the hall beyond the foyer to the visitors' coat rack.

"What am I going to do with the port?" whispered Elizabeth. "It will kill me to sit through dinner with this bottle digging into my gut."

Edna peeked around the doorway to make sure they weren't being watched. "Give it to me. I'll slip it in with the sherry."

Elizabeth worked the bottle out of her corset as Edna hung her coat on a hanger. She squealed when Edna removed the bags of apricots from her brassiere cups.

"You're a genius, Eddie. I had no idea," she said, staring up at Edna with undisguised admiration.

Edna pushed the apricots into the brown paper sack along with the port. "If we leave this bag here on the floor, nobody will notice. And I'll hide it under my coat when we go upstairs."

The friends blended into the crowd waiting for the five-thirty dinner-bell as Diana Mallory entered the foyer carrying a large canvas tote and book bag. Edna watched suspiciously as Bernice greeted the young writer and led her around the corner to the coat rack. She wanted to follow, if only to assure herself that Bernice didn't notice their brown bag on the floor, but instead accepted Elizabeth's arm casually as the crowd surged into the dining room at the sound of the bell.

A short, plump, red-headed woman bustled up to them.

"Who was *that*?" she asked Edna, obviously impressed by the young writer. "You always keep your finger on the pulse of things around here." The woman smiled ingratiatingly into Edna's scornful face.

Whenever she heard Merle's voice, Edna thought of squeaky door hinges and wished she could oil the old woman. "I wouldn't know, Merle. Butting into other people's business is more in your line than mine."

Unoffended, Merle touched Elizabeth's sleeve. "That Edna," she said happily. "We wouldn't have nothin' to laugh about if she wasn't around." Her teeth clicked noisily as she spoke and a cloudy tear oozed from the inside corner of one of her eyes.

Elizabeth smiled, fascinated by that tear. "Our Edna's a laugh a minute," she agreed, rolling her eyes as Edna yanked her toward the dining room.

"Don't encourage her," Edna whispered. "She's such a simperer."

"Charity, Edna," Elizabeth chastised. "Charity."

They reached their table for three beside the large curtained windows through which Bloor Street traffic could be seen and heard diffusely. "Oh shut up," Edna said happily, sliding out her chair and dusting it off with a sweep of her hand before sitting down. She picked up her linen napkin and wiped each piece of cutlery, her water glass, and the inside of her teacup vigorously.

"I don't know why you do that," Elizabeth said, archly observing Edna perform her customary cleaning ritual. "The cook has an autoclave. Everything is sterilized."

Edna ignored her. "I wonder where that young thing will sit tonight. I certainly hope Bernice lets her make the rounds. She isn't going to do us a damn bit of good if she spends all her time fraternizing with the enemy."

Elizabeth shook out her napkin before arranging it daintily on her lap. Absently fingering her delicate choker of pearls she said, "Let's see. Monday. What was it yesterday? Roast beef or roast turkey?"

"I have no idea. The cook smothered whatever it was in that axle grease she calls gravy."

"I think it was turkey," Elizabeth reflected. "That means turkey hash."

"I hate hash. It's common."

"So are we," observed her friend.

 "Speak for yourself!"

The women exchanged their pleasantries as waitresses filed out of the kitchen carrying broad trays with five dinners on each. The routine was always the same. Those farthest from the kitchen were served first. Edna and Elizabeth received their turkey hash in silence. Each looked down at her plate before looking at the other's.

"You got more than I did tonight, Edna."

"You're lucky. They're probably trying to get rid of me faster."

"I should think so." Elizabeth glanced at her black bag where it rested by her feet. "Are we going to eat tonight?"

"There's no point in starving or in taking more risks at the mall than we have to. The only thing I'm dead set against is the goddamned creamed tuna on toast on Wednesday nights."

"Good. I didn't line my purse tonight. But I'll remember to line it on Wednesday."

"See that you do. Do you think we should warn that little thing over there about the tuna?" Edna gestured to Diana Mallory where she sat with Bernice at a table just outside the kitchen doors.

"Absolutely not, Edna. That was the most legitimate complaint you've made yet. Imagine trying to tell someone that a great big brown hairy spider was a piece of tuna-fish skin."

"I once met a woman who found a dirty finger bandage in a package of cookies," Edna said, wanting to hold her hubris over the spider in check.

"I'm always glad I baked my own."

"Well, complaining didn't do a bit of good. We still get that goddamned creamed tuna on Wednesdays. I wish I'd thought to dig out the spider and send it to the Board of Health."

Elizabeth laughed. "They would have run tests on it and told you it was well cooked."

"Poke through that mess in front of you carefully. I still have hope that something specific will turn up."

"Optimism is a fine virtue, Edna, but I don't think the cook sees herself as readily employable. I bet she's been on her toes since you found that spider."

"That was the one time I should have kept my big mouth shut. I should have just put it in a tissue and given it to someone important. But the shock of finding first one leg, then another . . . ."

"Edna, please! I'm not going to be able to eat this, and then I'll be hungry in the middle of the night."

Edna put her knife and fork down. "It's going to be like when we were young and had a friend over to sleep. We'll have such fun."

Elizabeth looked at her blankly.

"You haven't forgotten? I'm going to be rooming with you this week."

"Oh, yes." Elizabeth remembered to be cross. "I don't like change, Edna."

"And you're always spouting charity to me. Don't be so mean, Lizzie. Look on it as an adventure."

"I never much liked adventures. I like . . . peace. That's it. I've always been attracted to peace."

Edna began to eat again. Every now and then she glanced over at Bernice and Diana, curious about their conversation. Edna watched as the writer ate, listened, and occasionally pointed at something in the room. Bernice, controlled and inscrutable, spoke between mouthfuls.

"Lizzie!" Edna exclaimed suddenly. "Look at that. Bernice is actually eating! She never eats in here."

Elizabeth looked over at the manager. "That is odd, Edna. Why do you suppose she's doing that? I thought she always ate in her own suite when we were finished in here."

"She's deliberately trying to make that girl think she eats like the rest of us. I know very well she has the cook grill steak for her almost every night," Edna said, knowing no such thing but finding plausibility at least as valuable as fact in her case against the manager.

"Oh, well, what does it matter? Maybe she's just eating with the girl to keep her company on her first day here, to be polite."

Edna put down her knife and fork again and poked her finger

into her mouth. "This stuff sticks like glue to my upper plate. I can't wait to get upstairs and soak it."

Elizabeth started to laugh.

"What's so funny?"

"Do you remember when Mr. Wallace burst into our lounge after he stumbled into Bernice's apartment? I thought he was going to bust a gusset." She sobered suddenly. "Oh, I forgot. I didn't mean to speak ill of the dead."

"Good riddance to that one."

Elizabeth gave Edna a disapproving look.

"Don't be sentimental," Edna said. "I don't think God will hold it against us that we didn't like him. He was intolerable – oozing fat and pieties – I bet what sent him off about discovering Bernice and her steak was that she didn't ask him to join her."

"Edna! That's enough. You're being blasphemous. You have no idea how God feels about Mr. Wallace."

"I know how He feels if He's smart. He'd probably like to send him right back. Maybe the reverend is on his way to a new life already."

"Now that sort of talk makes me giddy with fatigue. I'm overburdened with this life."

Still studying Bernice and Diana Mallory intently, Edna picked up her knife and fork. She noticed for the first time that the older woman's grey hair did not move when she bent her head to listen to the writer, as though it might be made of a solid sheet of aluminum.

"Do you remember what else he said about that night?" Edna asked.

"Who?"

"Wallace."

Elizabeth thought for a moment. "Just that she was eating steak. Goodness, Edna. You look peculiar."

"He said Bernice didn't look like herself. That she didn't have her regular hair on."

"What?"

"He did. She wears a wig. Look at her. Her hair doesn't move like real hair. It must be made of some kind of plastic."

"I don't remember him saying Bernice didn't have her hair on. Besides what if she does wear a wig? Ninety percent of us could use a wig to cover what we don't have anymore, including me."

"Why doesn't she wear a short curly wig or perhaps a nice chignon?"

"Edna! Let the woman alone. What do you care about what she wears on her head? There are far more important things to complain about. Like the craft classes she vetoed and the roof garden she keeps locked."

Edna sat quite still, mesmerized by the sight of Bernice in conversation with Diana.

"I don't know, Elizabeth. There is something so fishy about her."

Elizabeth ignored her. "Ah, tea," she said to her waitress. "Is it cold?"

The young girl delivering the tea smiled into Elizabeth's expectant face. "Stone cold, Mrs.," she said, returning the smile.

"Just like always."

"Are you being good?"

"What chance do I have to be anything else?"

The girl touched Elizabeth's shoulder on her way to the next table. Elizabeth bent over her cup. As usual, the tea was hot and strong. She smiled to herself at their shared joke.

Edna looked from Diana Mallory and Bernice Wilson to the tables in the centre of the big room. She watched people bend over their dinners, desserts, tea, as though what they were doing with the small blobs in front of them was the most important thing in the world. As she watched, hands – normal, veined, liver-spotted hands – became clutching, grasping claws, eyes jealously guarded individual portions of this and of that, and ordinary shoulders distorted, hunching in animal concentration. She was sure she could hear a few low, warning growls. She shook her head.

"What is it, Eddie?"

Tears filled Edna's eyes. "Don't ask. I can't tell you. It just . . . makes me sick." She stood abruptly. "If that bitch wants to know where I've gone, tell her I'm packing a few things for my week in your room." She rushed out of the dining room, watched, she knew, by eyes behind dark lenses.

Elizabeth sat at their table staring into her tea. Edna's growing unhappiness puzzled her. Elizabeth wanted to help, but there seemed to be nothing for her to do. She sipped her comforting tea. It mystified her that Edna should be so unhappy when she could afford to live in a place where all their needs were taken care of – well, she thought, the obvious ones at least – and where life was so convenient. She had a momentary feeling of guilt as she thought perhaps Bernice Wilson was right when she confided her fears regarding Edna's senility and suggested that her friend's profound dissatisfaction marked an insufficient supply of oxygen to her brain when the manager found Elizabeth alone outside the doctor's office waiting for a prescription refill.

Thinking of the doctor, Elizabeth temporarily forgot Edna's troubles. She loved going to see him. His office, right next to the tiny two-bed infirmary on the third floor, was so pleasant, and the doctor so cordial, so understanding. He never asked her to remove her clothing after she'd told him she'd rather not, and he never embarrassed her by asking questions she couldn't answer. He simply gave her what she wanted.

Many times she'd done her best to persuade Edna to see the doctor because most of the lodgers found his pills very helpful. When her husband died and she was alone in the world, it was the doctor and his pills that made everything right again. But Edna was pig-headed about advice. Elizabeth even said this to Bernice when the manager asked her to talk to Edna about getting a little help from the doctor. Bernice seemed to understand about needing help.

Elizabeth recollected the manager saying something about the doctor helping her, as well, something about a bad time in her life ten or fifteen years before she'd come to the lodge. Yes, Elizabeth remembered. The manager said her daddy had died. Daddies dying, husbands dying, the doctor understood. Without the doctor's pills, and without Edna and the sherry, life would be an overwhelming burden, and without tea. She sipped as she looked around the room at the other lodgers comforted by tea and routine. They all shared this feeling, she felt sure. Without the doctor, without the tea, life would be impossible. They were such a comfort, these simple things. But Edna would not be comforted.

Elizabeth turned her attention to Bernice and Diana Mallory. There was something frightening about the manager, Edna was right about that. Elizabeth remembered looking forward to a new craft class in their lounge. Someone, she forgot who, was going to teach them paper flower sculpture. Bernice burst into the group, looked at the supplies – mere coloured paper and scissors – and told them that she could absolutely not be responsible for people who handled sharp objects. That was the end of the flower-sculpture classes. Then there was the roof garden. To know that small oasis existed and was denied to them felt worse than having no place to go at all. Despite her constant supply of pills, Elizabeth always awoke in the night. She closed her eyes to conjure a younger version of herself, sitting in her garden – under stars or clouds – whenever she was unable to sleep. The night was different from the day, better, full of replenishing whisperings, secrets only trees and owls knew. She longed to sit outside at night on Sunset Lodge's roof.

Elizabeth finished her tea, shook her head to clear it of the tendrils of memory and longing, and glanced around the room once more. People, her friends and acquaintances made over her ten years at the lodge, were pushing back their chairs and preparing to expend the energy necessary to travel to their rooms where they could remove their shoes and belts and feel comfortable with the load of food sitting heavily in their bellies. She would do the same. She would read tonight. Yes, she would read. She tried to think of something wonderful to read.

"Where's your pal gone?"

Elizabeth looked up, startled. There was Mrs. Wallace, large and tidy, smiling her evangelical, praise-the-Lord smile.

"Hello, Wally. Edna's gone up to pack a bag. She's going to be rooming with me for the week."

Hearing this news, Mrs. Wallace sat down and leaned close to Elizabeth. "Why? I hope neither of you is poorly, as it were."

"It's a long story, Wally. You know Edna – complaining to anyone who'll listen. Well, she complained just once too often to Marion, and now we've been sent a writer." She turned to Bernice's table. "She's over there with Wilson." Elizabeth said, pointing intrepidly. "She'll be using Edna's room for the week she's here."

"Imagine that," said Mrs. Wallace. "I always feel gratitude's important, as it were. Mrs. Carver's a dear soul, but she sometimes wants gratitude. This place isn't perfect, but we're warm and dry, aren't we? And well fed. Wasn't that a lovely hash?" Her broad smile revealed large yellow teeth.

"I'm not a hash fan, Wally. But how are things with you? Are you making the adjustment?"

Mrs. Wallace's eyes misted over. "I miss him, of course. But I bear it knowing he's in better company, as it were. God must have had need of staunch support in the heavenly realm." She dabbed at her eyes with Edna's soiled napkin. "One must find the positive to emphasize until called from this vale of tears. I keep busy with my missionary work. You'd be surprised how many in here have never embraced the Lord, my dear. You are one of the few."

Feeling sheepish, Elizabeth looked down at her empty cup remembering the day she fibbed to Mrs. Wallace so the woman would stop her interminable harangue about receiving Christ into her black heart. "You're lucky to have a purpose in life, Wally. That's what Edna needs. She'd feel so much better if she just felt useful."

"That is entirely her fault, Mrs. Schmidt. You don't know how hard I've tried to include her in my work. All she'd have to do is come down to my room. The Lord would fill her heart immediately and she'd have His work to do for the rest of her days."

"I don't think evangelism is in Edna's line, Wally." Elizabeth smiled into the woman's horsey face. "Not everyone is blessed with your faith."

"How true," said Mrs. Wallace. "Oh, there's Mr. Martin. I must speak with him before he runs off and locks himself in his room. I feel he's very close to seeing the light, as it were. I might be able to share the joy of a conversion with Mr. Wallace later on this evening, when I say my prayers." She jumped up to pursue the bird-like man into the foyer.

Elizabeth sighed with relief. She chuckled as Arthur batted the big woman away before covering his ears with his small hands. With a return of her contemplative mood, she surveyed the stragglers dawdling over their tea. She waved at Merle, who was gesticulating madly at Vera Potts and rolling her eyes so Elizabeth would notice the woman's change of clothing. Elizabeth nodded, getting up stiffly to make her way to Vera's table.

"My dear Miss Potts," she exclaimed, breathing heavily with this small exertion. "You look wonderful. Is this a new dress you're wearing?"

Vera Potts stared down into her teacup. She was used, by now, to the special brand of snobbery practiced by some of the lodgers. She held herself rigidly as Elizabeth spoke, just as she did when she was a young girl at school and felt the first intimations of human cruelty because she was not like the others, because she was poor. In her mind, the pattern begun so many years earlier had changed only insofar as her persecutors' faces changed. Resigned to her role in life, she knew she would always be an object of pity and scorn. She bore Elizabeth's callous interest with dignity because she had decided that very morning she would not endure her fellow lodgers taunts much longer. Unable to discover how to change the fact of her poverty, Vera Potts took comfort from knowing that at least she could end it.

Elizabeth, seeing this skirmish as light-hearted fun and intending no real harm, went on. "Now, Vera," she said, wishing Edna was with her as witness. "You mustn't be shy. You look lovely. Have you been dieting?"

Merle rescued Elizabeth from Vera's silence by sidling up to her, linking arms, and leading her toward the foyer while talking loudly about her son's new condominium in Florida. When Vera was well out of earshot, Merle dropped her voice. "I swear they had to chisel the old dress off. She was months in that thing."

"Years," said Elizabeth. "I'm sure someone had to call in a gravel truck to haul away the remains. I'm so sorry Eddie missed it."

"Well," said Merle, "Vera don't have it easy, you know. She ain't got a soul in the world. Not like us. Family's so important." She flashed her rings at Elizabeth. "My son gave me every one of these. He spoils me rotten."

Elizabeth looked with distaste at the large, glittering gems. "I'd say you're certainly spoiled, Merle." She smiled when the other woman looked pleased. "But Eddie will be sorry she didn't notice Vera's dress. She prides herself on keeping up with everything."

"Do you suppose Miss Potts got it at the Goodwill? I think that's all she can afford, seeing how she seems to spend all her money on food. At least that's my opinion, judging from the size of her. 'Course finding something in her size'd be a problem, too. She'd have to wait for somebody as big as her to clean out a closet."

"Maybe she bought two and sewed them together," Elizabeth offered wisely as she and Merle joined the last of the lodgers waiting for the elevator.

Merle winked suggestively at Elizabeth as the elevator doors wheezed open. "Are you girls readin' anything hot and heavy these days?"

"We took our Mickey Spillanes back to the library last week and couldn't find anything even remotely exciting. Edna's sure the librarian hides all the good stuff when she sees us coming."

"That bookmobile ain't much better. I'll get my son to send up a box of paperbacks. He sent me some Harold Robbins books last time. Now *they* were entertaining." She winked again. "But you know, I took them over to the lounge for the others when I finished them — you know how I like to share my good fortune — and they disappeared. I heard a rumour that Mr. Wallace was burning them the night he died."

A fleeting frown furrowed Elizabeth's brow. "I thought he died of heart," she said.

"Gee," Merle mused. "I could've sworn somebody told me he choked to death in a fire in his bathroom."

"That's odd," said Elizabeth. "I've never heard that before. I wonder if Mrs. Wallace would set us straight although I do hate to bring up the subject."

"I know what you mean," said Merle. "Life ain't easy for the widow."

Elizabeth looked at Merle sideways and, discovering her earnestness, suppressed her smile. She walked slowly into the waiting elevator at the last of the group, shook off Merle's arm so the woman would not make more of their friendly chat than Elizabeth wanted her to, and yawned. "I'm going straight to bed," she said comfortably. "I've had a full day."

Taking the hint, Merle patted Elizabeth's arm. When the elevator door opened onto the fourth floor, Merle said grandly, "I'll let you know when them books arrive," and disappeared into her room.

"Thank you," Elizabeth called after her. "Sleep well."

Once the doors closed and the elevator began its ascent, a voice boomed out from the back of the elevator. "I can't stand that woman."

"Nor can I," another agreed.

Elizabeth smirked. "Now, now, people. We're all God's children," she said, imitating Mrs. Wallace. She laughed at the chorus of boos that welled up behind her. When the doors opened on the seventh floor, she walked into the hall and turned to face those remaining inside. "Good night all," she called airily, blowing the familiar, smiling faces a kiss as the doors wheezed shut.

Edna was in the lounge, waiting for Elizabeth. "You missed a time," Elizabeth told her exuberantly. "If you'd hung around, you would have seen Vera's new dress. The tent maker's been at it again."

Edna shot her friend an icy look. "For someone who's always preaching charity to me, you can certainly display a great lack of it."

"Come on, Eddie," Elizabeth said, exasperated. "You make fun all the time."

"I don't. Not of Vera. She can't help it if she's poorer than the rest of us."

"How do you know she's any poorer than the rest of us?" Elizabeth asked. "She just doesn't spend her money on clothes. Merle says she eats it all up."

"Merle is an idiot, Lizzie. She doesn't know anything about anyone except her fifty-year-old baby, if she knows anything about him. Maybe Vera feels so empty she has to overeat to fill up that big hole inside of her. There was an article in . . . ."

"I'm sick to death of your quotes from that silly magazine, Edna. Vera's fat and she doesn't change her clothes. I don't like it. People should take pride in their appearance."

"Around here that's about all people do take pride in," Edna answered sourly. "It doesn't do us a damn bit of good. What does it matter what we look like on the outside when on the inside we're dead?"

"Speak for yourself, Eddie. And I'd like to know why you can walk around criticizing everyone and everything to me, but when I open my mouth just once about Vera, you act like I'm a monster."

"Because Vera can't help it," Edna snapped.

"Edna, you're a hypocrite. Just this afternoon you said there was something wrong with that little writer. She's come to help and you treated her as if she were in league with the devil."

The contradiction in her attitudes toward people bothered Edna but she wouldn't admit this fact to Lizzie. "There's a big difference between criticizing somebody who obviously makes her living off the pain of other people and criticizing someone who's poor and lonely," she said. She was delighted to feel a sudden wave of self-righteousness.

Elizabeth snapped her fingers. "That is absolute nonsense. If Vera's so poor, how can she afford to live here?"

Transported by her powers of invention, Edna took pleasure in supplying Elizabeth with details. "She can't, Lizzie. She's subsidized." The effect of her story further delighted Edna. Elizabeth slumped against the counter of the lounge's Pullman kitchen.

"How do you know that?" Elizabeth asked, overwhelmed with guilt.

"I just know," Edna said.

"Really, Eddie? Like on welfare?"

"Welfare, old-age supplement," Edna said, tossing out the words like so much loose change. "There's not much difference."

"You mean she needs the supplement?" Elizabeth shook her head with shame. "She mustn't have a thing."

Edna continued to spin joyfully. "She wasn't married, so she couldn't have her husband's pension."

Elizabeth's shame lifted momentarily and she smiled wickedly. "Yes," she said. "That's the one thing mine was good for."

Wanting to rekindle Elizabeth's pity, Edna forged ahead. "You know where she'll have to go when they toss her out of here? A Home for the Aged."

"That sounds like something out of Charles Dickens."

"It very likely is," said Edna, pretending wisdom in such matters. Reluctantly, she left the subject of Vera Potts to attend to more practical concerns. "Come to my room. That young woman will want to move in. I'll get my things."

Elizabeth followed Edna across the hallway and through her open door to discover a heap of photographs in the centre of Edna's bed. "Why did you have all those out?" she asked, glad to forget Vera for a time. She and Edna had taken the photographs out of the needlepoint-covered footstool numerous times to sift through Edna's past caught in tin-type, sepia, and black and white.

Edna answered crankily. "I don't know. I suppose I was looking for something." Her mood lightened as she catalogued her supplies for the move to Elizabeth's room: "Nightie, Polident and brushes, soap, facecloth, sherry, port, apricots . . . ."

Elizabeth interrupted the litany. "I left my coat downstairs," she said, very much annoyed at her forgetfulness.

"I brought it up when I got mine."

"You're a pet," Elizabeth answered. "I got so engrossed with

Merle I forgot we'd been out. She's going to give us some dirty books. Her son sends them from Florida."

Staring down at the photos, Edna shook her head. "I wish what's wrong with me could be fixed by a smutty book or two." She swept the old pictures into the seat of the footstool but left the lid on the bed. "I'm even going to take a fresh dress for tomorrow," she said, rummaging in her closet. "Diana Mallory will get tired of this old work horse. *If* she's still here to notice anybody's idiosyncrasies."

Elizabeth didn't defend Diana because she was thinking about Vera Potts again. She wondered what she would do if faced with similarly bleak circumstances. Her children were settled in British Columbia, a place as distant to Elizabeth as China because she'd never travelled outside Ontario. She wondered if she'd have the nerve to follow them out to the coast if she needed to move, wondered too if they would welcome her. They wrote regularly – girls always did, she said – but they were married with families to care for. It was because of this that she'd moved to the lodge soon after it opened its doors. A neighbour, also recently widowed, had moved in and Elizabeth missed her company. She didn't know where else to go when running her house became bothersome after her husband died.

"Did you know I sold my house furnished?" Elizabeth asked suddenly. "I wonder where all my things have got to?"

"Marion kept all of mine that were any good and gave what she didn't want to the Salvation Army," Edna said. "I didn't want them to go, but I couldn't bring them here with me."

"Why did you move in, Edna?"

"In a moment of weakness I let Marion talk me into it. She was sure some thug would kill me if I lived in that big house alone. Ran around saying it's not Toronto the Good anymore. I got so tired of seeing her frenzied face, I capitulated. I was a fool. I could have handled any thugs. It's the viper downstairs I'm not so sure about."

"Well," said Elizabeth. "You just listen to me and keep your nose clean. There's no reason Bernice has to be a problem if we're clever. We'll have our fun on the QT."

Edna sat on the bed, thoughtful. "I don't think I'm after fun," she said. There was a tap at the door. "Come in," she called, glad of the diversion.

Diana Mallory pushed the door open with her foot. "I've come to drop off a few things before I go on a walking tour, Mrs. Carver," she said brightly.

Edna studied her. "How did you like dinner?"

Diana made an unpleasant face. "I've had better."

"Me, too," Edna said. "Just put your things on the bed. I'm almost finished collecting my belongings."

"Will you give me a key?"

"What ever for?"

"Don't you lock your doors when you leave your rooms?"

"If I thought there was the remotest chance someone would come prowling around, I'd leave the door open and a light on so they could find their way in." She laughed at Diana's absurd concerns. "You don't need to worry about anyone coming in when you're not here. Except for Arthur Martin. And I don't think you're his type. You can lock the door once you're in for the night if it makes you feel better."

Diana brought her things to Edna's bed. "Do you have two beds, Mrs. Schmidt?"

"No, but Bernice keeps a couple of rollaway beds on hand for emergencies like this."

"One of the girls set it up during dinner," said Edna. "I met her in the lounge just after she'd finished."

"I hope you won't be too inconvenienced."

"That has yet to be seen," said Elizabeth.

"Oh, come on, Lizzie. It's going to be fun." Edna pulled a large cosmetic bag out of a bureau drawer and filled it with toiletries. "You'll have to ask Bernice to get someone to bring you fresh towels, Miss Mallory. Don't worry about the bed. It was changed this morning."

Edna noted Diana's envious look. "Do they do that for you every week?"

"Yes," said Elizabeth. "And they make them for us every day, as well. To my mind, the vacuuming is the best service. It's so delightful, Miss Mallory. We never have to lift a finger to clean up after ourselves."

"It sounds wonderful. I haven't had my bed made for me in years." The young woman laughed at this childish desire for permanent room service.

Edna frowned. "It's a waste of our poor little girls' time, if you ask me. They've got enough to do without bed making."

Listening to Edna as she tossed her dress over her arm and picked up her overnight bag, Diana sensed that she'd failed the older woman in some way. "Are you sure . . ." she began.

"I'm ready, Lizzie. Let's go down to your room and let Miss Mallory settle in." At the door, she turned to a bewildered Diana. "By the way, are you going on your walking tour alone?"

"Miss Wilson is taking me."

"I thought so," said Edna smugly. "Well, sweet dreams, dear." She opened the door. "Oh, Lizzie, I hung your coat in my closet. Your hat is on the shelf."

Elizabeth went to the closet and pulled out her grey, light-weight wool coat and stood on her tiptoes to reach the cranberry-coloured hat. Diana walked around the bed to help her.

"May I carry your things for you?" she asked, still hoping for a friendlier parting.

Edna laughed grimly. "Really, we're being killed with kindness as it is. Leave us to do one or two things for ourselves, or our muscles will vanish altogether." She walked haughtily down the hall.

Elizabeth smiled, understanding a little of what Diana was feeling. "Don't mind Edna, Miss Mallory. She doesn't mean to be rude. It's just . . . . Oh, I don't know. She's got more spirit than the rest of us, I guess. This forced slow-down doesn't sit well with her. She's a good soul, really."

Touched by Elizabeth's loyalty, Diana reached out, letting her hand rest lightly on the woman's arm. "She's very lucky to have you for a friend," she said.

Elizabeth laughed. "Oh, no, Miss Mallory. You've got it wrong. I'm the lucky one, and most of the time I'm smart enough to know it."

"Lizzie!" Edna called from the hall.

Watching Elizabeth take careful steps toward the door, Diana reflected on humanity's fragility. This would happen to her if she lived into old age. Her strength would ebb and she would shrink in stature. When Elizabeth made her exit, Diana felt the inevitable loss with surprising force. Searching for comfort, she noticed her typewriter, a small portable, peeking out of her canvas bag. She took it out and decided to work at the vanity next to the wall mirror in which Edna's doppelganger tidied her hair earlier that afternoon. The room seemed far more depressing now that Edna and Elizabeth were gone from it. The bureau beside the old rocker seemed especially alien since Edna had removed her silver brush set from its veneered surface.

She set her typewriter up quickly, wanting to dispel the gloomy thoughts brought on by old age and cheap furnishings. The furniture offered an apt metaphor for life at the lodge and, she thought with a shiver, life generally. She looked at her face in the mirror and found her own exterior depthless, thin. It worried her, this sudden cynicism. She sat down on the edge of the bed, her hands cradling her smarting abdomen. Since dinner, she had been bothered by a tiresome ache that came and went. This ache wasn't as troublesome as the cramps she'd experienced earlier, but its pulsing nature wore her down. She searched for something to take her mind off her belly and noticed Edna's photographs in the open foot stool. Picking up three, she stared at the handsome features of Edna's younger self. She'd been a beauty, far more so than her pretty, well heeled daughter.

A fleeting impatience quivered around Diana's mouth as she thought of Marion's description of her mother. The woman's superficiality had always annoyed Diana, but now that she'd met the mother Marion referred to in martyred tones she thought she might come to dislike her if fate brought them together more frequently. She suspected Marion had never allowed herself to imagine her mother's desolation at the loss of her freedom – what amounted to her essence. No wonder Edna Carver hated Sunset Lodge. She was not a person to settle for church work, tea parties, and television shows, as Diana knew Marion was. Lost in these musings, the writer didn't hear Bernice Wilson enter Edna's room. She looked up, startled by the manager's polite cough.

"Are you ready for your tour?" the woman asked in her whistling, hollow voice.

Diana replaced the photos guiltily and shouldered her bag with its comforting pen and notepad. With a sense of purpose, Bernice led the reporter to the elevator.

"We'll go down to the basement and work our way up," Bernice said. She pushed the button to call the elevator with an elaborate flourish of her hand. "We have a laundry facility with ten washers and dryers, commercial of course. Residents observe a very strict laundry schedule, with no deviation, to avoid disorganization in personal habits of cleanliness." Diana felt the woman's smugness grow as she described her organizational accomplishments. "I do everything alphabetically here: A to E on Monday; F to J on Tuesday; K to O on Wednesday; P to T on Thursday; the last on Friday, along with dining room linens. Of course, the help does their laundry. Residents simply have to have their laundry bags ready on their specific day." She thought about her well organized approach to laundry for a moment. "Oh, yes, on weekends, we do the linens to have ready for the following Monday's change of sheets and towels."

"You're very well organized," Diana observed dryly.

"Organization is the key to running a place this size successfully, Miss Mallory," the manager answered, missing Diana's tone. The elevator doors opened. "Here we are." Chatting quietly, the women stepped inside. From the far end of the hall Edna watched, waiting for them to disappear into the elevator.

"They've gone," she whispered to Elizabeth conspiratorially. "I think now is the time for a little chat with Vera. I'll make sure she knows you meant no harm."

Elizabeth radiated sheepishness. "I suppose *I* should do that, Eddie," she said wearily. "But I've not got the strength. I need my bath before I apologize."

"I'll tell her how badly you feel, Lizzie. Just leave it to me." She left her friend to run her bath and walked the short distance to Vera Potts' door.

"Vera? It's Edna Carver." She listened intently for an invitation to come in but heard nothing. She tried another tactic as she rapped softly. "I'm going to make a nice pot of tea. Shall I set out a cup for you, Vera?" She listened again. "We have a little port," she said, remembering their newest acquisition. "Would you like to take a little wine with Elizabeth and me?"

Edna moved quickly into the shadows when the elevator doors opened at the far end of the hall. Unseen, she observed Arthur Martin get off the elevator and head for her room. "You old fool," she mumbled as she charged down the hall. "Get away from there," she called. "What do I have to do to make you leave me alone?"

Arthur grinned as Edna barreled down on him. "I'm having a little celebration, Edna. My daughter sent me some chocolates and I want to share them with you."

"I don't want your chocolates. And stay away from my room. I know damn well what you mean when you say celebration. Why don't you invite Merle? She's ripe for this sort of shenanigan."

"I don't want Merle," Arthur whined. "I want you. Come up to my room and let me give you a chocolate."

Edna tapped his shoulder and the little man fell against the wall. "The only reason I'd come up to your room would be to push you out the window. Stay away from me, Arthur. You make me sick."

"If you don't come, I'll tell Miss Wilson you tried to hurt me. She'll send you to Tranquil Time, like she does all the ones who don't know how to behave."

"You don't scare me. I've handled bigger men than you in my day."

"What on earth is going on out there? Who's doing all the shouting?" Elizabeth's voice wafted down to them from the other end of the hall.

"I'll be right there, Lizzie. I'm getting rid of some vermin in the hall."

Arthur's wizened face turned malevolent. "You can't treat me like this, Edna. You're no better than anybody else."

Edna leaned over him. "I'm a hell of a lot better than the likes of you. Feeling people up in elevators for a cheap thrill," she said, shaking with indignation. "You're just lucky I didn't report you. But I will, Arthur. If you ever touch me again, or come snooping around to buy me with chocolates, I'll make you miserable for the rest of your inconsequential life."

Arthur slid sideways along the wall. "I'm going to tell," he whined, inching away from Edna. "I'm going to tell that you talked dirty to me and tried to steal my chocolates."

Edna laughed. "Nobody in their right mind would pay attention to a lecherous beast like you. But if you open your mouth to Bernice, I'll make you very, very sorry."

The elevator opened again, prompting Edna to hurry down to Elizabeth's room. Arthur shouted something after her but she was too angry to listen. She slammed Elizabeth's door and slumped on the rollaway.

"Really, Lizzie," she cried through the bathroom door. "Sometimes it's more than I can bear."

But Elizabeth had the water running and didn't hear her. Edna thought of her plans to talk with Vera but didn't dare leave Elizabeth's room until she was sure Arthur was gone, afraid she would give in to the temptation to strangle the man. She turned bright pink remembering the first time he'd caught her alone in the elevator and, without any warning, grabbed her breasts. She'd knocked him backward, almost off his feet, but he was hardly discouraged. A few days afterward, in a moment of self pity, she'd told Mrs. Wallace about the incident. The newly widowed woman, not wanting to pass judgment, told Edna she should take his overtures as a compliment, assuring her there were many lonely women who would be thrilled by Arthur's attention. Since Mrs. Wallace's disappointing response, Edna kept the fact of Arthur's impudent behaviour to herself.

She sat up to listen. Whoever came up in the elevator had gone and the hallway was quiet. She suspected Arthur would be gone as well since in the past his persistence manifested in little bursts of energy rather than long sieges. She peaked into the hall, and, finding it empty, called on Vera again.

She rapped softly. When she got no response, alarm prompted her to rap sharply. "Vera! Vera? It's Edna Carver. Vera! Let me in!" On an impulse, she tried the door and found it locked. A sudden, unexpected wave of dread washed over Edna. She had planned to simply smooth things over with Vera, but now she suspected something sinister had caused the woman to lock herself in her room. She rushed down the hall and waited impatiently for the elevator. Finally downstairs, she dashed into the kitchen for help. Terrified for Vera's safety, she cried, "Who's got the keys to the rooms?"

The lodge's cook, thin, wary, looked up through the trail of yellow smoke drifting up from the cigarette she held between her lips.

"Miss Wilson," she said, untroubled by Edna's obvious agitation.

Edna banged the stainless steel counter. "We've got a terrible problem on the seventh floor," she cried. "I have to find her. Where is she?"

"I don't know," the cook answered in the same indifferent tone.

Edna ran into the dining room and discovered a waitress vacuuming the floor. "Where's Miss Wilson?" she cried. When the woman shrugged, Edna decided to visit the manager's private suite, pleased to violate what she called Bernice's pathological demand for privacy. She wound around the circuitous hallway to the manager's apartment and banged loudly on her door.

"Miss Wilson. Miss Wilson!" She was shouting now. "I need your keys. There's an emergency." She remembered Diana's tour of the building and rushed back to the foyer just as Diana and Bernice stepped out of the elevator.

Seeing them somehow validated Edna's fear. "Thank God," she cried, impulsively touching Bernice's arm.

Diana watched the manager change from house-proud hostess to patronizing caretaker. "What are you doing down here at this hour, Mrs. Carver? You should be in bed." The tour left Diana overwhelmed by Bernice's compulsive need to order the people who made the lodge their home. Now she was overwhelmed by the manager's need to shrink Edna, to tuck her away neatly, as if she were a sweater, in one of the moth-balled trunks in the basement storage room. Diana couldn't understand why Edna didn't instantly shrivel into a pile of dust.

Despite the manager's psychic assault, Edna remained her formidable self. "Vera's locked her door and I can't get her to answer," she cried. The acoustics of the foyer were meant to mute sound but Edna's voice was loud, louder than anything Diana had heard since coming to the lodge.

Diana felt the manager's pointed look but refused to collude with her. She heard Bernice say with obvious condescension, "Miss Potts is probably resting, Mrs. Carver. Let's not bother her." The words sounded kind enough but beneath the kindness, obliterating it, the manager continued her assault.

"No," the older woman said. "There's something wrong in there." Fascinated, Diana watched Edna play her trump card. "Are you going to open the door or shall I call the police?"

The tension between the two women prompted Diana to step back. Bernice looked like a woman preparing to strike a naughty child. Moving closer, Edna stared her challenge into the manager's immobile face.

"Why don't you go upstairs and make a nice cup of tea?" the manager suggested after she recovered from her surprise at Edna's persistence. Diana shivered with revulsion at the sound of the coldly hollow voice.

Edna responded to this suggestion as if some gauntlet had been flung down. "You have tea if you want it, Miss Wilson. I'm calling the police." She brushed past the manager to claim the elevator. Bernice followed.

"I'll go up with you to prove there's nothing wrong," Bernice said in an artificially polite voice. "And you'll tell her you're sorry you made a fuss and bothered her, like a good girl, won't you."

As the elevator doors closed, Diana continued to sort through the emotions she felt as she watched the women's battle of wills. Suddenly she knew she had to be with them when they met with Vera Potts. She dashed for the stairs. By the time she reached the seventh floor she was badly winded and in pain but she ignored her abdomen. She arrived in time to hear Bernice call out before fumbling with the keys on a large ring attached by a chain to the belt of her thick tweed skirt. With a key poised, she tried the door. It was unlocked. She looked at Edna pointedly. Diana peered in. Vera Potts' door opened into a room exactly like Edna's but missing any trace of individual personality. To Diana, it looked as though no one had ever lived there.

"Mrs. Potts," the manager called pleasantly.

Edna rushed past her into the airless room.

"Vera," she cried. "It's Edna."

Diana watched the manager's face settle into a triumphant smirk. "Shall we go along to Mrs. Schmidt's room for a rest now?" she suggested, infinitely kind.

Still agitated, Edna opened the bathroom door and stalked inside as if she might be a tightly wound toy instead of a flesh-and-blood woman. Diana feared there would be no way to calm Edna and that she would charge around the building in this state for the rest of her life.

But Edna came out of the bathroom far calmer than she'd entered. "I wouldn't have wanted to surprise her naked in the tub," she said with a joyless laugh. Before Bernice could respond, Edna dashed out of the room and down the hallway.

The manager spoke directly to Diana for the first time since the episode with Edna began. "I am so sorry about all this, Miss Mallory," she said. She shrugged her shoulders in a plea for sympathy. "She will be so much better off at Tranquil Time. Our Edna's a dear when she's not deluded, but those moments are fewer and fewer." The manager waited for Diana's sympathy. When she received none, she followed Edna down the hall.

Edna hurried to the lounge, expecting to find Vera Potts sobbing on the sofa. She planned to embrace her, include her in the magic circle she and Elizabeth formed, but when she arrived, she found the lounge empty. In an instant she noticed the open balcony doors and the chair pushed tight against the high railing. She stood for a moment, confusion dissipating the powerful energy that had insisted she rescue Vera. She walked to the railing and looked down. There, seven floors below, people were gathering around a small, light-coloured form on the rain-washed pavement. Edna blinked, uncomprehending, and then she knew. The street had become a long black river that would carry Vera Potts to a kinder destination.

It seemed to take years for the others to join her. Hearing a high, whispered cry, Edna turned, imaging a baby had just wakened and needed tending. But it was only Bernice, pale and still, staring at the chair beside the railing, and the other one, the young woman Marion had sent. After she collected herself, Bernice rushed to the balcony.

"Good God," the manager muttered. "Now I'll have to lock these doors as well." As soon as she said the words, she wanted to call them back, but they'd flown out of her mouth too quickly and with too much force.

Diana could not make herself walk to the railing to look down. When Edna stumbled to the sofa to collapse, the writer sat beside her, tentatively putting her arm around Edna's shoulders. She was grateful for something to do.

Bernice turned on them. Diana jumped guiltily, as though she had been the cause of it all. "Mrs. Carver," said the manager with deliberate slowness. "You must go back to Mrs. Schmidt's room. I don't want anyone else upset by your difficulties."

Diana wanted to defend Edna, wanted to shout that this was not her fault. She turned to the older woman, her face close enough to kiss, seeing the fine network of lines as so many scars made by previous battles with Bernice Wilson. She felt the weight of these battles shift to her own shoulders as they sat together, mute, upon the sofa.

Edna found it difficult to accept Diana's tenderness, to bear the heat of the young, strong arm clasping her shoulders. Awkwardly, she stood. She walked, strangely numb, from the lounge to Elizabeth's room. Without looking back, she slipped inside and noiselessly closed the door. Inside, Elizabeth was putting on a short red robe over her nightie. Hearing the door open, she looked up.

"What's the matter, Eddie? You're white as a sheet. I heard a terrible ruckus in the hall."

"Lizzie," Edna said quietly, still not quite believing the reality of what she'd seen. "I'm afraid Vera has killed herself."

"What?"

"She jumped off the balcony," Edna said. She lowered herself to the rollaway bed and buried her face in the pillow. The room was silent save for Edna's mournful howls.

Finally, Elizabeth spoke. "I've killed her," she whispered. "I pushed her over when I made fun of her new dress."

"No," said Edna. "This goddamned place killed her."

Elizabeth wanted to share the blame for Vera's death but knew with a terribly clarity that she couldn't. Overcome with shame, she invited the full weight of her guilt to fall on her shoulders. Silently, she contradicted Edna's indictment of the lodge, knowing she would have to deal with what she'd done later, alone, when Edna was asleep. For now, she looked at her friend tenderly. All at once, Edna removed the pillow. Fury distorted her fine features.

"Bernice is blaming me, of course."

"Why?" Elizabeth asked, surprised she had not yet been struck dumb. "Was it Vera you were fighting with out there?"

"Fighting? Oh," Edna said, remembering. "I had to fight off Arthur. He tried to buy me with some candy."

"I don't think Vera would kill herself over that," Elizabeth said.

"Don't be obtuse, Lizzie. Arthur had nothing to do with Vera. He was just out there lurking in the hall when I went to call on her. I was going to ask her to have tea with us." Edna looked up at Elizabeth for a moment before abandoning herself to another fit of weeping. "Lizzie, if only I'd persisted. Vera must have sneaked out when I went downstairs to get the key for her room. I'm such a fool.

I thought . . . ." She stopped herself, realizing she had not known what she was thinking as she charged around feeling Vera was in trouble and needed her. It terrified her to think that she might have inadvertently sent Vera over the balcony with her hysteria.

Deep within her own dark halls of recrimination, Elizabeth did not notice Edna's terror. She wanted to beg Vera for forgiveness even as she understood she was beyond redemption. She sat opposite Edna and looked down at her small white hands, so seemingly serene in her lap.

Edna's whispered question came from a long way off. "Could I be to blame, Lizzie? Is Wilson right about me? Do I upset everyone?"

Elizabeth put aside her own grief to comfort Edna. "What have you got in your head now, you crazy old woman?"

"You didn't see me," Edna said. "I ran around the place as if I *knew* something like this was going to happen."

"Perhaps you did know," Elizabeth said. "You're very perceptive about people, Edna. Maybe you knew, but didn't want to know you knew."

In spite of herself, Edna began to giggle.

"Perhaps if *I'd* been more perceptive, I wouldn't have made those remarks at dinnertime." Elizabeth shook her head forlornly. "Oh, Eddie, what have I done?"

"You didn't do anything so terrible."

"But I did," Elizabeth cried. "I made fun of Vera. On purpose."

"She's been made fun of at least a hundred times before. Why would it make such a difference tonight? No," Edna added firmly. "That's not what did it. I didn't mean to, but I caused this catastrophe. Somehow my panic got away from me. It leaked out of my head and contaminated Vera."

"Edna," Elizabeth said with quiet matter-of-factness. "You sound nuts."

Edna smiled suddenly. "*That* would be a blessing. I think we should get out the port."

When Bernice excused herself to notify the authorities, Diana shut herself in Edna's room and locked the door. The tour she had taken with the manager replayed itself as she lay on Edna's bed fighting pain. She squeezed her eyes closed tightly, saw again the nine floors identical to Edna's, pictured each frail inhabitant she'd been introduced to, heard the same polite response to her intrusion into their sanctuary. That's what Bernice had called the lodge over and over again, but what it was a sanctuary from the manager hadn't said. Diana wondered if the lodge was more a refuge for Bernice Wilson than the lodgers. Bernice's thick white scar expanded in her imagination.

The young writer opened her eyes, rubbed her sore belly with the palms of her hands, and stared at the plastic ceiling fixture cradling the dim overhead light. Patiently, she waited for the jumble of images she'd gleaned from her tour of the lodge to form a theme. Every floor was the same, except for the main floor – where dining room, foyer, manager's office, washroom, and manager's suite were situated – and the third floor with its small two-bed infirmary and doctor's office along with the usual resident rooms.

On the roof of the building was a patio of sorts, grandly labeled ROOF GARDEN. To Diana, this "garden" appeared to be an afterthought among the lodge's heating and cooling fans and exhaust housing. The garden took its name from the few window boxes and hanging plants positioned strategically among the patio tables and chairs that were tucked into a tiny corner of the roof.

Diana fastened upon these few differences with relief. Upon reflection, they were evidence of the possibility, little felt anywhere else in the lodge, of nonconformity. As the manager spoke proudly of the shopping service she had created for the lodgers' convenience, of the bookmobile, of the mobile Chest X-ray Unit that visited every six months, of the hairdressers, nurses, and psychologists, of the clergy visits weekly, bi- and tri-weekly, Diana felt she'd inadvertently stumbled into the presence of someone who unconsciously set out to control the natural ebb and flow of life itself. She was at first amused by the manager's complacent pleasure in stifling her clients. When her amusement ran its course, she felt nothing but pity for a woman so obviously terrified of life.

Diana stood to undress, still puzzling over the manager's pride in creating this strange, air-tight fortress. Even the deviations in the floor plan were safe ones. The doctor, Diana was sure, did little to encourage the lodgers to rebel against the stifling atmosphere. If anything, she speculated, he abetted the manager's need to control the lodge population. After all, he owned the lodge. If he were displeased with the manager's need to control everything, he could easily replace her.

Nor was Diana surprised to find the roof garden, such as it was, under strict supervision. The doors were locked for the entire winter, and when they were opened in the spring, the lodgers were allowed to enjoy it only for very short, supervised periods. She stood with her hands resting lightly on the buttons of her white shirt, doing her best to fathom the rigidity of the lodge's routine. Thinking of Vera Potts as she undid her buttons, she wondered if the manager's scar might be the remnant of her own attempted suicide. Perhaps Bernice Wilson's hold on life was so tenuous she had to create this fortress as defense against the compulsion to try to end her life again. Replaying the discovery of Vera's suicide, Diana felt sure something was very wrong with the manager because she hadn't expressed the natural emotions well adjusted people express when someone they care for suddenly commits suicide.

The writer laughed bitterly as she hung her blouse on one of Edna's hangers. Bernice had deflected, quite neatly, Diana's attention away from the person who'd brought her to the lodge. Edna Carver might very well appear to be crazy now and again, but to Diana Edna's craziness had purpose. It was the only way to escape the lodge's deadly monotony. She pulled off her boots, knickers, and underwear and went to the mirror, looking at herself differently than she had before she'd come to the lodge. Her smooth, naked body with its clear skin and clean lines had always been something she had taken for granted. Since meeting Edna a fresh lens had been added to her faculties of perception. Her body's strength, she now saw, was fleeting, its beauty temporary. This new lens sharpened her intuition, too. She knew with absolute certainty that on a spring night forty or so years before, Edna had looked at herself in such a mirror and through such a lens to acknowledge her own youthful beauty and mourn its inevitable end.

Diana touched the long, angry incision that ran across her pubic bone, a cut she'd ordered her surgeon make to end the possibility of having children. Before the operation, before this night in Edna's room, the decision seemed uncomplicated by any wistful dreams of motherhood. Now, aware of the inevitable time when the strength and beauty of her maturity would be gone, she touched the incision with regret. It would all end soon enough. She needn't have rushed to hasten the end of her fertility.

Tears slid down her smooth cheeks as she grieved, not for her unborn children, but for her aging self. She turned from the mirror quickly, knocking over the opened footstool and unearthing Edna's past from its small, tidy grave. She stooped to retrieve the photographs, her eyes gliding over Edna at ten, at twenty, at thirty. She dropped to the floor to pore over Edna's mystery, willing some connection with her own.

In some of these photographs, Edna stood alone, strong, straight, and directly facing the camera with a laughing audacity. In some she found Edna as Madonna, cradling Marion in swaddling clothes, her manger a lovely old wooden cradle. In others she found Edna in the midst of some task, a relentless, determined, unyielding woman whose eyes seemed to defy the camera's ability to capture anything soft in her nature. These harder images comforted Diana. She thought perhaps this Edna, like herself, was unsentimental in biological matters. Back then, Diana knew, choosing not to have children was far more difficult for women than during her lifetime.

Diana relaxed with this determined Edna, her conscious mind flooding with unexpected joy. If Edna could resist the manager's attempt to control her, to snuff out her determination to live the life she desired, perhaps Diana might one day be victorious in a similar battle. She felt hopeful despite the pain in her gut. She scooped up the photographs tenderly, replaced them in their hiding place, and turned out the overhead light. Crawling into Edna's bed, she relished the feel of the cool, stiff sheets on her hot skin. Sleep came to her as easily as she had slipped into Edna's life.

Bernice finished with Vera Potts quickly, even down to the details of having her room cleared out by the night staff. Tersely, she instructed Maintenance to arrange to have all the balcony doors fitted with safety locks the very next day. There would be no further incidents.

Her emotions, however, were more difficult to manage. Despite her attempts to attend to mundane tasks, the manager began to remember fragmented images of her own earlier attempt to rush away from life. She had not thought of these events for many years, believing she had successfully managed her past as she now successfully managed lodge challenges. Vera's suicide opened a door to that earlier time. Feeling haunted, she remembered far more than she wanted to.

She shook off these distressing memories when the lodge's owner appeared in the foyer. The doctor grinned at her boyishly. "I thought you might need a little company," he said. "Let's have a drink. You look like you could use one."

Diffidently she followed him to her suite, both pleased and angry at his assumption that she needed comfort. At the same time, she resented that he took her need for him for granted after all her years of running the lodge. Her resentment made her turn a cool cheek to him when they reached her apartment. She was disappointed when the doctor seemed not to notice.

"God, I've had a day," he said. "This Potts business is the perfect way to end it."

She turned on him. "I couldn't help it. There was nothing to indicate she planned this."

He frowned at her. "Take off that damned outfit. You know I hate to see you looking like one of them."

Bernice dipped her head to hide her smile. "I told you why I dress like this. It gives me more authority."

In the beginning, dressing as her mother had dressed before she'd died, even to the detail of the wig, lent credibility to her role of manager at the lodge. Believing the lodge's residents would feel more comfortable with an older woman in charge boosted her confidence as manager. Now she was almost fifty, her mother's age at death, the disguise had become more habit than necessity with the deferential lodgers. Now it was the doctor's reaction to her disguise that prompted her to perpetuate the dowdy image. At the best of times thinking about her motives exhausted her. This evening she had little desire and less energy to work at untangling the emotional brambles of their relationship. He was here, handsome, solid, and as comfortable as her tweed suit and wig. Whatever quirk in her nature fed her delight in annoying him would wait until another day to be parsed. She slipped off the wig and fluffed her short brown hair with the lazy confidence of a cat.

The doctor poured a drink and slumped in a large wing chair. "I still can't understand it," he mused. "I make it as easy as I can for them. There was no reason for her to go this far. She could have come to me."

"Ah, yes," Bernice said smiling cruelly. "The doctor fixes everything with his medicine."

He snorted at her sarcasm. "You'd be lost without it."

She continued to smile. "Oh, I know, Doctor," she said, pretending contrition. She slipped off her glasses, letting them drop to the pile of magazines on the coffee table. "I'd be the first to admit how much I need what you can give me." She stood up, slipped off the bulky tweed jacket, and began to undo the buttons of her too-large, polyester blouse.

He watched her grimly. "Christ, Bernice, why do you always make me feel I should be doing more? Pavlov's dog is no more predictable than a patient on Metaphin. I don't know what more I can do to make your life easier," he said, his voice rising to an unpleasant, childish whine.

She slipped off the blouse and tossed it to him. "Yes," she said. "You're wonderful. They all say so." She unhooked the keys at her waistband and jangled them. "Vera Potts was quite thoughtless to jump, wasn't she?" She undid the button of her shapeless skirt's waistband, allowing the weight of the fabric to take the ugly garment to the floor.

"Shit!" the doctor said, disgusted. "I don't know why I come here. You always try to make me into some kind of ogre."

His manager stepped out of the skirt to sit daintily in his lap. "I'm mean, aren't I?" she whispered. "Not to show how grateful I am to the big, wonderful doctor."

He jumped up then, making her scramble for balance. "I'm getting out of here," he cried. "You make me sick with these goddamned games."

She put a finger to her lips. "They'll hear you, Doctor. You wouldn't want them to know their paragon is down here playing house with their manager." She followed, relentless, as he moved to the door. "Going home to the wife and kiddies? Do they make you feel more perfect?" As she spoke, she tilted back her head, exposing the thick, white scar.

Seeing the symbol of his power, he stood poised between revulsion and desire. He had kept this woman alive against all odds, had rehabilitated a hopelessly dependent and neurotic personality, afterward transforming her into a capable business woman, efficient and reliable. She made the transition from patient to manager to mistress as effortlessly as he thought any healthy woman should. Still, there was in her this need to bring out the very basest in him. Staring down at her, he was torn between grinding her into the carpet with his rage and elevating her to goddess.

He cried out despairingly, lunging at her, shaking her, pushing her to the floor and ripping at her slip. He felt her arms slip around him, her hands grasp his head, pulling him down until his lips rested against her scar.

"There, there," she whispered. "I've been a bad girl. I won't be naughty anymore."

Desire overwhelmed the doctor, blotting out the other, more frightening emotion. His tongue travelled up the white road to her ear and when she moaned, he picked her up and carried her to the bedroom. She seemed as insubstantial as the air he breathed.

Without saying anything to Edna, Elizabeth made her decision to give up the doctor's pills as an act of atonement for killing Vera Potts. Her decision emerged from a muddle of thought and conversation with Edna over glasses of port and a tin of sour candies. Even though Edna had done her best to change her friend's mind, Elizabeth knew the truth. She had killed Vera with her cruelty.

She lay in the darkness listening to Edna's regular breathing, weeping silently, and feeling deeply she was sure, for the first time in ten years. It pleased her to discover the courage to live without the doctor's small shining pacifiers — especially after he'd impressed her with the risk of abandoning them abruptly. Surprised that she suddenly decided to be like Edna and face life head on rather than work to make Edna like her, Elizabeth Schmidt wept with relief. She dabbed at her wet eyes, understanding now that she'd always had the potential for courage. Silently, she railed that she'd had to kill someone in order to summon it now. A flash of insight followed her fear that she had murdered Vera. All her life, the alternative had been to kill herself, not literally, as Vera had done, but just as efficiently. The difference was that she could hide her death in the pretense of living a good, respectable life.

Lying in the dark Elizabeth felt that her life had been nothing more than a desperate attempt to live up to others' rules and expectations. Her mother wanted a dutiful daughter, someone she could point to with pride, even at the end of her life when Elizabeth was well into her forties, as someone who always did as she was told. Her husband wanted – and got, she knew, enraged – a servant, cheerful and uncomplaining, though overworked with childbirth and the drudgery of running a household on little money and less respect. Lying in the comforting darkness, Elizabeth understood that while she had always been aware of her anger at the injustices she experienced, she now understood she'd turned this anger inward. It wasn't her mother, strong and domineering, or her husband, her mother in a man's body, who had thwarted her dreams and sold her into bondage. It was she who'd done that. She wept softly when she admitted that she'd never resisted either of them because she had not known real living required she resist them to honour her own needs, even as they reduced her to a convenience whose sole purpose was to meet theirs.

She brought her fist down on the narrow bed and muttered, "Never again."

Edna stirred in her sleep.

"Hush, hush, Eddie," Elizabeth soothed. "It's all right now. You've got a real friend." She stifled a sob as she recalled her ten years at the lodge, ten years of pill taking to control her justifiable emotions of indignation, anger, and fear. She pushed down the urge to escape into masochistic recriminations. "I've got a little time left," she said. "It's not too late."

"What?" Edna said, grumpy with sleep.

Elizabeth smiled into the darkness. "I think I've had a revelation, Eddie." Her voice, full of wonder, delighted Edna.

The younger woman propped herself up on her elbow to peer into the darkness. "From God?" Edna asked.

Elizabeth cackled happily. "Sort of," she answered. "Only this God doesn't get to church much. She stopped attending ten years back when her husband dropped dead and she tried to hide the joy she felt about it all, even from herself."

"What on earth are you talking about?"

"It doesn't matter that you don't understand, Eddie," whispered Elizabeth. "I do. That's what counts."

Edna flounced to her side and gave her pillow a few good punches. "You sound as crazy as I do, Lizzie. That's not a good sign."

"Oh, you're not as crazy as you'd like everyone to believe, Eddie.

You just use that act as a way out, a way to avoid responsibility. But you'll get over your nervousness. You're right most of the time. One day you'll stop being scared about it. You'll just thumb your nose at the world and get on with your business. You won't need all these poses anymore."

"Do you really think so?" Edna asked.

"I *know* so!" Elizabeth said. "Didn't I just tell you I've had a revelation?"

"I wonder why it's so hard to admit when we see clearly. Even when I was young and painting every single day, getting better and better, it was only good when I was alone. Somehow, when someone else would look at what I'd done, I could feel myself shrink from their praise. I always wanted to hide behind something. 'I'm just an amateur,' I'd say, 'I've never taken a lesson in my life.'" She broke off, too full of emotion to go on.

"But that wouldn't make any difference to anybody else. They'd see your talent, even if you tried to hide it."

"I suppose so. But I'd never let anyone pay for a painting. I always gave them away, almost . . . apologetically."

"You must start again, Eddie. It's not too late to learn to feel comfortable with your gift. That's where your power lies."

Edna snorted. "How would you know? You've never seen a thing I've done."

"I know, Eddie," Elizabeth said quietly. "And so do you. One day, you'll find a reason to admit it. You'll take up where you left off and stop all the excusing and apologizing. You'll just get down to doing the thing you do best – seeing."

Edna tried to resist Elizabeth's belief in her. "Who would want to see that fart Arthur in watercolour?" she asked. "What is there around here that's worth painting?"

"Life's here, Eddie. You already know that. That's why you wanted that writer to come. You want to change the way things are done so life has more of a chance. But you haven't the nerve to do it yourself, yet. You think this young thing will do it better than you will. But no one can do it for you. You see that already. That's why you steal, and have these scenes with Bernice. That's why you take on responsibility for someone like Vera – who's responsible for herself, as we all are – instead of summoning the nerve to start your real work."

Edna was quiet for a long while. At last she said, "Not another word, Lizzie. If we don't get any sleep, I won't be strong enough to assume the mantle and become the Albert Schweitzer of the old folks' home."

"Sweet dreams," Elizabeth whispered. She turned her back to Edna and willed her body to overrule the doctor's threats.

Feeling pleasantly replete, Bernice snuggled into the bed made warm by the doctor's lovemaking, to fall into a triumphant sleep. As she drifted into a dreamlike trance between wakefulness and sleep, she felt sure he was beginning to feel the new truth of their union. Originally, he'd seen himself as her creator, but the power, initially all on his side, had slowly passed into her until now she exulted in her ability to mistreat him and have him remain in her thrall.

In this mood of exultation she drifted into sleep, the overhead light playing on her eyelids. In no time that external light became an internal moon casting its beams on the opalescent marble statue that was her when she dreamed. Seeing the familiar image she moaned with fear, but the moon, relentless, shone its light upon her marble self. Her heartbeat quickened, anticipating the ritual she had performed in dreams for fifteen years. The arms reached up – the right hand holding the sharp, shining blade. It severed the head in one neat stroke. As it fell, doves flew up, up to the source of light. When she heard the doctor's heavy footsteps she moaned again. That sound meant he was returning, the dead birds that had only moments before been alive and flying in his grasping hands. She fought to waken before he could stuff their broken bodies inside her, replace her head, and seal them inside. But she couldn't waken. He was looming over her, imprisoning them inside her with his special magic. She could feel their dead weight. She could smell them as they rotted.

She cried herself awake, her present terror and confusion as sickening now as they had been the first time she'd had this dream. Dreams were the reason the doctor always kept her prescription for sleeping pills filled. Humbled, she crawled out of bed and staggered to the bathroom to take four of them now, admitting, shamefully, how much she needed his medicine. Back in bed, she searched but could find no trace of the doves or the statue. At last she slept, empty and dreamless.

TWO

At breakfast, Mrs. Wallace rushed to Edna to whisper excitedly. "Is it true?" she asked. "Did Vera Potts die last night?" Edna nodded. "What was it?"

"Heart," Edna said soberly. "Broken beyond repair."

"I feel a great failure," the widow confided. "I should have provided balm for her wounds. Mr. Wallace expected that of me."

"She was beyond your help, Wally," said Edna. "You did your best, as you do with all of us."

Mrs. Wallace pressed Edna's hand before returning to her table.

Edna sat down across from Elizabeth, looked her over frankly, and then smiled. "You look better today than I've seen you look in years."

"I feel wonderful, Eddie. Like a girl again."

As they sipped their coffee the pair studied their fellow lodgers. Elizabeth gestured to Arthur. "He looks a bit under the weather today."

"Don't even look at him," Edna hissed. "After last night, I'm not going to bother with civility. I've reached the end of my patience. And if you say 'charity,' I swear I'll bean you."

Elizabeth chuckled. "I wasn't going to say a word. Arthur is entirely your affair."

"Please!" Edna snapped.

Bernice Wilson, sexless in a navy double-knit, three-piece suit, her silver wig shining and her smoky-lens glasses in place, hesitated on the threshold of the dining room before making her morning rounds. She did a quick head count and then made a notation on the clipboard she cradled in her left arm. Diana Mallory walked out of the elevator into the foyer behind the manager. Bernice turned at the sound of the closing doors. She did not smile when she saw the writer.

Edna inclined her head toward the writer. "I bet she's about to catch it for being late. Let's see what she thinks of Bernice after she's been given a tongue lashing."

Elizabeth studied the women in the dining-room doorway. "That young woman looks ghastly. What do you suppose is the matter with her, anyway?"

"The meaning of life – or lack of it," Edna answered. "I bet she doesn't like the idea of growing old."

"Well, that's a laugh. Does she think we invited the process?"

"She probably didn't think much about it at all, before meeting us."

"Stupid lump," said Elizabeth.

Edna smiled jubilantly. "You've stopped taking your pills!"

"If you gloat, I swear I'll run upstairs and take the whole bottle."

"I promise not to say another word." Edna turned her smile to the window.

Diana limped to their table. "Miss Wilson said I should eat with you this morning." she said, sitting slowly. Her voice was more like an automaton's than a young reporter's on the brink of journalistic excellence.

"Lizzie and I would love your company, Miss Mallory," Edna said with a graciousness that unnerved the writer.

Elizabeth looked critically at the young woman. "You look like you've been hit by a truck."

"That's how I feel," Diana admitted. "I'm not sure why."

Edna looked at Elizabeth significantly. She called to a passing waitress. "Could you bring our guest some coffee, dear?" The harassed woman nodded and rushed to the kitchen. "I'd get it for you myself, but the cook would flatten me for stepping into her private domain. They don't appreciate initiative around here."

"I don't know where you get the energy for initiative," the writer said. "I feel I'll never have the strength to do anything again."

"That feeling will pass," said Edna.

"That's the trouble," Diana muttered. "Everything does."

With a pleasant sense of the manipulative nature of what she was about to say, Edna took Diana's cold, limp hand in her own. "A little hard work will make you feel better. Perseverance is invaluable at a time like this."

Diana shrugged helplessly. "I don't know what I'm supposed to persevere at."

"Put one foot in front of the other for a while. Think of this dark mood as a tunnel you've entered. If you don't keep moving, you'll never make it through to the . . ."

Elizabeth interrupted Edna with a cry of indignation. "What the devil is this supposed to be?"

Instantly, a waitress hovered over them. "It's what it always is on Tuesday mornings, Miss," she said with bogus enthusiasm. "It's oatmeal."

Deeply offended, Elizabeth pointed accusingly at her bowl. "No oatmeal *I* ever made looked like this!"

"Well *I* don't make it, so don't yell at me," the young woman snapped.

"I will yell at you. You've got no business serving food like this. Would you eat it?" Without answering, the girl rushed to the next table.

Edna examined the oatmeal. An odd, brownish colour, she bent low to smell the contents of her bowl. "Whatever it is, it has no odour," she said. "It must be something new they're trying out on us."

Elizabeth stood. "Miss Wilson," she called peremptorily. "Come over here."

Astonished, the manager almost sprinted to their table. "What is it, Mrs. Schmidt?" she asked, disguising her alarm.

"What's this supposed to be?"

"You know very well what it is," Bernice said. "The menu hasn't varied since you moved in, Mrs. Schmidt. We know how you count on routine." She smiled at Elizabeth as she would a wayward child. "It's oatmeal."

Infuriated, Elizabeth persisted. "It doesn't look like oatmeal," she said, her cold rage directed at the small bowl. "It doesn't smell like oatmeal." She filled her spoon. "You tell me, does it taste like oatmeal?" Surprising herself as well as the manager, she thrust the spoon into Bernice's open mouth.

Fighting her gag reflex, the manager managed to swallow the tepid, soupy liquid. "Mrs. Schmidt," she mumbled, straining to control her impulse to shout. "We're all upset by last night's events. And I know sharing your room with Mrs. Carver must be difficult," she said, indulging Edna with one of her dazzling smiles. "But today is a fresh start. I suggest we all help to make it a better day by tucking in." She patted Elizabeth's chair invitingly.

Elizabeth pulled herself up to her full five feet. "And I suggest you ask that strange creature who passes herself off as our cook to get out here and tell us what we are being served for breakfast."

Bernice looked around the room nervously. Seeing other lodgers murmuring in agreement, there seemed to be nothing to do but comply. As the manager rushed to the kitchen, Elizabeth nodded happily to those encouraging her in her stand.

Presently, their cook came out of the kitchen carrying an envelope in her hand. Significantly, she'd left her ubiquitous cigarette behind. The lean, bent woman cleared her throat several times before she spoke. "This is good oatmeal," she said, brandishing the envelope in the air. "It's something new, flavoured with brown sugar and apple. They say it's even more nutritious than that other kind." She looked into the faces of the lodgers in a plea for sympathy. "I bought a whole case of it," she said in a wheedling tone, "so I hope you get used to it." She shrugged her shoulders before returning to her steamy sanctuary behind the swinging doors.

"I am not eating it," Elizabeth said, disgusted. "I want real, cooked oatmeal, not this brown fake food."

"This oatmeal is fine," Bernice contradicted gently from the kitchen doors. "It's just as good as the oatmeal you've always eaten, and it's so much more convenient for the cook because it's instant." She smiled benignly. "And we all understand the need for convenience."

Over the capitulating murmurings around her, Elizabeth called, "I'd like to know why, when we pay exorbitant rates for room and board here, the food here has to be convenient for the cook. It should be good tasting and nourishing for us. As you well know, Miss Wilson, it is neither."

Terrified of the possibility of public humiliation that would undermine her authority, Bernice resorted to her deadliest weapon. "Shall I call our children? Shall I worry them because mother and father refuse to eat a perfectly good breakfast?"

Hearing their manager's threat, many lodgers picked up their spoons.

"Just a minute here," said Elizabeth. "We pay for this food. We don't have to eat it if we don't like it. It has nothing to do with our children."

Edna stared up at Elizabeth with shining eyes, until, out of the corner of her eye she saw Mrs. Wallace obediently eating her oatmeal. Indignant, she cried, "Shame on you, Wally!" She leapt to her feet.

"I'm sorry," the widow said, cringing over her bowl. "The Lord's work takes a full stomach."

"Phaugh!" cried Edna. "The Lord's work – and ours – takes courage."

Mrs. Wallace bent low over her breakfast, pretending not to hear Edna's chastisement over the growing din. Edna threw her hands up in disgust.

"Let's go," she said, turning to Elizabeth. "We'll eat out today."

"No, Eddie," Elizabeth said with uncharacteristic defiance. "I've paid for my breakfast. I want something decent to eat right here."

The manager returned to their table. "Mrs. Schmidt," she said, stern now. "As you see, you've created quite a disturbance. The cook has explained that the oatmeal is perfectly good, nourishing food. They wouldn't sell it if it wasn't. Please sit down and eat your breakfast like a good girl or I'll have to call the doctor in for an assessment."

Elizabeth looked up at the cold unmoving face, terrified of this very real possibility. Still, something in her refused to back down. "I will not eat it. It isn't right."

Diana had been listening to this conflict as though it played out in an adjacent room. She looked up at Elizabeth and Edna and Bernice, her elbows resting heavily on the table, her hands cupping her swollen face. She saw Elizabeth's mouth turn down at the corners, heard Edna cry, "Don't you dare bully her. She doesn't have to eat it," so indifferently she wondered if she were watching a television program and not eye witnessing an unlikely insurrection.

She closed her eyes. All at once, she became aware of her fever. "I'm sick," she said with relief. "I'm really sick. I've got a fever."

Edna and Elizabeth took no notice of her. Bernice did her best to stare the women down. When she couldn't, she walked quickly from the dining room. After she'd gone, Edna impulsively hugged her friend.

"You were wonderful," she whispered.

"Fat lot of good it did me," Elizabeth lamented. "Damn. She's calling the doctor to make an assessment. What does that even mean?" Shaking, she sat down to stare into her coffee cup.

"That's just posturing. She's making empty threats," Edna assured her. "She's gone off to nurse her bruises, Lizzie. She can't do anything to you. You really told her."

Elizabeth looked around the dining room. "I might have told her, but look." All around them, lodgers hunched over the instant oatmeal, eating silently.

Edna walked to Mrs. Wallace's table. "How could you, Wally? Lizzie needed your support. Besides, you've got enough fat on you to live through a week of fasting." Mrs. Wallace went on eating. "Damn," Edna cried. "Put down that spoon and fight for your rights."

Mrs. Wallace offered Edna a feeble smile. "We must be positive, Mrs. Carver. This oatmeal isn't that bad." She swallowed noisily. "Now please sit down and eat yours," she pleaded. "I don't want any trouble."

"You've got it anyway. We've all got it." Edna turned this way and that in her desire to address her fellow residents. "Elizabeth is right. We shouldn't have to eat anything that isn't good, honest food." Because he was the closest to her, she touched Arthur Martin's arm, willing temporarily to forget their differences in her desperation to unite the group. "Tell us honestly, Arthur. Is this like the oatmeal your mother used to make?"

"Better," Arthur cried in a high shrill voice.

Edna stood open-mouthed for a few moments, disbelieving his pettiness. "You, Arthur Martin, are a liar, a contemptuous, evil liar," she said at last.

The waitresses stopped gathering up dishes, stunned when Edna turned over Arthur's bowl, spilling oatmeal over the tablecloth and onto the floor. "That's what all of you should do with this mush – and all the mush they feed us. We have teeth!" she cried. "I have teeth."

Looking around, Edna understood at last that their collective fear was greater than her power to persuade them to fight. She saw this fear plainly in their pinched and anxious faces. Defeated, she shrugged. "Maybe you're all getting what you deserve. Maybe you don't merit anything more than whatever it is they're willing to give us." She walked back to her table and sat down heavily.

Alarmed by Edna's quiet fury, Elizabeth whispered guiltily. "Oh, Eddie, I didn't mean to make you so upset."

"Shut up, Elizabeth. You didn't upset me. It's this place. These people," she said, raising her voice so everyone might hear. "Men and women acting like frightened children, no, like horrid, bloody cowards!" She turned on Diana venomously. "And you," she said. "Are you going to write about the superficial niceties of the place? The sanitation? The organization?" She pointed to Bernice who had returned to the doorway. "Do you applaud the way she *manages* us? Are we to be managed?"

Edna's words fell like blows on Diana's shoulders. "I'm sorry, Mrs. Carver," she said feebly. "I'm sick. I've got a fever."

"How goddamned convenient for you."

Elizabeth put her hand on Edna's arm. "Stop, Eddie. Look at her."

Edna stared at the round, pale face. "She's sick because of what she sees. She doesn't want to see it. She came here thinking about white gloves and hats, cribbage and pleasant memories. She should be sick, sick of lies, sick of pretense."

Diana slumped against the table. "I'm going to have to lie down," she said, weakly.

"Oh, yes, have a little sleep and all this unpleasantness will disappear. Throw yourself into your career. Get married. Have babies." She smiled unpleasantly at the way Diana sat so passively under this assault. "One day you won't be able to run from it. One day you'll find yourself in a place like this and curse yourself for not doing what you could to change things."

"Edna, enough," Elizabeth said. "Leave her alone. She's sick. Any fool can see it."

Edna looked around as lodgers began walking into the foyer. "Come on, Lizzie. Let's go out to buy a box of biscuits."

Diana dragged herself to her feet. "I have to lie down," she said again and stumbled from the room.

Alone in the dining room, Elizabeth and Edna looked at one another. Elizabeth smiled unhappily.

"I was afraid I was going to die of fright, Eddie."

"I know," Edna whispered. "Your legs were shaking. But you were wonderful. You didn't give in."

"No, and I'm not going to. You're absolutely right about this place. Just because we're old doesn't mean we can't make a few decisions for ourselves."

"I wish you'd come with me. I don't think they're going to feed us anything now."

"It isn't the food," Elizabeth said. "It's the principle. They take our docility for granted."

Edna observed Bernice speaking to one of the waitresses. In a moment, the young woman scurried to their table. "She says I'm to clear this away," she said nervously.

"How much do you get paid?" Elizabeth asked.

"Please!" Obviously frightened, the young woman went on, whispering, "Don't make trouble for me. I'm here, you know . . . ." She snatched up their cutlery.

"What do you mean?" Edna demanded.

"Please," the girl said. "You'll get me fired. And I can't get another job." She rushed to the next table.

Edna frowned. "What on earth is that about?"

"I don't know," Elizabeth said wearily. "But I think you're right. I'm not going to be fed here. I'll have to feed myself." She stood, ostentatiously throwing back her frail shoulders.

Edna linked arms with her, pinching the loose flesh on the back of Elizabeth's upper arm. Elizabeth pinched her back. The friends walked past Bernice and Diana, still standing in the doorway, carrying off the pretense that neither of the younger women existed.

Maternally, Bernice placed a cool hand on Diana's brow. "That's a dreadful fever," she said. "I won't hear of you going up to Mrs. Carver's room." She checked her watch. "The doctor will be in later. You can rest in the infirmary until he has time to have a look at you."

Diana leaned against Bernice Wilson, her mind empty. She wanted only darkness, only sleep. Her stomach and abdomen ached so fiercely she couldn't wait to be drugged, to escape into unconsciousness.

On the way to the third floor infirmary, Bernice became uneasy. "Perhaps you'd best go to a hospital," she said. "You might have something contagious. I'm worried about you, of course, but I don't want my lodgers taken ill with anything that might spread."

Diana explained about her recent surgery. Relieved, the manager unlocked the small, cool room and led the reporter to the closest bed. She helped the young woman lie down and then removed her shoes before covering her with the standard thermal blanket found at the foot of every bed in the lodge. Diana seemed to fall asleep immediately. The manager took a moment to study her pretty face. After a few moments, she turned off the overhead light and slipped out, quietly closing the door behind her.

The manager returned to the foyer, stopping on the second

floor to ask one of the cleaning staff to gather Diana's belongings from Edna's room and take them to the infirmary. Back in her office, the lodge manager stared down at the blotter on her desk. Absently, she picked up a ball-point pen, and, tapping, she considered what she might do next.

Out on the street, Edna and Elizabeth talked comfortably. "I hope we really put the fear of God into her," Elizabeth said.

Edna looked dubious. "I'd be happy if we could begin by filling her with the fear of Edna Carver and Elizabeth Schmidt. I'm not sure God wants to have anything to do with us. Maybe He hates old people, too."

Elizabeth shook her head vehemently, firmly holding on to her cranberry coloured hat when a spring gust threatened to send it sailing down the street. "I don't think we need to worry about God, Eddie," she said. "We've got each other now. We'll fight the good fight."

Edna grinned at the prospect of further battles. "Ah, yes," she agreed, tucking her arm into Elizabeth's as they walked slowly along under the bright April sun. "We'll fight a very good fight."

Elizabeth thought for a moment. "What will we do at lunchtime? Will we toss those pasty white-bread sandwiches on the floor and trample them under foot? Or will we tell everyone to put them in envelopes and send them to loving children or nieces and nephews and ask them what they think of our fodder?"

Edna laughed. "Can you imagine Marion opening a parcel containing a three-day-old turkey sandwich?"

Elizabeth grew thoughtful. "We laugh, Eddie, but they should care. Think of all her lunches you cared about."

Edna shook her head. "I don't like to think about it. She already drives me crazy with her caring. Besides, I didn't care about her lunches so I could blackmail her with my love when she grew up and I grew old."

"Of course you didn't. But wouldn't it be wonderful if she did care? Oh, not in that horrible is-everything-all-right-mother way of hers that always sets your teeth on edge, but really cared, because you're who you are."

"And not because I'm her rapidly deteriorating mother?"

"Exactly."

"I'm not sure."

Elizabeth's stomach rumbled loudly. "I think this may be the first time I've actually felt hungry in years. It's rather pleasant. Maybe I won't eat after all."

Edna pounced. "You mustn't do anything to make yourself sick, Lizzie. I'm delighted you stopped taking those pills, but I don't want you to starve yourself to death."

"You needn't worry about me, Eddie. I have everything I need." She was thoughtful for a moment. "But there is one thing I'd enjoy. I'd love a manicure. Let's go down to the school and get our nails done."

"You know what Bernice said about going over there. From her second lecture on respect for neighbouring institutions, I gather the principal was apoplectic that we took some of the others over with us the last time."

"What do we care what Bernice thinks? We can bloody well go where we like and do what we like."

"Yes, we can! And if you want a manicure, then a manicure you shall have." Edna squeezed Elizabeth's arm to strengthen their spirit of defiance.

They arrived at the school entrance and walked boldly into the cool dim hall. In front of them, at the top of a T-intersection, a large sign hung on the wall: ALL VISITORS MUST CHECK INTO THE OFFICE. Edna thumbed her nose at the sign, pleased to disobey it each time they visited the school. The principal, she vividly remembered, had been horrified to find three or four lodgers milling about in the corridor outside the hairdressing room in the basement, and as many more drinking tea and coffee in the cafeteria opposite it. Edna chuckled, recalling the man's shock when she'd told him to respect his elders. He'd rushed off to complain to Bernice.

They navigated the stairway to the basement classrooms, noting the signs exhorting students to GET INTO THE 'YES SIR!' HABIT! The pungent scents of setting lotion and singed hair announced their arrival at Hairdressing 101. Edna knocked on the open door, and several youngsters looked up from their demonstration heads in surprise.

"Hi," said an approaching tall, blond girl with a mouth full of bright pink gum. An older man rushed up behind her.

"I'm afraid Mr. Fathers doesn't want you here," he said. "It's because of the stairs. We're liable if you fall."

"Nonsense," said Elizabeth. "He wants what is best for the common good. We need our nails done and your students need to practice doing nails." She bustled past him into the large bright room with its curious students.

Thinking of the students, Edna looked at the teacher wisely. "You mustn't let him bully you, you know." She oozed sympathy in what she hoped was a decent impersonation of Bernice.

Torn between calling Mr. Fathers on the intercom or doing their nails and rushing them out before anyone found out, the teacher followed his own good judgment and opted for the latter course of action.

Elizabeth found a young girl bent over a tray of polishes, chose a bright red colour, and plumped herself into the manicure chair. Edna observed her choice of colour with a shake of her head.

"I think that colour is garish," she said, her nose in the air.

"Nonsense," said Elizabeth. "I want my toes done, too."

"Lighten up, Miss," the chewing-gum girl said to Edna as she joined them. "What's wrong with a little colour?"

Edna was pleased to be overruled. "Yes," she said. "Roses are red, aren't they?" She sat down to wait her turn.

Elizabeth was pleased with the girl's firm handling of her hands as she soaked her nails, pushed back the cuticles, filed the tips, and then applied the colour. Entranced, the old woman followed the entire process avidly. When it was complete, she held out her hands to admire the bright red nails. "They're lovely. But I won't be able to let you do my toenails after all. I forgot – I'm wearing pantyhose."

The girl blew dry Elizabeth's nails before retrieving a large screen from the corner of the room and setting it up in front of the chairs. Delighted, Elizabeth kicked off her shoes and wiggled out of her stockings. She was especially pleased when the girl separated each of her toes with fat cotton ball.

Edna removed her shoes and stockings, ready for her turn. She looked down at her feet, studying the large bunion that protruded on the inside of her right foot. Her left foot, she noted indifferently, sported two corn plasters, one on the baby toe and one on the fourth. As she studied them, her feet became the perfect things they had been when she was young woman.

She shook her head, but no matter how she tried, she couldn't see the bunion or the corns. She looked over at Elizabeth, absorbed in the polishing of toenails. When she looked back at her own feet, the bunion and the corns were there again, but the vision of her perfect feet made her wonder if perhaps they still existed somewhere, like those tablecloths and napkins she had tatted as a young woman that were now the property of strangers who shopped at the Salvation Army. She sat, lost in the possibility of opening a door one day, a secret door to a secret room, where she'd find everything she thought she'd lost. When the girl set to work on her toes, she wondered if her young and perfect feet were benefiting from this pedicure as well.

After the girl finished and both women had been thoroughly charmed by her attention, they each gave her the dollar the school charged to cover the cost of materials as well as a handsome tip.

"You don't have to do that," the girl said, blushing and blinking her intense blue eyes. "I'd do it for nothing, but they make us charge for the supplies."

"Put it toward something you really want," said Elizabeth. "But make it something wonderful, something . . . ." She lost her train of thought to a dizzy spell.

The girl grinned at her disjointedness. "Be sure you come back. On Thursday, we're having an Open House. I can do your hair for nothing."

"How lovely!" Edna exclaimed. "Will all the rooms be open?"

"Yeah," said the girl. "But this room and the shop room are the best. They got some good stuff up there from the wood working classes. My brother Frank will show you around."

"We'll bring a gang," Edna promised, gleeful about the consternation such a visit would cause the principal and Bernice.

Elizabeth sat quietly, trying to work out the numbness in her hands and feet. Initially distracted by a persistent ringing in her ears, she found she could concentrate on what was being said if she made an effort.

"I'll get my demo ready while you put your stockings on," the young girl said.

As the girl slipped out from behind the screen to join her classmates, Edna pulled up her stockings and fastened her garters.

"You know," she said, her voice reverent, "I've only seen this done in magazines. I had no idea that was how real people painted their toenails. Did you know you were supposed to do it like that?"

Elizabeth shook her head to dispel the ringing and then cautiously leaned over to remove the cotton from between her toes. "Real people, the people in magazines, they're all the same, Edna."

"Yes, I suppose they're all real," Edna said, amazed that she was only just discovering such an obvious truth.

"Or unreal," said Elizabeth.

Edna looked up sharply. "Are you all right? You seem funny. Perhaps you've inhaled some fumes."

Elizabeth laughed. "*I* seem funny." They linked arms, nodded at the teacher who was watching their departure with anxious anticipation, and strolled out into the empty hall.

When they managed to leave the school without running into Mr. Fathers, Edna took their success as a sign. "We'll go back to the lodge and tell them about the open house. Everyone must come – everyone. We'll show these little tyrants they can't scare us."

Elizabeth walked along in silence, smiling as she clenched and unclenched her fists.

"And maybe afterward," Edna continued, "we can persuade the whole lot to go out for something to drink." She pulled Elizabeth along when the small woman lagged behind. "We'll get Mrs. Wallace, and Merle, and maybe even that little fart Arthur. We all could do with a change of scene. It does my heart good knowing we'll upset Bernice *and* the principal. We'll show them they can't push us around."

"I don't think I'll be going," said Elizabeth.

"Why not?" demanded Edna. "You're the hero of the hour. You stood up to her this morning."

"It has nothing to do with her, Eddie. I think I'll be otherwise engaged, that's all."

Edna looked at her, exasperated. "If you start that dying business, I'll be furious. Why on earth would you die now, when you've discovered the right way to live? We should persuade everyone to stop taking those pills he gives out like candy, whatever they are. How do we know what he's been giving everyone? Look at the change in you already. You'll be doing the Charleston by Thursday night. I won't hear any more talk about dying."

"I don't think you've got it quite worked out yet, Eddie," said Elizabeth. She straightened her hat after Edna knocked it askew.

"Oh, pooh," said Edna. "I've got everything worked out. I feel so good, like one of the immortals in that Yeats poem." She walked in time to the rhythm of the lyric she remembered.

> We who are old, old and gay
> O so old!
> Thousands of years, thousands of years,
> If all were told:
>
> Give to these children, new from the world
> Silence and love;
> And the long dew-dripping hours of night,
> And the stars above:
>
> Give to these children, new from the world,
> Rest far from men.
> Is there anything better, anything better?
> Tell us it then:
>
> We who are old, old and gay,
> O so old!
> Thousands of years, thousands of years,
> If all were told.

Edna clapped her hands at the end of her recitation, delighted to remember it all.

"You've got one for every occasion," said Elizabeth. "Where ever did you learn them all?"

"Here and there," Edna said. "I'll tell you a secret if you promise not to laugh at me."

"Go ahead, Eddie. I'm too tired to laugh at anything just now. You're safe."

"Well," Edna began rapturously. "When I was young, I dreamed of going around the world."

"What on earth for?" asked Elizabeth, exhausted by the thought of the few steps it would take to reach the lodge.

"I wanted to study. Painting, poetry, whatever there was to learn. But my father didn't believe in education for girls and my mother needed me at home. So I taught myself to paint and memorized all the poetry I could lay my hands on." She pulled open the lodge door for Elizabeth. "It's funny. I only seem able to remember those poems when I'm with you."

Elizabeth walked slowly into the elevator and slumped against the far wall. "Eddie," she said, mustering her enthusiasm for Edna's sake, "it's very pretty when you say it."

"I've been reciting poetry to you for three years," Edna said. "Isn't it odd I've never told you why I learned it before now?"

"I've enjoyed it all, Eddie. I was never much good at memory work, even though I've always loved to read. Mother thought it was very important that we all speak well – I suppose because she was sensitive about our German heritage and anxious for us to blend in during all that anti-German sentiment around the time of The Great War. Some of our relatives changed their names to Smith and even Smythe back then. Oh, yes, I read and read and read. But I don't recall ever memorizing something for the sheer love of it. Not like you."

When they got off at the seventh floor, Edna was seized with fresh resentment against Diana. Someone had taped a scribbled sign on the open door: Down in Infirmary. As she was about to launch into yet another tirade about Diana's cowardice, Elizabeth collapsed on her bed.

"What is it? You look so pale." Edna plumped the pillows under Elizabeth's head and shoulders.

"I'm cold, Edna. Cover me up." Edna took an angora afghan from her bureau, covering Elizabeth before she went to make tea.

In the lounge, she banged the kettle around, feebly cursing Diana to release a little of the worry she felt about Elizabeth's condition. "Stupid girl," she muttered. "I knew any friend of Marion's wouldn't be able to help us. What a dud." She set the cups on the tray with a vengeance, but even as she did, she felt ridiculous, suspecting her irrational anger at the young woman stemmed from a jealousy borne of her own confined life. Contrite, she looked into the small refrigerator for something for Elizabeth to eat. There was a small package of cheese and an apple, which she took, thinking the owner would want Elizabeth to have them after her morning's display of courage.

She returned to her room full enthusiasm. "Here we are," she said cheerfully. "This will fix what ails you."

Elizabeth had turned her face to Edna's open closet. "I want you to steal the roof-garden key for me," she said. "It's mean to ask you to do it alone, but you know I'd do it for you if the circumstances were reversed."

Edna bustled about, pouring tea, slicing cheese and apple, and retrieving cloth napkins from her bureau drawer. "I think you should rest right where you are. I don't think you should go traipsing up to roof feeling sick."

"I'm not sick, Eddie." She turned her head to smile mischievously at Edna. "If you won't get the key for me, I'll get it myself."

"Don't threaten me, Elizabeth Schmidt. If I say you're sick, you're sick. You're to rest until you feel better."

Elizabeth's eyes filled. "You've been a good friend to me, Edna. Better than you know."

"Oh, yes," said Edna, afraid of Elizabeth's sentiment. "A friend who's taught you the real virtues of old age – thievery, profanity, and bitchiness."

Elizabeth laughed. "If you knew why you were so angry all the time, you could revolutionize old age."

Edna set down the tea cups, shocked. "Lizzie," she said, very serious. "Please don't make me into something I'm not. I'm just a querulous old lady, willful and . . . ."

"But you're on your way to being something better," said Elizabeth.

Edna flushed with pleasure. "I wish I could believe you."

"You can, Eddie. I know."

"The scales having fallen from your eyes," Edna said archly. "Oh, yes, I forgot about your recent nocturnal revelation and ascent to the Right Hand. You're omniscient now, I suppose."

"Something like that," said Elizabeth.

The women sat quietly, drinking tea, and nibbling cheese and fruit.

"There's something else I want you to do for me," Elizabeth said after a time. She finished her tea and set her cup and saucer on her abdomen. It rattled a little with her breathing. "When you go to the school on Thursday night, I want you to promise me that you'll talk to the children. Tell them not to be discouraged by all the signs and rules they have over there. Tell them real life's not like that."

Edna shook her head. "I wouldn't be telling them the truth if I told them that, Lizzie. I think it's just as well they get used to it as soon as possible."

"No," Elizabeth said. "Real life's not like that." She closed her eyes. "I want to go up to the roof, Eddie. Promise you'll get the key for me."

"I'll get it," Edna assured her. She placed her tea cup on the bureau and went to the mirror to tidy her hair, pulling out the several pins holding the knot in place and shaking her head so her hair fell to her shoulders. She rummaged in the top drawer for her favourite brush. After a vigorous brushing, she caught her hair in one hand and twisted it into the simple knot she secured with her hair pins. She looked at herself critically wanting to feel confident at least of her appearance if she happened to meet Bernice. On the way downstairs she decided to pretend to be inquiring after Diana if she found Bernice in her office.

As luck would have it, Edna found the foyer empty. Nervously she smoothed the nylon of her pale green dress and plunged her hands into its deep pockets before stepping behind the information counter and walking quickly to the open office door. She could see immediately that the room was empty. Glancing behind her once, she stepped inside to survey the plaque where the manager kept her keys. She found several, each efficiently marked with a printed tag. All were arranged alphabetically. The roof-garden key was in the last row, next to the storage-room keys. She tucked it into one of her pockets, filled its empty space with a duplicate from another hook, and quickly returned to the elevator.

Upstairs, she held out the key to Elizabeth and shook her head as she spoke. "It's against my better judgment, Lizzie. But if you're determined . . ."

"Thank you, Edna." Gratefully, Elizabeth took the key and dropped it into her bag on the floor beside the bed. "I think I'll snooze here for a bit. But you go down to eat."

"Shall I get the cook to prepare a tray for you?"

"No, I'm fine. You go now."

In the hallway, Edna saw Mrs. Wallace standing in the midst of a group of lodgers.

"Hi," she said, wanting to smooth over their earlier argument. "No hard feelings, I hope, Mrs. Wallace."

"I haven't learned much in this life," the big woman said, smiling a genuine smile. "But one thing I know for certain. The Lord doesn't want anyone to hold a grudge. Besides, you spoke from your heart, Mrs. Carver. You're right about us insiders. It's pretty easy to become self-righteous, as it were. Mr. Wallace often cautioned against smugness."

Edna touched her arm. "You know, Wally – it isn't you. It isn't any of the lodgers – it's this place. It's the feeling that Wilson doesn't quite see us as human beings."

"I know, Mrs. Carver. But we must fight the good fight. However she may see us mustn't affect the way we see her."

Astonished, Edna blinked. "Well, of course, Wally," she said absorbing the widow's wisdom. "I never thought of it like that. How did Blake put it? 'We become what we behold.' I must be more careful to behold her in the right way – or I'll be just as bad as she is."

Mrs. Wallace's smile broadened. "That's it, my dear," she said warmly. "I won't say our manager isn't odd about a good many things, but she has her good qualities, as well. Only an hour ago she called me into her office to tell me about that young writer your daughter sent to us. Apparently, she's not feeling well, and Miss Wilson tucked her into the infirmary so our good doctor can have a look at her."

Edna opened her mouth, tempted to express the vitriol she felt, the source of which she was only just beginning to examine. Instead, she clamped her mouth closed and waited for Mrs. Wallace to continue. "She's asked me to look in on the poor thing for as long as she's in the infirmary. I think that's very thoughtful, don't you?"

Edna was saved from responding when the elevator arrived full of lodgers from the higher floors. She and the others from the seventh floor joined the noisy group.

"More lambs for the slaughter," someone quipped from the back of the car. They all laughed. "Where's Mrs. Schmidt?" a woman asked.

She's resting," said Edna. "She's feeling poorly after this morning."

"She was a corker down there," said another woman. "I expected Miss Wilson to shout, 'Off with her head!'"

Arthur Martin cleared his throat. "You'll get us all into trouble."

"Shut up, Arthur," said his male tablemate. "You give us all a bad name."

Edna radiated goodwill as the elevator's doors opened and the lodgers disembarked, smiling, chatting, and wishing one another luck with the meal they were about to be served.

Merle caught hold of Edna on her way into the dining room. "Where's that writer gone?" she asked. "I wanted to show her my jewels."

"She's come down with a convenient case of something," Edna said.

"I ain't surprised," Merle said in a tremulous, world-weary voice. "Young people today. There ain't many like my boy."

Edna suppressed a smile. "Aren't you lucky to have him? It just shows how good mothering pays off." Merle was delighted by the compliment and rushed over to Mrs. Wallace to repeat it.

Edna pulled out her chair and dusted off the seat. She was engaged in wiping her cutlery with her napkin when one of the lodgers whose name she couldn't remember, an energetic old woman with hair like electrified steel wool and a face set in a perpetual clown's smile, bent over to whisper in her ear.

"Did you hear about the nutty group that meets on Tuesday afternoons in the lounge on three? You should send that writer in for an earful."

Edna smiled conspiratorially. "The poor thing's come down with flu," she said. "Maybe I'll come and take some notes for her."

"We meet right after lunch."

Hoping she might entertain Elizabeth with a story or two after her nap, she nodded brightly. "I'll be sure to be there."

"Good," said the woman. "This is our third session, but we're still not sure what we're paying for." Edna looked at her, puzzled. "We pay five dollars a visit," the woman said, "so bring your pocket book." She scuttled back to her table when Bernice entered the dining room.

"I'll see you there," Edna called after her.

Lunch was abysmal. The canned tomato soup, made with water, was cold, and the processed-cheese-slice sandwiches on stale white bread were dry. After the lodgers received their bowls and plates they looked expectantly in Edna's direction. Aware that some act of defiance was required of her, Edna determined to rise to the occasion. She called one of the waitresses over.

"My soup is cold. Please have the cook warm it up."

The girl stared at her, apparently too frightened to move.

Edna decided to take the soup to the kitchen herself. On her way, she asked if any of the other lodgers would like their soup warmed. Many of them nodded. She got a tray and began to gather bowls. "I want a nice tip for this," she said to the woman who'd told her about the group meeting in the third-floor lounge. The woman's laughter sent her wild hair into motion.

In the kitchen, Edna smiled at the startled cook. "The soup is cold," she said sweetly.

The cook answered indifferently. "It wasn't when it left here."

"It was when we received it," Edna countered. "Just show me which pot you used and I'll heat this up myself."

"I don't think Mrs. Wilson would like that," said the cook.

"I'm sure Miss Wilson wants us to have warm soup." As she spoke, Bernice walked into the kitchen, her face tense with the prospect of yet another difficult scene. Edna smiled at her. "You've got enough to do, Miss Wilson. Just leave this to me."

Bernice stepped between Edna and the stove. "Please leave, Mrs. Carver." Her low voice whistled more than usual. "If the soup is cold, the cook will warm it. You know perfectly well that our safety regulations forbid lodgers access to the kitchen."

"The cook will warm it? Thank you so much," Edna said loftily. She pushed through the kitchen doors, raised her arms, and offered her fellow lodgers two victory signs. The company burst into applause. Those who had not given her their bowls called for the waitresses to take them to the kitchen as well. Edna sat down at her small table feeling very fulfilled.

Ten minutes later, the waitresses came out of the kitchen with steaming bowls of soup. When Edna received her bowl, she wrinkled her nose. It smelled burnt. She tasted it. It was scorched. She looked up to find many of the lodgers looking at her helplessly.

She stood up. "Shame!" she called, wanting the cook to come out of the kitchen. Instead, Bernice pushed through the swinging doors.

"Lunch will be cleared away at the regular time," the manager told them evenly. Some of the lodgers picked up their spoons.

Edna pushed her bowl away, disgusted, before standing to face the manager.

"Miss Wilson," she said pleasantly. "When I was cooking in my own home, I always found the preparation of soup, especially canned soup, to be the simplest operation. Why is it that our cook can only serve it cold or burnt?"

Bernice's face expressed no emotion. "Another of your exaggerations, Mrs. Carver," she said. She looked around at the expectant faces before walking from the room.

Edna shook her head and looked around. Everyone seemed to be looking to her for direction. Impatient with all of them, she said, "You can do what you want, but I am certainly not going to eat it." She sat down and received her tea graciously.

"Miss," said her waitress nervously. "You're going too far. She makes trouble for all of us."

Thinking she understood, Edna smiled at the young woman and picked up her tea cup, crooking the baby finger of her right hand in exaggerated fashion. "It's perfect, my dear," she said after her first sip. "I am so glad the cook knows how to boil water."

Waitresses soon began clearing tables although many of the lodgers complained that the soup was still too hot to eat. Despite their protests, every bowl was taken away.

Edna rose, deciding to return to her room to check on Elizabeth before attending the group on three. On her way to the door, Merle grabbed her arm. "I think you make it worse when you complain," she said. "Before you started all this, we got to eat."

Edna did not disguise her sneer. "A woman needs more than food to live with dignity."

"Oh, yes," said Merle, forgetting her empty stomach. "Did I show you this?" She held up her arm to display a wide gold bracelet studded with large red gems. "My son sent it, special delivery. These here are rubies."

Edna considered the bracelet for a moment. "I bet if you sold that," she said after a moment, "you might have kept Vera Potts here for another year."

"Probably two," replied Merle with a smirk.

Feeling impotent and angry, Edna moved with the crowd to the elevator.

On the third floor, a few lodgers converged on the lounge to wait expectantly in strategically arranged straight-backed folding chairs. Edna joined them after splashing cold water on her face in the main floor bathroom, to get rid of what she thought of as Merle residue.

"How long has this been going on?" she asked.

Arthur Martin jumped from his chair. "You've no business butting in. It's only for people the doctor refers. And it costs money, five dollars a week. No freeloaders allowed."

"Button up, Arthur," said Edna. "I'll pay like the rest. But it's a free country. I can come if I want." Edna turned to the woman closest to her. "What's it all about?"

"Darned if I know," she answered. "He told me to come because my regular psychologist was cutting back on lodge visits. I don't much like this setup, but a body needs *somebody* to talk to."

Edna knew many of the lodgers had been having private consultations with psychologists who seemed always to be in and out of the lodge, but as far as she knew this group was a new addition to the doctor's remedies for the ills of those who made Sunset Lodge their home.

At last a plump young woman in her early or mid twenties joined the group. Dark haired and nervous, she wore peculiar looking corrective oxfords and a grey, hand-made skirt that had come down at the hem in two places. She looked at the floor until she'd navigated the tight passage to the chair facing the group. After she'd sat and carefully arranged her bulging, tattered briefcase beside her on the floor, she looked up, Edna thought, reluctantly.

"Good afternoon," the young woman said in the high sing-song voice some professionals use with those they assume to be of limited intellectual capacity. "How are we all today?"

No one answered.

The girl cleared her throat. "You remember in the first session I told you how important it is to get in touch with your feelings?" She stared at the rug when the lodgers remained silent. "When I ask you how you are, I expect you to tell me about your feelings."

The lady with the steel-wool hair and clown's smile burst forth. "I'm starved, that's how I am. We're trying to make the cook give us better meals, and we're being punished for complaining."

The girl looked as though these were not the feelings she was hoping to discuss. She looked at the speaker for a moment and then returned her gaze to the rug. "So you're hungry and you're angry," she said.

The woman laughed, her hair bobbing merrily. "That's what I said all right."

"Do you think the meals are intentionally bad?" the young woman asked, carefully measuring each word.

The lodgers murmured together. Finally another woman spoke. "I don't think it's intentional. More like carelessness, I think."

The girl smiled with relief. "And do you ever make careless mistakes?"

"Sure," said the woman, happy to be engaged in conversation. "All the time."

Just as she was about to expand on her last careless mistake, Edna groaned loudly. The leader of the group took no notice of either Edna or the other woman. She addressed the group. "I'm sure you can all see how someone cooking for so many people might make a careless mistake now and then?"

Edna jumped in. "I'd like to know who pays your salary and why."

The young woman looked into the faces of the lodgers, searching for the person who had spoken. "Pardon me?" she asked, not quite believing the tone of the question.

"Who pays you?"

Locating Edna, the young woman smiled patronizingly. "The people in the group pay me."

"Who suggested you come here?"

"I'm sorry," said the young woman, her face losing colour now. "I don't remember you from our earlier meetings. Are you new today?"

"Yes," said Edna. "Please answer my question."

The girl looked around, chagrined by the expectant faces. "The doctor invited me to complete a practicum here, for my doctorate." she began. "All clinical psychology students have to . . . ."

"And what did he tell you to do in this little group?"

"What all psychologists do," she said. "I help people adjust."

"What if you help them adjust to something they shouldn't adjust to?"

The young woman took off her glasses and placed them in her lap before rubbing her eyes. "We live in an imperfect world," she said, replacing her glasses. "We all need help learning to cope with it."

Edna snorted. "Has it ever occurred to you that perhaps the imperfect might be improved upon? Instead of making the people who live in it lower their standards and expect less?"

Relief, sudden and unexpected, animated the young woman's face. "You're making a value judgment," she said quickly. "We don't make value judgments in this group. We work with feelings."

Arthur Martin came alive. "She's a bigmouth and a trouble maker," he said, pointing at Edna. "She shouldn't be here."

"How many of you agree with this gentleman?" asked the girl.

No one spoke. She turned to Arthur. "I'm sorry, but you're the only one who seems to feel this way. Let's go with your feelings of hostility for a while."

Arthur blanched. "Go with someone else's feelings. I've had my say."

"I understand," said the young woman, earnestly supportive. "It's very hard to be odd man out. But honour your feelings. You have them for a reason."

Edna laughed. "He has them because he's an old fool. But let's not get off track. What are you supposed to do for these people who pay you?"

"I told you," the girl said, impatient now. "I help them adjust. Statistics prove institutional life can result in depression if inmates don't find a release valve."

"Inmates," repeated Edna. "I like that."

A few other lodgers murmured their protests.

Sensing that she was losing the support of her group and angry with herself for using clinical terms instead of the customary euphemisms, the young woman decided to change the subject. "Are there any other feelings we need to talk about?" She tried valiantly to sound cheerful.

"They've locked all the balcony doors," said a soft spoken tall man with a bulbous nose. "I like to take the air after lunch, before my rest."

"And you feel sad that the doors are locked?"

"Vera Potts threw herself off the seventh floor balcony last night," Edna said. "Help us to adjust to that."

Horrified, the young woman blurted, "Oh, my goodness. Did she die?"

Someone giggled nervously.

"Of course she died," Edna said. "Who could survive a seven-storey leap?"

"I'm very sorry," said the girl. "I think I can see why they lock the doors though," she added cautiously. "I'm sure you wouldn't want anyone else to jump, would you?"

The man who made the complaint cleared his throat. "Oh, I'm not interested in jumping," he said calmly. "I just like to take the air."

The girl smiled tightly at him. "Perhaps you could go for a walk after lunch."

"Impossible," he said. "My joints aren't good. Daily walking is out of the question."

Furious, Edna tried again. "You're missing the point entirely. You called us inmates, and now you seem to expect we should adjust to being prisoners. This isn't jail – at least it isn't supposed to be."

"That's another value judgment," the young woman insisted. "We don't make them here."

"I'd like to know why not," Edna cried, bristling.

"Because value judgments are purely subjective," the young woman answered, her voice becoming higher and more whispering as she continued. At the end, she sounded to Edna like a child chanting a prayer to banish a looming phantom.

Edna moved to the door. "I've heard enough. This is tommyrot! And regarding your fee, what I've heard isn't worth five cents, let alone five dollars."

The girl looked around the room. "Would anyone like to comment on this lady's feelings of hostility?" Edna marched out without waiting to hear if anyone responded.

Strong, swift strokes took Diana out to the centre of a cold, bottomless lake. Her arms propelled her, moved of their own accord, while her brain whispered caution. 'You're going out too far,' it warned. Sensing she'd reached the deepest point, Diana stopped swimming and flipped to her back. Sculling lazily, she opened her eyes to an arch of pale blue. She felt a gentle protectiveness until the water suddenly sucked her downward.

Descending dizzily, Diana tensed, but her resistance accelerated her downward fall and she panicked to be under so much water. A great, pressuring weight told her she must get used to it, that she'd never be able to return to the surface. And then Edna's battle cry, "I'd like to know why not!" reached down like a giant hook to yank her to the surface at a dizzying speed. Once more she saw the sky, the sun, and, with great relief, a cliff of land peering over the distant, watery horizon. Slowly, she began her journey toward shore.

Upstairs, Edna found Elizabeth awake, the bag of apricots open and beside her on the bed, the Gideon Bible from her bedside table resting on her abdomen.

"You look better," Edna said, relieved. "I was going to check on you right after lunch, but had Merle business to scrub off. Just let me run across to put the kettle on before I tell you all my gossip."

In the lounge, she found someone had already boiled the kettle. She quickly filled one of the small brown pots, refilled the kettle, and returned to her room before she was seen.

"That was fast," said Elizabeth, eyeing the pot.

"The Lord provides," said Edna. She poured out a cup for Elizabeth. "Did you know there's a group that meets every Tuesday in the third-floor lounge?"

Dismayed, Elizabeth erupted. "Don't tell me they got around Bernice with flower sculpture and didn't tell me about it."

"Nothing so elevated," said Edna. She sat in her rocker and kicked off her shoes, suddenly smiling at the sight of her toenails. "The doctor's told some poor lost soul to come in here and oil all the squeaky parts en masse."

"What?"

"It's a group therapy session run by a psychologist-in-training. She's practising her craft on us, but I don't know how she could help anyone. She didn't look dry behind the ears. She's meeting some research requirement for grad school while she aids and abets our doctor. Like so many, she's likely filled with theories and good intentions but not a grain of wisdom from experience."

"How did you get wind of the group?"

"You know that dear soul who looks like she's stuck her finger in a light socket?" Elizabeth thought for a moment before laughing and nodding. "Well, she bustled up to me at lunch and told me about it, thinking the writer might be interested. They have to pay five dollars a shot to get told that even though they don't like it, this is the best of all possible worlds. She's helping them adjust."

"It doesn't sound like they're adjusting if they think the writer should know about it."

Edna smiled. "Doesn't it do your heart good? It makes me feel the human spirit might be indomitable after all."

"The human spirit runs this place, Eddie. Don't give credit unless it's due."

"What have you been doing while I was gone?" She eyed the Bible suspiciously.

Lizzie tapped the book. "I've had a wonderful rest. Do you know there's a psalm called 'The Prayer of an Old Man'? I don't see why we old women shouldn't read it." She set her tea cup down and began to turn its pages deliberately. When she found her psalm, she smiled shyly at Edna.

> My lips will shout for joy,
>> when I sing praises to thee;
> my soul also, which thou has rescued.

"See? We're not alone in this."

Edna took the Bible from her friend. She read the psalm to herself as she rocked slowly back and forth, closing the book when she'd finished and studying Elizabeth with tender curiosity. "When you were young – you know, Lizzie, a girl – did you take religion seriously?"

"The only place I ever felt in the presence of something that might love the universe and be purposeful, perhaps even include me in its purpose, was in my garden."

Edna nodded. "With me, it was my painting."

"I still can't understand why you gave it up."

"I think the desire to do it died when I moved in here."

"Ha!" Elizabeth cried. "There's nothing dead in you! It's just been pulling backward so it can shoot farther." Edna opened her mouth but Elizabeth silenced her with a wave. "I want you to promise me that you'll start again. Get your things from Marion. Do a little every day."

"Goodness, Lizzie. My painting supplies were probably among the first of the things she got rid of. She never could understand why I didn't sew and knit like other mothers. She resented the time I spent on painting and tatting. She used to make fun of me."

Her hands shuttled back and forth as she spoke, imitating her daughter's parody of the tatting motion. "She wanted me to make pretty clothes for her but I made tablecloths and undergarments. Worse, I painted pictures."

"Start again," Elizabeth said. "You know damn well Marion's opinion doesn't matter in the least. We all have to work out our own salvation."

Edna looked at her friend, her head to one side, her eyes concentrated. "All right," she said. "Don't upset yourself."

"Good," said Elizabeth. "Now tell me about this group on three."

Edna picked up her tea cup. "She told us she came, at the doctor's request, to help the inmates adjust."

"Inmates?" Elizabeth repeated. "Surely she didn't say inmates."

"She did. That's exactly what she said. God knows what they call us behind our backs."

"It seems the adjustment has not been entirely successful."

"No. From the noises the rest of them were making, I don't imagine they'll be shelling out their five dollars for much longer."

"Good." Elizabeth leaned back on her pillow and closed her eyes. "I'm sure psychologists mean well, but they often muddy the waters. A person can't be helped from the outside to adjust to something. That's an internal process. Although coming here might do the psychologist some good." She opened her eyes and smiled at Edna. "Was she awful?"

"She was pathetic, as green as grass, poor child." Edna sipped her tea to oil her storytelling powers. "Her skirt was coming down at the hem and she wore shoes even I wouldn't be caught dead in."

"Her clothes have nothing to do with anything, Edna. Remember Vera."

Edna blinked, feeling small and mean. "You're right, Lizzie." She stared frankly at her friend. "You know," she said after careful scrutiny. "You haven't got a bad head."

Elizabeth closed her eyes. "It's a wonder, considering all those pills I've taken."

"You know what I mean," Edna said, jumping up to rummage in her bureau drawer. She returned to the rocker with pencil, paper, and telephone book and resumed her study of Elizabeth's features.

Elizabeth dozed while Edna struggled through several false starts. After an hour the neglected connection between her eyes and her hands seemed less tenuous and Edna was sure she'd begun a sketch she'd finish. When Elizabeth awoke, she found the floor littered with balled paper and Edna hunched in concentration over something in her lap.

"I think I could eat a little something," Elizabeth said sleepily.

"Ah," Edna said, holding up the sketch. "If you hate it, you've only yourself to blame."

Elizabeth found it difficult to focus on the feathery strokes and eased herself off the bed to have a closer look. Finally she took the paper from Edna.

"Well," she said after a long time. "It's me all right. I bet there isn't a soul in the world that wouldn't look at it and say, 'There's one angry old lady.'"

"Do you like it?"

"No," said Elizabeth. "But it's me. You make me feel like Moonwort, more transparent than I want to be."

Edna laughed. "Moon warts!"

"Lunaria, Honesty, The Satin Flower," Lizzie corrected. "Some people call them silver dollars or silver pennies, but I like Moonwort because its seed pods look like tiny moons."

"Oh, that," said Edna, seeing in her mind's eye a papery disc containing a small seed. She looked at the sketch. "A Moon Wart," she said, laughing again. "That's you all right."

"*Moonwort,* Edna, if you please," Elizabeth insisted. "What did you find out about that writer, anyway?"

Edna chuckled. "She looked worse than you did at breakfast." She ignored Elizabeth's impatient glance. "Mrs. Wallace told me Wilson's stuck her in the infirmary. Do you think our manager has a supply of oleander she draws on to keep snoopers under control?"

Elizabeth laughed. "Our manager may not be as extreme in her solutions as you are, Edna. No," she said, two deep fret lines separating her pale eyebrows as she tidied herself in the mirror. "I think that little girl is really ill. Let's look in on her after dinner. I bet she's in need of more than aspirin."

Edna felt rebuke in Elizabeth's kindness. "I suppose we should," she said. "I guess she can't help having everything."

Elizabeth laughed again. "Nobody has everything, Edna. You

of all people ought to know that. Or if they do have everything, it isn't all good. She must tote around her fair share of despair and confusion. Would you like her better if she were homely?" Before Edna could answer, Elizabeth opened the door. "I hear the gang assembling," she said, taking Edna's arm and leading her out to join their friends in a grumble about the slowness of the elevator.

Dinnertime noises filtering in from the vent above his head distracted the doctor from the stack of files in front of him. He looked at the files, searching for the satisfaction that used to come at the end of his busy days as owner and home physician of Sunset Lodge. When Bernice intruded, he felt caught out in his profound dissatisfaction. He turned on her.

"Goddamn it, Bernice. I might have been with a patient."

"I knew you weren't. I keep track of things around here, remember?"

"Do you want something?" he asked. "I still have a lot of files to complete."

"We have a patient in the infirmary," she said. "I think you should look at her."

"Why the hell did you wait until now to tell me? It's quitting time."

"I thought our people's appointments should come first," she answered.

"She's not one of ours?" The doctor rose to his feet.

"No. She came to visit one of our people and decided the lodge would make a good subject for an article. She's a writer. I told her she could stay for a week."

The doctor stared at her in disbelief. "I don't like you making that sort of decision without my input, Bernice. God!" he moaned. "A journalist snooping around after a suicide is just what I need. Does she write for newspapers?"

"I think so, and magazines."

"For God's sake," he sputtered. "What the hell were you thinking?"

"Doctor," the manager said quietly. "Lower your voice. Do you want her to think there's some reason she shouldn't see this place? I think I've done a fine job in covering for you. She'll probably help you to fill your beds. But then, you don't need any help with that."

He was out the door before she could say more. When he entered the dark infirmary, he found Diana curled in a fetal position, her temperature still high. She moaned in pain when he jostled her as he sat on the bed. Silently, Bernice appeared in the doorway.

"Hi," he said, unaware of the manager behind him. "I'm the doctor here." Diana opened her eyes. The doctor turned on the bedside lamp, illuminating her halo of blonde hair spread out on the pillow. "What seems to be the problem?"

"I had a tubal ligation last Thursday. Could this have something to do with the surgery?"

"Let's see your incision," the doctor said, pulling the blanket back and loosening her belt buckle so quickly Diana flinched. Unnerved by the intimate note in his voice and by the way his hands exposed her flesh so quickly, the writer squirmed away. She heard a sharp inhalation of breath and turned to see the manager in the doorway, almost muttering 'Thank God' when she discovered she wasn't alone with him.

"Ah," he said, lightly touching her hairline incision. "This is a nice neat phantom steel. Why didn't you have it done via laparoscopy?"

"I didn't want a general anesthetic," she said.

The doctor's eyes glittered in the small circle of light. "A spinal's tricky, too," he said, pushing gently on her tender abdomen. "But you got through it." His fingers moved down to the incision again with a sensuality Diana found horrifying. "A bit angry here. That's the trouble with the laparotomy. All these hair follicles." He brushed her growing stubble with the tips of his fingers. "They make the risk of infection greater."

"Infection?"

"I'm sure it's just a little post-op one and nothing to be concerned about if you take your medicine like a good girl." He grinned at her, intentionally making his eyes crinkle boyishly as he revealed his even teeth. "So you're a reporter," he said, still touching her pubic hair lightly.

Diana pulled up her underpants and knickers. "Can I go home?" she asked, covering herself with the blanket.

"I don't think that's a good idea," he said. "You'd be unwise to move until this thing clears up. I've got some samples in my office. We'll get you started with an antibiotic tonight."

"I want to go home."

"Another liberated woman," the doctor whispered, "who doesn't like to take advice. You'll make yourself pretty sick if you don't relax. I'll take good care of you."

Diana pulled the blanket under her chin as armor against his searching, probing hands. Her tongue felt swollen, her eyes too large for their sockets. She closed them against the glaring bedside lamp.

The doctor's footsteps ebbed in the hall, a door opened, water ran. She drifted. All at once he was beside her again, holding four capsules in his large, clean hand.

"Take these," he said. "Eat a light diet and drink lots of fluids." He cradled her head unnecessarily close to his chest as he put the water glass to her lips. "Drink it all. I bet you haven't had a thing to drink all day."

Bernice felt sure he made this remark to shame her. As she watched his tender ministrations to the beautiful young woman, it occurred to her for the first time since they'd entered their peculiar liaison that she was no longer as important to him as she once was. The thought made her desperate. She wanted to break him before he broke her.

Unaware of his manager's terrors, the doctor bid Diana a good night's rest, turned out the lamp, and brushed past Bernice.

"Will she be all right?" the manager asked, following him.

"She'll be just fine," he said. It seemed to the manager that he wanted to smile, maybe even laugh out loud.

Although it was five-thirty and she had never before missed the supervision of an evening meal, Bernice could not leave the doctor alone on the third floor so close to the helpless, beautiful young woman. In a panic, she grabbed his arm, pulled him into his office, shut the door, and locked it. Without speaking, she took off her wig and glasses and placed them on his littered desk. Willing him to watch her, she removed her jacket slowly, dropping it on his chair before pulling her jerkin over her head. She drew her slip straps down, unclasped her bra, and leaned her heavy breasts against his chest.

His astonishment gave way to excitement when she undid his belt and trousers, pulled their pelvises together, and rotated her hips. He bent to bite each nipple, undid her skirt, and yanked her pantyhose down. Finally, feeling flesh against flesh, he slumped against his desk and pulled her onto him as she lifted his shirt and rested her breasts against his naked chest. Like seaweed in a stagnant pool, they began their steady undulations, each thinking of the beautiful young woman in the next room.

When they finished this compulsive coupling, Bernice tried to kiss him, opening her mouth to his chin, nibbling her way to his lips. He turned his face away, gripped her at the waist, and pushed her away. She stared at him for a moment and then understood. Dismissed, she thought. I've been dismissed.

Furious, she turned quickly, snatching up her clothes on her way to the office bathroom. "I need a bed at Tranquil Time," she called sharply over her shoulder. "Mrs. O'Shea promised to take a patient this Friday."

When he didn't answer, she looked into the mirror to see what he was doing. Distracted by her own image, she found her pretty face, a small oval dominated by large brown eyes, was no longer young. It was not the only face he looked at, she felt sure. "I won't think about this," she muttered. "I'll get her out of here."

"What?" The doctor stood smiling in the doorway. She spun around. "Are you talking to yourself now? You must be spending too much time with the natives."

"You've got a problem, too," she said. "One of your star experiments shows all the signs of Metaphin withdrawal. If she isn't crazy within another twenty-four hours, or dead, I'll be surprised."

He stiffened. "Who?"

"Schmidt."

He relaxed somewhat. "She's years older than the last one who took matters into his own hands. Walters?" he asked.

"Wallace," she said, disgusted. "You're pathetic. You can't even remember your victims' names."

He ignored her. "She's in her eighties. And her heart's erratic anyway. Whatever happens, it's not traceable after twenty-four hours. I don't think we'll need a bed for her."

"Let's just hope she doesn't follow the pattern. Two suicides in one week won't look very good at the coroner's office."

He grabbed her arms. "Were you giving it to that Potts woman?"

Bernice laughed. "Maybe I was. It wouldn't be too hard to get in here and do a little doctoring of my own."

"Are you crazy? We could go to jail if anyone suspected I was still prescribing Metaphin."

She laughed again. "Don't worry. I haven't been dispensing your precious meds." She eyed him coldly. "Just remember that I could. Three or four breakdowns a week wouldn't help your reputation."

He let her go. She quickly picked up his jacket and helped him on with it as if they'd been talking about the weather. "I'm sorry," she said lightly, pretending contrition. "It's been a bad day."

Diana stood on the other side of the door, confused by their conversation and fearful of their angry voices. Unable to hurry, she inched along the wall to the open infirmary door. Just as she heard the muted tumble of the lock a few feet away, she shut herself inside the room next to the doctor's office.

She'd gotten out of bed to find more water for her unquenchable thirst and had stood outside the doctor's office listening, a woman in a dream. Her fever still high, she doubted that the last few minutes could be anything more than hallucination. She lay on the bed and covered herself with the blanket as the doctor and his manager stepped out of the elevator to exchange pleasantries with the lodgers in the foyer.

Edna looked up from her meal to discover the doctor saying goodbye to the manager in the dining room doorway. She studied him carefully, noting his leanness, his medium height, his dark hair, and his rather expressionless eyes set in his bland face. She'd never heard his voice but imagined it would not be deep or high, just somewhere in the middle range and entirely forgettable.

After he'd made his brief, cool exit, she fell to musing. It was a pity that the human body could reveal so little. Elizabeth touched a nerve when she'd asked about Diana's looks. Edna realized she had unwittingly held the young woman's youth and opportunities against her. As a beautiful young woman, Edna too had met people who assumed her life was better than it really was, or shallower – depending, she discovered, on their own beliefs about conventional good looks. Some felt it was synonymous with virtue, others with vice. She knew it was neither of these. And here she was at seventy-five, perpetuating the same damnable prejudices. She was ashamed of herself, and out of her shame grew the desire to see Diana clearly. She knew there was enough in life that divided people from one another. She wanted real relationships now and silently blessed Elizabeth for inspiring her shift in purpose.

"You're awfully quiet this evening," Elizabeth said as the waitress poured their tea. She was saddened when the girl rushed away without indulging in the playful banter they usually enjoyed.

"I've been thinking about how much I don't know," reflected Edna.

Elizabeth chuckled. "Isn't that supposed to be the beginning of wisdom?"

Edna sipped her tea, afraid to hope Elizabeth might be right. She longed for wisdom. She longed to believe that before she died she might see some tiny, indestructible corner of universal knowledge in spite of her human failings. Instead of saying this to Elizabeth, she smiled devilishly and whispered, "What are you going to wear for our party on the roof?"

"I hadn't thought about it. But now you mention it, I'm going to wear something festive. Remember that gorgeous blue suit I lifted when you got your slacks and jacket?" Edna nodded. "I'll wear that. I think it's appropriate to wear the colour of starlight when visiting a roof garden at night."

"You're going to let me come up with you, aren't you?"

"I suppose I should share the wealth, Eddie. After all, it was your idea to steal the key and you who stole it."

"Let's take what's left of the port up there, and maybe some cheese and crackers."

Elizabeth's face grew pink with pleasure. "I can't tell you how much I'm looking forward to this, Edna. I know it seems very commonplace, but . . . ."

"You don't have to explain. Once, when I was much younger and Marion was just a toddler, I took her down to the lake, to Sunnyside Park, for a picnic. She was playing in the sand and I was spreading the cloth — such an ordinary thing — when I was overwhelmed by the conviction that everyone who'd ever made any headway in enlightening humankind was out there, borne along by the current." She looked at Elizabeth with a mixture of defiance and embarrassment. "It sounds crazy. I knew they weren't physically there, but somehow, I felt she just had to get in that water, that I needed to expose her to all those sources of wisdom."

"What did you do?"

Edna laughed ruefully. "I picked her up and waded in with her. She kicked and screamed, terrified, but I held on to her and dangled her legs in the water until that feeling of urgency passed. To this day, she blames me because she never learned to swim."

Elizabeth laughed. "You can lead a horse to water . . . ."

"But you can't tell him Socrates is floating around in it." They laughed uproariously until they noticed that many of the lodgers were studying them. Edna mopped her eyes. "It's too bad you can't tell people how to have a good time."

Elizabeth sniffed loudly before searching her black bag for a handkerchief. "Ah," she said after blowing her nose. "You can't tell them anything at all. Marion will have to discover that feeling of oneness all by herself."

"What if she never does?" asked Edna, her eyes filling.

"Then her life will be different from yours. She may never know there's meaning – beyond material satisfaction – to be found."

"It's such a pity. I hope it isn't my fault."

"The sins of the fathers aren't visited on the children any more. Remember Ezekiel?"

Edna growled. "You're getting as bad with the Bible as I am with *Psychology Today*." She stood. "Let's beat the rush. We can look in on the invalid then have a little time to rest upstairs before we change for our party."

"As long as you don't make any wart jokes," Elizabeth said, getting to her feet and taking Edna's arm. She nodded at the lodgers as she walked to the door, laid a hand on Merle's shoulder and told her not to forget Edna when the dirty books arrived, and then let go of Edna to embrace Mrs. Wallace.

In the elevator, Edna whispered, "What was all that about?"

Elizabeth smiled. "She's fun," she said. "She always gives me something to laugh about."

"You make it sound like she's about to join her husband." The elevator stopped at three, interrupting their conversation. Edna moved to the front of the car and held the door open while Elizabeth stepped out and turned to bow gracefully to the people inside.

"It's been lovely," the small woman said breezily.

"You didn't get the same dinner I did," someone called. Elizabeth blew her fellow lodgers a kiss and set off down the hall waving her right hand over her head in a jaunty parting gesture.

They found the infirmary dark when they opened the door. Elizabeth called Diana's name quietly. When the writer answered, the women went inside. The reporter struggled to sit up, glad to escape another drowning dream. Elizabeth propped pillows behind Diana's back and placed a cool hand on her forehead.

"You're still very warm," she said. "What have they done for you?"

"Please, turn on the light," Diana said. "I want to convince myself you're really here."

Edna fumbled with the switch. "Damn," she muttered, but turned it on at last, catching Diana in its pale circle of yellow light. "Miss Mallory, you don't look at all well," she said.

Diana was grateful for the unexpected sympathy in Edna's voice. "If I look as bad as I feel, maybe someone should call a priest. May I have some water?"

"Has the doctor seen you?" Elizabeth asked.

"He's given me an antibiotic," Diana said. "I still feel sick, but I'm better than I was a while ago. I think I've been hallucinating. It must be because of the infection."

Edna returned from the lounge with a glass of water. "Infection?" she echoed.

Diana drank and rested against the pillows. "I had a tubal a few days ago. He says this is an infection caused by the operation."

"What on earth's a tubal?" Elizabeth asked. "It sounds like trouble."

"I thought it was the end of trouble," Diana muttered.

"There's no end to that," Edna said matter-of-factly. She sat primly at the foot of the bed, carefully avoiding Diana's feet.

"So I'm discovering. A tubal ligation," she explained. "I had my tubes tied, you know, to make me sterile."

"Goodness," said Elizabeth. "Imagine that. In my day being sterile was a curse. I had a cousin who couldn't bear. We all felt sorry for her."

Edna stared at the writer wondering if university had given the young woman this confidence, or if she were simply one of those people born knowing what she wanted and how to get it.

Elizabeth poked her arm. "Eddie. Where in heaven's name are you? She asked you a question."

Edna blinked. "I'm sorry. I was just thinking about not going to university. I'm sure attending would have made such a difference."

"I know a lot of people whose schooling left them as ignorant as they were before they started," Diana said. She looked into Edna's face, empathizing with the mixture of longing and anger she saw in her expression. "We take these things for granted now. I know it was different for you."

"Yes," said Elizabeth, tenderly touching Edna's hand. "Eddie's always had a yearning."

"It's not too late," Diana said. "You could go now, if you wanted to."

"I know," replied Edna. "But it's not quite the same." She looked at Diana curiously. "Tell me. Why did you decide to have this done?"

"My decision didn't come from failed love or anything like that," Diana answered. "I didn't meet anyone I wanted to have children with when I was younger, and then this writing thing took hold of me. It's grown and I've grown with it. There are lots of ways to be fertile."

Edna turned away to hide her filling eyes. Elizabeth felt Diana's forehead again. "Can I get you anything else?"

"More water, please. Oh, and another doctor. The one who works here gives me the creeps."

"I can manage the water," Elizabeth said, taking the glass and heading for the lounge.

Edna looked at Diana curiously. "Why didn't you like him?"

"Maybe it wasn't him. Maybe I just didn't like being ill and powerless with a strange man in the room." She laughed at herself.

"This place is full of strange men," Edna said. "There's one who tries to get familiar with me every time I turn around."

"No!" Diana said. "Don't tell me you have to put up with that at your age."

"I'm afraid so," Edna said as she gently tapped Diana's feet. "You'd better get used to strange men. Whether you're fertile or not, they aren't going to go away."

Elizabeth returned with the water. "You know very well that the men aren't any stranger than the women, Eddie," she said, laughing. "Especially us." Feeling stronger than she had in days, she walked around the bed and pulled Edna to her feet. "Let's let Diana get some rest," she said. "I need a little, too." She took a halting step toward the open door but changed her mind, returning to Diana to kiss her lightly on the forehead. "Take care of yourself. If you don't, our doctor might." She smiled into the pale face.

Edna envied Elizabeth's ease in expressing her feelings and while her resentment and anger were gone, she still felt a distance between herself and the younger woman that made her sad.

"Good night," she said quietly. "We'll be back tomorrow."

"I'd like that," Diana said, fighting the urge to beg them to stay. "There's strength in numbers."

Edna laughed. "I used to think so, too, and then I moved here." She followed Elizabeth from the room missing the fear in the young woman's eyes as she closed the door.

On the seventh floor, Elizabeth refused Edna's offer of her bed.

"I'll lie down in my own room for a while, I think," she said when Edna opened her door. "Come for me around ten. Everyone should be tucked in by then."

Edna nodded. "Put a sweater on under your suit. It's bound to be chilly up there."

Mugging, Elizabeth put a finger to her lips as she walked down to her room, hunching her shoulders and looking from side to side as if for spies. Edna laughed and disappeared into her room, thrilled they would soon be breaking another rule.

Too excited to rest, Edna put the sherry, glasses, and apricots into a bag and set it on the dresser. Finished with this task, she looked through her laundry bag for hand washables and set to work in the bathroom. When slips and stockings were hanging over the towel racks and shower-curtain rod, she changed into her black slacks and tweed jacket, taking another forty-five minutes to decide what to wear under the jacket for warmth. She finally settled for a heavy white cardigan turned back to front so the buttons wouldn't show. She felt very smart, but not as smart as she might have felt in a proper turtle neck. That was what she needed, she decided, to complete the outfit. The next time they visited the Eaton Centre, she would find a bright one, perhaps red, and maybe some big hoop earrings like Diana's as well.

Moving restlessly to the bureau, her eyes fell on the sketch she'd made of Elizabeth. She began to laugh until she picked it up for a closer look. Elizabeth had been right; her anger was unmistakable. Edna realized that she'd never thought of Elizabeth as angry, even when she was sketching her earlier. And yet here it was in plain sight, her quiet fury. "My eyes see more than my brain acknowledges," she said, looking from the paper to the fingers holding it. "And my hands are in league with them." She laughed at herself. "Doesn't that sound just like a moon's wart?" She put the sketch away and set off with the picnic things to scratch on Elizabeth's door. Rested and excited, the older woman opened the door and turned a graceful circle so Edna might admire her blue ultra-suede suit.

"It really is the prettiest thing I've ever seen," Edna said. "I'm sorry they didn't have one in my size."

Elizabeth shook her head. "No, Eddie, you're not as prim. The slacks are perfect for you. If I had a behind, I'd have snitched a pair for myself." She felt the wool of Edna's trousers. "They'll wear forever. It's too bad you have to dry clean them."

"I'm going to wear them until they're filthy and then give them away," Edna said grandly. "Someone else can dry clean them."

Elizabeth picked up the remaining apricots, a box of lemon creams, and a small jar of mints. "Do you have room in your bag for these?"

Edna took all but the mints and put them in the bag. "I hope it's not too cold up there. Maybe we should take a blanket." Elizabeth folded the thermal blanket that lay at the foot of her bed and draped it around her shoulders.

"That's it," she said.

They left Elizabeth's room like the thieves they were, tiptoeing quietly to the stairwell at the far end of the hall. Once there, they climbed slowly, resting at each landing. Finally, on the top floor, Elizabeth retrieved the key from the pocket of her suit jacket. She unlocked the large glass door and gave the key to Edna. They didn't speak until the door closed behind them and they looked around to make sure no one lurked behind the trellises.

Edna put the brown bag down and took out sherry, glasses, and food before she arranged two of the patio chairs side by side so she and Elizabeth could both sit under the blanket. It was a beautiful night, cloudless, starry, made perfect by the mild temperature and the full moon hanging above them like a giant pearl against a dark, sequined dress.

"Are you warm enough?" Edna asked when she had settled Elizabeth beneath the blanket.

"I'm fine. Pour me a glass of wine, will you?"

"It's too bad we don't have some paper plates."

"It doesn't matter. We've got everything we need." Elizabeth sat very still as Edna poured the wine and arranged the food on the nearby table. After a few minutes, she patted the chair next to her and ordered Edna to stop fussing and sit. Edna sat, pulled the blanket across her knees, and looked up at the sky.

"Oh, Lizzie," she said. "Isn't it glorious? I forgot things like stars existed. If only we had a pail of water!"

"Whatever for?"

"To reflect them," she said, opening her arms to embrace the night.

> The Dog, and the Plough, and the Hunter, and all
> And the Star of the Sailor, and Mars
> These shone in the sky, and the pail by the wall
> Would be half full of water and stars.

"That's lovely," said Elizabeth, clapping her hands. "What's it from?"

"Damned if I know," said Edna. "But I'm sure it's Robert Louis Stevenson. I used to know all of *A Child's Garden of Verses* by heart. I'd recite them to Marion while she played." She frowned suddenly. "So much of what I used to know is gone."

"Don't fret. You still know more than most."

Edna straightened her shoulders, remembering the pact between her eyes and hands. She picked up her glass. "I think we should drink to something. What will it be?"

Elizabeth thought for a moment and then raised her glass to the moon. A gust of wind ruffled her cap of curls. "Let's drink to the light," she said. "Let's drink to reflecting the light as perfectly as that dead ball up there does it."

Edna's eyes filled. She sipped her sherry as the first tears slid down her cheeks. "I've done precious little reflecting, Lizzie. I've done a lot to be ashamed of."

Elizabeth laughed. "What terrible things have you done? Burned a pie or two. Forgotten a birthday. Pinched a few things. Used foul language. Those things don't matter, Edna."

"Much worse than that," said Edna quietly. "You really don't know the worst about me. I've never told anybody. And now that we've talked to that young writer, I'm not sure whether I think I'm a sinner or whether I've got more courage than I know."

"Now you've piqued my curiosity. What are you talking about?"

Edna sipped her wine before speaking. "Why did you only have two children?"

"Hah!" said Elizabeth. "I had ten, but two were stillborn and six died shortly after birth, all before I celebrated my thirtieth birthday. All the babes who died were boys." She shook her head sadly. "My husband moved to another room after the eighth died. He said there was no point in having relations with a woman who only produced girls."

"Oh, Lizzie, I'm so sorry."

"He was very hard. But I think I understand him now in a way I couldn't when he was around to hurt me. It wasn't that he didn't love the girls. It's just that he was old school and wanted sons as well. I'm sure he thought eight chances were enough. Maybe after the eighth boy died, something in him died as well. He never touched me, not even on the arm, after that. I was too stupid to fight with him. And I was exhausted by the strain of bearing them and hoping and then having them die."

The women sat in silence for a time. Finally, Edna spoke.

"I was twenty-five when I had Marion, exactly nine months after I married," she said. "I think I must have conceived on my wedding night. But I wanted her. I was so full of hope before she was born. Still, I had no idea how it hurt to have a child. When I got pregnant again, she was only four months old. A friend of my mother's looked into my eyes and gave me something." She heard Elizabeth's breathing alter but did not look at her. "I almost bled to death. It was the last of my worries about pain from child birth."

Elizabeth reached over to take Edna's hand in her own. "You did what a lot of women did and do in extremity. And what's worse, I'd like to know? Giving birth to seven children and neglecting them out of fatigue and hardship, or giving birth to one and really caring for her?"

"But that's just it. Even though I cared for her, even though I gave her all my time and energy, shared what to me was joyful, mysterious, and tender in the world, she grew into a selfish, dismal woman who can't see beyond her own desires. I didn't want to create a child like that."

"You didn't create her, Edna. People create themselves. She took what she chose to take from you. Leave her with her own soul, Edna. You don't blame your parents for your shortcomings."

Edna looked from Elizabeth to the moon. "I often wonder who that baby was destined to be. Do you think I might have had a friend if I'd been a little less willful? Can a child be a friend?"

"Ah, there's a riddle. I often wonder what my life would have been like if I'd married the man my mother chose for me. He was older and lived next door to us. She thought I would have a little security with an older man who owned his own farm and was making a good living. She was probably right. Our lives would have been more comfortable. The man I chose to marry appealed to me in a way no other man did." She smiled into the darkness. "But he thought it was unseemly for a woman to want a man the way I wanted him." She laughed suddenly. "Men," she said. "They had some mighty peculiar notions about women back then."

Pensive, Edna said, "After what I did, I thought it was wrong to enjoy myself that way. I think I was full of the devil for a long while – mean with my husband, as though it was his fault – and after a while, the desire wasn't there anymore. I had my daughter and my painting. Goodness," she said. "I thought I locked all this up and threw away the key. I never thought I'd be touched by it again." She looked at Elizabeth suddenly. "Do you still think about your husband that way?"

"Yes," said Elizabeth. "That's another reason those pills were such a help. Even though I hated him most times, I wanted to love him, too, even after he was gone. The pills made me numb to all that longing."

Edna opened the apricots and passed them to Elizabeth. "Do you suppose the others feel like you? Merle? Wally? Wilson? Do you suppose they'd like a man?"

"It's hard to tell. I suspect Wally misses the reverend very much, because they had all that time together. How did Shakespeare put it? 'The beast with two backs'?" She laughed. "Of all the things I read as a young girl, that's the only phrase that made a deep impression on me. I suppose there was some of that going on between them."

Edna shivered. "That's a revolting thought. Imagine having to snuggle up to an oleaginous preacher every night."

"I believe Wally really loved him, Eddie."

"Just the thought of the two of them together in bed gives me the creeps. I guess I've turned into something of a cold fish," Edna said.

With delicacy for Edna's feelings, Elizabeth said, "Maybe your energy got channeled in another direction. Maybe that's why you painted. Diana's right about there being many kinds of fertility."

"I didn't paint anything like that, I can tell you," Edna said haughtily. "I liked still life, wild flowers, and portraits."

"No naked bodies writhing on beds?" Elizabeth asked with demonic hilarity.

"Don't be disgusting, Lizzie."

Edna threw the blanket off her lap and stood to stretch, then set her glass on the table before examining a nearby planter. "Before we know it, these boxes will be brimming with petunias. Remember the show we had last year? And the hanging baskets of fuschia and ivy?"

"I've seen the last of them. The only plants I'll be seeing are the ones in my garden. They live in my heart so they can't die. Did you know I had trilliums, Edna, and May apples? I even had one glorious jack-in-the-pulpit in my shade garden."

Edna moved to the high railing and looked down. "All those cars look like fireflies zipping along down there. I wonder where they're going in such a hurry."

"Here and there," said Elizabeth. "You look positively beautiful in the moonlight. I wish you could see yourself. If you painted what I see, you'd have a masterpiece."

"Some masterpiece that would be, Lizzie. All folks would see is a crazy old lady with two chins and three eyelids over each eye."

"Nonsense, Edna. You're good to look at. You refresh people, the way you carry yourself and move your hands."

'Stop it, you old fool."

"You don't know what you've got," Elizabeth persisted. "Most people our age are finishing up on the losing side of a battle, but you haven't even begun to fight. You can inspire people, Edna."

Edna returned to her chair. "I'm not going to change a damn thing. I'm just another old lady, shunted off to a rest home to be out of everybody's way."

"No," said Elizabeth. "You're like the moon up there. You shine and shine in all your phases. But don't get puffed up about it all. You're going to have to shine on some pretty horrible sights before your light goes out."

Edna clucked her tongue. "You sound like you can see into the future."

"You'd be surprised at what I can see." Elizabeth shivered. "I'm getting cold, Edna. I think we'd better start packing up."

While Edna was busy folding the blanket and putting the furniture back where she'd found it, Elizabeth walked over to the railing to whisper to the sky.

"What are you mumbling about?" Edna wanted to know.

"None of your business," said Elizabeth. "This conversation is between the moon and me."

Laden down with their things, Edna joined Elizabeth at the railing. "It's a mystery, isn't it?" she said reverently.

"What is?"

"How all that dead stuff can appear to be alive, shining, glorious."

"It is," Elizabeth agreed. "It certainly is."

"I wish I could remember that Shelley poem." Edna closed her eyes as she searched her memory. "Pale for weariness?" Smiling, she opened her eyes and addressed the moon.

Art thou pale for weariness
Of climbing heaven, and gazing on the earth,
Wandering companionless
Among the stars that have a different birth, –
And ever changing, like a joyless eye
That finds no object worth its constancy?

Elizabeth's face reflected the reflected light of the moon. "Edna, that was wonderful. You say the words with such feeling.

You might be a poet, catching a little of the wonder of the world so others can see it, feel it, make it part of them. "

"That doesn't sound like a bad ambition."

Elizabeth gave the moon once last glance. "All ambition's bad except the ambition to get home," she said softly.

"What?"

"Oh, never mind. I'm wandering. I'm weary. Let's go in. I've had enough." She shivered and leaned against Edna for warmth. "'No object worth its constancy'," she repeated. "Get me downstairs, Edna. I'm all in."

Edna moved the blanket and bag to her left arm and closed her right around Elizabeth's shoulders. Slowly, the friends walked to the glass doors and slipped inside.

THREE

It was six-thirty when Edna pulled back the drapes and said good morning to the world. She ran her bath awash in happy roof-garden memories, taking out her upper plate and putting it in a glass to soak while seeing Elizabeth in her lovely suit as clearly in her mind's eye as she'd seen her in the flesh the night before. Smiling and humming, she climbed into the hot water for a soothing soak. As the water cooled, she thought of the pleasurable things she and Elizabeth would do on this glorious new day.

After her bath, her hair brushed and tucked into its top-knot, she looked into her closet for something spring-like to wear. A neglected flower print caught her eye. She decided she would forgive it for being a gift from Marion and pulled it on over an intricately tatted cotton slip, one of the few relics of her past she had managed to hold on to when she'd moved to the lodge. The dress was white jersey with a spray of navy and red flowers set into nests of green leaves. The belt was navy leather. She pulled on her navy Naturalizers and felt so smart she hoped Elizabeth would be inspired to replace her usual winter drab for something equally in tune with life's burgeoning possibilities. Turning a gentle circle, she felt like one of spring's offerings.

Impatient to be out and about, Edna decided to call for Elizabeth and persuade her to go out for a walk before breakfast, something they had never done before. She went down the hall thinking she must remember to put the roof-garden key in her satin money pouch. While they were out, she decided, they would visit the hardware store to have a duplicate made. That way, the original could find its way back to Bernice's office before it was missed and they could visit the roof whenever liked.

She listened before knocking on Elizabeth's door, expecting to hear her friend belting out "Bringing in the Sheaves", something she did when she was particularly happy, but the room was silent. She knocked softly and then more loudly. When Elizabeth didn't answer, Edna opened the door and called gaily, "Lizzie, you sleepy head. It's a beautiful spring morning." She went into the darkened room where Elizabeth lay in her bed, her drapes still closed.

"That's enough of that," Edna said sternly. "Get up and get dressed. I've already had my bath." She opened the drapes and turned to the bed. Elizabeth, pale and still, did not move. Edna went to her, knowing, wanting to shriek with what she knew. "Lizzie?" she whispered. "Oh, Lizzie."

She took one of Elizabeth's small, cold hands in her own before taking up the paper lying beneath it. She surprised herself when she didn't cry. Dully, she squinted and read.

Dear Edna, I know you're not going to like this, but I think this is the end. I'm sorry, but there are one or two things you must do for me.

Edna looked from the page to the still face, relieved to discover that wherever Elizabeth was, she was not here, on the bed, in this impossibly still body. She resumed reading the letter.

I want you to have my black bag, dear. Don't forget to line it before you go into the dining room tonight. Otherwise, you'll have to eat that awful tuna and I wouldn't want that. I still have hope that you may find something in it reminiscent of the spider. If you do, send it to the Board of Health. I'm sure they'd love a scandal. It would give them purpose.

In the top drawer of my bureau, you'll find a large, flat key. It's for my safety-deposit box in the bank across the street. There is some cash in an account there, four hundred dollars I think, which you're to spend on my remains. There are to be no undertakers, Eddie. I don't want any strangers touching me, just a serviceable wooden box to get me from here to that lovely crematorium on St. Clair. You remember the one in the big cemetery with lots of trees. If they'll let you, I'd like to be scattered afterward. Find someplace surprising for my ashes. I'll leave the location to you since you have a better eye for that kind of thing than I do.

Have the bank send my will and other papers to my daughters. Don't worry about any objections to my instructions. I long ago told them what I planned to do, and, in truth, I think they'll be relieved not to have to see to any of this. It's all in the will, in any case. But don't you dare leave it to anyone else. You're the only one I trust to put aside sentiment and follow instructions. You always have, better than you know.

And don't forget that business at the school on Thursday night. Get over there and get your hair done. If you want to know the truth, it's getting ratty at the ends and should be seen to. And tell those children what I said about real life. It's not rules and regulations. It's what we felt when we were up there, under the moon. No matter how mean and pinched it sometimes seems to be, it's really all that mystery and wonder. We just have to open to it.

Be sure to tell them not to worry about the bullies. They're good for us because they give us something to measure ourselves against. Take as many as you can from here. Get them out. Get them moving. Get them mad. Afterward, go out and have a party. Drink something wicked and make a toast to me. That's the way I want it. I want to imagine you all sitting at a table laughing and having fun, and plotting against the ignorance that says a human life is valuable only under certain circumstances.

Oh, I almost forgot. Return the key to the roof garden. You're not going to need it anymore. But don't forget the moon. If it can reflect light, so can you. You're going to think it's all over because you've lost me, but believe me, for you it is just beginning. You gave me a green old age, Edna. You'll do the same for others. You'll make them laugh. You'll . . . . I'm tired and muddle-headed. Before I realized I didn't have as much time as I hoped for, I took off my suit. Lay me out in it, will you? I'm too tired to put it on myself.

Edna folded the letter and tucked it into her bra. She went to the closet and pulled the starlight-blue suit off its wooden hanger, placing the skirt and jacket at the end of the bed before going in to the bathroom to run a sink full of warm water. Back at Elizabeth's bedside, she folded back the covers and undressed her friend.

With a face cloth and some lavender soap, Edna bathed Elizabeth's body, toweled her dry, and found fresh under things in the bureau. Awkwardly, she pulled up what Lizzie called her Marks &Sparks and then a new pair of panty hose. With expanding grief, she fitted the amazingly small brassiere and maneuvered a slip over Lizzie's head and shoulders. At last, she dressed Lizzie in the suit. At the end of it all, she combed her friend's hair before applying a little lipstick and rouge. Satisfied that she only needed shoes to complete her task, she went to the closet and pulled out Elizabeth's finest pair. She wept a little as the red toenails disappeared into the black suede pumps. She stared at the shoes for a moment. Finally, she picked up the phone.

"Miss Wilson," she said in her most matter-of-fact voice. "Elizabeth Schmidt died in the night. She left instructions that she wanted to be cremated, but not embalmed." Edna expected a sigh of exasperation from the manager but heard none. "I suppose you're familiar with the routine when one of us has the temerity to die on the premises. Could you set the wheels in motion?" She hung up the phone with a bang and looked at Elizabeth. "If I had the nerve, I'd put you in a wheelchair and push you over to that place on St. Clair myself. But I think there are laws in these matters. You wouldn't want me to go to jail, would you?" Elizabeth's stillness enveloped her.

She walked to the bed and sat down before taking a cold hand in her own. Gradually, the lodge came to life around her. She heard the elevator taking the first breakfasters to the dining room as the cleaning people descended onto the seventh floor. The vacuum's whine filled the hall, but over the motor's noise she heard the gossiping. She imagined Bernice lost little time in letting everyone who might have business on the seventh floor know that they were not to enter Elizabeth's room. Edna was grateful. She didn't yet know how she would respond to sympathy.

The room was very still as she sat with her friend. And then the door opened and Bernice and a man Edna had never seen before entered the room. Here was living proof of the reality of Elizabeth's death. Edna took a deep breath and stood to face them.

"Ah," said Bernice cheerfully. "Here she is."

The man nodded at Edna. "Are you her next of kin?" His voice was unbearably kind. Edna shook her head. "A good friend then." He closed the distance between them to put a hand on Edna's shoulder. She looked into his open face, grateful for the humanity she found there.

"Do you need me for anything else, Miss Wilson?"

Bernice was looking down at Elizabeth curiously. "You'd better tell Mr. Franks her wishes in the matter."

"She wants to be cremated, but not embalmed, in a plain wooden coffin. As simple a process as we're allowed, if you please."

"Because it's a cremation, there must be a coroner's examination," Mr. Franks said.

"I'll take care of all that," the manager said efficiently. "I have all her information on file downstairs. And I'll take care of the payment for your services as well as the cremation. The next of kin are always very prompt in matters of funeral charges."

"Thank you, Miss Wilson." He turned to Edna. "After the coroner completes the necessary paperwork, and after the forty-eight-hour waiting period, we'll take your friend to the crematorium of her choice."

"I want her ashes," Edna said.

"Of course," said the man. "But since you're not a relative, I suggest you call her family members before the forty-eight-hour waiting period is up. I'll need some sort of . . . ." He stopped seeing that Edna understood. After a moment, he continued. "I'll take care of the burial permit, of course. Where would you like your friend sent when we've seen to the formalities?"

"She likes that place on St. Clair Avenue," Edna told him. "I'll want to be there. On Friday?" The man nodded.

Doing her best to imitate the man's tenderness, Bernice walked around the bed to Edna. "Would you like to pack up her things, Mrs. Carver? It would be a help to me, and I know Mrs. Schmidt would like it if you did."

"I'll do whatever needs to be done."

"Good. I keep a supply of empty cartons in the basement for just such situations." Edna noticed the man look away from the manager's zestful approach to the process. "I'll have the help bring some up for you." She walked to the door and then turned, remembering something. "Did she say anything to you about a will?"

"It's in the bank across the street. In a safety-deposit box." She went to Elizabeth's bureau for the key and handed it to Bernice. "Might her money be transferred to a bank near her daughters?"

"That's not your concern," Miss Wilson told her. "I'll notify the bank and they'll see to everything."

"Will you call her daughters?"

"Yes, Mrs. Carver. We've spoken on the phone a few times. I'll call this morning for cremation approval. I'm sure they won't mind what's done with her."

"Good," Edna said with relief. "They don't know me from a load of hay. I won't be going down to breakfast this morning. Could you . . . ?"

Bernice offered the smile she reserved for visitors. "Certainly, Mrs. Carver. I'll inform the kitchen. The boxes will be up shortly. Please take care of this as quickly as possible. There's such demand for our rooms." The manager went out briskly, leaving Edna and Mr. Franks alone.

"May I do anything for you?" he asked.

She shook her head. "Not unless you know how to raise her from the dead."

"Let me walk you back to your room, Mrs. Carver. We'll be finished here shortly."

At last Edna was able to cry a little. "I've bathed her. I've changed her clothes. Please," she whispered. "Don't let anyone else touch her."

On the way to her door, Mr. Franks cradled Edna's shoulders lightly. The pair walked slowly, Elizabeth Schmidt's modest funeral procession. "If you like," Mr. Franks said, "I'll inform the crematorium that you'd like to light the retort on Friday. Would nine be too early?"

"Nine is fine, thank you," Edna answered, opening her door and holding the man's hand for a moment. When he left, she closed the door and pulled her drapes, wanting the room as dark as possible when she sat down to rock.

"I should be doing something," she chided herself after a few minutes. "I should be doing something other than talking about funeral arrangements and wills and packing things away." After another few minutes, she opened the drapes and retrieved the Gideon from the bedside table. Sitting once more, she riffled its pages looking for something she might read before she lit the fire that would burn away the body of Elizabeth Schmidt. A soft knock at the door interrupted her.

"It's open," she called.

Mrs. Wallace came bursting in, her face the picture of sadness.

"I'm so sorry my dear. I was with Miss Wilson when you called down to let her know. I would have come up with her but she absolutely forbade me. What might I do for you?" She nodded her approval at the Bible in Edna's hands.

Edna put the book back in the drawer. A mysterious stoic forbearance eclipsed her terrible grief. "You can help me pack up her things if you've got the time, Wally."

"Of course, I will Mrs. Carver. What's faith without works, as it were?"

"Indeed," said Edna.

"What was it? Heart?"

"Old age, I imagine," said Edna.

Mrs. Wallace blinked back tears. "She's in a better place. When are we going to have the service?"

"She doesn't want a service, Wally. She wants to be cremated without any fuss."

"Oh, dear," said Mrs. Wallace. "The Lord will sound the last trump and Elizabeth's body won't be found."

"Don't be an ass, Wally," Edna said tiredly. "If the Lord can wake the dead, He can recreate Elizabeth out of a few cinders."

"Yes, of course He can," the widow agreed mechanically. "But there is nothing about . . . ."

Edna sighed. "I don't want to argue about this. It's what Elizabeth wants."

Mrs. Wallace studied her shoes for a moment, glad to bolt to the door at the sound of a sudden knock. It was one of the cleaning women wanting to let Edna know the boxes were in Mrs. Schmidt's room.

"She's in a rush, isn't she," Edna snarled. The woman patted Edna's hand and went back to her vacuuming.

Mrs. Wallace walked down the hallway with Edna, trying to think of something comforting to say. In the end, she offered Diana's comfort instead. "I told the young writer about Mrs. Schmidt on the way up here. She cried, Mrs. Carver. Really, the poor dear was quite overcome . . . ." Mrs. Wallace stopped talking when she observed Edna's weary shrug.

Back in Elizabeth's room, Edna became efficiency personified. "You take the closet, Wally. Put the shoes in the bottom of one of those large boxes and then fold the dresses and sweaters and put them on top." Mrs. Wallace nodded. Edna closed the door before opening the drawers in Elizabeth's bureau.

She felt her breath catch only once as she lifted the underwear out. From her place in front of the closet where she folded quickly, Mrs. Wallace said, "You're like me now, Mrs. Carver. You're one of the bereaved."

"Yes," Edna answered politely but feeling that no matter what life circumstances they might share, she could never be like Mrs. Wallace.

"You'll find the strength to go on. I did, even though my

partner of fifty years was taken from me." She banged some shoes into the box before making a high, piercing animal sound. Edna turned in alarm. The minister's widow had collapsed on the bed in a fit of sobbing.

"Wally? Oh, my dear, I had no idea you were that close to Elizabeth."

Mrs. Wallace fought back tears. "It isn't Mrs. Schmidt. It's my own hell, Mrs. Carver, my own torture."

Edna's eyebrows shot up. She wanted the woman to close her mouth so she wouldn't have to look at her enormous teeth. "Do you want to tell me . . . ?"

"Mr. Wallace killed himself," the widow cried.

"Oh, my goodness," said Edna. "There must have something to him after all."

"What?"

"Nothing," Edna said quickly, hating herself for speaking aloud. "I thought he died of a heart attack."

"He did. The smoke affected his heart." Another convulsing sob escaped from Mrs. Wallace's heaving chest. Edna looked away from the teeth in order to thwart a building impulse to laugh. "He locked himself in the bathroom and set fire to some books. He put them in the sink, mind you, and rolled up a damp towel so smoke wouldn't escape under the door. He didn't want me to be any danger."

"How peculiar," said Edna. "Lizzie told me something about smoke. I think Merle told her . . . ."

The widow rushed on, eager to share the details of her tragedy. "Miss Wilson was very good. She came up right away and had the night watchman jimmy the door off the hinges. He was slumped over the tub, all purple and horrible."

"There, there," said Edna. "It must have been terrible for you."

"The terrible part is that he's damned because . . . I don't even know why. He was a good minister. But when he came here, he felt useless. The doctor was very kind. He gave him medicine that seemed to help for a time, but the reverend was uncomfortable with prolonged material help. I tried to tell him how loved he was, how needed, but the day before he . . . did it . . . he seemed to fall to pieces, accusing God of deserting him and the good doctor of all sorts of devilry. He . . . did away with himself, Mrs. Carver. And now he's damned," she cried. "It says so in the Bible."

"It says a lot of things in the Bible, Wally, but what does it say in your heart? That a man should live a good life, get to the end of it and be forsaken? What kind of a god would behave like that?"

Hope shone in the widow's eyes. "You don't think Mr. Wallace is damned?"

"If he is, I don't think it's because of the way he spent the last couple of days of his life."

Quiet now, Mrs. Wallace retrieved a handkerchief from her pocket and blew her nose loudly. She grinned girlishly at Edna. "This is a fine howdy-do. Here you've lost your best friend in the world and you have to comfort me."

"We have to comfort each other, Wally," Edna said tenderly. Feeling entirely under Elizabeth's sway she embraced the widow. "Now we'd better get back to work."

Mrs. Wallace picked up Elizabeth's large black bag to put in with the shoes.

"No," said Edna. "She left that to me. I'll put the contents in with her underwear."

There wasn't much in the old purse – a bank book, a small green change purse, a wallet, two lipsticks Edna remembered they'd stolen on one of their trips to the Eaton Centre, a purse-sized packet of Kleenex, a few pens, two paper clips, and some loose Digestive Biscuits at the bottom.

"We'll miss her bright and shining face in the dining room," Mrs. Wallace said, resuming her folding.

Edna smiled and nodded. She opened the second drawer and began to take things out to pack. The sweaters she put into the box first and then the hot water bottle in its little knitted jacket. She recalled how she'd laughed like a lunatic when she first saw the thing, accusing Elizabeth of playing with dolls. She added two old garter belts, small enough to fit a child, stockings and panty hose, and last of all, an old chocolate box full of empty pill bottles. Edna packed everything without saying anything until she'd closed the second drawer and started emptying the third. "Were you a regular visitor to the doctor's office along with the reverend?" she asked.

"He went down every week for his pills," Mrs. Wallace said. "But I've always had the constitution of a horse, so I didn't need them." Edna couldn't help but smile.

Without warning, Bernice barged into the room. "Ah," said the manager, apparently very pleased with their progress. "You're doing a fine job. I'll tell Mrs. Robertson her mother can have the room tonight if she'd like." Edna didn't look up. "How are you feeling, Mrs. Carver? Would you like me to call the doctor? He can give you something to help bear the strain."

"I'm fine, thank you," Edna said. "The doctor can't help me."

"We were just talking about him," said Mrs. Wallace.

"Oh?" Bernice's whistling voice conveyed alarm. "What were you saying?"

"Mrs. Carver was asking if I saw the doctor regularly, the way Mr. Wallace did." She smiled, missing the manager's sharp intake of breath. "I told her how the doctor helped him with his moods."

Bernice peered critically into one of the boxes and muttered something about calling the Goodwill Store to arrange a pickup. She surprised the women when she left as abruptly as she'd arrived.

"Oh, dear," said Mrs. Wallace. "She's got a bee in her bonnet. I hope I didn't put it there. I do so like to stay on the good side of people, as it were." She put Elizabeth's cranberry-coloured felt hat in the big box and closed the lid. "That's it over here. Shall I check the bedside table?"

Edna nodded absently as she wondered how many of the other lodgers used the doctor's pills to take refuge from life.

"Nothing but the Gideon," Mrs. Wallace sang. "And it's almost lunchtime. I'm famished."

"You go ahead, Wally. I've got one or two things to do up here. Besides, I'm not very hungry. I'll see you later." Remembering Elizabeth's request, Edna paused in her folding. "You might mention a party for Elizabeth after the open house at the school tomorrow evening. See how many people you can persuade to come."

"Of course I will." The big woman smiled. "Thank you, Mrs. Carver," she said warmly. "Those were healing words you spoke."

Edna returned her smile. "Thank you, Wally. I wouldn't have wanted to do this alone."

"No. There is altogether too much that has to be done alone in life." She leaned forward, impulsively kissing Edna on the cheek. "Maybe you and I," she added shyly, "now that we're all alone, maybe . . . ."

"Yes," said Edna, but without conviction. "We'll have lots of good times, Wally."

Mrs. Wallace hugged her before slipping out into the hall. Alone, Edna surveyed the cluttered room. The bureau and closet were empty, she noted as she sat on the edge of Elizabeth's bed. "So this is how we wrap up a life. It only takes a few boxes, a little business at the bank, and a death certificate." Her voice came from the chasm of emptiness within her.

Edna felt the quilt where Elizabeth lay only a few hours before. It was still damp from the bath she had given her friend. She pulled it off the bed, not wanting anyone else to touch it. Picking up Elizabeth's black bag, she walked out into the hall where she discovered one of the young women had parked the laundry hamper. Edna gently placed the quilt in it before returning to her room to take up her meditation in her rocker.

The morning began badly for Diana when the doctor crept into her room just as she wakened. The pulsing tenderness in her abdomen made her feel more vulnerable than she usually did. As prelude to his examination, he sat beside her, took her hand, and brushed the hair off her forehead. She felt like an animal in a trap. When Mrs. Wallace burst into the room, Diana wept with relief. Smoothly, the doctor pronounced her temperature normal and left Diana with her visitor.

The day before, when Mrs. Wallace had introduced herself as the minister's widow, Diana sneered inwardly, but this morning, when the big woman promised to come back later in the day to read the Bible to her, Diana felt genuine gratitude. Before she left for the seventh floor, Mrs. Wallace shared the news of Elizabeth Schmidt's death. Diana's grief surprised her.

Alone again, Diana recalled snippets of the bizarre conversation she'd overheard the day before between the manager and the doctor. She remembered accusations about breakdowns, and pills leading to suicides. Straining to remember, Diana glanced at the capsules on the bedside table and determined to call her gynecologist before she took any more of them.

Seated at her table for the evening meal, Edna accepted the inevitable rush of attention Elizabeth's death brought.

Automatically, she thanked people for their condolences. The woman with the remarkable hair continued to smile ferociously as she told Edna how sorry she was. "Some folks just love a place like this," she said. "They don't do anything their whole lives through, so coming here's just more of the same. I could tell you and that little woman weren't like that." She winked devilishly, but Edna felt a million miles from any sense of connection with her or the other lodgers. "If you ever want anyone to, you know, go somewhere with, I love a good time." She winked again.

This time, Edna made herself smile. "Thank you," she said. The offer of a good time made her remember Elizabeth's wishes. "Will you be coming to the open house at the school tomorrow night?"

"The one down the road? Oh, yes. I think so. I won't bother about my hair, though. It's entirely natural," she confided, touching the silver, kinky spikes with pride. "Where's the party afterward? The minister's widow told us about a wake at lunchtime."

"I haven't thought of that. Perhaps we can find a tavern within walking distance."

The woman's smile expanded. "There's a nice enough one, you know. It's not too rowdy and it's only a couple of blocks from the school."

"That sounds like just the place," Edna said. "We've all been good for far too long." The old woman nodded with enthusiasm for both of them. She returned to her table when the waitresses came out of the kitchen laden with trays.

A few minutes later Edna made herself smile as Mrs. Wallace leaned over, whispering. "I asked Miss Wilson if I might be permitted to join you this evening, Mrs. Carver. I thought you might like the companionship, as it were."

"As it were, I wouldn't," Edna said tiredly. "No offence, Wally, but I've had it with the social whirl. I hope you understand." Mrs. Wallace pressed her hand before returning to her usual table.

When a plate was set before her, Edna speared a piece of tuna and looked at it critically before shaking it off her fork. She pushed the creamed mass this way and that, then pulled Elizabeth's black bag onto her lap. She opened the purse and arranged the plastic liner. Without bothering to see if anyone was watching, she dumped her dinner into the bag and shut the clasp tightly. It sounded like a satisfied burp.

Her tea arrived, and while she did not want it, she made herself stay at the table for a few more minutes to stave off gossip. Elizabeth's favourite waitress touched her shoulder on her way to another table.

"I liked her," she told Edna sadly. "I really did. Not many have a sense of humour around here."

"Well," Edna snapped, hating herself for her meanness. "It's not like there's a lot to laugh about around here." The girl rushed away with her load of tea pots.

"I think I've had enough socializing for one night," Edna said far louder than she'd intended to. A few lodgers looked at her curiously. She stood, inadvertently knocking her tea cup to the floor with Elizabeth's unwieldy purse. "Oh, damn," she exploded. "How did such a little woman pack this thing around so gracefully?"

Bernice walked over to her quickly. "Don't bother with cleaning it up, Mrs. Carver. We understand how it is when the body goes out of control." Edna didn't bother contradicting her as she walked haughtily from the dining room.

On Thursday morning a wave of vitality broke over the dining room as the lodgers anticipated their evening out. Fifteen minutes late because she'd overslept and then taken pains to dispose of the previous evening's creamed tuna by flushing it down the toilet a little at a time, Edna discovered Merle shouting at Bernice. "I ain't gonna stand for this. I got money. My son will find me a nice place in Florida, near his condo."

Infinitely patient and smiling her most indulgent smile, Bernice said, "Please sit down, Merle."

"Not until you bring me bacon that ain't burned."

Edna offered encouragement as she passed Merle on her way to her usual table, but it was more from habit than actual support. Arthur leapt to his feet as Edna sat at her table. "Why don't you throw yourself off the balcony like Vera did, Merle!" he shouted. "Nobody would miss you either."

Bernice quickly walked to Arthur's table. "Mr. Martin," she said loudly. "I appreciate your support, but what happened to Miss Potts is most regrettable."

Arthur would not be subdued. "Nobody can stand Merle. Flashing her rings. Bragging about her son." He pointed a vicious finger at Edna. "And that one! Thinking she's too good for everyone."

"Certainly too good for you, Arthur Martin," Edna said regally.

Lodgers offered a staccato burst of applause.

'Well, I think we'd be well rid of the both of you." Arthur countered feebly. "A couple of trouble makers."

Bernice did her best to control the situation. "Please, Mr. Martin. Be a good boy." She turned to Merle. "I'll take care of this," she said, patting Merle's back as she would a well behaved puppy's. She whisked her plate away and disappeared into the kitchen.

Edna summoned the energy to address the room. "As you know," she began. "We're all invited to an open house at the high school down the road this evening. I know Mrs. Schmidt would be pleased if you would join me for a party afterward, to give her a good sendoff."

Bernice flew out of the kitchen. "You naughty girl," she said with forced merriment. "You know Mr. Fathers has asked us to leave those children alone. We're all going to be very good and stay away from their school." She stared down the lodgers who had the temerity to look directly at her.

With no appetite and less fight, Edna attempted a cheerful smile and exited the dining room. Once upstairs, she closed herself in her room, took out her Bible, and flopped on her bed intending to spend the time before lunch looking for something appropriate to read before Elizabeth's cremation the following morning.

Hours later, she awoke with a start, the closed Bible heavy on her chest. It was quarter to seven. She rushed into the bathroom to prepare for her evening out.

Merle, Mrs. Wallace, Arthur Martin, whom she was very sorry to see, the old woman she thought of as electrified, the tall, elegant man with the bulbous nose she'd met in the third-floor therapy session – she recalled his bad joints and wondered how he would make the trip to the school and manage the stairs – as well as three women who sat near her in the dining room were waiting for Edna in the foyer when she stepped off the elevator. Mrs. Wallace took Edna's arm proprietarily.

"Ah, here you are," she said, smiling. Edna looked away from the large, gleaming teeth Mrs. Wallace displayed far more now that they were bereaved together.

"Is this all?" she asked   "Did the rest of them decide to be good?"

"When two or three are gathered," began the minister's widow.

"Oh, can it!" Arthur sniped. "I'm only going to keep an eye on you for Miss Wilson. She wants me to tell her everything you do."

"Shut up Arthur," Edna said. She held out a hand to the woman with the shocked hair. "It's high time I learned your name."

"Miss Jones," the woman said, delighted to be admitted into Edna's inner circle. "I was a school teacher for fifty years. Started in a one-room school house when I was just fifteen."

"You poor thing," said Edna. The woman offered her a high, squeaking note of pleasure. "I'm Edna Carver," Edna said formally.

"Oh, I've known who you are since I moved in a few weeks ago. There's a rumour afoot that your days are numbered here. That's why I'm coming along tonight. It might be my last chance for a little fun with you."

Edna appreciated her frankness. "Promise you'll remember me when I'm gone," she said. The woman squeaked again.

They set off slowly, Arthur and the tall, elegant gentleman labouring to lead the way, the three familiar diners next, and Merle, Mrs. Wallace, Miss Jones, and Edna crowding one another on the pavement at the rear. As they walked along, Edna tried to convince herself they would have a good time. She smiled stupidly and watched, fascinated, as Merle oozed, Mrs. Wallace worked her big teeth, and Miss Jones's hair bounced up and down with each step she took. She was glad they seemed to be having a good time despite her own lack of joy. She only wished Elizabeth could enjoy the occasion.

When they arrived at the school, Edna tried to break the grip Mrs. Wallace had on her arm, but to no avail. The woman hung on to her as though one or both of them were drowning. Edna acquiesced, suspecting she needed the widow's attention more than she realized.

Miss Jones broke away from the group in main foyer. "I'd like to see the Home Economics room first," she enthused. "I imagine I'll see some changes. That's where I finally specialized." Her voice trailed after her as she walked decisively toward the source of the kitchen aromas perfuming the hallway. The group watched her go, envious of her sense of purpose.

"Shall we go down to the basement classrooms?" asked Mrs. Wallace. "I believe that's where the hairdressing room is."

Edna looked around. "There's no one here," Edna said. "Maybe I got the night wrong."

Exasperated, Arthur pointed at a sign on the wall. "It's says right there, 'Open House, Visitors Welcome'."

"Why don't you find a machine to throw yourself into, Arthur," Edna offered cordially. "I'm sure the students would find it very entertaining to see what happens to a human body when it falls into a buzz saw." Arthur followed close behind when Edna and Mrs. Wallace headed for the basement stairs.

In the hairdressing room they found eight students, all looking very bored until Edna and her friends walked in.

"Jeez," said the tall blonde girl who'd given Elizabeth her manicure. "I'm so glad to see you. We thought nobody was gonna show." She ushered Edna to one of the chairs. Where's your friend?"

Edna looked at her hands. "She couldn't make it tonight. She said to say hello to you," she paused for a moment, to swallow her tears. "And to tell you that real life isn't like this."

"God, I hope not," the girl answered. She studied Edna's hair while cracking her gum vigorously. "What do you want me to do with it?" she asked as she fingered the long grey strands dubiously. "Lizzie said it was getting ratty at the ends. I'd like a shampoo and a trim."

"A precision blunt cut," said the girl. "That's my favourite and I need the practice." She slipped the plastic apron around Edna's neck before fitting a piece of cotton inside it and fastening them both with a large hair clip. She gestured with her head toward the shampoo area at the back of the room. When she noticed Mrs. Wallace, she whispered, "I don't think there's a thing anyone can do for her."

"Have someone give her a manicure," Edna said. "I don't think she's had one in her life."

"Gotcha," said the girl. She called one of the other students over and pointed at Mrs. Wallace. The boy went off to get the minister's widow, leading her by the arm to the manicure trays despite her loud protests. "He'll take care of her," the girl assured Edna. Edna sat in the chair in front of the basin. The girl ran the water and then pointed to the group in the doorway. "What do they want?"

"I wouldn't know," Edna said.

"You all want a trim, or what?" the girl called, and then turned on four girls who were gossiping animatedly in the opposite corner. "Hey, I'm not gonna do everything. Get the lead out." Slowly, the girls smirked their way over to their visitors.

"What's your name?" Edna asked as the girl worked up the lather.

"Anna," said the girl. "Bertini. My brother, Frank, he's upstairs in woodworking. Remember? I told you to see him last time you were here. They got some neat stuff up there. Some sucky stuff, too."

'Why did you decide to come to this school? Why hairdressing?" Edna was surprised by her interest in this friendly young girl.

The girl sighed dramatically. "I'm an immigrant. Know what that means?"

Edna said she thought she did.

"Well, you don't," Anna said matter-of-factly. "People think it means that your family comes from somewhere else to Canada and you get to be Canadian and you fit right in like everybody else. But that's bull shit. What it really means is that when you're in grade eight, teachers and puke-faced guidance counselors make decisions for you about your future. I kid you not." She cracked her gum. "I'm used to it now, but it used to bug my ass."

"Don't you want to be a hairdresser? You're very good at this. I feel like I can trust you, that you listen to me when I explain what I want."

"I like doing hair, but they think everybody they send here is a dummy. I can't fight it. My mother doesn't speak good English and she thinks teachers know best. It's okay for me. I hate school anyway and I can train with a hairdresser who knows what's what. But my brother, he's real smart." Disgusted, she added, "They got him building boxes."

"I bet they're beautiful boxes," Edna said as Anna wrapped her hair in a towel, turban style.

"Better than anybody deserves." The young woman guided Edna back to the mirrors, checking the cotton strip around her neck for leaks and smoothing down the protective apron once she'd settled Edna into the big red chair. "You must feel like we do," she said suddenly. "Everybody saying they know what's best for you."

"Yes," answered Edna, her eyes filling.

"So your friend says real life isn't like this."

Edna studied their images in the mirror as she would a pair of strangers, the girl combing and parting the long wet hair, the old woman pensive beneath the capable hands. "She said to tell you it wasn't all rules and regulations. That you need the bullies to help you to choose who you want to be."

The girl laughed. "We need bullies like a hole in the head."

"I don't know exactly what Elizabeth meant," Edna said thoughtfully. "But I do know – and you've probably already heard this a million times before – that you learn to really value the things that people try to take from you. Like freedom. And self respect."

"Sure," said the girl. "I'll take a couple of inches off, okay?"

"That's fine," said Edna. She picked at the plastic apron. "I live just down the street."

"Yeah, I know," said the girl.

"If you ever feel the impulse for a change, you could come to visit. Bring your brother. I get pretty tired of looking at all those wrinkles, I can tell you."

"Got any kids?"

"One. She's got wrinkles now, too. But she tries to hide them."

The girl laughed, cutting Edna's hair with amazing speed. "Can I blow it dry for you? You don't want a set."

"I'd like that," said Edna. "I've never had it done before."

The girl picked up the blow dryer and aimed it at Edna's head as she pulled up sections of hair with a brush. "You got a good head of hair. What colour was it when you were young?"

"Dark brown."

"Oh," said Anna. "You Italian?"

"No," said Edna. "I'm English. On both sides."

"Both sides of what?"

"On my mother's side and my father's side."

"Oh, I guess I'm Italian on both sides. But everybody thinks I'm something else because I'm blonde. Nerds. They don't know Italians can be blonde, too."

"I don't usually have a part," Edna said nervously.

"Let me do it my way tonight. You can change it back to the way you want it next time you wash it. You know Maria Callas?" Edna nodded. "This is how she sometimes wore her hair. Elegant."

Anna parted and re-parted Edna's hair then set to work with the blow dryer again. When she was finished, she gathered the silky strands at the nape of Edna's neck to fasten in an intricately looped chignon. While she was fastening the chignon in place, Mrs. Wallace, her fingertips blazing red, rushed to Edna.

"I feel as if I've gone to the dogs." She flashed her teeth at Anna, along with her red nails. "That young man was very persistent."

"What happened to Merle?" Edna asked.

"I think she went up to find Miss Jones in the cooking class. Something certainly smells good, doesn't it? I didn't have my dinner," Mrs. Wallace confided to Anna. "Are they giving away free samples up there?"

"They've been baking for a week. I'll take you up. It doesn't look like anybody else is gonna show anyways." She surveyed the room. The men were being shaved and trimmed and the other women from the lodge were in the midst of permanent waves.

"I really thought you'd be overrun."

"Naw," said Anna. "Hardly anybody's parents come to these things. It's too depressing. Most of them can't understand English, and those who can just hear how lazy and good for nothing their kids are. What's the point?"

"What kind of school is this?" asked Mrs. Wallace.

"Vocational – for dummies."

"Pardon me?"

The girl laughed. "You want something done with that?" She pointed at Mrs. Wallace's short-cropped hair.

"No, thank you, dear. I've been vain enough for one day." She smiled, wanting the girl to know she was on her side. "Who calls you dummies?"

"Nobody who matters," said Anna.

Edna was turning her head this way and that, trying to decide if she liked the new style.

Anna frowned, her critical eye scrutinizing the chignon. Abruptly, she turned to the door. "Hey, Francis! Here's my brother," she said proudly. "I was just telling this lady about you."

A tall, slim, dark-haired youth walked toward Edna, his tanned hand outstretched. "You live at the senior-citizen's place?"

Edna couldn't take her eyes off him. He was beautiful, Donatello's David come to life. She nodded stupidly.

"Our sister-in-law's cousin got a job there."

"Shut up, Frank," said Anna.

"Why?"

"You know," said his sister. She unclipped the plastic apron and helped Edna stand. "Why don't you take them up and show them your room? Give them a souvenir."

"Sure. Ya wanna see it?" he asked Edna.

Edna was studying his hair – dark brown, almost black, it fell in perfect waves to his shoulders. He was unconscious of his beauty and couldn't understand why she didn't answer him. "She bonkers or what?" he asked his sister quietly.

"Just take them upstairs. They have less fun than we do."

He shrugged and headed for the door. In a haze of appreciation, Edna followed. "Wait for me," called Mrs. Wallace but Edna ignored her. Mrs. Wallace paused at the door, smiling at Anna. "You're not a dummy, you know."

"If you say so," said the girl. She resumed chewing her gum with vicious little bites.

"People who call you names shouldn't be allowed to . . . ."

"Breathe."

Mrs. Wallace waved an ineffectual goodbye.

Edna followed the boy as he took the stairs two at a time, all the while watching the muscles in his back moving beneath his thin T-shirt. He looked over his shoulder when they reached the landing. "You know why she didn't want me to tell you about our sister-in-law's cousin?"

Edna shook her head and continued to stare.

"She's here illegally. My sister thinks everybody's a stoolie for the immigration department. They pay her way below minimum wage at that place, but she can't complain. Most of them are in the same boat. They're just glad to have the work."

A flash of understanding released Edna from her trance. "What's her name?"

"Why? You think you know her?"

"I might," she said, remembering the strange nervousness of her young waitress during confrontations with Bernice.

He gestured for her to follow him into the empty woodworking room. Here and there, set out on the long wooden workbenches, Edna saw examples of the students' handiwork – bread boards, large letters and numerals, small hinged boxes, several three-legged stools. She wandered in between the tables until she came to a small carving of an old man. About nine or ten inches high, it was carved in extraordinary detail. Edna picked up the statue amazed to feel veins in the tiny hands. The boy walked over to her. "You know about Don Quixote?"

"Of course," said Edna, smiling. "I've tilted at a few windmills myself."

"Take him."

"No, I couldn't. He's wonderful."

"I don't get any marks for him anyway. The jerk in here only gives marks for what we make from that list up there." He pointed to the front of the room. Edna read the list quickly and then turned to the boy.

"You carved this?"

"Yeah."

Edna touched the statue reverently.

"I used to paint," she said. "I haven't done anything for years . . . ."

"Oil? Acrylics?"

"Water colours."

"That isn't easy. I've tried."

"I told your sister to visit me. If you want to come, too, I could teach you what I know, if I remember anything."

"I hear you don't ever forget what you really know."

Anna bounded into the room. "I took that big lady up to the Home Ec room so she wouldn't get lost. They're all piggin' out up there. You wanna go, too?"

Edna nodded. "Your brother, he's . . . ."

"Michelangelo," the girl said in musical Italian. "Nerds. They think he should make boxes."

Obviously embarrassed, Francis Bertini changed the subject. "What's to eat up there? Think they'd let me have something? I'm starved."

"Maybe four parents have come," Anna said, disgusted. "And the old ladies that came with this lady with the gorgeous hair." Edna smiled. "If you don't eat it, all the teachers will rip it off."

Edna placed the carving on the table. "No," said the boy, picking it up and handing it to her. "I mean it. I want you to have it. You know who Don Quixote is. He belongs with someone who tilts at windmills."

Edna took the scarf from around her neck and lovingly wrapped the carving in it. "Believe me," she said. "This is the most beautiful sculpture I've ever owned."

He grinned sheepishly and walked out to the hall. Anna walked to the door and waited for Edna. "My brother's too good for this place, he really is. It burns my ass."

"Tell him to transfer. He should go somewhere where they'll develop his talent. He's good enough for the Ontario College of Art."

"It takes bread," said Anna. "And parents who agree. He's already got a job and saves his money, but I don't know how he'll manage to get out of this hole. It's like quicksand. Once you're in, you need help getting out."

At the top of the stairs, Anna pointed to an open door about halfway down the hall. "There's Home Ec. I better get back to Hairdressing in case anybody needs me for anything."

As the girl turned to leave, Edna grabbed her hand. "Seven-o-one." The girl looked at her blankly. "My room number at the lodge," she said. "In case you ever want to come by."

"Sure," said the girl. Edna watched Anna sprint down the hall before following Frank to the Home Economics classroom.

Edna and Francis Bertini, Frankie to his female fan club, stopped at the door of the Home Ec room and peered inside. Merle and Mrs. Wallace sat at a long table bent over a variety of delicacies. Miss Jones stood by the stove stirring something while enjoying an animated conversation with one of the students. "It's safe," Frank told Edna. "Hatchet-face isn't here."

Edna laughed. "It's funny, isn't it, how the names for teachers never change. We had a Hatchet-face when I was a girl. She used to smash people over the head with large, heavy objects. "

"I think this one just turns the electric knife on students." He left Edna for a beckoning girl.

"Hi, Frankie," she said with a smile that dimpled her cheeks and ignited her eyes. "Want some tarts?"

"Which one of you is putting out first?" All the girls laughed as he helped himself to a plate of butter tarts and returned to Edna with a napkin. She took one and sat down with Merle and Mrs. Wallace.

"Where did *you* get to? I've been looking for you everywhere," Mrs. Wallace mumbled as she chewed.

"Here and there," said Edna. "What have you got there?" She looked at Merle's plate.

"I ain't got a notion but it tastes *de*-licious." The students twittered. "I think these kids should cater the lodge and maybe give the cook a few lessons."

Miss Jones joined them. "I've been making strawberry jam. Do you know how long it's been since I made strawberry jam? That's what I miss most," she said, her eyes brimming. "Poking around in the kitchen, making pastry or meatloaf. I wonder if the cook would let me come in to help now and again."

"Never mind helping," said Merle. "Take over for her."

"I'd love to," said Miss Jones. "I used to do a superb duck. Very crisp, not at all greasy. And Floating Island. And oh, goodness, I forget what all. I'd put roses in your cheeks."

Merle licked her fingers noisily. "I think every single one of us should be able to plan a day's eats – say once every coupla months." She took another noisy bite. "Nothin' fancy, mind, but wouldn't it go a long way to makin' us feel part of it all."

"What a splendid idea," said Mrs. Wallace. "Mrs. Carver, why don't you suggest it to Miss Wilson? You're the only one who's not afraid to speak up. In her peculiar way, she respects you."

"Peculiar is right," said Edna, annoyed the lodgers were so intrepid when Bernice wasn't around. "I'd like another one of those," she told Frank. He brought the plate of tarts over and she took two. "This is the first food I've eaten since . . . ." She put the tarts down.

Mrs. Wallace, quick to sense the need for spiritual support, chided Edna. "Now, now. This is the night you're to celebrate her reunion with her Creator."

"Yes," said Edna. She put on a brave smile and picked up a tart but didn't want it any more. She looked at her watch. "If we're going to get out and have a drink before they lock the doors at the lodge, we'd better get a move on."

"Where's Arthur?" asked Merle, trying to sound casual.

"Oh, let's not bother with Arthur," Edna said. "Let's just get going. Whatever happened to the other women?"

"They must still be having their hair done," said Mrs. Wallace.

"Do you think they want to come?"

"Who cares if they do," said Miss Jones. "Let's just us go. We can have a good time at that place and nobody will be around to squeal on us." She returned to the bubbling jam.

Feeling an urgent need to move, Edna helped Miss Jones on with her coat. "Are you going to leave the jam? It smells awfully good."

"The girls let me have a few stirs. It's a project they're to be graded on."

Edna tried valiantly to recapture the old spirit of thievery. "Take it anyway," she said.

"Oh, no," said Miss Jones. "Strawberries are awfully dear, even in season. Their teacher would be furious."

"Yes," said Edna absently. "Old Hatchet-Face."

Miss Jones bristled. "How did you know that's what they used to call me?"

"You too?" Edna studied her for a moment. "But you don't look like a Hatchet-Face."

"I lost the hatchet when I stopped teaching." The students who had been listening to the old women laughed discreetly.

Edna picked up her carving and rewrapped it tenderly. "Thank you again," she said to Frank. "I'll treasure it." He nodded, taking for granted that she would. "Don't forget. Room seven-o-one at Sunset Lodge. Come by anytime and we'll talk art."

Francis Bertini nodded and returned to his conversation with the girls. Merle and Mrs. Wallace began to button their coats. "I don't know about this drinking business," said Mrs. Wallace. "Can't we just go out for something to eat?"

"Wally!" Edna cried. "You've just had a three-course meal. Come and have a drink. We have to toast Elizabeth."

"I'm afraid Mr. Wallace wouldn't like it," the widow protested feebly.

"Well, he ain't invited," Merle snapped.

Ready to do battle with the principal should the need arise, Edna marched through the empty halls to the school entrance, the others burbling in her wake. Once on the pavement, Miss Jones took Edna's arm and led the way. The tavern turned out to be three long blocks from the school, and by the time the women arrived, they were tired from walking and thoroughly chilled by the damp spring air.

The posters out in front, hand-painted in wild fluorescent colours, showed voluptuous women with opened red mouths, their bodies in various seductive poses. All had tiny stars covering their nipples and sentimentalized kitten faces painted over their pubic hair.

"Look at that!" said Mrs. Wallace in disbelief. "I'm afraid this place may be far too dangerous for us to patronize."

"Yes," said Edna. "Especially if this very poor excuse for art is any indication of the establishment's tone."

"Don't be silly," said Miss Jones. "I've been here before. The place is harmless." She sensed their disapproval and, pleased she could lie on such short notice, invented a fictionalized version of her first visit. "One afternoon on my way home from a long walk I stopped in to rest. The place was fine and I was fine," she said smiling innocently. "I had a hot meal and some cold liquid refreshment and walked home a new woman."

Merle licked her lips and narrowed her eyes. "This looks straight out of Harold Robbins. Do you think we'll see a strip tease?"

Edna pointed to a professionally printed flyer. "Only on Friday nights. I'm far too tired to go all the way back without a rest. Bad art or no, I have got to go in and sit for a bit."

Hearing Edna's decision, Merle heaved opened the wooden doors carved with satyrs and nymphs in all positions of sexual precocity. The women followed her into an atmosphere permeated with the perfume of spilled beer, stale smoke, and ancient vomit. The room was brightly lit and not yet full, and from the far corner of the room the women heard a piano player banging out a Scott Joplin rag. Sudden, noisy enthusiasm over a game of darts infused the otherwise bleak room with a festive air.

The women walked to a badly scarred, round wooden table not far from the door. Miss Jones was the first to sit. A waiter laden with a full tray of draft beer appeared instantaneously and plunked eight frosty glasses on the table. Miss Jones's companions looked as if they were trying to decide if the young man might be a visitor from Mars.

"Good evening, Ladies," he said affably. "It is pay as you drink here at The Biffy. That's two bucks. It's on special on Amateur Night. Two bits a draft. Who's buying the first round?"

Edna reached into her cleavage and pulled out a perfumed ten.

"That's class," said the man with genuine admiration. "Are you here for the competition?" Edna, Merle, and Mrs. Wallace stared at him open mouthed. "See the sign? Best act gets all the money in the pot. On a good night there's close to a grand in it. This place'll be jammed by nine." He made change quickly, throwing eight singles on the table.

"Give him something," whispered Miss Jones.

"Like what?" Edna asked loudly.

Miss Jones picked up a dollar bill and gave it to the waiter. "Thanks," he said and bustled to the bar to restock his tray.

"You're awfully free with my money," said Edna.

"It's the way it's done," said Miss Jones. "I'll tip him when it's my turn."

"You're turn! Just how much of this swill are we supposed to drink? I've never had beer in my life."

"Oh, it's very refreshing on hot summer nights," said Miss Jones. "I started to drink it during Friday-night staff outings. . . ."

"What did he mean by best act?" asked Mrs. Wallace.

Edna glanced around looking for the sign the waiter had mentioned. At the farthest end of the room near the dart board and piano sat a dais and beside it a large sandwich sign proclaiming:

EVERY THURSDAY
AMATEUR NIGHT
ALL WELCOME
ENTRY FEE $10
WINNER TAKE ALL

She pointed to the sign. "Well, opportunity knocks. Can any of you do anything besides crochet?"

"I used to sing for Mr. Wallace," said the widow. "He was often moved to tears by my rendition of 'Just a Closer Walk with Thee'."

"I bet he was," said Merle. She picked up a glass of beer and drank half of it. Edna raised her eyebrows. "Oh, I've had this stuff before," Merle assured her. "It's harmless. I used to nurse my son on it." She shook her head and laughed. "I mean he drank milk while I drank beer. They started me on it in the hospital. My doctor said it calmed nervous mothers. He prescribed stout for all of us. I swear my son is the man he is today because of it. Stout and macaroni and cheese. And roast beef every Sunday. Dr. Brown was world famous because he invented Pablum." She held up her glass with a flourish.

Edna picked up a glass and sniffed it. "It smells bitter," she said. She tasted it, Merle and Miss Jones watching eagerly for her verdict. "Not bad," she said after swallowing. "But not near as smooth as a good ruby port."

"It's cheaper," said Merle.

"Yes," agreed Miss Jones. "Beer is far more refreshing on a night like this." She smiled a mischievous smile. "And of course it's full of vitamins."

"Come on, Wally," said Edna. "Drink up. It'll oil your vocal cords."

Mrs. Wallace picked up a glass and giggled. She took a large gulp. Her upper lip began to perspire and her eyes watered. She licked the foam from her upper lip.

Edna loosened her coat, placed the carving in her lap, and prepared to settle in. "We mustn't forget why we've come," she said. "Raise your glasses, everyone." She waited until four glasses trembled in the air. "Here's to you, Elizabeth Schmidt. I . . . ." she began. She paused for a few moments to compose herself. Finally she managed to whisper, "I love you."

Everyone drank. Mrs. Wallace's face grew very red. "Are we going to enter this contest?"

"It doesn't begin till nine. The doors at the lodge will be locked," Merle said.

"We can always ring for the night watchman," said Miss Jones.

Edna nudged her. "You sound like you've done this sort of thing before."

Miss Jones smiled a Mona Lisa smile. "I get out now and again," she said. "I like to see what I missed out on back when I was toeing the line."

As the smoky room filled, Edna delighted in discovering contrasting members of the crowd: young, blue-jean clad students, well dressed older men and women wrapped in robes of fragile gaiety, odd mixtures of boys and men who whispered over their tables and held hands in a way she was sure Mrs. Wallace would find alarming, and poorer looking middle-aged people she suspected frequented the pub because they lived nearby and had limited resources for entertainment. Miss Jones warmly greeted a woman with rollers in her hair sporting a pair of men's overalls whose bib shielded outsized breasts and an interesting assortment of shirts with sleeves of varying lengths. When the former teacher finished greeting the woman, Miss Jones embraced the woman's partner, an Orson Wells of a man with dark bristle sprouting from his heavy jaw. Edna envied her new friend's easy sociability and was pleased when Miss Jones invited the pair to join them, but they declined her offer to accept one much closer to the low stage where the amateurs performed.

"What do you suppose they do?" asked Edna when the man and women were out of earshot. "I mean in the way of entertainment up there, of course."

"I used to play 'Swanee River' on the kazoo," said Merle with a beery smirk.

Miss Jones became uncharacteristically somber. "You'll find the competition is very stiff, Merle. People here are accomplished. They sing, dance, and recite Shakespeare like true thespians. No one plays the kazoo." Merle sniffed and moved her hands elaborately to make her several gemstones sparkle in the overhead lights. Feeling as generous as the expanding atmosphere, Edna reached across the table to pat the smaller woman's sparkling hands. Before she knew it, she'd emptied her second glass of beer.

Miss Jones raised a wiry arm to catch the waiter's eye. He returned in a flash, scooping up empty glasses and replacing them with eight more. Mrs. Wallace rolled her eyes as Miss Jones pulled out three one-dollar bills from her pocket book. "I think I'm getting drunk," Edna whispered to the widow. "I don't know why. Lizzie and I drink like . . . ." She stopped in mid confession. "How are you doing, Wally? Isn't this the high life?"

In the tavern's lurid lighting, the widow's face had taken on the colour and sheen of canned salmon, and when Edna spoke to her, she blinked pink in her friend's direction. "It's only for Mrs. Schmidt," Mrs. Wallace said, finishing her second glass. "I really don't think the reverend would like it if he knew I was drinking alcoholic beverages in a house of ill repute."

Miss Jones laughed raucously. "This is just a tavern, dear," she said in a kindly voice.

"Oh," said Mrs. Wallace, embarrassed to be ignorant but clearly not understanding the difference.

Delighted to share her modest store of worldly wisdom, Miss Jones explained. "A house of ill repute is where persons sell their sexual favours for filthy lucre."

Mrs. Wallace's hands flew up to cover her ears. "Hear no evil," she said quickly.

"Right-o," said Miss Jones. "Nothing is, but thinking, thinking, thinking." She clinked glasses with Edna, carelessly sloshing beer on the table.

"Pipe down," said Merle. "Something's about to start up there."

The women turned to the stage. A burly man, his outsize handlebar mustache waxed at the tips and his sideburns fluffed to performance perfection, blew into the microphone. Shrill whistles blasted the crowd. Dressed in what looked like a referee's striped shirt, the coifed man's attire prompted Edna to wonder if perhaps amateurs might be predisposed to fisticuffs.

After making several adjustments to the neck of the microphone stand, the man coughed significantly. "Testing," he said suavely. "Testing. Testing." Delighted with the sound of his own mellow baritone, he began his introduction.

"Welcome old-timers and newcomers, welcome. We're glad to see you at The Biffy, where every Thursday evening talent has a chance to be seen and rewarded." Applause, sharp but light, like firecrackers in an amphitheatre, exploded here and there. "We're not formal here. If you want to try your hand at the big one, don't be shy. Just drop your ten spot into the pot and step on stage. Remember! You can't win if you don't give yourself a chance." He detached the microphone from its stand and held it out, his voice lost in the shuffling and talking of nearby patrons. Drawing the microphone back to his mouth he said confidentially, "I see a lot a talent out there. You there," he called, pointing at a table near the piano. "You look like you may be able to do something unusual." A woman at the table laughed wildly. "C'mon," he coaxed. "Who's gonna be first? Who will break the ice and let the rest flow up natural and nice?"

A short, stocky man, red of nose and sad of eye, walked to the dais and made an elaborate show of taking out his wallet and extracting a bill. He dropped the money into the large glass bowl, jumped up on the small platform, and bowed with what Edna found to be surprising grace. The room reverberated with applause and cat calls. Edna and her friends joined in, tentatively at first, and then more enthusiastically. The man held up his hands to quiet the room then took the microphone from its stand and began, in a high, sweet tenor, "My Wild Irish Rose."

When he'd finished and the ladies paused in their clapping, Merle confided to Edna that she thought the man as good as Dennis Day. Edna nodded and added her own benediction. "It was lovely, Merle," she said. "It was truly lovely."

A young girl took the microphone next. Her blonde hair, loose and hanging past her shoulder blades, swung back and forth as she puffed on a cigarette and sang, with incredible weariness in a low, sultry alto, "Won't You Come Home, Bill Bailey" as none of the women had heard it sung before.

"Imagine that voice coming out of that little girl's body," Mrs. Wallace said when the young woman had finished and applause thundered.

"I'll bet she's studied," said Merle.

"I bet I know where," said Miss Jones.

The next contestant, Miss Jones's particular oddly-shirted friend, took the microphone dramatically and said in a Londoner's accent, "Do ya know? They're changing the guard at Buckingham Palace," suitably altering the remainder of the children's poem for a sophisticated evening crowd at the pub.

"That might have been the dirtiest thing I've ever heard," said Edna, awed by the woman's flagrantly blue delivery.

"Oh, not me," said Merle.

Miss Jones smiled at the women with an air of world weary experience before turning to Mrs. Wallace. "Are you ready to perform, Mrs. Wallace? Let's hear what moved the reverend. Go on, dear, you can do it."

"Oh, no," said Mrs. Wallace. "I'm terribly awkward in public. I couldn't. I need an accompanist."

Miss Jones grinned fiendishly. "I play! If we win, we can split the pot."

"Oh, no, no," said Mrs. Wallace, turning to Edna with pleading horse's eyes. "Tell her I mustn't, Mrs. Carver. Remind her I'm newly widowed . . . ."

"Do it," Edna said. "Oh, Wally, I'd love to hear you sing."

"So would I," Merle chimed in.

Offended by Merle's sarcastic tone, Mrs. Wallace rose with great dignity. "I suppose you think I can't do it. Well, fifty years in the choir says I can." Belligerent with beer, she marched to the stage.

"Shall I come?" Miss Jones called after her.

"'Just a Closer Walk with Thee', key of E flat," Mrs. Wallace said over her shoulder.

As Miss Jones scurried to the piano, Edna broke into encouraging applause. "This is wonderful," she said to Merle. "Better than the Leafs playing on the TV."

Disgusted, Merle muttered to no one in particular, "I'll believe she can do it when I actually hear music comin' out of that big moutha hers." She drank more beer and jealously watched as a young man at the next table tore into a bag of potato chips.

Miss Jones played a brief, somber introduction. Mrs. Wallace cleared her throat and put her head down. Edna wondered if she was praying for courage when, all at once, the widow began to sing, her voice a clear, rich soprano. Edna closed her eyes and listened rapturously. The performers' timing suggested they had worked together for years so beautifully did the women weave lyrics and accompaniment together.

At the end of the hymn, with the harsh glare of lights playing on Mrs. Wallace's homely face, she closed her eyes and offered the crowd her very best rendering of bliss. Tears slid down her oily cheeks. The place went wild. People from all corners of the room shouted "Brava!" and "Encore!" Miss Jones rushed to the stage to confer. Mrs. Wallace composed herself and waited for the second introduction. She began the old show tune tentatively, searching for the words as she sang them. Soon everyone was singing "Lucky Old Sun" with Mrs. Wallace providing a strong lead.

When the widow returned to their table, she was shaking with excitement and drenched in perspiration.

"You were wonderful!" Edna exclaimed. "Oh Wally, what a gift you have. You should be singing all the time."

Merle wiped her mouth with the back of her hand. "Not bad for an amateur. Say, anybody want potato chips?"

"They make my diverticulitis act up," replied Edna coolly. "But you go ahead, Merle. It seems absolutely nothing affects you."

Mrs. Wallace smiled at Edna gratefully. "You don't think I was too forward, do you?"

"A voice like yours is meant to be heard," said Miss Jones. "I can't remember when I've had more pleasure playing. It makes me wish we had a piano at the lodge. What a time we could have."

They stopped enthusing over their performance when the next contestant pulled a chair onto the platform and sat down to play spoons on his knees. He was a sunburned, thin man of about seventy, and as his hands beat out the rhythm he hummed a familiar Irish Jig. A group of East coast exiles leapt to their feet to step dance in the space around their table and, watching them, Edna found herself longing to dance. Instead, she sat where she was and kept time to the rhythm with Miss Jones, the pianist's hands moving like the dancers over the sticky table top. Mrs. Wallace fanned herself with a beefy hand, her eyes registering delighted surprise as her red nails flashed by.

After they clapped for him, Edna asked Merle what she was going to do.

"I was always good at recitin' poetry when I was a girl. I even won a prize for it." She sucked her cheeks. "But I can't think of a thing right now."

"Perhaps you might recite something from Shakespeare," prompted Miss Jones. "When I was a girl, we all had to learn something from the Bard."

Merle shook her head. "I know you'll be surprised, but I never went far in my schoolin'."

"Then give us a childhood rhyme or a skipping song," offered Mrs. Wallace, determined to be charitable despite Merle's frequent un-Christian behaviour.

Merle screeched. "There was a silly one – it used to give me the creeps. Know what I mean?" She raised her penciled eyebrows at Edna as though remembering an esoteric truth. "What was it now? 'One bright day in the middle of the night, two dead boys began to fight'."

"That sounds promising," said Edna.

Merle stood up, looking to the other women for encouragement.

"Go ahead," said Miss Jones. "They find everything entertaining after the first four or five numbers, so long as it's not played on the kazoo."

Merle shrugged happily. Like an elegant showgirl, she swayed to the empty platform, dropped her money in the pot, and stepped onto the dais. Barely tall enough to be seen over the heads of the people in front of Edna and her friends, the women cheered when the master of ceremonies placed a chair on the platform and lifted Merle on to it.

Merle took the microphone and giggled. "I have a little pome for you," she said, obviously in her element. "Let's see if any of you have heard this little ditty before." Clasping the mike like a pro, she winked, then, swaying from side to side, began to chant in a singsong voice . . .

"One bright day in the middle of the night, two dead boys began to fight."

Merle paused, offering her audience a look of disbelief before reaching up dramatically with her left hand to offer her rings to the light.

"Back to back they faced each other." She took a long pause for effect.

"Drew their swords and shot each other." She lowered her voice to a whisper, making everyone lean forward to hear.

"A deaf policeman heard the noise and came to arrest the two dead boys." Merle grinned as applause rocketed up from her listeners.

"It was nothin'," she said. The MC helped her down from the chair and clapped loudly into the microphone as Merle sashayed back to her friends.

"A newcomer," he said over the din. "Give the little lady a big hand." The audience needed no prompting, clapping and clapping for Merle's Mae West delivery.

Edna held out a glass of beer as Merle sat down. 'Well, Merle," she said happily. "You seem to have hidden talents, too." Merle waved the compliment away, suggesting she did this sort of thing all the time.

"Now it's your turn, Mrs. Carver," said Mrs. Wallace, slurring slightly. "What are you going to do?"

Edna put a beautiful finger to her numbed lips. Someone was about to sing. The women turned to the stage again, delighted to be invited to clap through a long session of "When the Saints Go Marching In." Centre stage stood the woman who had laughed so exuberantly when the MC suggested she might know some interesting things to do. She was dressed in an imitation leopard jacket and black Lycra pants. Edna marveled at her hair, long, blue-black, and as wavy as a country singer's. Her lips glistened with what Edna thought might be tomato-paste and wished with all her heart that Elizabeth could see the woman's performance sure her friend would agree that here stood the epitome of exotic beauty.

"I think she's better than Judy Garland was," Merle cried during the chorus. Edna nodded, clapping along joyously and thinking she had never seen anyone so outrageously beautiful or had had a grander time. She pinched her nose occasionally, to make sure it was still in the general area she thought it should be and marveled at the taste in her mouth as it fluctuated between vile and delicious, depending upon whether she had not sipped her beer for a while or had just taken some. When the leopard-coated lady finished her song, Edna called, "Marvelous, marvelous." She watched in absolute rapture when the striking woman flung herself from the stage into the arms of an appreciative fan.

Those strong arms lifted the woman more capably than Edna thought possible and planted her so firmly on the solid floor that Edna cried out with the shock of witnessing such unexpected strength. Seeing in the swift decisive action an irrefutable testament to other people's competence, she rested against the back of her chair, the worn wooden slats comforting as she looked from Miss Jones, to Merle, to Mrs. Wallace, and, beyond them, to the room full of revelers. They don't need me, she thought. Everyone is just fine without me.

Her companions chatted noisily but Edna couldn't play the game anymore. Elizabeth, the one person who might really have needed her, was dead. Quietly, making no outward sign, Edna followed the truth to its core. Elizabeth had not needed her, either. It was she who had needed Elizabeth. Her friend had provided the space for Edna to create herself. Now that space was gone, creation was over. Even though she breathed and moved and seemed alive, Edna felt sure the essential part of her had died with Elizabeth.

She sat very still, understanding that there was no room for pretense anymore, no necessity for courage, defiance, or curses. Elizabeth was dead. No one else wanted her poetry. These people could sing, play the piano, recite poetry, and fight for their own justice. Or, like Vera, they could end the fight. Edna couldn't pretend any longer. She was powerless without Elizabeth.

Wretched with weariness and despair, Edna pulled on her coat and gently took up Frank Bertini's carving. When the others moved to do the same, she shook her head. "Please stay," she said. "Enjoy yourselves. See who wins and tell me all about it tomorrow." Without another word, Edna walked out through the wooden doors into the cold, clear night.

The moon, still full and only a little blurred at its bottom edge, hung above Edna as she walked the several blocks to the lodge. Her heels made a pleasant sound as they struck the pavement, but she would not be distracted by their music. She remembered instead the sound a wagon's wheels made as she pulled young Marion along on the many adventures of her childhood. Hearing that sound, Edna completed her discovery. Even her child had no need of her.

She walked on, the weight of the old red wagon behind her, her weariness reminding her of the futility of the miles she'd walked with Marion, pointing out patterns, enthusing over colours, explaining all the whys of the world. She stopped to look up at the moon. Except for the tides, it wasn't needed either. It gave no heat, caused nothing to grow that she knew of, except perhaps warts.

"Round and round and round we've gone," she whispered to it. "Round and round and round we'll go." She remembered reading somewhere, many years before this cold, clear night that people in ancient times believed the souls of people on earth flew to the moon to feed it at death. Looking up, her head to one side and sad beyond comfort, she saw in this belief its perfect logic. "Where else could we go?" she asked the moon. "Of course, we belong together. Like unto like." She pulled the roof-garden key from her satin purse and threw it into the gutter.

On Friday morning, Edna awoke at five. Numbly, she ran a bath and chose very carefully what she would wear. In the end, she selected a favourite of Elizabeth's, a yellow cotton shirtwaist with large red poppies growing up from its hem that was pinched at the waist with a red silk scarf. She went to her bureau for her white cardigan but chose instead a thick yellow one she had stolen with Elizabeth on one of their first shoplifting expeditions. She arranged dress, sweater, and under things meticulously over the rumpled covers before opening a box containing yellow and red shoes she'd inherited from Marion. Each year, at the end of the summer season, Marion sorted through her clothes to make a donation to the Salvation Army. Any items she felt would look good on Edna she brought to the lodge. The shoes pinched her feet, Edna remembered. Knowing she would have much walking to do, she took them out of the box and placed them on the bed with her other things, intending for this masochism to remind her of the discoveries she'd made the evening before.

After putting her upper plate in its soaking solution, she took off her nightie and stepped into the bath. Almost too hot to bear, the water almost instantly turned her skin bright pink. She soaped herself, unaware she cried until she felt her tears dripping onto her breasts.

At seven, Edna looked at herself in her vanity mirror, smiled wanly at the yellow and red garden growing beneath her haggard face, slipped on the tormenting shoes, and walked silently down the hallway to the elevator. The lodge was very quiet, and no one was about as she made her way through the foyer and unlocked the door to the street. The day, humid and already uncomfortably warm, seemed perfect for what she had to do. She walked west, looking forward to visiting with the Humber River before she traveled north. Only vaguely aware of the cars and trucks zipping along Bloor, she suddenly found herself on the bridge looking down into bottle-green waters rushing to the lake.

She was surprised to see the river and did her best to recall details of all the shops she must have passed, streets she must have crossed on her journey. She remembered nothing. Leaning against the rough cement railing, she shook her head to clear it. A pigeon swooped down, perching a few feet from her on the narrow sidewalk. "Did he say nine?" she asked the bird. "I think he said nine." The pigeon cocked its head to one side, inching closer. "I don't have a thing for you. Lizzie's the one who carries the biscuits in her purse." The pigeon moved closer still, its head moving from side to side. "I can't chat all day," she said. "I've got one last appointment. I think it's at nine."

The bird pecked at something on the sidewalk. She looked at her watch, surprised to find the familiar face in its usual position on her wrist. "Was it nine?" she asked the bird. When the pigeon didn't answer, she walked back the way she'd come, trying to decide how she would get to the crematorium.

At Jane Street she went into the subway station to enquire about the best way to get to St. Clair. The man mentioned so many possible routes she stumbled back to the street overwhelmed by her choices. After eight now, she began to worry that if she didn't get there precisely at nine, they would take care of Elizabeth without her. Recklessly, she stepped out onto Bloor Street to flag a taxi. In a moment, a Diamond Cab made a U-turn to pick her up. She got in, telling the driver about the crematorium and the general area where she thought he might find it. The car lurched forward, swinging into traffic and pitching her away from the door. She straightened, leaned her head against the back of the seat, and closed her eyes.

The driver watched her curiously in the rear-view mirror. When her mouth dropped open, he asked, "You okay, Lady?"

"What?" Edna opened her eyes. "Oh. It's you. I forgot you were here."

"Think this car moves by remote control?"

Edna took a little comfort from her smarting feet. "Have you ever been to a cremation?" she asked.

"Nope," he said. "I don't go in for that morbid stuff."

Edna took a good look at him. His blond hair curled over the collar of his shirt. "You look too young to be that wise."

He laughed. "I'll be forty next month."

"Forty?" She looked at his picture on the visor. "You don't look much more than a boy."

"I plan to stay that way, too."

"As do we all," she answered. She closed her eyes again.

"You don't look too good," he said. "Should I stop?"

"No," she said tiredly. "I was out late last night, drinking beer if you can imagine. And I got up at the crack of dawn this morning. I'm so tired I'm having lapses. And I'm sad." She looked out the window feeling that life itself was rushing by along with the buildings and people. "If I'm late, do you think they'll start without me?"

"What's this you're going to?"

"A cremation, but I'm going to be the only one there."

"That's a shame," said the man.

"That's the way she wanted it."

"Who?"

"Lizzie, my very best friend in the world. She wanted to be cremated."

"Oh," said the driver sympathetically. "If it's just you, they'll probably wait." He offered this information tentatively, as if he believed they might indeed begin without her. "What time are you supposed to be there?"

"Nine I think although I can't be sure. I used to be so good when it came to keeping appointments. God knows why."

"Don't you worry," he said. "We'll be there before nine. It's just a few blocks over." He turned onto St. Clair and sped through thickening morning traffic.

Edna retrieved her money from her satin purse so the man wouldn't have to watch her fumble for it after they parked. She craned her neck searching for the stately green iron gates that marked the entrance.

"Out in front okay? Or do you want me to take you in?"

She glanced at her watch. "Out in front is fine. It's only quarter of."

He parked in the driveway of the cemetery and leaned over the seat to open the door for her. "I'd say have a nice day, but somehow, that doesn't seem right."

"No," she agreed, handing him several bills and waving the change away. "But you have a good day."

"Hey," he said, reluctant to see her enter the cemetery alone. "Would you like me to go in there with you? I can turn the meter off."

Edna smiled, wanting to be touched by this stranger's kindness but feeling as isolated from it as she'd been from the scenery speeding by on the way to her destination. "No, thank you," she said politely. She got out of the car stiffly and shut the door with an unintentional slam. The cab driver watched her for a moment. She turned to wave at him after taking a few halting steps. He returned her wave before reaching for his radio.

Once inside the crematorium's manicured grounds, Edna headed for a small stone cottage marked OFFICE. Inside, she found a pale young man drinking coffee at a long counter that reminded her of a bank. She laughed at the comparison. "I'm afraid I'm a bit early," she told the young man. "I've come to help Elizabeth Schmidt get what she wants."

The man put down his coffee mug and walked around the

counter. "We've been expecting you. They brought her over at eight." He offered Edna his arm after opening the door for her. "It's just a short walk to the chapel, Miss . . . ?"

"Mrs. Carver," she said. "This is very nice." She gestured to the beautiful grounds.

"Are you interested in our interment services? The funeral-home people weren't sure." He spoke quietly as they walked along the winding road.

"No," Edna told him. "She wants to be scattered."

"I'm afraid that's against the law here," he said. "There's a scattering garden in Ottawa, but here . . . . "

"Against the law? Why?"

"Pollution," he said. "Human remains . . . ."

"I see," said Edna, patting his hand. "That's all right. We'll put her in a nice pot and I'll take her with me. We're in no rush." At the chapel's entrance, the Funeral Director held the door for Edna and then guided her to a room to the right of the entrance way. There he took out a ring of official looking keys.

Edna smiled. "You weren't afraid she was going to run away, were you?"

"This is where we keep the urns, Mrs. Carver," he said, opening the door. "If you'd like to choose something from in here . . . ."

"I can't imagine why you'd be worried about people stealing this sort of thing," said Edna as she watched him unlock two cupboards and swing the doors open. She ran her hand over a small marble box. "This is nice, but I want something more portable. Let's see that shiny one in there." The man retrieved a brass urn from the cupboard's depths. It was about nine inches high with a narrow neck and tapered bottom. "Yes, I could just tuck that under my arm." She put her hands out.

"It's heavy," he said, giving it to her.

She staggered forward under the unexpected weight of it. "My," she said. "It weighs as much as she does. Or used to, or . . . ." Her eyes filled. "May I see the inside?"

He removed the lid and Edna peered inside. "What's in there?"

"A liner. They blow it in."

"That won't do," Edna said, untying the red silk scarf at her waist. "When it's all over, could you wrap her in this before putting her inside?"

"Of course," he said.

"Well," she said all business now. "Let's get to it."

The man guided her out into the chapel where the tongue-and-groove paneling exhaled its strong cedar breath. Edna followed him through another doorway to the back of the building.

"You're going to let me . . . ."

"Yes," he said. "This is the retort room. The casket is inside. Mrs. Schmidt is in the first chamber."

"You have two?"

"Yes, M'am."

"For couples I suppose? It's very thoughtful for you to arrange it like this." The man opened the door to a long rectangular room made of cement blocks. The floor, cement, had been painted a copper colour, and the cold, airless room smelled of disinfectant. Edna looked around at the stainless steel counters lining the walls, one with a sunken metal tray. A vacuum cleaner stood nearby. She studied this arrangement for a moment, gradually understanding the wisdom of the floor colour. "You don't just get cremated and popped into a jar, do you," she observed.

"No, M'am," he said, guiding her to the first retort. There, inside the chamber, Edna could see the plain chipboard coffin Elizabeth had requested. The man swung down the door and as he did, two weights on either side of the chamber door glided noiselessly up from the floor. "Move this one to the right and this one up," he directed Edna, indicating two toggle switches.

"I was going to read something from the Bible as I did this, but I've left it at home," she said, suddenly agitated. She waved his offer of a Bible away. "No, I must think of something for her." She stood as the pigeon had an hour before, her head on one side, her eyes reflecting a worried search. Her face grew calm as she put her finger on the first switch. "She has lived, unseen, unknown, unlamented she has died; stolen from the world and not a stone tells where she lies." She flicked up the second switch and heard the burner leap into life. "It's a gross paraphrase," she said to the young man cordially, "but I think Mr. Pope would have given his consent, don't you? Besides," she added, a small note of satisfaction creeping into her breaking voice, "I'm goddamned lucky to remember it."

Calmly, the young man took her by the elbow and guided her

from the cold room back to the chapel. "Would you like to sit in here for a while?"

"How long does all this take?"

He looked at his watch. "Everything will be ready at two-thirty."

"It takes as much time to leave the world as it does to arrive," Edna reflected. "She's very tiny. I didn't think it would take so long."

"Cremations take about three hours, M'am," the young man said in his soothing voice.

Edna thought about the counter with the sunken metal tray and of the nearby vacuum cleaner. "Please be sure you get all of her. You won't let any of . . . ."

"Don't worry," he assured her in his comforting, professional voice.

"Fine," Edna said, sitting in one of the pews at the rear of the chapel. "I will sit for a while, if you don't mind. I've been up a long time. I'm tired. And my feet are killing me."

"Of course," he said. "Goodbye now." She heard him walk across the flagstones and then stop, heard the clinking of his keys as he locked the small room where the urns were kept, listened to his footsteps as he walked out the door, leaving her alone with the music, magically piped in as from heaven, and the low growl of the fire consuming Elizabeth Schmidt.

She looked around the chapel approving its austerity. The only religious symbol was a wooden cross at the front where she supposed the caskets were placed when a service was held for the dead before cremation. The paneling was to her taste, glowing, auburn, and while the windows were not the glorious cathedral windows of the main Christian religions, she found them pretty enough. She wondered if they were going to have a service that morning, wished she'd thought to ask the young man who was so pale and so kind. If she was to have the chapel to herself for the morning, she'd lie down for a little rest while Lizzie's business was being taken care of. Her head ached and her eyelids drooped. She knew Lizzie wouldn't mind if she dozed, but she'd feel a fool if people came in and found her stretched out and snoring on a pew.

She stood up abruptly, determined to find a bench where she might rest unobserved. Outside, a few yards from the chapel, she discovered a secluded stretch of green grass with a few headstones scattered about. She stooped to feel the ground and was pleased to discover it had already been warmed by the sun. Sitting heavily, she paused before laying full out, the sun on her face and shoulders, the rest of her body in the shade of one of the stones. She kicked off the pinching shoes.

Unseen, Edna slept through two services and one interment, a deep satisfying sleep undisturbed by exploring ants. When she awoke in full sun, it was two o'clock. Carrying her shoes, she walked back to the chapel to find a washroom. In the mirror, she discovered the sun had coloured her cheeks and a few obliging twigs had decorated her hair and sweater. She thought she looked much better than she had when she'd arrived. At the threshold of the chapel entrance, and still carrying her shoes, Edna met the man who'd been with her earlier. He greeted her with the urn.

He held it out to her. "It's very heavy. Do you think you can manage?"

"If you could call me a taxi . . . ." she said, letting him carry the urn for her.

Politely looking away from her stockinged feet, he guided Edna to the office and offered her a chair. He placed the urn on the counter and made the call she imagined he'd made thousands of times before. Edna stood, walked to the urn, and ran her hands over the smooth, cool surface. "I thought it would be warm," she said.

"The cab will be here shortly," he said. "Would you like to wait outside?"

"Yes," she replied, suddenly cheerful. "I think we will." She took the urn in both hands after dropping her shoes on the counter. "Throw these away, please. I don't' need any other reminders." She shook the heavy urn, pleased with the muffled sound. "She's in there."

"Yes," he said. "Would you like me to carry it for you?"

"No, you've done enough, thank you. I'll wait at the curb." As she walked out the door the young man held, a robin flew down from one of the old maples at the entrance. "Look at that," she said. "That's the first I've noticed this year." The man nodded. Edna thanked him and set off, the young man waiting until she was at the roadway before shutting the door and returning to his work.

The cab pulled up a few minutes later to whisk Edna back to the lodge. No one was in the foyer so she was able to get up to her room without fielding comments about her whereabouts or shoeless feet. She put the urn on her bureau next to Don Quixote and then opened her bureau drawers with manic energy. "We're getting out of here, Lizzie. I can't very well scatter you if we're all this way off the ground."

She pulled out her suitcases and began to pack: first toiletries, then underwear, then shoes, Elizabeth's purse, a couple of her own, old ones she hadn't used in years, sweaters, blouses, her tweed jacket, dresses, and finally, her two coats. When Bernice came by an hour later, the room was strewn with her belongings but Edna was nowhere to be seen.

The manager peered anxiously into the bathroom and found Edna sitting on the toilet seat holding a bottle of aspirin. "Mrs. Carver," she began, "I was concerned . . . ."

Edna stood up tiredly. The two women were only inches apart. For the first time since moving to the lodge Edna understood the meaning of the thick white scar on the manager's neck, raised her hand to touch it, but touched the lacquered hair instead. "So that's it," she whispered. "You're not so very different from us – from Vera, from Mr. Wallace, from me."

Bernice stared at the bottle in her hand.

"I was just trying to decide how many of these I'd have to swallow before I joined Elizabeth on the moon," Edna said.

Unmoving, and with Edna's hand still touching her wig, Bernice continued to stare, first at the bottle, and then into Edna's eyes, startling Edna when she removed her glasses and pressed closer. Edna broke the spell by slipping past the manager to re-enter the chaos of her packing. "I guess I'll have to finish the job," she told the mess before her. "But I can't do it here. I have to get down to the ground."

A needling doubt shook Bernice. "I don't understand," she whispered. "I've tried to make this place a haven. It's a good place, safe, well organized, comfortable. Why can't you be happy here?"

Edna blinked in surprise at the manager's tears.

Bernice fought for composure. She replaced her glasses and with her disguise complete, found her professional voice. "You'll be leaving today, Mrs. Carver. We've found a lovely spot for you."

"Is it close to the ground?" Edna asked, wanting to forget the manager's lapse into humanity.

Miss Wilson launched into an enthusiastic description of Tranquil Time. "It's a lovely Victorian home with beautiful gardens . . . ."

"How many storeys?" Edna asked.

"Three," said the manager.

"That sounds just fine."

The manager put her arm firmly around Edna's shoulders. "You'll be so much happier there, Mrs. Carver. Don't you worry about all this," she said. "I'll take care of all your things. Between your daughter and me . . . ."

"I don't need anything but these," Edna said, picking up the urn and the carving. "It can't take that long to scatter so little. And once that's done, I'll just sit and wait."

"Of course you will," said Bernice. "But you'll want all your pretty dresses to sit in. You always look so nice. You want your daughter to be proud of you, don't you? We'll sort through this and once you have your pretty clothes you'll feel at home in the new place in no time."

Edna let Bernice ramble on without contradicting her. In an unexpected flash of insight she understood that the manager needed the details of everyone's lives to convince herself of the value of her own. In this moment, she was content to allow Bernice to live with her illusions, as she herself had done until the previous evening. She walked to her rocker while Bernice fussed and folded and checked drawers, sitting down with the carving and the urn and thinking there might be an interval of waiting before she could finalize things for Elizabeth.

Edna rocked, drifting from memory to memory, the difference between past and present obscured until there was simply time she'd marked as now she rocked. Bernice chattered away as she emptied the dresser top, bathroom cabinet, and closet shelves.

The ambulance came at five. Edna was taken through the foyer just as it was starting to fill for the evening meal, one attendant carrying the smaller suitcase Bernice had packed, the other pushing Edna in the mandatory wheelchair. Edna clasped the urn to her stomach with one hand and held the carving in the other. When several people called out to her, she raised the small Don Quixote above her head to wave him to and fro.

Diana watched Edna's departure from her place next to Mrs. Wallace, the big woman's arm tightly linked through her own. The previous day the minister's widow had returned as promised but refrained from reading the Bible when Diana suggested she help the writer with her research. The widow confessed her grief about her husband's disorientation and death and shared with Diana her new found sense of peace, thanks to Mrs. Carver's unusual perspective.

During this conversation, Diana learned that the minister had become alarmed when he could no longer remember Scripture. Sure it was his medication he grew more and more morose and finally flushed it down the toilet. Mrs. Wallace told Diana that he grew much worse once the pills were gone, becoming completely irrational over the next twenty-four hours. Diana listened quietly, putting this together with her knowledge of Elizabeth's death and the surreal conversation between the doctor and the manager she'd overheard on Tuesday afternoon while she listened at the doctor's door.

When Edna disappeared down the back hallway, Diana disengaged her arm from Mrs. Wallace's firm grip. "You'll have to excuse me, Mrs. Wallace. I've got an appointment with the doctor," she said, making her escape.

"But you seem so much better today," Mrs. Wallace said, disappointed to lose what she hoped might be her dinner companion. "I hope you're not having a relapse.

Diana smiled. "I'm pretty sure I'm on the mend, but if I do take a turn for the worse, will you call someone for me?" She scribbled hastily in her notebook, tearing out the page and putting it in Mrs. Wallace's open hand. "It's my gynecologist. She wants to be alerted if I have any further problems while I'm at the lodge."

"Of course," said Mrs. Wallace, clutching the paper eagerly. "I'm so glad to be of service." Diana entered the elevator fighting the fear she felt at the idea of returning to the doctor's office.

PART TWO

TRANQUIL TIME

FOUR

From the stop and start motion of the ambulance as it crawled through heavy Friday evening traffic, Edna felt the city's permanent evening carnival come to life. Supine on the gurney and only vaguely aware of the tightness of the straps across her chest and abdomen, she heard the hurly-burly, felt the stop and start, the creeping pace of this journey serenely. In no rush, she turned her head and saw the urn, tipped over on its side, rolling backward as the ambulance made headway and then stop for an instant before rolling forward when the driver jerked to a stop. The movement, so like waves lapping a sandy beach on a calm, windless day, made her smile. She could hear the driver and his companion attendant talking quietly, their voices mimicking the rustling material of a beach blanket spread over warm sand.

Happiness flooded Edna's heart. Elizabeth's death, she understood now, had simplified her life. Relieved of all responsibility, she felt like a child on some carefree outing, a picnic perhaps. She laughed joyfully, remembering these men were taking her to a fine old house, Victorian, Wilson had said. The queen died at the turn of the century, and yet so many buildings continued to testify to the vastness of her influence.

An old lady marking time, moving into a house built in the style of another old lady who had marked it. She delighted to discover that disillusionment hadn't crippled her imaginative leaps. Instead, she discovered that the lifted veil freed her to see the marvelous jokes life played. The car crept forward. Edna listened to the hum of the surrounding traffic and another more distant sound – wagon wheels as she pulled . . . . When? Could it have been only last night? Did she pull her daughter along in her wagon only last night? Her happiness shrank to make room for a little worry. What did I do with that wagon, she wondered, and – she was embarrassed by her priorities – that child? She shook her head, fretful now, pulling her hair from its tidy knot as her head brushed against the pillow. She resolved to redo her hair as soon as she arrived. She would ask for the powder room, wash her hands and face, tidy her hair. And when she was presentable, she would ask to see her room, no doubt an elegant Victorian parlour that had been converted tastefully, one with leaded windows, of course, and perhaps, if her luck held, a canopy bed curtained with tapestries, a bed like the one she remembered Scrooge slept in when he was visited by his ghosts.

Scrooge, she thought, happy again, was old like herself, like Queen Victoria. Perhaps he would have rooms in this fine old home. Perhaps they would mark time together. That would be fine, she decided. He was all right after he'd learned a lesson or two. Not like Arthur who seemed never to learn. Remembering Arthur would not be at this new home she forgot the lost wagon and child in the pleasure of anticipating life without his surprise attacks.

They were sailing along now that they'd left the mad rush of downtown traffic behind. The dining room would be very elegant, she felt sure. Really fine old houses were well built, wainscoting – gumwood, rosewood, oak, it didn't matter which – highly polished like the paneling in . . . . She remembered breathing in the scent of tongue and groove, cedar it was, but . . . . She closed her eyes to form a picture of the place. Ah, yes, that wooden cross . . . some church or other.

The attendant opening the doors at the rear of the ambulance disrupted her reverie, but she wasn't at all cross. "I like fine things," she told him. "I'm happy to get away from Sunset Lodge. It didn't have much that was fine, except my Lizzie." Edna didn't mind that he was silent, that he tipped her narrow gurney at an awkward angle as he maneuvered it out of the ambulance with the other silent man. She looked beyond them to the house.

"Gorgeous," she cried, seeing the house's three full storeys created from what she was sure were custom-made bricks, and, before the magnificent house, a circular drive! And the gardens, at least half a city block of green grass and rich black beds warmer weather would fill with flowers and shrubs. And around it all she saw, her amazement growing, a magnificent wrought-iron fence. She looked again at the splendid red-brick house, entirely taken with the lovely stone arches of its portico, the grand coach lights on either side of the fine old door, and the red tile stairs that led up to its beveled glass and shining brass hardware.

Edna squinted at the inscription above the door. It was Tennyson! Oh, and ivy everywhere. "Is this a university?" she asked one of the silent men. "I've always wanted to go to school. Father didn't believe in educating girls, so he insisted I leave in first form to help my mother at home. Knowing one's place was his motto, but times have changed, haven't they. I might as well wait here as anywhere. May I walk up? I'd like to walk inside myself." She was mystified when they did not answer. She frowned. Despite her obvious displeasure, they did not speak to her as they stood staring at the wonderful door, waiting for something as they held her dangerously tilted bed. Had she not been strapped in, she felt sure she would tumble to the ground. "I'd like to walk," she repeated. "Please. Let me down."

Without warning, the impressive door swung open and the men trotted up the stairs. Edna's head jerked back to the pillow. "My urn!" she cried. "My carving! I want my things. I want to walk." As they jostled her through the door, an unpleasant smell assaulted her nostrils and Edna hunched her shoulders in the effort to breathe less deeply. A woman in white spoke to the attendants, snatched forms from them, read cursorily, and then glanced at Edna with indifferent hazel eyes. Edna stared into the unsmiling face. "Who are you?" she asked. "Do you teach something here?"

"Mrs. Carver? Edna Carver?" the woman said more to herself than to Edna, "the Sunset Lodge troublemaker Wilson sent over." She motioned for the men to transfer Edna to the waiting gurney.

Edna smiled when the woman seemed to recognize her, remembering Diana, thinking the young woman thoughtfully registered her here. "What's that awful smell? Has a student had an accident?"

The woman in white remained silent as she walked to a narrow counter and rang a bell. Two more women, these dressed in pale green hospital scrubs, came rushing in. The hazel-eyed woman said in an unnecessarily loud voice that did not disguise her boredom, "Third floor, Ward D."

"Where is the dining room?" Edna asked one of the green-clad women. "I'd like to see the wainscoting. I bet it's lovely."

One of the women – middle-aged, stocky, and worn down by the hardships of routine – patted Edna's hand. "Don't worry about a thing. We'll get you settled in, Honey. Dinner won't be for an hour or so."

"To hell with dinner," said Edna. "I just want to see the house. Lizzie can wait for a bit. Where will I take my classes?"

The woman in white grasped Edna's wrist as she studied her watch. After a minute, she said, "She's got a strong pulse. He'll want her started on Metaphin tonight. After the first dose, we'll see how it goes." The women nodded before wheeling Edna's gurney down the hall.

Edna did her best to turn her head, looking at first one woman and then the other as they pushed her along the dark hallway. "Someone should do something about the smell," she said. "It's frightful. Don't you have a janitor? It smells as though there's an outhouse on the premises." The women stopped in front of a small elevator. One pulled a key from her pocket and, magically, Edna thought, opened the door. This woman pushed Edna's gurney inside and squeezed in, leaving the other woman behind in the fetid hall. The woman who stayed with her inserted the key into a tiny slot and the elevator began to move.

Edna watched this process with amazement. "That's something new. I'd like one of those keys. Do all the students get one?"

The woman laughed and patted her hand.

"The elevator in the place I used to live worked with buttons," Edna told her, feeling her excitement bubble up once more. "It was damned slow, I'll tell you, and this one's not much better. But I like that key."

In what seemed to Edna to be hours, the elevator jerked into position and its door clattered open. The woman wheeled Edna into a dark green hall, dimly lit with old-fashioned brass sconces situated in pairs at six-foot intervals on the dingy walls. The smell was much worse up here. Edna felt her gorge rise.

"I'm going to be sick," she said, shocked by the admission. "I'm never sick, but I'm going to be sick. You should have this place fumigated."

As the woman briskly wheeled her down the hall past several open doors, Edna glimpsed still forms and heard unfamiliar noises. At last they reached a fluorescently bright room containing four beds. Edna strained against her straps trying to look around. Abruptly, the woman parked the gurney beside one of the narrow beds.

"Oh, no," Edna said politely. "This won't do. For one thing, that smell will kill me. And I must have privacy. I've had a room of my own my whole life, even after I married. I won't be staying here, but thank you for your trouble. I'll be leaving now."

The aide welcomed the attendants who appeared with Edna's things, telling them where to put the suitcase and the carving. She seemed amused by the urn and placed it on the floor of an empty metal locker. Edna huffed at the woman's nerve.

"I won't stay here," she repeated, thinking the woman must be dull or preoccupied. "This is not acceptable. I don't have to lower my standards just because I learned the truth. I'd like a room with a nice bay window." Her mouth open, her eyes wide with astonishment, she watched them unpack her things and pull down the bed clothes. "Now look here. I'm not going to bed. I'm not tired. I want to see the dining room." Their insistent silence began to unnerve her.

The woman in green, still busily tucking away Edna's things in the locker and a small metal bed-side cupboard, finally looked up to ask Edna if she could undress herself or needed help. Edna shivered with revulsion. She was at a loss regarding how she might straighten out this misunderstanding. Her friend had died, and with her all Edna's illusions about life. But then she had spent a lovely day in a park and the smell of grass told her that if she chose to live, she must take rooms close to the ground. If this place was not the beautiful old mansion Wilson had spoken of, then she would leave. But how, she wondered, could she leave when they strapped her to a bed and refused to acknowledge her in any way? The woman finished organizing her belongings and moved toward her. Edna watched her warily.

"I think there's been some mistake," she said, struggling to make some human connection with the woman. "I understood I was moving to a fine old home, a university residence. Wilson changed her mind about where she was going to send me because I didn't . . . you know." She dropped her voice. "End it all."

The woman smiled, Edna thought, most peculiarly. "I'll help you off with your things. Shall I call you Edna?"

"I haven't been formal for a long time," Edna said, shrinking from the woman's hands. "Please don't touch me. Let me up and I'll take care of myself."

"Here's your nightie," she said unfastening the gurney straps.

"But I don't want to go to bed. I'm neither sick nor tired."

"Calm down, Edna," the woman said mechanically. "You'll have to be examined. Don't worry. It's just admissions procedure. Nothing hurts here. You can trust me."

Alarm closed Edna's throat. She wanted to ask why anything should hurt, but her voice deserted her. The woman helped Edna stand. "Put this on, Sweetie," she said, thrusting the nightie at Edna.

Dumbly, Edna looked around for a means of escape.

"So we're modest, are we?" The woman laughed. "You'll soon get over that. Come sit on the bed and I'll close your curtains. No one can see you when they're closed."

Roughly, the woman pulled Edna to her bed. Just as the attendant wrenched the curtain out from the wall, Edna heard footsteps and a cheery voice sing out. "More Big Bats. More Big Bats. What's it look like, Susie-Q? Another geriatric Shirley Temple dollie?"

Safe behind her curtain, Edna listened as the woman in green responded. "No," she heard her say. "You'll like her, Mary. She thinks she's been enrolled in a university."

Edna heard an uproarious laugh. "Ah, yes," the cheery voice said. "We like a woman who's after higher education. What's she doing in there?"

"Getting into her nightie. Leave her alone. The nurse has to give her first dose of Metaphin."

Edna heard retreating footsteps and then a low, tragic sigh. "Metaphin," the voice repeated sadly.

Edna screwed up her courage and peeked around the curtain. A squat dumpling of a woman with sandy brown hair pulled tightly to the top of her head and shaped into a perfect doughnut was bending low to rummage in an exact replica of the cupboard beside her. Dressed in a short, floral-print housecoat with missing buttons and odd bedroom slippers, Edna thought she looked a fright. Despite this judgment, she felt immediately better for seeing this woman. She decided the tone of this place must be more casual than at the lodge and quickly slipped out of her cardigan, shirtwaist, and under things to pull on her nightie. After tidying her hair she opened her curtain and went to the locker for her housecoat and slippers. She smiled at her cheerful roommate. "Hello," she said warmly. "This place stinks."

Her companion stared, astonished. "My, but she is very tidy," she said as she looked Edna over.

"I try, but they insisted I put on this night attire." Edna made a little curtsy in her green robe. "I don't know why. It's only a little after five, isn't it?"

"Five what?" said the other woman.

"Five o'clock," said Edna.

The woman moved toward Edna, radiating curiosity and setting her body aquiver with each step. Edna frowned at her approach. It seemed everything jiggled except the tight little doughnut on the top of her head.

"Really, my dear," Edna said in what she hoped was a kindly voice. "You should do something about your girth. It can't be good for your heart."

The woman laughed a huge belly laugh that split her face in half then sobered quickly. "We don't sound like we've come to the right place," she said suspiciously. "Are we a government spy? Were we sent to see if we're getting more spending money than we should?"

Edna sat on the room's one chair. "I'd be happy if they offered me the job. I'd probably take it," she said. "I'm so bloody bored most of the time. I've had to steal and swear and get into all kinds of fixes just to prove to myself that I haven't died already. I'd be happy to work. Am I here for training?"

The woman set her tapioca flesh in motion once again. Edna marveled at these gyrations as she moved closer. She felt rude and yet couldn't look away from the jiggling flesh. A mere foot from Edna, the woman extended her hand as if she expected Edna to kiss it.

"We are Mary. Mary Stuart. Descendant of the bloody queen."

Edna smiled graciously. "I'll watch my step," she said and shook hands vigorously.

Edna's diffidence pleased Mary, and she immediately opened the curtain and made herself comfortable at the foot of Edna's bed. "Who is she?" she asked, indicating Edna with a gracious tilt of her head.

"I'm sorry to say I'm not related to royalty, bloody or otherwise. I'm Edna Carver. My best friend died. She's in an urn at the bottom of that vulgar closet. Would you like to see her?"

Mary's bright eyes followed Edna to the locker where she stooped to retrieve the urn. Impressed with the shining brass, Mary said, "We bet Edna has chocolates in there."

Edna laughed. "Oh, no, it's Lizzie." She shook the urn, letting Mary hear the muffled sound, then plopped the urn heavily onto her bed. Mary looked at the brass container sideways.

"Open it," she said. "Prove to us Edna isn't hoarding chocolates."

Edna sat on the bed, pulled the urn to her lap, and tugged at the cap. "It's stuck. I can't get it off."

Mary reached over to help. The two were puffing and twisting in an effort to open the urn when the woman in green returned, followed by a nurse pushing a cart.

"Oh, you've met your roommate," the nurse said to Edna. "You two are going to live in splendid isolation because they need those beds on two."

Mary looked pleased, but Edna remembered to be unhappy. "I want a single room," she said. "I was expecting a bay window and a canopy bed." She watched the nurse and the aide exchange amused glances before the nurse took a syringe from the cart and walked to Edna's bed.

"This will help you relax," she said crisply. "You won't have to have anything intramuscularly after tonight as long as you're a good girl."

"I won't have it intramuscularly tonight," Edna retorted. "I don't need relaxing. I think there's been some mistake. I only asked to move to a quiet place where I could scatter Lizzie. The place I used to live was sealed tighter than a mausoleum and every inch of ground was covered by concrete." She heard Mary laugh just before the nurse pinned her to the bed.

"If you don't hold still, we'll strap you down again."

Mary joined Edna, putting a cool hand on her arm. "Don't worry. Edna will get used to it. Just let them do what they want and they'll go away."

"Get to your own bed, Mary," snapped the nurse.

As Mary wobbled away, the nurse plunged the needle into the flesh of Edna's suddenly exposed leg. The aide stood by the cart inspecting her fingernails until procedure required she take the syringe from the nurse in exchange for Edna's chart. As the young woman wrote, she said mechanically, "That didn't hurt, did it. It never hurts so there's no point in fighting. Next time you'll get it by mouth."

Mouth, Edna thought. She longed to smack the impertinence off the nurse's small one. In shock, she watched the aide strip the bed across from her own, saw the other woman's critical appraisal of the aide's work as she dismantled the side rails, foot and head boards, and then unlocked the wheels to push the bed and its heap of linen from the room. In profile, the nurse looked like a child, not a line marking the perfectly smooth face, a pretty face if it had been animated, but a sullen face because, because . . . . Edna's mind drifted. She heard the nurse say, "Check her in fifteen minutes. If she's really out of it, bring her a tray later."

The aide asked, "Should I strap her in before I wash these down?" as she pushed a bed through the doorway.

In response to this question, Edna heard a disembodied voice answer, "You'd better. We don't want her falling on her face her first night here."

Edna smiled stupidly as the aide lifted her legs to the bed and strapped her down. Feeling its steady presence, Edna stroked the urn nestled close beside her as she would an affectionate cat. Beyond the bed, she was aware of a cloud of green and a cloud of white moving this way and that before disappearing through a funny hole on the other side of the . . . ." She forgot the name of the place she was in.

"Fight it," a voice whispered ferociously. "Fight it. It's the only way. Fight it."

Languidly, Edna turned her head in search of the source of the voice. Mary Stuart pressed her hand. "Edna must fight it, or she'll want it all the time. When they give her a pill, she can throw it away, but she'll want it if she doesn't fight it now." Edna smiled stupidly, unable to understand the woman's agitation. "Please," Mary pleaded, staring into Edna's eyes. "We want someone to play with. The doctor takes away all our playmates."

The doctor, Edna thought. Her smile disappeared. She wanted to ask Mary how to fight the drug, but her tongue wouldn't work. She grunted.

"Say the stupid times table. We'll help. Two times one is two. Two times two is four. Two times three is . . . ." She looked at Edna hopefully.

Edna tried to work her useless tongue. "Three?" she slurred. Mary smacked her hard on the chest.

"Two times four?" Mary raised her hand again.

"Don't hit me again," Edna cried, her words still slurred but comprehensible. "Eight. Two times four is eight. Why does this help?"

Mary's eyes shone conspiratorially. "We don't know. But every time they outsmart us," she said, burying her fingers in the abundant and rosy flesh of her bosom, "we manage to work a little of it off if we get mad. Do the hateful times table. Say the rotten alphabet." She smacked Edna suddenly, not liking the look on her face. "Two times five?" she demanded, pinching Edna's thigh.

Edna wanted to smack her back. "Ten," she cried, "And if you hit me again, I'll bean you."

Mary laughed, splitting her face in two again. "We like Edna Carver. She's good stuff. We might give her a title. Two times six?"

"Twelve," said Edna, enraged. "Two times seven is fourteen. Two times eight —"

Mary Stuart clapped her hand over Edna's mouth. "The aide is coming," she whispered. "Edna must do it in her head. Edna must bite her tongue."

Edna continued the times table silently. Mary shuffled back to her own bed. When the aide peered in, Edna thought to close her eyes, but as soon as she did she felt the unmistakable urge to drift. The numbers she recited seemed absurd bits of nonsense some silly person invented to fool people into measuring everything, but there was nothing to measure. Numbers were like the emperor's new clothes, a fiction of someone's imagination. Even their names were ridiculous to her. Mental images started surfacing to replace the hilarious numbers, but they were imperceptible, shadowy. She closed her fists, digging her nails into her palms and pressing with all her might. When she opened her eyes the aide was gone and four little red smiles decorated each of her palms.

"Look," she said, holding up her hands. "Stigmata."

This delighted Mary. "Edna Carver will get a title for sure. We Stuarts like good Catholics."

Edna laughed, closing her fists again. When she concentrated on the pain, Edna discovered the shadows were gone and she was able to sense her body and the urn at her side.

Feeling it safe to do so, Mary crept over to Edna's bed. "Is Edna in there?" she asked, her hand poised to strike.

"Yes," Edna said. "I don't think the numbers are going to work for me, though. They seem so absurd. Who made up numbers anyway? Was it a Stuart?"

"Very likely," Mary answered, frankly inspecting the contents of Edna's locker. She pulled out dresses, sniggering and sneering but Edna didn't notice as she mulled.

"I'm going to be the sort who has to bang her had against a wall, I expect. Pain has always had the effect of . . . ." Marion's birth popped into her head – a hard, dry labour with no anesthetic and months of pain because the baby had made her own way into the world, without the help of an episiotomy. Even though she had caused herself more pain when she'd ended her second pregnancy, it was a final hurt, the end of that sort of pain altogether. She increased the pressure in her fists, digging her nails harder into her palms, aware that Mary had abandoned the large locker to search in the small metal cupboard beside her bed.

"Mean little things," Edna said, her hands shaking with effort as she gestured to the cupboard Mary inspected. "I thought I'd be surrounded by burled walnut and inlaid oak. And this place stinks. What is that smell?"

"Pee and shit," Mary answered, surprised that she had to tell an intelligent person something so obvious. "Didn't Edna go to the bathroom where she used to live?"

"Well of course! But only in the toilets."

Mary stopped her search to express amazement. "Really? Well, the dollies do it everywhere here because they're tied to chairs and forgotten. We almost sat in a big pile in the sunroom this morning, and we in our best chemise, too." The way she stroked her gaping robe, it might have been ermine.

Horrified, Edna foolishly unclenched her fists. "Tied and forgotten! What on earth . . . ." All at once the horror faded and the seductive shadows returned.

Mary guessed what was happening and quickly pounded Edna's upper arm.

"Ow," Edna shouted.

"Edna was drifting. Try biting her lip."

Edna bit but couldn't remember why she was biting. She looked around the grimy room and felt quite lost. "Where am I? This isn't my room at Sunset Lodge."

"Edna lives at Tranquil Time now," Mary told her cheerfully. "And she's been shot full of stupidness because that's the way they like us here. Now look," she said, losing patience. "If Edna's serious about fighting the stupidness, she mustn't forget this. They'll have her if she just takes her pills and sits back and drifts." An animal cunning lit up Mary's round face. "If she drifts, we'll take that urn and throw it out the window."

The threat brought Edna sharply to her senses. She cradled the urn protectively. "What window?"

Mary gyrated to the wall beyond Edna's head. She yanked on a cord, sending the blind up until it stopped with a jerk. Beyond the house's shadow, sunlight rimed tree branches fuzzy with pale new leaves.

Mary closed the blind with the same sharp movement. "It's the rules. All the blinds have to be down. They say the sun makes the linen fade. "

"Turn the lights off and open that again," whispered Edna. Tears slid down her cheeks. "Turn the goddamn lights off and open it again."

"Settle down," Mary said imperiously. "Royalty gives the orders here. Besides, it's the rules. It's such a stupid one, our window faces east, but rules run this place, not intelligence. When Edna's here a while, when we're sure she can be trusted, we'll show her something really spectacular."

"There were bars out there." Edna was crying loudly now. "They've sent me to a place with bars on the windows."

Mary put a fat, cautioning finger to her lips. Edna sputtered, doing her best to control herself. The sound of crepe-soled shoes squeaking along the hallway grew louder. She wiped the tears up into her hair and composed her face. The nurse was at her bedside moments later. Her eyes closed, Edna felt the cold fingers press her wrist and then her chest. "You *are* a strong one," she heard the woman mutter. "Not much of a change at all. We'll have to get an elephant gun for you." Edna listened to the squeaking recede then opened her eyes again.

Mary crept from her own bed. "That's not good," she told Edna. "Next time she comes in, let go and drift. We'll smack Edna out of it when the nurse leaves."

"Oh, dear," said Edna. "I want to go home. How do you get out of here?"

Touched, Mary studied her new neighbour from the end of the bed. "Edna can't. Not unless she's got some family that will come in here, be appalled, and take her home."

"My daughter," Edna said wearily. "I have a daughter."

Mary's cheerful look changed abruptly. "Daughters," she spat. "It was our daughter who locked us up in here. And all because of our beautiful bugs. We hate our daughter. It's better not to expect anything from daughters."

"What bugs?"

Mary radiated happiness once more. "Our cockroaches! Our hubby and we lived in the same apartment building for the forty years that we were married." Mary leaned toward Edna and dropped her voice. "He wasn't royalty, but he was all right. We used to let him kiss our big toe now and then, and he was glad to do it." She looked into Edna's fascinated eyes. "Our building was nice enough to start with, but about the time the hubby retired, it started to go downhill. And we on a limited budget! We simply couldn't move. And then he died and we didn't want to move. The place was full of him and we couldn't leave him behind."

Mary placed a warm, dry hand on Edna's shin. "The bugs started coming in from the apartments on either side. We cleaned and cleaned. We even had the manager fumigate. About four times, too. Royalty has no truck with vermin. We like things nice. But no matter how hard we tried to get rid of them, they came back, like they liked us," she said. "Needed us. At last we understood. The bugs were our new subjects." Seeing the surprise on Edna's face, Mary laughed.

"Oh, yes, people are pretty squeamish about where they're willing to admit finding the miracle of creation. They say yes to flowers, but no to worms. It doesn't make any sense. Anyway, our bugs and we lived very happily together. They were very artistic company." She looked at Edna defiantly. "We bet you didn't know bugs can dance."

"No, I didn't," Edna said.

"Well, they can. And they're good enough for any palace, especially when we get them to give an impromptu performance by sneaking into a dark room and turning on the lights. They twirl and skitter . . . ," she moved her hands gracefully to imitate the cockroaches, ". . . and they do very well to almost any tune. We used to sing to them," she said, and then burst into a full throated version of "The Ride of the Valkyrie."

"And they did very nicely to 'Ain't She Sweet' or 'Silver Threads among the Gold' but weren't too fond of hymns. They were afraid of us at first, the best subjects are always respectful, but after a while they understood it was God's purpose for them to perform for we and perform they did. It was wonderful at night in the quiet kitchen. We forgot our dead husband and all our other cares as we watched those lovely shining beetles dancing their little legs off." Mary tapped Edna's shin sharply. "And then our meddling daughter walked into the palace unannounced and uninvited, saw the pleasure we had from our bugs, and had us locked up here. If we knew how to communicate with our bugs, we'd send for them. We'd be prettily amused. They'd help us fight off the stupidity. They don't like that sort of thing. We never found them in our bathroom, just the kitchen. They like good wholesome food." She knocked Edna's shin with her knuckles. "Is Edna drifting?"

Edna shifted her leg out of Mary's reach. "I'm going to be black and blue, for heaven's sake," she cried angrily. "Stop hitting me. I'm fine now," she insisted, but she knew she wasn't. Something, she understood, had gone terribly wrong. She tried to undo the tangle of knots in her head beginning with her present situation and working backward into the past, but the riddle's solution escaped her. Mary slipped off Edna's bed and waddled to her own.

"Drift," the queen commanded over the approaching sound of crepe-soled shoes.

Edna let go of the tangle to invite the shadows once more. As soon as she did she was aware of a thrumming sensation in her chest as if her heart were shifting to a lower gear. It was an odd sensation, one she'd never been conscious of until now, but it did not frighten her and she felt no pain. The squeaking sound suddenly stopped. A cold hand pressed her chest again.

"That's better," she heard the nurse say. "You're just a slow starter." Edna heard the words, but their meaning was lost in the rhythmic, shadowy pulsations crowding at the edges of her mind. A light, pale at first but growing stronger and emanating from a source deep within her, centred gradually, illuminating the outlines of peripheral images. She was puzzled by the fragile stocks at first, woody stems that had no meaning until the light reached the small satin circles they bore. As she watched, the circles turned, faced the light directly, and reflected it. All at once she felt a burst of inner warmth. So, she mused, surprised. Even though Elizabeth is dead, something still grows in me.

Mary slapped her hard across the face. Edna strained against the straps to retaliate.

"Edna's fine now," the fat woman said. "As her reward, she shall be Lady Edna from here on in." Mary's delighted smile canceled Edna's anger.

"How long are they going to leave me here to rot?" Edna asked. "I'd like to see the place."

"Don't be in too much of a rush," Mary advised, shoving the urn aside to make room for her left buttock. Edna wiggled, hoping to push her off the bed but found she couldn't budge the woman. Mary laughed at Edna's feeble attempts to move her.

"We spent a good many years building to our present girth. It was no accident. They leave us alone because it's damned hard to move two hundred pounds of slack. The little doves and wrens get shoved and wheeled and dragged without thought. But we," she said, burying her finger in her fleshy bosom, "we don't like to be pushed around and so we made it impossible for them to do it."

Edna admired Mary's genius. "When you know what you're doing, and why," she said, "you can be a dangerous adversary."

"The most dangerous," said Mary. She tapped Edna's knee. "We're going to have a good time, Lady Edna. She . . ." Mary confided, her finger dancing under Edna's nose, "is the answer to a prayer."

"Well," said Edna, as seriously as any newly appointed board chair, "suppose you tell me what I can expect when they let me up to explore this place."

"The worst. The very worst and then some," Mary whispered. "We're the only human beings among inconspicuous consumers. The dollies live to eat and take their pills."

The word *eat* triggered longing in Edna since she'd eaten neither breakfast nor lunch. "How's the food?" she asked.

"Cold," said Mary. "No matter whether you get it first or last, it's always cold. And tasteless. It doesn't matter to most of them. They're only going through the motions anyway."

"I'm hungry," Edna admitted. "I've had a bad few days. My diet's suffered."

Mary heaved her round cheek off the bed and waddled to her small bed-side cupboard. Pulling out shoes and books and baby powder in order to search at the back of the cupboard, she pressed her doughnut of hair into the closed drawer above. Edna's mouth watered at the sound of promising rustlings.

"Aha!" Mary exclaimed before awkwardly straightening. She offered Edna a package of unopened Carr's biscuits. "This is the first of Lady Edna's rewards as a faithful subject," Mary said grandly. "But we suppose she'd like cheese with them, and perhaps a pear. We have a nice Bosc somewhere." Mary placed a hand on her porcelain throat before swinging open her locker to sort through myriad articles on the top shelf, finally extracting a pear and an unopened package of Havarti. Edna gobbled a biscuit while waiting for Mary to finish slicing the cheese and pear with the pocket knife she apparently kept at the ready in her housecoat pocket. When fruit and cheese finally arrived on the lid of a pickle jar, Edna pronounced it the best food she'd ever tasted. After she'd eaten eight biscuits, half the cheese, and the entire pear, she quizzed Mary on her supplies.

"We're sorry to say the crackers came from our daughter," Mary said. "She thinks we should eat things with absolutely no food value when she knows we don't like anything that isn't sweet. Sugar used to be the only medicine used by royalty but our daughter has refused her heritage. The pear we got from Mr. Barren. His teeth aren't good — he leaves them in all sorts of strange places — and when he hasn't lost them, Mrs. Strowd wears them, so why his relatives bring him pears is beyond us. We got the cheese from the kitchen."

"They let you into the kitchen?"

"Of course not," said Mary. "But the queen needn't wait to be invited. We just go in when we feel like it. Nobody's in there after midnight. We help ourselves to what we want." She pulled out a tin of Quik from her locker to prove her point. Before she put it back, she opened the lid, inhaled rapturously, poured some into her palm, and licked greedily. Entranced, Edna smiled approvingly at Mary's initiative.

"Next time, we'll take Lady Edna with us," Mary said, seeing her new roommate's admiration. "We can always use another pair of hands." Edna snuggled down in her bed comfortably, deciding she hadn't been far wrong when she thought in her confusion that she was attending a university.

A loud rattle from the hallway made Mary bolt down the Quik

and stash the rest of her food in her locker. In a few moments, the nurse who had given Edna the injection pushed a cart into the room and then stood like a sentry in the doorway. The ominous sound of street shoes striking the linoleum alarmed Edna. When the doctor's bland face appeared behind the nurse, healthfully tanned above his white coat, she couldn't help the shriek of recognition that escaped despite her clenched teeth.

He was at her bedside in a moment, his warm hands exploring her body in a disgustingly familiar way. "Hmmm," he said, leaving her breasts to palpate her abdomen. "Unstrap her and close the curtains." His disinterested voice terrified Edna. She watched anxiously as the nurse carried out his orders. Seeing her willing compliance, Edna thought of well oiled machines. When the three of them were behind the large semi-circle of tired hospital linen, the doctor made a gesture. In response, the nurse unbuttoned Edna's dressing gown and yanked up Edna's nightie. Though she wanted to swear indignantly, Edna closed her eyes, searching for the small inner lights again. Finding them, she breathed shallowly to obliterate the doctor's violating hands. Then, with the courage of a deep breath, she extinguished the lights, opened her eyes, and looked at him. He seemed to be nothing more than an insubstantial husk a light breeze might blow away. Her fear was gone.

"You appear to be in stable health right now, Mrs. Carver," the doctor said at the end of his examination. "I'm sorry we never met at the lodge, but we'll make up for lost time now, won't we." Edna's silence didn't prevent him from continuing pleasantly. "You'll get lots of rest here. I'm sure I won't have to do this sort of thing very often." He gave her an obligatory smile before leaving as abruptly as he'd come, the obedient nurse at his heels.

Edna was thinking about what she'd seen when the nurse returned. "He says you're alert enough to eat with the others tonight. No tray. Get up," she said. In spite of the uncivil tone of its delivery, Edna was pleased with the news. She buttoned her housecoat to the neck, put on her slippers, and took several turns around the room before marching up to Mary as she savoured the lingering taste of Quik. "It isn't right, you know," said Edna. "It's like we're animals they hoard in a pen. Like sheep."

Mary raised her eyebrows, surprised at Edna's indignation.

"Of course," she said. "We can't blame them for treating people like sheep when they act like sheep."

Edna rubbed her hands together, absorbed in a new infusion of warmth.

"Look," Mary said, patience etched on her round sweet face. "Some of us are born to rule and some of us are not. We are the queen because we've got what it takes and we know how to make more of it. The sheep don't have it. That's why they need shepherds."

"Shepherds," Edna repeated. There flashed into her mind the image of a grove and beyond it a sloping pasture, green beneath a blue, blue sky, where lambs gamboled and a shepherd dozed in the luxurious shade of an ancient Sycamore. "But we're not sheep," she said defiantly. "I want to do something about whatever they give us that makes them think we are."

"Oh, that," said Mary, laughing. "Edna's already got that licked. She doesn't need to worry about Metaphin anymore. She'll count or bang her head or pull her fingernails out if they manage to slip a pill past her. She'll be fine," Mary assured her. "Most of the time it's very easy to slip the stuff into someone else's juice. Or stick it in our ear and flush it down the toilet when we have the chance. We have our morning and lunchtime doses right here," Mary said, thrusting her doughnut in Edna's face. Edna could see a white speck lodged firmly in the centre of the tight little ring of hair. "We've got lots of places to hide it," Mary went on, "but sometimes they think we're too much to handle and they give it to us with the needle. That's when we have to remember to fight it, because if we let it get into our soul, we'll start to need it and then we'll want to take the pills. It makes life a lot more pleasant for the sheep. They don't know when someone's forgotten to treat their bed sores, or wash them, or take out their catheters."

"We'll find some other way to make life pleasant," Edna said. "And just think, Mary. You could have real subjects if the people in here weren't drugged to the eyeballs."

Mary thought about this for a moment. "Lady Edna might be right," she said tentatively. "We've never thought of the dollies as our subjects. We suppose they could be, if we whipped them into shape." Skepticism flashed across her face. "But just remember. They love the pills. We won't have stupid subjects."

"I'll help you make them smart. We'll do it together. I don't think it's fitting that a queen devote herself exclusively to bugs."

Mary reveled in the idea of expanding power. "Lady Edna, we hereby make you the First Royal Advisor. We'll listen to advice in matters pertaining to the queendom's well being. But if we think the sheep can or even want to stop taking their Metaphin, we are a very Big Bat indeed."

"Maybe there's another way," said Edna. She heard the distant clanging of dining room preparations and thought she could even smell something like cabbage permeating the sharp fecal reek she feared had lodged permanently in her nostrils. "But before we do anything about the people, we have to do something about the way this place smells."

"Well," Mary began thoughtfully. "If we make the stupid ones smart, it will smell better because they'll be able to get to the toilets by themselves."

Edna left the bed for the window. "How about these windows? Can we open some of them?"

"Some," Mary said coyly. She waddled into position a few steps in front of Edna who immediately understood that protocol demanded this positioning. Her head high, Edna walked several paces behind the queen as they processed out into the hall.

On her first journey under her own steam in her new home, Edna discovered railings along the walls, at about hip level. Edna watched as Mary gravitated to the railing on the right, clutched it, and began moving slowly forward. She imitated her new friend, thinking it wouldn't hurt to have the staff think she was feebler than she was. The bar ended at a doorway, which, Mary informed her, was their bathroom.

"There is a very nice surprise in here for Lady Edna. When we see she's in need of a lift, we'll show her." Mary paused, suddenly remembering the pills in her bun. "We'll just get rid of these," she said, digging out the medication and stepping inside to flush them down the toilet. Edna admired Mary's ingenuity and touched her own knot with new respect.

Resuming their slow journey, the pair came to three more doors opening onto darkened rooms. Inside, Edna could barely see the still forms, white ghosts beneath whiter sheets, small protrusions under blankets that barely moved with the small life beneath them.

"What about them?" Edna asked, her eyes filling. "Do they just lie there like that all the time?" She was horrified by the apparent abandonment of these people, by their sexless, pale faces tilted back at awkward angles, by their silent gaping mouths. She began to cry in earnest.

"Don't," Mary commanded. "We will drive ourselves crazy if we look too closely."

But Edna would not turn away. She walked quietly into the last room to stroke the arm lying limply on the light coverlet. "What can I do for you? Might I bring you some soup?" she whispered. The phantom did not respond.

Mary guided Edna back out into the hall. "If the nurses find Lady Edna interfering, she will be strapped into her bed, shot full of stupidness, and before she knows it, become just like that." She touched the tears on Edna's face. "It is hard, we know, but there's nothing we can do for them now. Nothing, except maybe put a pillow over their faces to help them go. But we know what they'd do to us for our trouble." Gently, she took Edna's hand and resumed their journey along the hallway.

At last they reached the dining room. So unlike the dining room in her imagination with its pedestal tables, complete with lion's feet, and its wainscoting, and its fine old Tiffany lamps, Edna was sure Mary had somehow become disoriented and stumbled into some horror story. Three windowless walls and a low, crude railing where the fourth wall had been removed defined the space. A cluster of small arborite tables, smaller even than those at Sunset Lodge, and meaner, without tablecloths or little bouquets of plastic flowers or even salt and pepper shakers, stood in the centre of the space. Narrow vinyl chairs lined one wall. A dumb waiter, open and disgorging dinner trays into the hands of a green-clad aide, distinguished another.

For a time, overwhelm prevented Edna from noticing her fellow residents. When she finally focused on them she discovered that most were in wheelchairs, slumped at the mean, small tables, waiting. They were so quiet, so still, Edna imagined she could see through them to the dingy, green walls beyond. Mary guided her to a greasy table in their midst.

"We have to get our own chairs and put them back when we've finished," Mary informed her. "That way the aides can maneuver the wheelchairs in and out quickly. The nurses get furious when anyone blocks the way. It makes them do more work," she said, then added in a confidential whisper, "we're sure they'd like it much better if we were all in wheelchairs or strapped to our beds. Feeding tubes," she said with a pointed look, "are so much less fuss and muss to worry about."

When an aide dropped two trays on their table, Mary moved with surprising speed to retrieve a chair and get down to the business of eating. Edna watched her for a moment and then looked around at her as yet unknown fellow prisoners. She remembered Mary's name for the residents and shivered with its aptness. At first, the women looked alarmingly the same, with short, mechanically curled grey hair framing pinched grey faces that bobbed over pale nighties and robes that were similar enough to have been chosen for the same person. All wore ill-fitting glasses of the same type – bifocals in pale grey plastic half-frames.

After studying her neighbours for a while Edna was relieved to notice small differences – plumpness, thinness, a small nose, a large one. To Edna's great delight, one woman wore a red baseball cap. She thought the woman must have dropped something and was bending over to retrieve it, but then an arm found its way to the table top, groped for a spoon, found it, filled it with food, and brought it to her head as it rested in her lap. The hat convinced Edna Mary was wrong in her assumptions about these people. She could hardly wait until dinner was over to introduce herself.

Mary looked up from her plate and followed Edna's gaze. "That's Myrtle," she said. "She's not bad as dollies go."

"Myrtle," said Edna. "What a beautiful name." In her mind's eye she could see the deep green leaves and small blue flowers that had established beauty in the darkest, rockiest places in her long-ago garden.

A nurse holding two small white paper cups, each with a pill inside, startled her back to the present. As Edna reached for the cup, another nurse called out in exasperation. "Not her. She's the new one. She had it an hour ago." Wordlessly, the nurse whisked the cup away.

Edna watched the unfolding scene and discreetly asked Mary

if the nurses trusted everyone to take the medication. "We don't give them any reason not to," Mary told her. She winked before taking three half slices of soft white bread from Edna's plate to soak up the last traces of her own dinner. "We pretend to take it like this." Edna studied Mary's technique of palming the pill before raising the cup to her lips and tossing back her head as if she were swallowing a jigger of whiskey. In a minute or two, using the pretense of tidying her hair, Mary tucked the pill in the centre of her doughnut. Edna looked from Mary to the people around them. Unlike Mary, they dutifully took the medication with birdlike sips of sugary juice.

Mary grinned into Edna's pensive face. "If Lady Edna's not going to eat that, we'll be happy to help out." She reached out to exchange her empty plate for Edna's full one.

Edna slapped her hand. "You already pinched my bread. You don't want to starve your First Advisor altogether," she said as she picked up her fork and began to eat without her usual wiping down ritual. At that moment, she noticed the nurses abandoning their private knots of bored conversation with one another to bend over the diners with expressions of care and concern. The aides began to bustle, too, cheerfully filling cups that had been neglected for the entire meal. When one of the nurses turned on a hundred watt smile as she sprinted to the doorway, Edna sensed this was some kind of unscripted performance. She turned to see what precipitated this startling change of atmosphere. A visitor stood in the hall beyond the door. It was a woman. After a few seconds, Edna realized it was Marion.

"Oh, Mother," called Marion Andrews when she recognized Edna in the group of disheveled residents. Joining the nurses in their impromptu display of caring, Edna's daughter spoke in a volume everyone in the room could easily hear. "I've brought over more of your things. Miss Wilson explained that your move was efficiently expedited, but I wanted to see for myself that you were comfortably settled in."

"I bet she did," Edna whispered to Mary. "Efficiently expedited indeed."

"We told you," Mary said sadly. "Watch out for daughters."

"I'll see you in our room," Edna said, standing. "Oh, enjoy my dinner . . . consider it a trade for the feast you provided earlier.

When you get to our room, if you can think of something to give my lovely daughter a turn, I'll be grateful." Edna walked regally to greet her beautifully dressed, perfectly groomed fifty-year-old child.

After she'd shaken off the nurses and silenced Marion by hissing for her to stop fawning over them, Edna and her daughter, scrupulously maintaining a no-touch zone between them, walked down the hall together. Edna could feel Marion's distress about the home's looks even before she spoke.

"This was Miss Wilson's choice, Mother, because she thought it would be best if you remained in the lodge doctor's care, but if you don't like this place we'll move you anywhere. Robert and I will be happy to find you a more suitable place. You don't have to stay here."

"If you think this place is awful, why on earth did you treat those nurses as if they were innocents serving tea at a church picnic?"

Marion pretended not to understand her mother's question. "Really, Mother, we can put your name on the waiting list for that gorgeous place in Forest Hill."

"No, thank you, Marion," Edna said with easy dignity. "I'll stay right here. It might do you some good to come in and have a look around every Sunday. Unless you decide you can't stand it."

"Mother!"

"I'm sorry, Marion," Edna said, owning her mean spiritedness. "I don't want to move just now. But there is something you can do for me."

"Your laundry? Your shopping? Anything at all, Mother. Just tell me."

"Bring me my paints. And if you've given them away, buy a box of water colours. Any child's box will do, but with as many colours as possible. And a good sized package of paper. Make sure it's meant for water colours. Without good paper, I can't paint worth a damn."

"Mother," Marion pleaded. "Please don't swear. You know it isn't nice."

"Nice?" echoed Edna wearily. "You think this place is nice? You think people should be left to lie in bed day after day with little needles in their arms while their shit and piss drain into hidden plastic bags the staff neglect to empty and . . . ? Oh, never mind. Just bring me the paints and save your moral lessons for Robert. I'm sure he wants to be nice."

Marion's eyes filled. "No, Mother. I don't think this place is nice. The smell is awful, and I don't like the colour of the walls. The least they can do is give ambulatory people like you a private room a good distance from that disgusting communal feeding station. You should have your own television." Edna began to laugh. She wished she could pull one of the doctor's pills out of her pocket and explain to Marion that they didn't need television at . . . . She couldn't remember the name of the place and her forgetfulness frightened her. "What's the name of this place?" she asked.

Marion touched her mother's shoulder tenderly. "It's called Tranquil Time, Mother," she said gently.

"Thank you," Edna said, shaken. "I will try not to forget that again."

"Oh, Mother," Marion said. "It doesn't matter to me if you're forgetting things now. You've reached that stage of life when you deserve to have others remember things for you."

Edna wanted to tell her that it mattered to her very much, but her daughter's frosted blond hair, styled so that it fitted around her skull like a beautiful cloche, and her tailored suit of pale blue silk shantung, and her perfectly matched stockings and shoes depressed her. "Never mind, never mind, Marion," she said, longing to be civil. "Just bring me my paints."

"All right, Mother," Marion said in martyred tones. She leaned forward to kiss her mother's cheek lightly. "I'm glad to see you're enjoying your dressing gown. It reminded me of you when I saw it at Creeds last Christmas."

Wanting to rip the robe off her back and step on it several times, Edna stood, erect and proud, waiting for her daughter to leave. Marion made no move to the door. "I think we've finished our business now, Marion. Thank you for coming but I think it's time for me to rest," Edna said.

"Are you sure you wouldn't like me to stay and have a nice cup of tea with you?"

"Oh, yes," said Edna. "We'll buzz for room service."

"Can you do that?" Marion asked.

"No, Marion, we can't. We'll have tea some other time. This

has been a tiring day." The flash of inspiration came suddenly, making her stagger before she rushed to her bed. "I cremated Lizzie this morning. Here she is." She offered the brass urn to her daughter.

Revulsion spread over Marion's pampered features. "Mother," she said, "I think you'd better let me dispose of that."

"Don't be ridiculous. Lizzie's already been disposed of. Wouldn't it be nice if I were just as tidy? You could put me on your mantle and never give me a thought except when you had your *girl* in to clean on Wednesdays."

Marion walked to the door. "I'll be back on Sunday, Mother," she said, forlorn. "Please call if you can think of anything else you'd like me to bring." Edna waved goodbye, distressed that so many of their meetings ended as this one had. She didn't understand why every word her daughter spoke, every gesture she made, should grate on her sensibilities like a wire brush. She knew Marion felt the same way about her.

Mary agitated into the room minutes later, on the lookout for Edna's daughter. Seeing Edna's slumped shoulders, she began to laugh and shake her finger at her new roommate. "Lady Edna must change her expectations. When she does, when she remembers her daughter is simply a sheep in training and not at all capable of higher development, she'll be fine." Mary's brown eyes shone with wisdom. "Constant disappointment saps our strength, Lady Edna, and our First Advisor must be strong."

Edna looked into Mary's eyes, wishing she could share the grief and disappointment that separated her from her daughter.

"Come on," Mary soothed. "We'll introduce Lady Edna to the few dollies who know the difference between a person and a bedpost. Don't be gloomy, Lady Edna. It is time for our First Advisor to meet the sheep."

Hoping the diversion might help to soothe her aching heart, Edna followed Mary to the hallway. As they walked to the rooms in the wing beyond the eating area, Mary spoke animatedly, hoping to cheer her new friend. "Supposedly we're all Big Bats up here. But if they call this crazy, they've led sheltered lives. This one here's Mr. Barren," Mary confided, pointing into the first private room in the north wing. Edna discovered an old man bending low over a metal cupboard identical to hers and Mary's.

"Looking for the teeth, Mr. Barren?" Mary called.

The old man stood upright and, seeing his visitors, bowed elegantly. "No," he said in a high quavering voice. "I'm sharing them with Mrs. Strowd this evening. I was looking for a fresh corset, but I'm afraid I've run out."

"We're taking this new lady around," Mary told him. She pushed Edna at the old man, who shook her hand warmly as he looked her up and down.

"She's got nothing for you, Mr. Barren, as you can see. Perhaps Miss Jenkins might let you have something tonight." Edna's confusion made Mary laugh. "He likes the ladies' undies," she confided as they left the old man, shrugging when Edna balked at the idea of a strange man wearing her corset. "Nobody seems to mind. If we're missing anything vital, he's the man to come to."

Edna turned to study Mr. Barren, wanting to be able to identify him as the culprit should any of her under garments go missing. He was tall and very thin, with wisps of white hair barely covering his pink scalp. She watched him search through some handkerchiefs and ties, his hands stroking the material before discarding each article. He used his hands as if they were organs of sight. They were beautiful hands, she thought, musician's hands. As she watched them explore the various fabrics, Edna determined to sketch them. He looked up as she stared and offered a warm, disarming smile, as if to say he didn't think much of his proclivities and hoped she would forgive him for them. Impatient to continue their rounds, Mary called her to the next room.

There, Myrtle Jenkins received Edna by resting her chin on her bony knees before whipping off her red baseball cap. "Howdy-do," she said, apparently delighted with the company.

Edna waited until Myrtle had replaced her cap before shaking her hand and sitting beside her on her bed. "Tell me, Myrtle, may I call you Myrtle?" Myrtle nodded. "Good. I'm Edna. Tell me, Myrtle. What's the name of your condition?"

Myrtle studied her quizzically. "Oh," she said, as if startled that Edna should notice her posture. "This is just arthritis. They give me pills for the pain, but I'm tiptop. Tiptop." She tipped her hat at Edna a second time, conveying the end of their interview. Before they left, Mary searched through Myrtle's closet for something Myrtle said she could have. The gift turned out to be a pound box of chocolate-covered almonds. Mary exploded with gratitude.

"Really?" she exclaimed. "For us? How kind, Myrtle. Is she sure?"

"Nuts and I don't get along at all well," said Myrtle. "They all know that, but they bring me nuts just the same." She eyed Edna, who was crouching down to make eye contact. "What's the matter with your legs?" she asked.

"My legs are fine," Edna said. "I thought it might be easier for us to talk if I were down here."

Myrtle laughed. "About what? The weather? I don't want to talk about the weather. I don't want to talk at all." She tipped her hat three more times in the effort to send the women on their way.

"How long have you been like this?" Edna asked.

"Like what?" Myrtle snapped.

"So crippled?" Edna said, sorry for the sharpness in her voice.

"God, I don't know. Does it matter?"

"I just wondered if they were doing anything . . . corrective for you."

"They do fine," said Myrtle, dismissing Edna. "I get my pills morning, noon, and night. They do just fine."

Mary moved to the door restlessly, her large body aquiver with the excitement of an unexpected sugar feast. "Come, Lady Edna. Mrs. Strowd is just next door."

Edna stood, wondering how Myrtle managed to get into bed at night, or go to the bathroom, or open a door. She told Myrtle she hoped they would become friends, and for this sentiment received two more tips of the red baseball cap. Despite these flourishes, Myrtle did not look happy about Edna's intentions to befriend her.

Edna stifled a shriek when Mary introduced her to Mrs. Strowd. A little thing, built like Lizzie but wearing teeth so large her chin almost rested on her breast bone, she looked as ferocious as a piranha. The woman wore a perpetual smile far more maniacal than Miss Jones's clownish one. This insanely happy expression together with the enormous teeth made her look quite mad. Edna clutched Mary's arm for protection. As Mary chatted about her almonds, Mrs. Strowd nodded, blinking cloudy blue eyes and muttering viciously through what Edna learned were Mr. Barren's teeth. Relief flooded Edna when Mary could no longer resist the chocolate-covered nuts and began the walk back to their room.

"Why would anybody do that?" Edna asked when they were reclining on their own beds. "She'd look so different if she'd only use her own teeth."

"She's not interested in looking different," Mary said. "She likes looking that way. Nobody fools around with her when she's got those teeth in. The aides and the nurses are afraid of her. The doctor, too." She ripped the cellophane off the chocolate box and tore at the lid, sending a spray of almonds onto the floor. Unconcerned about what she might catch from the grimy linoleum, Mary gathered up a handful of nuts and began to eat. With her mouth full and working hard, she bent down to retrieve the rest of the almonds from the floor. Once she was sure she had them all, she swallowed noisily and resumed her tone of friendly conversation. "Because of her daughter's visit, Lady Edna missed the best dessert they serve here – chocolate pudding with whipped cream and a cherry on top. We ate hers." Mary laughed. "We feel good tonight. Chocolate has such energizing properties."

Edna lay on her bed and touched the urn wishing she knew an energizing property that might conjure a live and mischievous Lizzie out of it. Before she could drift into her private world of comforting memories about Elizabeth, a nurse rushed in to wrestle Mary for the few remaining almonds in the box. Edna propped herself up on her elbow to watch, delighted to see Mary shove the last handful into her mouth, chew, swallow, and triumphantly laugh her split-faced laugh. Furious and bruised, the nurse limped to Mary's chart to record this malfeasance. No sooner had she left than one of the aides appeared in the doorway.

"Do you need help?" she asked Edna. Edna blinked her confusion. "Can you get into bed yourself?"

"I'd like to wash before I do," Edna said. "May I?"

"Tub?" the woman asked wearily.

"I beg your pardon?"

"If you want to have a tub bath, someone has to be with you."

"Not on your life," said Edna. "I'm fine on my feet. And I like my privacy."

"Not in the tub," the aide said. "You can do your hands and face and teeth alone, but that's it."

"Please," Edna pleaded. "I'd like a bath."

"Look," said the aide, doing her best to help Edna understand the rules and regulations of her new home. "I'd be liable if anything happened to you. I have to supervise all baths on this floor. We schedule baths on Tuesdays. This is Friday. And I've got two complete overhauls to take care of."

Edna appreciated the girl's efforts to help her fit in. "What if I left the door open? You could check on me if you hear any funny noises. But honestly, dear. Nothing will happen. I'm very strong. They only locked me in here because they think I'm crazy."

"And if I'm not yet, I soon will be," said the aide. Furtively, she looked over her shoulder. "All right, but bathe as quickly as you can. I'll supervise you from Room C."

Mary waited for the aide to leave before putting an arm around Edna's shoulder. "Lady Edna's beginning to feel the place. Lots of rules, she thinks, and not much freedom." She patted Edna's cheek. "Come. We'll help run the bath. There's something we want to show our First Advisor."

Edna followed Mary into their bathroom, noting numerous signs of the house's grander days. In an effort to save money, the speculators who'd converted the old Victorian mansion had salvaged as many of its original fixtures as possible. This bathroom had been left entirely in its original state except for the addition of a couple of steel handles bolted to the white tiled walls to assist bath and toilet use.

Once inside with the door closed, Edna looked around. The room was as big as a smallish bedroom. A grand old pedestal sink sat below an old float-glass mirror that made Edna grin at her distorted reflection. The tub, gently oval and reminiscent of a giant inverted turtle's shell big enough for at least three Lizzie-sized people, rested on huge claws. She was glad to see that the support handles didn't mar the beauty of the room the way the long, ugly fluorescent tube over the mirror did. She looked up to the ceiling where the patched plaster in the centre of a ring of laurel leaves announced the original light fixture's removal. She felt the house's tragedy as acutely as she did all magnificent old creatures' and lamented it's exploitation by ravagers.

Mary hissed, "Quick. Come here, Lady Edna. The aide will return in a moment. Ever since they let one of the dollies scald to death, they've been pretty nervous about anyone having a bath alone."

Mary tugged at something, pushed once or twice, and finally sent the window up with a muted screech. The smell of hyacinths drifted into the room. Edna thrust her head into the dusk. Below, the gardens beyond the house's shadow were aflame with early evening sun.

"Why isn't it as cared for on inside as it is on the outside?" Edna whispered.

"Nobody sees the inside," Mary said, surprised she had to tell her First Advisor something so obvious.

"Are we allowed to sit out there, or do we spoil the view?"

"We're allowed, but not alone," Mary answered. "We can only go out when someone takes us."

"Like a daughter?"

Mary sneered. "More like a volunteer."

"Are there many?"

Mary cocked her head to one side. "Oh, they come once or twice but they get discouraged and find more enjoyable ways to spend their time . . . at day care centres and after-school programs with cute little children. We can't blame them."

Edna craned her neck, taking in as much of the garden as she could. "It's enclosed. They could take everyone out to sit."

"If they did, it wouldn't look so grand, would it. You don't want Mrs. Strowd scaring away Toronto tourists." Mary pulled Edna back suddenly, shut the window, and replaced the long spike that appeared to nail it shut. "The girls sneak in here for a smoke and the view. They don't know we know, so don't let on. That aide will be back in a minute, so Lady Edna better run her bath."

Reluctantly, Edna turned to the tub. "A person could do a fair bit of damage, jumping out that window."

Surprise animated Mary's features. "Why would anyone want to?"

"It's just good to know it could be done, if a person were inclined to end it all."

"Lady Edna won't be feeling like that in a week or two. Just wait and see. A couple of midnight trips to the kitchen and she'll be feeling right at home." Mary wiggled out of the big bathroom, leaving Edna to gaze at the swirling water and consider her options if she chose to end her life. The pills she would begin to collect the next day might do the trick, or refusing to eat or drink, or escaping and wandering into traffic came to her as possibilities. Leaping from the window took more courage than she thought she had, but perhaps if she drugged herself first . . . .

She longed to soak away the despair she felt. Sunset Lodge, for all its faults, at least afforded her the small but exquisite pleasure of an afternoon in her tub sipping sherry and reading. As she was pining for this lost joy, the aide returned to turn the water off. She felt the temperature and told Edna she could get in. Hesitantly, because of the open door, Edna took off her robe and nightie and inched into the water. Once submerged, she discovered there was no soap.

"I suppose they're afraid I'd eat it," she said, liking the echo the big room threw back at her. She sloshed back and forth, making a great wave of water splash over the end of the tub to puddle on the patterned white and black ceramic floor. The waves she made inspired her.

Dipping her long forefinger into the warm water, she brought it to her forehead. "I have no soap, but I'll be damned if I'll let all this good water go to waste. Edna Carver, Lady Edna, I hereby baptize you in the name of the little bit of wisdom that's left in these old eyes and hands." She began to relax, and soon she was humming, then singing, "Show me that river, take me across, wash all my troubles away . . . ." She stopped to search for the place where she last heard the song. "Of course," she said. "Wally led us, last night, at The Biffy." The moment in the pub when she'd acknowledged the strength of other people returned. "Perhaps their strength doesn't diminish mine after all," she whispered. As soon as she spoke, she felt the beautiful room welcome her.

Edna looked up where the window framed tree branches ablaze with early evening sun and, beyond them, the sky where the moon would rise. "You old trickster," she muttered, "sneaking around in the dark. Driving us crazy with your games of hide and seek. Well, I'm not nuts yet," she said defiantly, closing her eyes and conjuring. "Yes," she said after a long while. "I can see a thing or two even when it's black as pitch." Feeling as clear and calm as her bath water, she pulled the plug and, reborn, stepped into a fresh new world.

At five, Edna awoke with a start to discover a nurse roughly taking her pulse. "Mrs. Carter," the woman said briskly. "It's time to get up."

"It's Carver," Edna corrected sleepily. "But you may call me Edna. There is no need to be so formal." She found her robe, pulled on her slippers, and then dangled her legs over the side of the bed, waiting for the fuzzy haze to lift. Gradually Mary, inert in the next bed, became familiar. Edna patted the urn, warm from sharing her bed, and stepped to the floor.

"May I wash?" she asked.

The nurse shook Mary impatiently. "I can't help right now," she told Edna over her shoulder, "and the aides are setting up the dining room for breakfast."

"Oh, that's all right," Edna said. "I can manage on my own." She shuffled into the hallway with her bag of toiletries feeling a little like a world traveler suffering from jet lag. The sharp smell of ammonia assaulted her nostrils and the first cries of stiff, bedridden patients rang in her ears. She walked quickly to the bathroom.

When she finished her morning routine, she entered the room she'd passed with Mary the day before. Edna leaned against the bed railings, pleased to see open eyes. "I'm Edna," she said, smiling.

A nurse rushed in. "Get out of here. If I catch you bothering anyone, I'll have you strapped to your bed."

"I was just introducing myself," Edna said calmly. "After all, we're neighbours and should at least know one another's names." When the nurse stared at her, Edna guessed she was assessing how crazy she was.

"You're the new one," the nurse said at last. "What's your name again?"

"Edna Carver. They think I'm crazy, and while I'll admit to being difficult, I'm still in my right mind, at least most of the time." She smiled at the nurse. "Maybe I could do something constructive for you. I give a great back rub," she said, indicating that she might perform this service for the woman in the bed.

"Thanks for the offer, Edna. But that's my job." Edna could feel her soften a little. "Maybe you can help Mrs. Stuart get organized. She's slow this morning after that chocolate binge last night."

Edna nodded, returning to her room feeling she'd made a small but significant connection. Mary was sitting on her bed when she returned, combing out her fine brown hair. When she saw Edna she stuck out a fat, bare foot. "Lady Edna can kiss our big toe," she said.

"Like ducks I will," answered Edna. "You can kiss my arse."

Mary laughed as she created a pony tail on top of her head, twisted it into a thin ringlet, and then wound it into the tight little doughnut that served as her nest for pills.

"Do we have to stay in our night things?" Edna asked, peering into her closet for something bright.

"Why bother to get dressed?"

"It's no bother," Edna insisted. "I'm going to wear something pretty today. It's my first. I want to make a good impression."

"Don't be surprised if no one notices."

Edna dressed, furtively pulling up underpants and panty hose beneath her nightie so that Mary wouldn't feel excluded by her drawn curtain. Her bra was a little more difficult to manage, but she finally got it into place by pulling her arms inside her night dress and working blind beneath the makeshift tent. After she wiggled into one of her more elaborately tatted slips, she threw her night things on the bed, not minding who saw her now. She decided on the white jersey with its navy and red flowers.

Seeing Edna's transformation, Mary thought better of remaining in her night clothes. She couldn't have her First Royal Advisor looking better than the Monarch and selected a fuchsia caftan. Not bothering with underwear, Mary wriggled the stretchy material over her ample body and thrilled to see its revelations as it tightened over her breasts and buttocks. Edna tried not to stare at the nipples poking out like thimbles but found them too wonderful to ignore, especially when Mary moved.

"Do we go down for breakfast now?"

Mary huffed and puffed as she pulled on gold lamé, Cuban heeled slippers. "Of course not," she answered. "It's only a little after six."

"Why do they get us up so early?"

"By the time they rouse those that need help and get them ready, it will be eight-thirty." She went to her locker. "We usually use the time to check our resources and plan our day."

Edna understood Mary was talking about food. She slipped out of the room, leaving Mary to fondle supplies and revise her list.

Down the hall, she found the woman she'd spoken to earlier lying on her side, her raw back and buttocks exposed. Edna hadn't planned to re-enter the room, but seeing the scalded red flesh changed her mind. The nurse was nowhere in sight.

"Those sores look so painful," she said kindly. "We need to find you some zinc oxide." The woman howled softly into her pillow.

Just then, the nurse returned, furious to discover Edna in the room again. She'd forgotten to pull the woman's curtain in her rush to bathe her and was not at all pleased to find Edna inspecting the woman's bed sores. "Please leave," she said, forgetting their earlier cordiality.

"These look so sore," Edna said sympathetically. "She must be in terrible pain."

"Oh, no," said the nurse, drawing the curtain out from the wall. "She's senile. She doesn't feel at thing."

"What?"

"It's true," the nurse said, impatiently shooing Edna from the room. "That's why they get as bad as this. They don't feel anything, so they don't complain."

Edna stared at the young woman in disbelief. "I don't know about any of the others," she said, "but this person doesn't complain because she can't. Listen to her. That is the sound of pain."

"Please leave," the nurse repeated. Edna noticed her tone had changed, as though the young woman clarified the sort of person she was dealing with.

"Are you going to put something on that?" Edna persisted. "Zinc oxide helps."

Without another word the nurse pressed a button that brought one of the green-suited aides on the run. "Take her back to Ward D. Strap her in if necessary."

Edna frowned at the woman but walked back to her room without further complaint, at the doorway throwing off the aide's arm. Once seated in the chair by the window, she lifted the blind to peek at the garden, all the while mulling over her encounter with the nurse. "This place," she muttered, "is a torture chamber disguised by an exquisite floral façade."

Seated at the table she shared with Mary the night before, Edna discovered Myrtle Jenkins, her baseball cap askew, in an obvious stupor. Mr. Barren was wearing a corset over his blue and white striped pajamas and matching robe although it was so large it was in danger of sliding to the floor each time he moved. When Mrs. Strowd joined the group Edna nodded and smiled, but the woman stared through her with blank, flat eyes.

Breakfast consisted of artificial orange juice, instant oatmeal, and cold white toast saturated with margarine. Edna suspected that the cook from the lodge was doing double duty but she was so hungry she ate every bite. Mary, saddened by Edna's hearty appetite, looked covetously at the full plates all around her.

"Today is Saturday," Edna said, finishing her toast. "Last Saturday Lizzie and I walked to our neighbourhood mall to steal some sherry. We often went downtown as well. Have you been to the Eaton Centre? We stole some lovely things from there." Mary leaned closer, fascinated. "We were the salespeople's favourite shoppers because they could pretend we were invisible." She interrupted her story to thank a nurse for her morning pill, making an elaborate display of taking it before tucking it discreetly into her satin purse during a fake brassiere adjustment.

After breakfast, aides herded the ambulatory patients into the small elevator to visit the first-floor sunroom. Mrs. Strowd, still wearing Mr. Barren's teeth, stood next to Edna during the journey. Edna hoped the woman would resist devouring a piece of her upper arm.

The sunroom was bright and inviting with its hanging plants, comfortable chairs, and ancient upright piano. Edna ran her hands along the keys. As the sound died away, a very old woman appeared in the doorway and told Edna to stop making a racket. Edna thumbed her nose at her as she comfortably plumped into one of three basket chairs. Disappointed in Edna's lack of fighting spirit, the old woman disappeared.

With deep satisfaction, Edna breathed in the aroma of warm foliage. Sunlight streamed through the glass, dazzling her eyes and warming the top of her head until it nodded forward. Catching herself before she nodded off, she stood to amble around the room in hopes of shaking off the room's narcotic effects.

The old lady returned to watch her from the doorway. "You damn crazies," she muttered just loud enough for Edna to hear. "They just bring you down here so they can hose down your rooms. Everybody knows you nuts on three make messes everywhere you go."

Edna immediately sensed the hierarchical nature of Tranquil Time and decided to have some fun. "Big Bats," she corrected the woman graciously. "If you intend to have an intelligent discussion with me, please use the correct nomenclature." She took another turn about the room.

Furious, the woman banged her cane on the floor and cried, "I'll call you what I feel like calling you. Crazies. Ding-bats. Cuckoos. I don't know why they bring you down here. They should lock you in broom closets and throw away the keys."

"How unenlightened of you," Edna answered, tossing the woman a sympathetic smile.

The old lady's face turned a deep pink. "I'm the oldest in here, and the smartest," she sputtered. "Don't contradict me."

Edna's smile broadened. "What on earth is the matter with you?" she asked earnestly. "Didn't your mother love you?"

The old woman's eyes flashed fire. "How dare you speak to me about my mother?   She was a saint and I was her darling."

"How unfortunate for her," Edna said, her calm growing in direct proportion to the other's agitation. The old woman whacked the heavy wooden cane supporting her small weight against the door frame before shuffling down the hall shrieking. "Get these crazies out of here," Edna heard her shout. "You have no business bringing crazies down to my floor."

Edna looked to her companions for a response to her performance. Even Mary ignored the old woman's tirade and at least pretended to be preoccupied with the banana she found on top of the piano.

Just then, a tall heavy nurse bounded into the room. Her face only vaguely familiar, it took Edna a few moments to arrange the woman's features into that of the admitting nurse of the evening before.

"Who has been upsetting Miss George?" she demanded. "I won't have Miss George upset. If you can't be civil, we won't invite you down to enjoy this lovely sunroom. Remember. This is a privilege, not a right."

Edna turned away so the nurse would not see her smirk, but the old woman joined the head nurse and pointed at her accusingly. The nurse marched over to confront Edna. Edna, understanding this game, turned an expressionless face to the nurse.

"You're the new one from Sunset Lodge. We have a few rules around here and the first is that if you can't be civil, you shouldn't say anything at all."

Edna continued to stare at her, careful to keep her expression neutral. The nurse frowned and turned to Miss George. "You know you shouldn't come down here when they're using it."

"But it's *my* sunroom. These crazies shouldn't be allowed down here."

"Come on, Auntie," the nurse soothed. "We'll have a game of gin till they go. I got a nice letter from Cousin Bill I'll read to you."

Edna watched as the head nurse led the old woman down the hall. She tapped Mary's knee. "Is she the head cheese?"

The reference to food made Mary garrulous. "The cheesiest is the doctor, the second cheesiest is the director. That one's the third cheesiest, but she's the one who really counts. Mess with her and we've had it. She's the one who gives the orders about what's to be done with us. We think she'd like us dead but knows the government would stop the subsidies if she killed us off. We hope they take us up soon. We're starved."

Edna etched the head nurse's features into her imagination: little hazel eyes too close together in a round face framed by short, serviceably cut salt-and-pepper hair. She looked to be about fifty, Marion's age, but Edna knew chronological reality sometimes differed from external signs. She decided then and there that this woman would be the subject of her first portrait. She laughed as she compared the head nurse's face with the image taking shape in her mind's eye and hoped that Marion would remember her paints when she visited on Sunday. She looked about the room and then went to the piano. "Does anyone play?" she asked, lightly touching the keys.

Everyone except Mary stared at her languidly.

"The piano," she encouraged, patting the bench. "Does anyone play?"

Mr. Barren smoothed his corset and adjusted his empty cups. "Mrs. Strowd has been known to tinkle the ivories," he said with great dignity.

Edna turned timidly to the woman wearing Mr. Barren's teeth and smiled into the distorted features. "I love music," she said. "Would you do me the honour of playing?"

All at once, as if Edna were the conductor at Roy Thomson Hall, Mrs. Strowd rose gracefully and walked to the piano. After she sat and adjusted the bench, she closed her eyes and then allowed her fingers to rove sensually over the keys. Edna stared at her grotesque profile. All at once, her eyes still closed, Mrs.

Strowd began to play the familiar opening notes of the "Moonlight Sonata."

Silently, the hall beyond the sunroom began to fill with people responding to the exquisite music. Edna saw how the delicate vibrations wrapped themselves around the listeners, soothing pain and worries and filling the terrible emptiness created by boredom with indestructible beauty. The slack was gone from the lined old faces and while what replaced it might not be joy or happiness, Edna thought it just might be contentment. She sighed deeply.

"What if we had a fire?" a shrill voice cried. "Get back to your rooms. I won't have the hall blocked like this." The head nurse bullied the listeners back to their rooms.

Edna leaned over to whisper in Mary's ear. "Just listen to that," she said, gesturing to Mrs. Strowd. The toothy old woman continued to play, unaware of her dwindling audience. "Did you see the others in the hall?"

"Oh, them," Mary said, dismissing Edna's optimism. "Everybody likes a good toe-tapper. But we're surprised at Mrs. Strowd. We didn't know she could play."

"You mean she doesn't do this regularly?"

"Not that we know of," Mary said. Her stomach rumbled ominously. "Her main interest has been teeth."

An aide came into the room. "Up we go," she said pleasantly. She turned to Mrs. Strowd. "You're very good," she said, smiling. "I didn't know you could play."

Mrs. Strowd stopped playing to stare into the aide's face. The aide guided her from the piano and stationed her at the doorway before returning to the sunroom to help those third-floor visitors who were less steady on their feet.

Edna held out her arm for Mr. Barren. The aide nodded gratefully. "What's up now?" Edna asked her.

"Not much till lunch. Then naps, then snacks, then supper."

"Gee," Edna exclaimed, laughing. "I don't know if my heart can stand all this excitement."

FIVE

In the shadows adjacent to the sunlight's glare, Diana Mallory watched and listened to Edna as she moved around the airy sunroom. The reporter slipped in through the big front door at the same time that Edna's group dribbled into the bright room and, seeing Edna, decided not to follow orders and check in with the head nurse. Instead, she walked quickly to the deep hall shadows, leaned against the wall, and fought the revulsion that made her want to run away from the stench and the torpid people glimpsed in rooms she passed on her way to invisibility.

The previous afternoon, after her interview with the doctor, Diana packed and left the lodge, anxious to begin her article. Unsettling facts gleaned from an interview with her personal physician and a quick study of a pharmaceutical compendium quickened her concern for Edna Carver's well being. She'd come to Tranquil Time to warn Edna.

Studying the older woman as she waited for her opportunity to speak to Edna alone, Diana was shocked when the nursing home's deadened atmosphere carried Beethoven to her ears. She was more shocked when seemingly lifeless spectres from the first-floor rooms responded to the music, shuffling closer and closer to its source. From her place in the shadows, she observed the group until the head nurse stormed from her office to berate the listeners and herd them back into their rooms. The reporter waited until the hall was clear before she navigated the dim hallway to the head nurse's office.

Mrs. O'Shea, momentarily startled by Diana's sudden, silent entry, greeted the young woman with an adversarial, "Yes?"

"I'm a friend of Edna Carver's. I'll be visiting her this morning."

"Edna Carver," Mrs. O'Shea repeated, trying to place the name. "Oh, yes," she said. "The new one. She's in the sunroom now. She'll be going up to her room in a moment if you'd like to wait until she's settled in."

"No, thank you. I'll see her now," Diana said, staring at the woman, wanting to intimidate her on Edna's behalf. She understood her efforts had no effect when the woman abruptly returned to her paperwork.

The reporter arrived at the sunroom just as the aide organized the group to return to the third floor. Silently, she slipped into their midst and nodded to Edna as if she belonged to the group.

"How was breakfast?" she asked, smiling.

"I've had better," Edna said, returning her smile.

"I'll bet." Both women laughed.

When the elevator shunted into position on three, Edna accompanied Mr. Barren to his room before walking Diana down the hall to her own small space in the dirty, reeking house. After she'd determined unequivocally that Edna's guest had come empty handed, Mary set off to scrounge for food in the north-wing ward. Edna insisted Diana sit in their one chair and perched at the end of her bed for their conversation.

"This place is dreadful," Diana said.

"What are you going to do about it?" Edna wanted to know.

"I'm not sure yet. How about you?"

"I've already asked Marion to bring me my paints. Poor darling. She wanted to move me someplace 'nice,' in Forest Hill I think. She thinks I'll be happy in a clean room with a television." The women laughed easily together.

Edna daubed at her eyes. "What brings you here? I thought you'd be sampling the cook's fare for another couple of days."

Diana sensed the change in Edna and trusted her impulse to tell her the truth. "I interviewed the lodge doctor yesterday," she said. "Did you know that he owns this place as well as Sunset Lodge?"

"Yes," Edna answered. "I discovered that unpleasant fact last night, when he examined me. We're intimates now." She telegraphed her revulsion with a shiver of disgust.

Diana looked around the room, her eyes coming to rest on the brass urn. "I'm so sorry about Mrs. Schmidt," she said.

"Don't be," Edna said. "I couldn't stand the thought of her in a place like this."

"But it's all right for you?" Diana asked quietly.

"Some people need pain for life to quicken in them – not that splashy kind I hit you with when we first met, but a quiet, tenacious inner life that gives no outward sign."

Diana leaned closer. "Did the doctor give you any medication?"

"No," Edna answered. "He leaves that dirty work for the nurses. My roommate saved me from the worst of it. Why?"

"I can't tell you much just now. Nothing's been confirmed," Diana said. "But things could be far more serious here and at the lodge than you suspected."

"Don't you worry about me," Edna said. "I've no intention of becoming one of the dollies." Diana smiled thinly at Edna's description of her over-medicated peers. "See?" Edna took a pill from her hidden satin purse. "My new roommate taught me how to take care of myself."

Diana stood excitedly. "May I take that with me?"

"By all means, have it. I was going to flush it down the toilet."

The reporter wrapped the pill in a tissue before tucking it into an inside pocket of her bag. "I doubt my having this analyzed will have a tranquilizing effect on Bernice Wilson," she said, squeezing Edna's hands. "I've got to run. Promise you won't underestimate them here."

Edna waved her off. "Not to worry. I'll be all right. Thanks for coming, Diana," she said. "I'm counting on our keeping in touch."

As she lay on her bed waiting for lunch, Edna did her best to figure out the floor plan of the two lower floors. The house, she knew, had been built on a centre-hall plan, and given this fact reasoned that the stairwell must be opposite the dining area, behind one of the unmarked doors she'd seen the night before. On her floor, there were two identical wings, one on either side of the dining area. Her wing had three single rooms with baths, the large bathroom where she'd created her small oasis of peace, and the room she shared with Mary – a room designated a four bed ward but that currently housed the two of them. She speculated that the far wing would have a similar layout.

When Mary returned from her hunting and gathering expedition, Edna sat up to quiz her. "Is the second floor just like this one?"

"Good God, no!" cried Mary. "The second floor is all ward. They're too poor to afford private rooms, like the ones down our hall, or the semi-privates, so they're lumped together. You should have heard them howl on bath nights when they used to hose them down."

Edna lay back and closed her eyes. "The first floor is the best," Mary went on. "It's for people who have lots of money. They all have private rooms down there and some of them think their you-know-what doesn't stink. That's where the staff put their relatives. They have nice rooms and hot food."

"So all the daughters aren't bad," Edna said.

"We suppose not," Mary answered, wistful.

"How many of us are there on the first floor?"

"Just ten. Five in each wing. And they have the sunroom."

"It's lovely," Edna said. "I wish we had one of our own."

"At least we get to go down there. The second-floor sheep hardly ever get down to it."

"How many people on the second floor?"

"Sometimes as many as twenty. They're supposed to only have four beds per ward, but we've seen them stuff five and six beds into a room when too many resist dying and have to be *cared for.*"

Edna did her best to absorb this new information. "Doesn't anyone ever complain about the filth, or the food, or the understaffing?"

For a moment Mary looked as though she doubted Edna's sanity. "Who would they complain to? If we get put on the second floor, everything's against us. No money and nobody to check on us now and then. Besides, the second-floor sheep take their pills. The queen doesn't go down and tell them not to."

"Well, you should," Edna said.

"Lady Edna oversteps her bounds," Mary said. "The queen decides what she should do. Besides, they're happy," Mary added with a shrug. "The doctor gives them everything they want."

"Want?" Edna repeated.

"Sure. It is a lot easier to drift. Remember how hard Lady Edna had to fight the urge to drift yesterday? We bet she was tempted to take that pill this morning."

Edna acknowledged the accuracy of Mary's intuition with lilting eyebrows. "My daughter is bringing me my paints tomorrow. I am going to paint your portrait, you wise old thing."

Hearing this plan, Mary admitted Edna back into her good graces. "We'd like that. We'd also like a great big cockroach portrait to hang over our bed."

"I've never painted bugs," said Edna, but Mary ignored her in her excitement over the familiar sounds of lunch.

After finishing grilled cheese sandwiches that both women enjoyed despite the processed cheese, Mary and Edna discussed a few creative possibilities for the Jell-O dessert. During this amusement, a nurse approached them with their medication. "Something's up," Mary whispered as she studied her pill. "It's different." She pretended to pop it into her mouth and wash it down with cold, acrid tea.

Going through the same motions, Edna slipped the pill into her satin purse. Once she completed the charade, she walked very slowly to her room, wanting her jailors to believe the new pill worked well. To pass the time, she lay on her bed to reconstruct Tranquil Time's exterior in her mind's eye, even down to the detail of the ivy, both Boston and English, covering its red-brick walls. She chuckled as she recalled how, on the brick work of her own home, the more reserved English Ivy left spaces for the intrepid Boston to fill at spring's invitation.

The house's appearance, she mused, was such that a passerby could never suspect it no longer served a single family. And then it struck her. Tranquil Time's illusion reflected a larger truth. They were a single family.

Edna smiled an odd little 'ah, yes' smile. Fear of growing old built Sunset Lodge and Tranquil Time, and that same fear destroyed all sense of the residents' humanity by seeing aging as some kind of disease to be stamped out. And when aging could no longer be denied, the old had to be put away as painful reminders of the failure to stay young forever.

Theirs was a new story. Somehow, within a very short time, each person alive had and would become, if he or she lived long enough, an undeniable reminder of the passage of time and the fact of death. Edna straightened her spine and closed her eyes. Instead of seeing the miracle of this aging-and-death design as their ancestors had, some terrible distortion of modern mind and heart had re-invented old age as something shameful. And so it became an unlimited market for medical services.

Perhaps they were an unlimited market, but she knew they were much more as well. With utter humility Edna felt for the first time how the genius of aging made the residents a family, a strong, loving, and resourceful one heading for the inevitable next adventure together. It was only the modern fear and hatred of aging and death that destroyed their familial relationships. No, she thought, fear hadn't destroyed their connections to one another.

Fear and hatred assaulted them individually and collectively, it was true, but they remained connected. Despite everything, they had one another. She smiled with new faith.

The absence of noise in the hallway assured Edna she could explore without being bothered. With renewed vigour, she left her room in search of the stairway to the lower floors. Her imagined floor plan proved correct and she slipped down the stairs to the second floor without notice.

The second-floor hallway was darker than the hall on three, its dining room far more cramped and disheveled. Lunch trays had not been cleaned away and pudding bowls and greasy plates lay about on tables and chairs. She tiptoed to the first room on her right. There were five empty beds in a room smaller than the one she shared with Mary. Close to each bed sat a chair, and in each chair sat a person. All were utterly still with mouths agape, hair unwashed and uncombed, and blank eyes riveted on nothing at all.

Edna walked to the person nearest the door to put a gentle hand on the unmoving shoulder. The person mumbled. "Salvation Army?" Edna heard.

"Absolutely," answered Edna. "Might I bring you something?" The person did not respond.

Having verified Mary's description of the second floor, Edna returned to her own room. There she found her roommate lying on the floor, her legs at right angles to her torso and resting against the end of her bed. She was reading a Harlequin. Edna couldn't help but notice through Mary's flimsy shift that her massive, slack breasts were like great pseudopods, inching away from her bloated body, the nipples leading a charge in opposite directions. Mary acknowledged Edna with a nod. "This is great for the back," she said. "Come on down."

"This floor is filthy."

Mary laughed at Edna's squeamishness. "Been down to the second floor?"

"Yes. Doesn't anybody work down there?"

"The nurses from the third and first floors run through every now and then to make sure the sheep haven't choked on their own vomit, or if they have, to cart away the evidence. The aides tidy up when they can. Aren't we glad we're up here with the Queen of the Big Bats?"

Edna returned to her bed to think. From a great distance, she heard an unanswered buzzer persist in some far away hall. Calling and weeping subtly underscored the inhuman noise. She pressed her hands over her ears and stared at the drawn blind, thinking of Elizabeth's prescience when they sat under the moon sipping port. She had indeed begun to look upon sights more horrifying than she ever dared to imagine. She dozed until Mary's shining, quivering face suspended a few inches from her own startled her awake.

Edna thought she must be inhuman to eat her dinner, but eat she did, and with relish. She even asked for a second dessert and received it graciously, returning the aide's accompanying smile. She felt remarkably well, considering.

She received her pill from an unsmiling nurse who unnerved her when she stood sentry, waiting for her to take it. Edna put the pill into her mouth, pretending to swallow but pushing it into her cheek. Mary, Edna observed, did the same. When the nurse moved on to the next table, both women disposed of their pills into hands cupped discreetly over coughs. Mary tucked hers immediately into her bun. Edna decided her cleavage was the most efficient repository in this circumstance.

"It'll melt," Mary cautioned.

"I'll take it out as soon as we get back to our room." Edna stood, took her chair to the wall, and then wandered slowly down to their end of the dismal hall, flushing her pill down the toilet when she reached their elegant bathroom. Back in their room, she cast modesty and her clothes aside to pull on her nightie. The urn winked at her in the fading light and she lifted it from the floor to the bed, curled herself around it, and fell into a deep, trance-like sleep.

In a cream-coloured linen suit accented with a raspberry georgette blouse and soft, raspberry coloured, leather shoes and matching bag, Marion Andrews, her features tensed against the stench of Tranquil Time Nursing Home, walked down the dim, dark-green hallway to her mother's room. She carried a package of the best rag and a watercolour paint box in such a way as to leave her clothes uncompromised. Her high heels echoed sharply on the dull linoleum. A few feet from the door, she stopped to rearrange her frowning features into a pleasant smile.

When Marion entered, she found Edna sitting in the chair by the window, peering out through a lifted corner of the closed blind, lost in the myriad shades of green below.

"Mother," Marion exclaimed with forced cheerfulness. "I've brought your things."

Edna looked up absently. "Hello, Marion. Isn't this garden a sight?"

Marion delighted in her mother's appearance – Edna looked so trim and tidy dressed in one of her gifts, a yellow and red spring shirtwaist pretty even without the red sash. Her mother also neglected to wear the yellow and red pumps Marion had given her, a shame because they matched so perfectly. Smiling brightly, Marion set to work to improve her mother's appearance. "You've forgotten your sash and shoes, Mother," she said, putting the box and paper on Edna's bed before opening her bag with an elegant flick. "The man at Curry's said sable brushes are the very best. I've brought you six, of different sizes." She pulled out the brushes and placed them with the paint box. "I bought you an easel, too. It's down in the car."

"Let's go down and get it together," Edna said, anxious to begin her work.

A small furrow appeared on Marion's forehead just below her cap of blonde-tipped curls. "It's too awkward, Mother. I'll have one of the help bring it up for us."

"I won't make any friends if I ask them to do anything more than they're already doing," Edna said in what she hoped was a kindly voice. "We'll manage."

Marion sighed. "All right, Mother," she said, determined to avoid a scene. "Will they let you come down with me?"

Edna laughed. "I can go anywhere I like if I'm in the company of a responsible adult. What are you looking for?" she asked as Marion opened her locker.

"Your red sash, Mother, and your shoes. You'd look much smarter in the complete outfit."

Edna laughed again. "I used the sash for Lizzie's winding sheet. And the shoes hurt so I tossed them."

"Mother," Marion said plaintively. "You know we could have had them stretched."

Edna took her daughter's arm and led her down the hall to the stairway, determined to leave all references to Procrustes' Bed out of the conversation. "Did you come up this way?" Edna asked her as she opened the stairwell door.

Marion smiled her best insider's smile. "The head nurse unlocked the elevator for me."

Glad for the absence of staff on this occasion, Edna led her daughter down the stairs to the wards on the second floor. Marion looked with horror into the untended rooms. "Where are we, Mother?" her daughter asked, terrified by the stillness and neglect of the place.

The patients were sitting as Edna had found them the previous day, mouths agape, eyes open but unseeing, arms slack and resting on protruding bellies, hands palms up and resting on wasted legs. Most were in their nightclothes, but one very thin old man sat naked in his chair, a puddle of urine at his feet.

"Goodness," Edna said, walking to his locker to find a robe. "Here you are, old fellow," she said. "We don't want you catching cold." She helped the man to his feet and wrapped the robe around him before lowering him to his chair. He seemed unaware of what she was doing. When he looked comfortable and secure in his chair, she went to the bathroom for paper towels. Marion stood in the doorway, disgusted and frightened. Edna finished mopping up the urine and returned to the bathroom to dispose of the towels and wash her hands. Marion followed her.

"Mother," she whispered urgently. "You shouldn't be doing this. It's a nurse's job."

Edna soaped her hands vigorously. "Do you still go to church?" she asked.

"Yes, of course. We had a lovely service this morning."

"Aren't the ladies always looking for good works to do?"

"My goodness, we're always very busy. Just now we're in the midst of a bridge marathon, to raise money for the Primate's Fund."

Edna dried her hands, thoughtful. "These people are primates," she said quietly. "Why don't you bring a few of the ladies here to volunteer? I know the staff would be grateful for the help." She guided Marion to the hallway.

The younger woman looked this way and that, utterly confused by the environment and her mother's suggestion. "I think we've lost our way," she said nervously.

"We certainly have," said Edna. She walked to the stairway and began the descent to the first floor. Marion followed, giddy with relief.

Downstairs, Edna observed her daughter chatting easily with the nurses and well tended patients on the first floor. The feeling of absurdity she felt when Marion visited Sunset Lodge returned and she found it almost impossible to control her rage as her daughter transformed into an accomplished actress, delivering ingratiating lines and avoiding all authentic connection.

The head nurse smiled warmly at Marion before turning her administrator's charms on Edna. "Going for a little walk, are we?" she asked in a tone Edna knew all too well.

Edna surprised herself when she returned the nurse's professional smile with a genuine one. "We're going to get my easel," she said brightly. "I hope when it's convenient you'll let me paint you. You have very good features for a life study."

It was not an invitation the head nurse expected and she flushed with the unexpected pleasure of it. "I might be able to find the time. Perhaps we can set you up in my office while I'm tackling my administrative duties." She sighed dramatically. "They never end," she confided to Marion. "For someone in my position, the opportunities for actual nursing are very few indeed." Marion offered her most sympathetic smile.

Edna walked through the inner and outer front doors and inhaled deeply. "What a day," she said expansively. "God's in his heaven. All's right with the world!" She turned to Marion. "Look at that. Whoever built this place was another poetry lover." She pointed to the inscription carved in the stone arch.

Marion looked up. "There is No Joy but Calm!" she read. "What a nice thought," she said.

Edna laughed wickedly. "It's from the 'Lotus Eaters', Dear. You should read it some time, when you're not too busy with your bridge marathon for the Primate's Fund." She walked regally to Marion's car parked in the circular drive muttering, "Given what goes on in this place, the stone carver had to be clairvoyant."

Edna's new easel's legs protruded from the trunk of Marion's daffodil-yellow Buick. Along with the easel, Edna was pleased to discover a large piece of plywood and sturdy clamps. As Marion carefully descended the tricky tile steps on her high, delicate heels, Edna took both easel and board from the trunk and leaned them against the Buick's bumper. "You take the board," she said when Marion joined her. "I'll carry this." She slammed the trunk and hoisted the easel to her shoulder, its legs jutting out in front of her.

"Let me carry that," Marion said.

"Nonsense," said Edna. "You'll tear your suit. You take the board. It looks clean enough." Edna walked up the steps, propped the easel against the wall, and opened both beautiful glass doors.

Mrs. O'Shea looked up from her desk to play the grand hostess. "Mrs. Carver," she trilled, remembering the offer of a portrait. "Do take your things up in the elevator." Edna accepted the offered key with a delighted smile. She turned to discover Marion struggling with the large board and walked back to hold the door for her.

Once inside the elevator, Edna took the board from Marion and rested it against the easel. "Do you know how to open this contraption once it stops?" she asked.

"Yes, Mother," Marion answered, exhausted with the physical and emotional effort this visit required.

"You don't look at all well. This has been trying for you, I know," Edna said with real sympathy. "Why don't you ask Robert to take you out for supper?"

Marion revived a little. "Would you like to join us? Oh, Mother, let us take you to Truffles."

Recalling what she could of the technique of her craft, listing the stages necessary to produce a translucent fragment of the teeming, kaleidoscopic confusion of life all around her, Edna answered a completely different question. "I know you saturate the paper," she said. "But I bet I'm too rusty to wash without sketching. I'll have to find my lines again, and then apply the wash."

As soon as the elevator shunted into position on the third floor, Marion flicked the key and magically opened the doors. Edna marched off with the board and the easel leaving Marion to trail behind with the clamps. She set up the easel by the window quickly and placed the board on it.

"Mother," Marion said, revived by a sudden thought. "If you're determined to stay here, why don't you let me see if I can get you a room on the first floor? It's so much more cheerful down there.

You could have your own bathroom. I know you'd like that."

"I like the bathroom up here," Edna said, opening the package of rag. "Does Robert have any tools I could borrow?"

"He's a stockbroker, Mother. Why would he need tools? We hire people to do the kinds of jobs that require tools."

"I have to get Lizzie out of that damned urn. She wants to be scattered and I can't get the lid off."

"Mother!"

"What on earth is the matter, Marion?" Edna said, sensing she'd reached the limits of her goodwill for this particular visit.

Marion took a deep breath to regain her composure. "It's after four. I should be getting home."

"Yes," said Edna preoccupied with the colours in her paint box. "You run along now. It was very good of you to bring these things." Edna put her paints down and hugged Marion with real feeling. "You are a dear girl."

Overwhelmed by her mother's unexpected gratitude, Marion returned Edna's embrace. "I . . . know we sometimes have trouble communicating," she said. "But you do know I love you, don't you?"

There was something so pathetically childlike in her daughter's voice and eyes that Edna found herself moved to stroke her cheek. "Yes, yes. And I love you. But you're still a pain in the arse."

Marion smiled a sweet, tentative smile. "Well, I don't mean to be."

Edna kissed her. "No, you don't. And I don't mean to be such a thorn in your side, either. Perhaps it's not too late for us to come to some sort of understanding."

Marion nodded. "I'd like that," she said, checking her watch. "I really should go. Robert will expect me." Before Marion reached the doorway, Edna was busily cataloguing her new supplies.

"What's all this?" asked Mary Stuart on her return from a satisfying raid on the first floor. She was laden down with parcels of all shapes which she dumped enthusiastically on her bed. Edna was preoccupied with the sketch she'd begun.

"I was just thinking about that old polemic, Mary. Which does come first? The chicken or the egg?"

"We don't have either here," Mary answered. "But if we come to the kitchen tonight, we'll cook Lady Edna an omelet."

Edna laughed at Mary's single-mindedness. "The chicken or the egg?" she asked again. "God! I'm absolutely famished," she exclaimed.

Mary gyrated over to inspect Edna more closely. "We sound more Big Bats than usual."

Edna laughed again. "I've heard that chance favours the prepared mind," she muttered. "Tonight, I feel like my whole life has been one long preparation." She inclined her head to one side. "It never occurred to me that it added up to something whole. I used to think it was just a series of disconnected, random events that I endured or enjoyed. My perspective changed entirely today, Mary." She wagged a beautiful finger in the air.

"We'd like the perspective of a chocolate Digestive Biscuit," Mary remarked, turning away from Edna's energetic face.

The aide's squeaking shoes heralded her appearance in the doorway. "Dinnertime," she said wearily. "Are you well enough to walk down or shall I bring a wheelchair?"

Mary trundled purposefully toward the dining room, and Edna followed eagerly at her heels.

"We'll have Lady Edna's stew," said Mary, finishing her own in record time and reaching for Edna's. "She's much too crazy to eat today."

"Nonsense," said Edna, defending her bowl with her fork. "This smells heavenly." She deftly took the paper cup from the nurse passing their table at a trot and deposited the pill in her satin purse while pretending to fumble with her bra. When she returned to her stew, Mary watched her every mouthful with tragic eyes.

"Best food I've ever tasted," Edna enthused. "What's for dessert?"

"We don't know," Mary said. "But we wouldn't be surprised if it spoiled Lady Edna's girlish figure."

Edna curled her upper lip. "I think if I was going to lose it, I would have done so by now. It's very sweet of you to worry about me, but it's your girlish figure we're going to concentrate on now." Mary fidgeted in her chair. "Say," Edna said, remembering something she needed to clarify. "Those people you introduced me to Friday night seemed almost chipper. What's the matter with them today? They're all about as active as dead fish."

"Mary's eyes slid away from Edna's bowl to study their companions. "Oh," she said wisely. "It's the new stuff they're giving us. They've upped the dose. We'll have to watch our step."

"Yes," Edna agreed, remembering Diana's warning. She sopped up the stew gravy remaining in her bowl with a little of her bread ration and absently held the morsel dangerously close to Mary's mouth.

"We wonder why they've changed it," Mary said. "Aren't we going to eat our crusts?"

Edna offered Mary her remaining bread. "Maybe they thought we were too alert before?" Edna suggested. "Do you ever talk to the others about not taking it?"

"Look at them," Mary said through a mouthful of dough. "Could Lady Edna talk to them about anything?"

Edna surveyed her fellow diners. Mr. Barren, toothless and wearing what had to be Mary's bra over an unbuttoned shirt, sat stirring his stew as he hummed softly. Myrtle Jenkins slept, her head resting on her knees, her arms dangling to the floor. Mrs. Strowd sat rigidly in her chair, Mr. Barren's teeth in her mouth, her untouched dinner before her on the greasy table. They were the only other diners this evening.

"What about the others?" Edna asked.

"Probably in their beds."

"Don't they eat?"

"It looks like they won't be able to tell whether they've eaten or not," said Mary. An aide, a woman Edna hadn't seen before, filled her tea cup while studiously ignoring Mary's obsequious smile. She sloshed tea on the table as she moved the tea pot from one cup to the other. Edna observed her closely, wondering if perhaps the doctor had begun to medicate his staff as well.

"I wish I could do something for the others," she told Mary. Mary laughed at this impulse but Edna was not discouraged. "Did you ever try to persuade the others?"

"Every time we get a new roommate, we try. Lady Edna is the first who had any real fight. Old Shirley-Temple dollies, every one of them."

Edna leaned over their small table to whisper conspiratorially. "How do you manage to wake yourself for your kitchen raids?"

"We've always been a light sleeper," Mary answered, looking

around anxiously for signs of dessert. "Oh," she cried with relief. "Here it comes." She looked the picture of bliss when lemon tarts appeared.

"You know," Edna said, watching her carefully. "You're playing a dangerous game with your body. There are other ways to be immovable. I can help you find them."

Mary's placid features contorted into a sneer. "Who says we want help? Don't meddle, Lady Edna," she growled. "We can be as crazy as anybody, crazier, in fact. Just ask our daughter."

Edna dismissed her threat with a backhand wave. "Well, you'll thank me when the hot weather comes and you're slimmer. I imagine you must get horrible rashes under your . . . bosoms. You'll find life much easier when you shed a few pounds."

"We aren't shedding anything!" Mary cried ferociously. She snatched Edna's lemon tart out from under her nose and popped it into her mouth. Untroubled, Edna sipped lukewarm tea and thought about what she would do when she returned to her easel.

After supper, Edna set to work. "Will it bother you if I work on this sketch? I won't have to work this way after I get my feel for it again, but I'm rusty now."

"Draw a large chocolate cake for me."

"Absolutely not," said Edna. "I'm not working at cross purposes again."

Mary propped herself up to watch as Edna concentrated on the circular seed pods that made up her composition of Moonwort. "There," she said, after a time. She stepped back from the easel to assess her drawing before tilting it so that Mary could receive the full effect. "Not bad for an untalented old lady," she said. "What do you think?"

Mary had been hoping that Edna was drawing something succulent. "What is that supposed to be?" she asked. "Those don't look like they'd taste good at all."

"Moonwort," Edna said, smiling and thinking of Lizzie. She moved back to the easel and set to work again.

Disgusted, Mary cried, "Moon warts! No wonder Lady Edna wasn't squeamish about our bugs. She keeps far worse company than we."

When a nurse came by Edna had completed her first translucent wash and was contemplating the subtle seeds beneath the satin finish. "Bedtime?" she asked the nurse absently.

"Get undressed," the woman snapped. "I'll be back to take you to the bathroom in a few minutes."

As early as it was, Edna was anxious to get into bed. "Promise to wake me when you get up to get your snack," she told Mary as she changed into her nightie. "I want to work on this a little more."

"In the middle of the night? They'll see the light on. They'll see we're gone. No," said Mary definitely. "Lady Edna will have to draw the moon's warts during the day."

Edna muttered curses. "Why are they so attentive at night when they're so rarely around during the day? Can't a body have any privacy at all?"

Mary pulled off her fuchsia caftan to proudly expose her naked body. She grinned, held her arms like airplane wings, shimmied, and took a step toward Edna, every bit of her flesh in motion. "We hope to hit five hundred pounds before we die."

Edna no longer pretended to be taken in by Mary's apparent joy in her fat. She shook her head firmly. "No, Mary, no five hundred pounds for you. You know perfectly well you are a size fourteen."

Mary glided to her cupboard for her nightie. "We are the queen. We decide what size we are." She pulled out a sheer, pale blue sleeveless baby doll nightie and wiggled into it.

"You might as well not wear anything," Edna said. "Where is your modesty?"

"Why should we be modest?" Mary asked. "We worked hard to get to this size. We're not going to be shy about showing it off."

Edna closed her eyes and lay back on her pillow until she remembered she'd put Lizzie at the bottom of her locker for safe keeping before supper. She carried the urn to the window sill, raised the blind a bit, and then got into bed to wait for the nurse who would oversee her evening bath.

The head nurse was surprised to see Edna the next day with her board, clamps, and paper. Still, she enthusiastically fluffed her hair and straightened her collar when the artist reminded her that she would paint her portrait. Hearing Edna's voice, Miss George came to investigate.

"What's she doing here?" she demanded.

"Oh, Auntie, hasn't the Metamucil worked yet?"

"I hate that stuff. I want an enema."

Mrs. O'Shea held firm. "It's important your bowels learn to work on their own."

"My bowels are tired of working on their own." Miss George came into the office and leaned heavily on her cane. "They want an enema to do the work for them," she said, inching to the largest, most comfortable chair. "And I want a game of fish."

Mrs. O'Shea rustled papers. "I have a lot of work to do this morning, Auntie."

Miss George eyed Edna's equipment suspiciously and then resumed her assault. "You don't like me. You've never liked me."

"Now, Auntie," her niece answered patronizingly. "If I didn't love you, would I give you the very best room in the place?"

The old woman sniffed, unconvinced. "Why should I leave my money to someone who doesn't even like me? I'm going to call my lawyer and change my will."

"Maybe one game," Mrs. O'Shea said, doing her best to ignore Edna as she leaned over the desk to study her face.

"Get that crazy old bat out of here," said Miss George.

Mrs. O'Shea shook her head. "She's here to do my portrait. If it's any good, I'll hang it out there in the hallway so people will have something nice to look at when they come in. Did you meet her daughter yesterday? She's such a lovely woman, really lovely." The head nurse retrieved a tired pack of playing cards from her top drawer and dealt two hands before spreading the remainder of the deck in an irregular circle on top of her desk blotter.

As the women played, Edna began her sketch of the head nurse's face with feathery strokes, forming an oval before adding the centre line and the two horizontals where Mrs. O'Shea's eyes and mouth would eventually emerge.

Miss George soon forgot Edna in her gloating over card triumphs and gossip with her niece. "Is he coming today?"

"I should think so. He always does."

"Well, keep him away from me. I'm sick of the way he's always pushing those damn pills."

"You don't need to worry. I keep the charts."

"I don't trust him," Miss George said, putting her cards on her lap before grouping them according to suit.

Mrs. O'Shea delighted in this opportunity to grumble. "It's that other one that gives me a pain. Calling me up and ordering me about like she's my boss. I remember when they brought her in here, back when we were a convalescent home, even if she doesn't." She took an open box of After Eights from her desk drawer and began to eat the mints compulsively.

"Give me one of those," Miss George demanded.

"You know you shouldn't eat chocolate."

"Give me one," the old woman whined.

The head nurse pushed the box across the desk after taking several wafers and arranging them in a neat little pile next to her cards.

Miss George gobbled up mint after mint as she rambled on. "I don't know why you ever wanted to work at that lodge, anyway. You're a nurse. They don't need nurses over there."

"*She* certainly isn't a nurse," Mrs. O'Shea said. "I'd be surprised if she even got through high school. After her mother died, she had to take care of her father." She lowered her voice and leaned toward her aunt. "The ambulance driver told me that the moment after he died and she'd called the ambulance, she made funeral arrangements for two people and then did her level best to cut off her head."

Mrs. O'Shea glared at Edna when she paused in her sketching. Edna resumed her work, drawing a wide, generous mouth where the head nurse's tight, embittered one should have been. She widened the narrow space between the hazel eyes to soften them and create a compassionate expression.

Mrs. O'Shea returned to Miss George, satisfied that Edna was minding her own business. "The ambulance driver's timing was amazing," she muttered as she took another mint from its envelope. "That's when the doctor got involved. If it happened now, I'm sure he'd let her bleed to death, but in those days he was young and just had to show off his anatomical knowledge. He had the attendant continue to block her carotid artery while he scrubbed. She should be a vegetable. Lord knows she often acts like her brain doesn't get enough oxygen." She crumpled one of the small brow envelopes thoughtfully. "I liked the doctor until he brought her here to convalesce. I always thought we might get together but there was his wife and children to contend with. Still, he was awfully handsome in those days," she said, wistful. "He hasn't changed much over the years."

"I don't see it," Miss George said with disgust. "He's a pervert if you ask me. Aren't you going to play?"

Mrs. O'Shea looked at her cards indifferently. "Give me all your queens," she said.

This sent her aunt into a rage. "You're cheating!" she cried. "You must be cheating." She threw her cards on the desk. "I had three of them. You've marked these cards."

"Take my queen," her niece said quickly. "You probably meant to ask for my queens your last turn."

"Don't tell me what I meant to do," the old woman shrieked. She got to her feet by pushing down with all her strength on her cane. "I'm glad he gave her that job. You don't deserve nice things. You're a cheater. My sister was a cheater, too, and you're just like her." Muttering savagely, Miss George wobbled from the room.

Edna rustled her paper to fill the awkward silence before putting the finishing touches on the nurse's pert little collar and nurse's pin. Their conversation troubled her, and she longed for the quiet of her room where she might reflect on what she'd heard. She coughed to break the spell of Mrs. O'Shea's internally gyrating grievances against her aunt. Startled, the head nurse looked up.

"My goodness," she exclaimed, staring at Edna's sketch.

"I know," Edna said "I'm very rusty. I have no idea if I can still handle the colour."

Mrs. O'Shea continued to study Edna's sketch. "You know," she said after a time. "It takes me back years, as if you knew me when I was young and had my whole life before me."

"I'll get upstairs to begin the washes," Edna said. "I don't think I'll need to have you sit again, but perhaps if this one doesn't turn out, or if you'd like another, you might allow me to come down again. It's so challenging to draw in my room because of the closed blinds." Mrs. O'Shea gave her a questioning look. "To preserve the linen," she added.

"I wonder whose rule that is," the head nurse remarked as Edna moved to the door. "You come down here any time, Mrs. Carver," she said. "This really is an extraordinary piece of work." She recalled the good looking daughter. "How would you like to set up your easel in the sunroom permanently? We could use a little civilized company down here."

"I wouldn't want to be in anyone's way," Edna answered, smiling.

As Mrs. O'Shea returned her smile, Edna marveled when the head nurse's features took on the softer lines of the image she'd created. "You won't be a bother at all, Mrs. Carver. Come down anytime you like."

Edna thanked her and packed up her things. "Wait," Mrs. O'Shea said in afterthought. "You might as well have this if you're going to be up and down." She took a small key from her middle drawer. "I'll show you how to work the elevator. It isn't difficult, but mind you don't lose the key. If you have your own, I won't have to get someone to unlock the elevator for you when you travel up and down."

"I'll be very careful not to lose it," Edna replied.

She walked with Mrs. O'Shea to the elevator, listened intently to the woman's instructions on how to operate it, and disappeared into the tiny box feeling like an incarnation of Merlin.

When Edna arrived at the third floor, the nurses were shocked to see her get off the elevator alone. She smiled and held up the key. "Mrs. O'Shea wants me to paint in the sunroom," she said. "I have to get up and down." Leaving them to hiss their disapproval over their carts and charts, Edna walked to her room savouring the taste of her first small victory.

Mary was in her bed rather than on it, lamenting that some tidbit she'd pinched from the kitchen the night before disagreed with her. Edna put the drawing of Mrs. O'Shea on her own bed before turning to her roommate.

"I think from your colour you need me more than Mrs. O'Shea. Would you like to be upright or reclining?" When Mary could only groan a response, Edna gave her a little direction. "We had a very swish Edwardian chaise longue when I was younger. I covered it with an interesting Victorian tapestry when it came to live with me. The pattern might prove a challenge to reproduce from memory, but I can probably create a reasonable facsimile. I'll drape you over that." Taking Mary's silence for consent, Edna set out a fresh piece of paper and positioned it on the easel before walking to her roommate's bed. Studying the soft, round features, she smiled.

"You feel dreadful now," Edna said lovingly, "but just you remember. This is the beginning of a new existence for you." Mary closed her eyes after giving Edna a look of furious disgust. Edna left her only after she heard the sounds of lunch being served. She hoped the food would give her enough energy to make a start on her second portrait.

Anxious to get back to her room, Edna ate her soup so quickly she wasn't sure if it had been chicken noodle or chicken with rice. Back in her room, she was glad to find one of the aides coaxing Mary with a small bowl of what turned out to be chicken with rice, canned of course, but hot and salty, just what Edna had needed to revive. Now Edna watched as Mary turned her face from the soup as sadly as an alcoholic on Antabuse turns from gin. She chuckled. Burgeoning with possibilities, she returned to her easel and supplies. "Move a little to the left, please," she said to the aide. "From this angle, you're blocking my view of her head." The aide turned to see what Edna was doing.

"Oh," she said, putting Mary's soup on the small metal bedside cupboard and peering over Edna's shoulder. "I had my kids done by a young girl at Yorkdale. She was really fast. She did both of them in just half an hour."

"I'm afraid I can no longer work that quickly," said Edna. "What did she use? Pastels?"

"Yes," said the aide. "They came out all creamy with little blonde curls. The drawings didn't look anything like real kids, but I liked them. One day I'll get them framed."

The woman picked up Mary's lunch tray. "I'll be back in a while with a little weak tea and some crackers. We'll see if that will make you feel better." Mary groaned and put a fat hand over her pale, dry lips. She closed her eyes and allowed her round arm to drop dramatically over the side of the bed.

Edna finished her preliminary drawing in an hour, and standing back, checked the perspective. Satisfied that there was nothing terribly out of proportion, she went into the bathroom and ran water in the tub to soak the rag. Rolling the large paper carefully, she carried it back to her easel and re-clamped it, returning to the bathroom to fill her collection of plastic cups.

Back at her easel, the painter set to work excitedly. A crimson wash moved energetically over the paper below the face and shoulders of an emerging Mary. Satisfied that she could do no more with the background and clothing until the crimson dried, Edna began on Mary's face, yellow ochre flowing with the contours she'd made with her pencil. She dabbed here and there with red-orange, tinting cheekbones and forehead and nose where shadow and light met. Burnt umber flowed from her brush at the hairline to darken at the base of Mary's trademark doughnut.

Once she finished Mary's face, Edna stretched and took a break. Wandering down the hall, she discovered a cart laden with afternoon drinks and helped herself to two cups of clear, hot tea. Mary opened her eyes at Edna's return. "Lady Edna's brought the queen tea," she said cheerfully.

"You're feeling better. I can tell by your colour," Edna observed.

Mary allowed Edna to prop pillows behind her head and cover her legs with a light blanket. "We don't know why we should," she said with a sniff of self pity. "It's been ages since we've been able to eat."

Sitting in their one decent chair, Edna took a teacup from the bedside table. Mary peered into her cup. "But Lady Edna, it's clear," she said sadly. "We take our tea with cream and sugar."

"Cream in tea," exclaimed Edna. "How absolutely revolting. At least taste it this way." She watched as Mary snorted over the cup and followed the snort with a noisy sip. "See? It's quite refreshing clear," Edna insisted.

Mary sipped again. "We have to confess, we feel quite queer," she said. "Like when the hubby died and we found ourselves alone with our bugs."

"Something unexpected came from that," Edna reminded her.

Mary nodded at Edna's easel. "How's the picture?"

"You're not to look at it until I make the presentation," said Edna. "I think I'll be able to finish it by tomorrow morning. Can you manage to remain supine for a bit longer. It should be dry enough to work on a little later, and I'd like to get your robes done before dinner."

"Robes?" echoed Mary.

"Certainly," Edna assured her. "A queen wears robes. I think you'll be pleased with your First Advisor's work. You might even want to have your portrait properly framed." Mary wriggled down to her former position to relax under Edna's steady gaze.

After an hour of painting, Edna draped her green robe over the easel. Satisfied that nothing could be seen, she lay on her bed and asked Mary to tell her more about her bugs.

"Why?" Mary asked in a decidedly suspicious tone.

"I need detail for my work," Edna said. She closed her eyes and waited.

Mary hoisted herself into her nest of pillows. "If Lady Edna promises not to tell, we'll let her in on a little secret."

"Better than the window in the bathroom?"

"Lady Edna might not think it is as good as that," she said, delighted that Edna appreciated the window. "We hoped it would help to boost her spirits."

"I owe you a great debt, for the window and for the sparring match you put me through when they drugged me."

"We'll take our painting as payment."

"Well, now," Edna said, her eyes still closed. "What's this other secret?"

"Edna won't believe this," Mary started a little breathlessly, "but our bugs have followed us here." She rippled happily. "We found them last night. When we turned on the lights down there, they danced as beautifully as they ever did back home. Pirouettes and pas-de-deux and all that other fancy French stuff. But they weren't sure it was we and skittered off almost as soon as we turned on the lights."

"Cockroaches in the kitchen!" Edna exclaimed. "I suppose I should do something about them as well, but there are so many more important problems to tackle first. How's your tummy?"

"We're sure it's getting smaller by the second. We wish we knew what we ate last night that upset our system."

"It wasn't anything you ate," Edna told her.

"How would Lady Edna know?"

"Because I know. There are some things you think you ought to know, some things you think you know, and some things you know you know. This is one of those things I know I know."

"Whatever it is Lady Edna knows, we know we wish we felt hungry," Mary said morosely.

"You'll soon feel hungry for other things, Mary."

"Oh, leave us alone," Mary commanded. "We don't want to be hungry for anything but chocolate sundaes and peanut brittle and fudge."

"That's something you think you know. But you know what you really know."

"We don't know what Lady Edna's talking about. We know we know that!" Mary groaned a little. "Still, we're very glad Lady Edna is here. We've decided she can keep her title. There's no one else to give it to anyway."

"You'd better dream up more of them because before you know it, you'll have lots of playmates."

Mary looked dubious. "Really? How is Lady Edna going to manage that?"

Edna blinked her fine brown eyes. "I'm just going to paint. It's what I love to do and so I'm going to do it."

Mary rubbed her empty stomach. "We'll believe it when we see it."

"You will," Edna agreed. "Seeing and believing help us to know what we know." She jumped up suddenly and went to her locker. "I almost forgot my first project," she said, pulling out the sketch she'd put away earlier. "I want to finish this before dinner."

"Are those the warts Edna drew last night?"

Edna laughed on her way to the bathroom for clean water. In an hour she'd finished her first still life. She left it to dry when she went down to supper.

Later, Mary watched Edna daub first at her portrait and then at the head nurse's, wondering where her First Advisor got her energy. Edna kept working until eight o'clock when one of the nurses came in to give Mary a sponge bath. In a moment of generosity, the nurse asked if Edna wanted one. Edna told her that she preferred a proper bath. To her great delight, the nurse allowed her to soak for an hour, the door closed, the window opened and raising gooseflesh.

After her bath, Edna took up her painting with a frenzied energy that further exhausted Mary. Their lights should have been turned off at nine, but Edna kept working and, miraculously, no one interfered. By ten o'clock she had completed both portraits. When she was satisfied with them, she placed the paintings on the floor across from their beds, tidied her art things, and made one final trip to the bathroom to wash paint brushes and empty cups.

In bed, the blind raised and the clear, starry sky spilling in through the heavy wire mesh covering the windows, Edna was too excited to sleep. In just two days she'd completed three paintings, crude compared to the masters who could wash and wash and never muddy the colour that created their delicate landscapes but still, she was happy with them. She lay on her bed, clenching and unclenching her long-boned fingers, from time to time looking from them to her paint supplies next to the urn on the window sill. After an hour, she fell asleep, a study in light and shadow, the moon's light washing over her.

SIX

In the days that followed, Edna felt her technical ability grow around her life the way she'd seen ivy find purchase on an old, dying Black Walnut tree in her childhood garden. Some vital partnership animated her again. She would stand at her easel in the sunroom staring at her drawings and waiting patiently for the next tendril to hook into her flesh to infuse her with the knowledge she needed to capture what she saw hidden and yet yearning for expression in her subjects. Sometimes Mrs. Strowd would play the piano as Edna painted. No one understood the vagaries of her musical gift, but everyone enjoyed it when she sat, Mr. Barren's teeth in her wide opened jaws, the music flowing as effortlessly from her fingers as the washes flowing from Edna's brushes.

At the end of her second week at Tranquil Time, Diana found Edna at her easel absorbed in a study of Mr. Barren's hands. "They're wonderful, aren't they?" Edna mused. "I don't know why he never played. Those hands long for a cello, or perhaps a bass fiddle, maybe even a Stradivarius." She wiped her brushes on the skirt of her dress before sitting down in the sun with the young woman.

"I've got some news," Diana began. "But I'm afraid it's not good."

Edna laughed a little ruefully. "These days, what news is? Come on. Those hands won't wait forever."

"The pill you gave me," Diana said. "I had a hunch about the medication the doctor was using and it turns out I was right." She looked steadily at Edna. "It's a version of one of the first tranquilizers ever developed, effective if taken once or twice . . . ."

"Yes, yes. Please Diana, get to the point. I'm anxious to get back to work."

Diana continued. "Used over a long period of time, months, years, it produces symptoms that 'mimic' senility." She pushed her hair back from her forehead. "If stopped abruptly, the symptoms often escalate and the patients can become completely irrational. Sometimes they kill themselves, and sometimes . . . ."

"Is that what they were giving Lizzie?" Edna asked.

"I believe it was," Diana said.

"She stopped taking it . . . as you say, abruptly. Why didn't she become irrational?"

Diana closed her eyes, dreading the revelation she had to make. "The other thing that is known to happen with abrupt cessation is . . . death."

Edna was quiet for a long time. "She trusted him, thought of him as a son," she said with quiet rage. "And there he was, drugging her to the eyeballs to keep her compliant." She closed her eyes and then opened them in a flash of insight. "No wonder it's so damned hard to get a bed here. He dopes them up over there and takes them off the stuff when a bed over here needs filling. He's worse than Dr. Frankenstein."

"Far worse," said Diana. "Dr. Frankenstein was wrong, but he loved the Monster he created and took full responsibility for the damage it did." She reached for Edna's hand. "The story runs tomorrow. It doesn't change what he's been doing to all his patients, but at least it will raise awareness about over medicating residents."

"Has he left town?"

"I'm afraid so. I inadvertently tipped him off when I took the pill you gave me to Sunset Lodge and asked Mrs. Wallace if it looked the same as the reverend's medication. Miss Wilson caught me and must have told him we were checking out the meds."

"Ah," said Edna. "After what I heard about that poor creature's history, I'm surprised she managed the lodge as well as she did."

"You know about her suicide attempt? And how she met the doctor?" Edna nodded. Restless, the writer stood. "She's the key to possible prosecution. I hope she's stable enough – and courageous enough – to handle it."

"Did she cooperate with you?"

"Not initially. She was hostile and even defended him when I asked her about the medication. But when she learned that Mrs. Wallace confirmed it was the same stuff he'd been giving people for years – it's funny, I was all bluff because nothing had been confirmed at that point – she broke down and admitted she knew he was using it to the lodgers' detriment. As soon as she admitted that, all the misery behind that terrible scar came pouring out. In the end, she was more like a frightened child than a middle-aged, competent, professional woman."

"Well, that explains our new pills," said Edna. "I must tell Mary."

"You mean they've already changed the medication here?" Edna nodded. "Wow," Diana said. "That means that in spite of the way he used her, she warned him. He'll have covered his tracks by now."

"Do you think the people here will suffer with the change?"

"My lab contact tells me there's something on the market that ameliorates the effects of prolonged tranquilizer use. Gross damage can't be reversed quickly, but there is the possibility of recovery. I imagine that's what he switched to when he knew he'd been caught."

"Well, that's something," Edna said. "The new stuff knocked everyone out for a day or two, but most seem more alert now." She pressed her temples in the attempt to take in the fact that a medical doctor charged with supporting the health and well being of his patients had been intentionally over-medicating them. "Do you think he'll go to jail?"

"The CMA and government inspectors say there will be an inquiry. But time's on his side, and the fact that it's not illegal to prescribe something that is still on the market, even though it has been proved ineffective and even dangerous. With all the notoriety, he probably won't even attempt to practice here now. I wish exile were just the beginning of a life of shame, but he's a Canadian physician. No doubt he'll set up in some clinic south of the border and continue to rake in the money." The writer brightened suddenly. "Oh, I almost forgot. I brought you something to cheer you up. I knew you'd need cheering when you heard the news."

Edna eyed the small box Diana took from her bag. "I hope it's not a pill box," she said.

Diana laughed. Inside the small box Edna discovered copper-hoop earrings similar to those Diana had been wearing when the women first met.

"You'll have to have your ears pierced now. Maybe one of the nurses here will do it for you."

Edna stood. "Do you think I can trust them with a needle?" She embraced Diana, linked arms with her, and walked her to the door.

With a cry of delight, Diana stopped to admire Edna's first painting, a spray of silver pennies, each pod luminously revealing its interior seeds. After she completed it, Edna had taped it to the wall for inspiration. "You did these," Diana exclaimed. "Sell them to me."

Edna shook her head. "I'll do some others for you if you like. Each time I finish a sketch, I add another circle." Overwhelmed by sudden grief, she fought for control. "Lizzie called them Moonwort but I heard moon warts – she said I made her feel like them. I've thought of them as warts ever since. Just like us. It doesn't seem so funny anymore, now that I know people are actively attempting to get rid of us."

Diana embraced her. "Hey, just remember," she whispered. "Warts are practically impossible to get rid of."

"I suppose they are," Edna answered, but without comfort. Lizzie was gone. The doctor managed to get rid of her.

The following week, Mrs. Wallace arrived in a dither over Diana's article about the lodge. As luck would have it, when the minister's widow arrived Edna was in the sunroom adding the final touches to a portrait of Mrs. Wallace and Miss Jones commemorating their evening at The Biffy. Edna was thrilled to hear that Anna and Frank Bertini had come as well and were waiting outside to be invited in.

Edna led her young visitors to the sunroom, eager for news. After they'd arranged themselves in a tight little group, Anna and Frank told her they'd read both Diana's article and the doctor's rebuttal. Apparently the Canadian Medical College of Physicians endorsed the use of pharmaceuticals to decrease the distress of old age. He wouldn't be charged with anything, but Diana's story raised enough questions to prompt him to find greener pastures in which to practice his healing arts. Apparently Sunset Lodge and Tranquil Time were for sale.

"So," Edna said after listening to their various opinions of the articles and their rumbling aftershocks. "We've turned out to be quite a can of worms."

"It's just dreadful," said Mrs. Wallace, plumping herself in a basket chair like a broody hen. "Everybody is talking about the scandal, but no one seems to know what to do or whom to blame. I felt quite sick about Mr. Wallace's tragic end until you comforted me, Mrs. Carver. And then I read about the side effects of the drug the doctor gave the reverend and the whole thing made sense. He *was* getting on in years, and of course his weight didn't help." She blinked rapidly. "Still, it's hard to believe a little pill could overrule the Almighty's plans for a soul, as it were, and prompt him to take his life instead of letting the Lord bring him home in his own good time."

"What about Wilson?" Edna asked.

"The critical nature of Miss Mallory's piece came as quite a shock to her," confided the widow. "She picked up and left the very day we read the story. No one's seen her since. The Board of Directors hired an interim manager and is determining the next step. I've heard rumours about a questionnaire to be filled out by residents. Imagine that, Mrs. Carver. They might think to ask us what we'd like for a change."

Edna listened to this remarkable news as she watched Anna casually move to sit beside Mrs. Strowd at the piano, apparently untroubled by the oversized teeth. As the young girl picked out the melody of "Heart and Soul", Mrs. Strowd played the bass as seriously as she played her Bach toccatas. Edna felt a wonderful rightness at the sight of this unlikely pair. "Anna," she said impulsively. "How would you like to be resident hairdresser here?"

"Sure," Anna answered, playing with a delicacy that sharply contrasted to her usual violent approach to the keyboards she mangled during band practice.

Frank got up to examine Edna's work, looking from Mrs. Wallace to the easel. "If I come over after school," he said, "could you find the time to teach me what you do?"

"Of course," Edna said.

Hearing unfamiliar voices, Mrs. O'Shea bustled into the room. "Hi," Edna said, gathering the head nurse into their company as if she were a strand of cotton necessary to complete a tatted pattern. "Meet Frank and Anna, friends from my old neighbourhood. They're going to come by regularly. Anna's a hairdresser and Frank is very good with his hands. He'll make things for you."

"You and your plans, Mrs. Carver," Mrs. O'Shea said. "Don't forget, our people need rest. We can't have any unsettling noise."

"The weather's fine now," Edna said brightly, smiling as she helped Mrs. Wallace to her feet to officially introduce her to the head nurse. "He'll do all the noisy work outside. We need lawn furniture, you'll agree, and bookshelves and plant stands for all the rooms. According to *Psychology Today*, plants are marvelous air purifiers." Edna distracted the head nurse from her objections by introducing Mrs. Wallace. "Here is our social coordinator at the lodge. I'm sure she can be persuaded to work her magic here at Tranquil Time. She sings like an angel, as well. We might start a choir, Mrs. O'Shea. What do you think?" Mrs. Wallace blushed with pleasure.

Edna resumed her painting, working on the image of the piano that was central to the portrait while Frank stood behind her, watching intently. She finished just as Mrs. O'Shea and Mrs. Wallace concluded their long, rambling, and amicable conversation.

"It is inspiring to find that you are so finely tuned to the necessity of beautiful, stimulating surroundings for your residents," Mrs. Wallace was saying as Edna unclamped the portrait of Mrs. Wallace's performance with Miss Jones at The Biffy.

Mrs. O'Shea glanced at the painting and then at Mrs. Strowd. "I should think you'd be anxious to get rid of those teeth," she muttered more to herself than to their pianist. "How do you think it makes me feel to see things like this day in and day out?" She shook her finger at Mrs. Strowd before returning to Mrs. Wallace. "You see what I have to contend with? And she's not too bad compared to some of them." The head nurse straightened her spine. "When all the papers are signed and I'm officially in charge, I'll be making some changes, I can tell you."

The minister's widow, engrossed in Edna's gift, shook her head with wonder. "It is so beautiful, Mrs. Carver. I know Miss Jones will love it too," she said as tears rolled down her cheeks.

Edna hugged her. "Come again, Wally, and bring the little pepper pot with you." She turned to Anna and Frank. "I'm so glad you've found us. Do you think you might persuade anyone else at the school to come the next time you visit?"

Anna looked up from her examination of Mrs. Strowd's hair. "I can ask the kids in hairdressing. God, this place stinks! Don't they know about Lysol?"

Edna linked arms with the tall blonde girl. "They don't know half as much as you do."

Reluctantly, Frank returned Edna's most recent portrait to Mrs. Wallace and joined his sister and Edna as they walked down the hall. "Most of the guys have part-time jobs," he said. "But I'll ask around." A fey Mrs. Wallace followed them, completely under the spell of Edna's painting.

Edna breathed in the damp spring morning and studied her young friends as they accompanied Mrs. Wallace down the winding red-brick pathway to the street. She took a few moments to send her blessing out to the gardens and then returned to the sunroom to organize her afternoon work. Mrs. Strowd sat at the piano, her hands resting in her lap. Edna prepared her paper before joining Mrs. Strowd on the narrow bench.

"You've got your own teeth," she said quietly. "You'll find them somewhere." She made a quick sketch as Mrs. Strowd looked up at her, suddenly agitated. "There," she said, handing her the drawing. Mrs. Strowd began to cry.

Before dinner, Edna found Mary circling and bending in response to some inner music. She watched her roommate from the doorway, estimating Mary's current weight loss to be about ten pounds. "You look wonderful," she said, comparing the physical Mary to the Mary in the painting hanging over the queen's bed. "Why don't you get the others moving like that? Mrs. Strowd is playing fairly regularly these days. I bet Mrs. O'Shea won't mind if a few of us gather to dance in the halls. They're wide enough for a good sized group."

Mary stopped in mid-twirl. "Our own cucarachas!" she exclaimed, inspired. "Lady Edna is a genius. By the way, Myrtle's been working with that physiotherapist since you hung up her portrait in the sunroom. I don't think she knew how bad she'd gotten. Maybe exercise will be the new trend. And we," she said, burying an index finger in her talcum-powdered cleavage, "will lead the way."

"Mrs. O'Shea will probably balk at first," said Edna. "But what we heard is true. She's buying the place. When the deed is signed, she's likely to say yes to anything that makes Tranquil Time a great place to spend one's golden years. Her heart's good. She just kept questionable company for a while."

"That's it then," Mary said happily. "We'll begin dance classes." Mary rushed off to speak to the other third-floor residents about joining her cucarachas. Edna added to her growing list of art supplies for her sunroom sittings. When she felt organized, she lay on her bed, the urn tucked in to her side. She rested, daydreaming, until dinner time when Mary returned, triumphant with potential dancers. The women walked to the dining room together to feast on homemade spaghetti instead of their usual canned fare.

The next morning, Mr. Barren, Mrs. Strowd, Mary, and Edna descended in the elevator to participate in their first dance class. Mary requested something sprightly to demonstrate the dance moves, and Mrs. Strowd obliged with Tchaikovsky's "November Sleigh Ride". Edna danced for a while, and then wandered back to her easel to exchange somber glances with Mrs. Strowd before she began the pianist's portrait. As Mrs. Strowd played, Edna painted. In time, several of the first-floor residents joined Mary's dance or wandered in to the sunroom to watch Edna and Mrs. Strowd create their art.

After a meeting with her board, Mrs. O'Shea discovered the group with more surprise than anger. She watched for a few minutes before doing a couple of twirls and then saying to Mary, "I think you should be doing this regularly, now that you've decided to slim down." Mary ignored her to focus upon the imaginary scarf she trailed behind her as she ricocheted back and forth across the hallway.

The head nurse found Edna at her easel, nodding her approval at the puddling colours revealing Mrs. Strowd at the piano. She studied the painting for a few moments and then sat in a nearby chair, ostensibly studying the lawn beyond the windows. "You're daughter's such a lovely woman," she said quite casually after a time. Edna waited. "We could use her help here," the head nurse said finally.

"Do you think the doctor will go to jail?" Edna asked.

"Jail? My goodness, no. He'll likely take advantage of one of the many opportunities to join a few like-minded colleagues who've opened clinics," Mrs. O'Shea said, "in Myrtle Beach, or Miami, or Galveston." Her face expressed regret as she looked at Edna squarely. "Whatever you might think, Mrs. Carver, I never liked the way he ran this place. When it's officially mine, it will be a real home, one we can all be proud of. Do you think your daughter would help me transform the place?"

"Call her," Edna said, concentrating on the painting.

"I've already reviewed the budget," Mrs. O'Shea confided. "I hired professional house painters this morning." She waited for Edna's response, but Edna was too preoccupied to comment. "Mrs. Carver," she said again. "I need your daughter's help. I'd like this place to look respectable if it's going to be mine."

Edna laughed. "Well, looking respectable is certainly in Marion's line all right. And she and her church group are always looking for new projects to water with their river of good works."

Mrs. O'Shea beamed with anticipated pride of ownership. "With all that controversy over the Metaphin, I've put a hold on next month's meds until we've completed an assessment. You know," she added confidentially, "I've always been a great believer in warm milk in the evening and coffee in the morning." She sighed contentedly. "Cutting all the unnecessary medications from the budget will free up money for necessities."

"Like more nurses," said Edna, locking eyes with Mrs. O'Shea.

Mrs. O'Shea nodded. "Yes, staff, of course. And I have to make sure we meet all the safety regulations. We need to install new fire escapes before the inspectors come. Oh, that reminds me," she said, standing. "I must make some calls." She nodded at Mrs. Strowd and left Edna to her work.

A month later, the painters came, and the cold, dark-green walls warmed beneath a coat of Benjamin Moore's Sunflower Yellow latex. Paint fumes required open windows and before long the residual smells of ammonia and feces disappeared entirely.

In her zeal to beautify, Mrs. O'Shea had the painters paint the outside trim as well. To accomplish this, the workers removed all the mesh screens on the upper windows, whitewashing these in the large work area behind the nursing home. They were forgotten in the bustle of change and remained stacked neatly behind the old house until the day the building inspectors insisted they be re-installed. In the meantime, the house had recovered its dignity along with a full complement of increasingly comfortable inhabitants.

When Diana returned, she hardly recognized the place. She found Edna wool gathering in the sunroom, surrounded by the many portraits she'd done since moving to the nursing home. Edna delighted in the visit. "Just look what you've done," she said, suggesting the entire house and grounds with her wide open arms.

Diana laughed. "I only took care of the Metaphin. Besides, I've done too much research to be pleased with myself. At its worst, this place was much better, even before its change of ownership, than several I've seen since I left the lodge."

Edna sat quietly, her head to one side, absorbing Diana's tales of drug overuse, unsanitary conditions, and inadequate caretaking because owners pocketed excessive profits instead of re-investing them in the care of their clients. "It's turned into an odyssey," Diana told her. "I'll have something to write about for the rest of my life."

"Marion's being drawn into the same line of work," Edna confided happily.

Diana smiled at this irony. "How on earth did you manage that?"

"I didn't manage a thing," Edna said. "It's all Mrs. O'Shea's doing. Ever since she discovered the health benefits of beauty, she's been pestering Marion's church group to volunteer."

"Maintenance work," Diana said laughing.

Edna joined in the hilarity. "I wanted to be a fly on the wall when they visited the second floor, but I had my own visitors. I have to say, they handled the horror very well. And now they're changing the place with all kinds of loving attention to what residents want."

Just then Mary came in and did a little shimmy for Diana. "Queen Mary," Edna said, as proud as any mother, "now teaches dance three days a week to our ambulatory brothers and sisters. She's very good. You should stay for a class."

Mary smiled regally. "We just came down to tell Lady Edna that her daughter's here. And it isn't Sunday. What can it mean?"

"Damn," said Edna. "I planned to get started on something for Anna, but if Marion's here, it must be time for me to begin a volunteers portrait."

Diana studied the painted Myrtle Jenkins, smiling and upright, her baseball cap at a jaunty angle on her lovely old head. "One day," Diana said with admiration, "you'll have to paint me."

Edna gently touched the young woman's cheek. "If you like, but it won't hold any surprises. You see as well as I do."

On her way to the door, Diana stopped at the piano where Edna had placed the small carving of Don Quixote Frank Bertini had given her. Edna promised to make introductions. "You'll have to come back when Frank and Anna are here." She pointed to Don Quixote. "That's Frank's work."

With infinite tenderness, Diana touched the delicate carving, turning to Edna with brimming eyes. "You're wearing your earrings," she said.

"Mrs. O'Shea pierced my ears in exchange for her portrait." Edna's eyes shone. "I absolutely love them, Diana. You were a dear to remember." The women embraced in a puddle of morning sunshine.

By July's end, a variety of Frank Bertini's designs, including platform swings, chairs, sitting arbors, and rockers – dotted Tranquil Time's front gardens. When the weather turned humid and hot, several of Edna's fellow residents dozed beneath a large oak in an assortment of comfortable wooden chairs as Edna painted nearby. If her legs grew tired, Edna made herself comfortable on a bench Frank made especially for her.

Whenever Edna found herself in the garden, she surreptitiously scanned the flower beds and shrubbery for Elizabeth's perfect resting place. It troubled her terribly that no matter how tempting the increasingly beautiful grounds, she couldn't seem to find a suitable home for her dearest friend. One sultry day in late July Mrs. Wallace and Miss Jones surprised Edna in her search for Lizzie's final resting place, calling out as they walked spritely to her easel beneath the oak.

It was a wilting weekday afternoon when Miss Jones peered at the unfinished sketch on Edna's easel in search of the unexpected mystical quality she had discovered in her own portrait. Mrs. Wallace sat on an oversized rocker and rhapsodized over the lovely gardens. "It really is too beautiful," she exclaimed. "You must be so happy here, lolling about as it were, drinking in God's providence."

Edna found herself admiring her friend's compulsive optimism. "How's Sunset Lodge these days."

Miss Jones's hair exploded into motion. "You won't believe it, Mrs. Carver. We just found out this morning. We're going co-operative."

"And we have our own piano, a gift from a new resident's family," Mrs. Wallace said.

Edna brightened. "That is good news."

"Weird, I'd say," Miss Jones added. "Your painting of me playing and Mrs. Wallace singing arrived one week, and the piano arrived out of the blue the very next. It was as if . . . ."

"I wouldn't think a woman who patronizes The Biffy would find anything out of the ordinary," Edna said, laughing. "By the way, how is Merle?"

"You know she's set her cap for Arthur," Miss Jones said with enthusiastic disgust.

"Hah!" Edna exploded. "I can just see the pair of them sniping over dinner. That's what I call just deserts."

Mrs. Wallace said, "Charity," and changed the subject. "Have those lovely children been faithful in their visits?" Edna pointed to Anna at work combing out Myrtle's hair, the old woman sitting almost upright in her chair.

"How wonderful," Mrs. Wallace said, at once leaving her friends to encourage Anna.

Glad to be alone with Edna, Miss Jones leaned into her with a conspirator's enthusiasm. "Tell me, you old wizard. How do you do it?"

Edna continued to paint. "Do what?"

Miss Jones would not be put off. "We won the pot that night, at The Biffy, you know. I've got quite a bit of my share left. We could play the horses."

Edna laughed uproariously. "I'd say yes, but you'd lose all your money" she said, dabbing at her eyes. "That's not the sort of thing I see."

"It's a shame," Miss Jones said. She accepted Edna's invitation to tea in the sunroom with a decidedly gloomy, "Oh, tea, all right then," and walked with Edna to the house. Seeing them, Mrs. Wallace left Anna to follow.

Inside, they found Mary's cucarachas spinning and twirling in the bright yellow hallway as if someone had only that moment surprised them by turning on a light. Miss Jones slipped into the group to dip and twirl once or twice, but Mrs. Wallace, obeying the strict 'No Dance' rule of her religious sect, offered the group a stiff smile before slipping by the dancers into the sunroom.

After a quick survey of the portraits on the wall Mrs. Wallace and Miss Jones nodded knowingly at one another. "Do you like Merle's portrait?" Edna asked, noting the look that passed between them.

"That's her all right," Miss Jones said, studying the painting of Merle at the stove in the lodge kitchen. "And that's where she can be found helping prepare lunch every Tuesday and Thursday. Mrs. Carver," Miss Jones said and then lowered her voice. "It's such a pity you won't consider the race track. We'd make a killing."

Edna laughed again.

Mrs. Wallace quizzed Edna about a painting. "Who is this lovely man?" she asked, indicating a portrait she hadn't seen before.

Edna closed her eyes for a moment. "He was our resident transvestite. He died two days ago. These are his hands." She pointed to the pencil study she'd made when she first arrived at the nursing home.

"He looks as though he should be playing something," said Miss Jones.

The minister's widow was forming a question about transvestites when Marion Andrews interrupted her train of thought. Marion offered the minister's widow her most charming smile.

"Hello," she cried. "I haven't seen you since Mother moved. How well you look, Mrs. Wallace. I've been meaning to visit the lodge to say hello to all Mother's friends, but they have been keeping me very busy over here."

Mrs. Wallace embraced Marion as one of her own. "Mrs. Andrews," she said, nodding approvingly at her volunteer's smock. "You are bringing water to the thirsty."

Marion flushed with pleasure. "I read to a dear old soul on Mother's wing. She seems to enjoy it."

"Of course she does," Mrs. Wallace said as she touched the sleeve of Marion's smock reverently. "It is so very good of you."

"I belong to a group at my church and after Mother made her move, I encouraged our members to devote some of our time to her new friends. Not that I've forgotten her old ones . . . ," she added, taking Mrs. Wallace's hand. She dropped her voice. "But they're just so much needier here than at the lodge, Mrs. Wallace. For some, it's the end of the road."

Hearing this, Edna and Miss Jones couldn't help but laugh. Mrs. Wallace and Marion ignored their raucous response, politely murmuring about the sad state of some of Tranquil Time's more neglected residents. "Many of them never got out at all until we began to take them," Marion said. "It's shocking the way families neglect the people who've given their whole lives to them. Really shocking."

"I know," Mrs. Wallace agreed. "The reverend often used to preach about honouring thy father and thy mother. But the world has changed so much. People don't hold to the old values anymore."

Marion agreed absently, diverted by a dark smudge at the hem of her white eyelet skirt. She rubbed the smudge vigorously before remembering to advertise her newest project. "You must bring some of mother's old friends to our rummage sale. We're raising funds to frame her pictures and to buy little odds and ends that will make the rooms more like home."

"Like televisions," snarled Edna from across the room.

"I'm getting one," confided Miss Jones. "Now we're a cooperative, we can furnish our rooms the way we like. Most of the others are going to leave them as is to avoid the bother, but I'm getting a great big Sony Trinitron for my bureau. Come over and watch a hockey game any time you feel the urge to have a good time on Saturday nights."

"Thanks," said Edna, thinking she would just as soon watch Mary. She looked into the hall where her roommate shimmied, her face pink with effort and pleasure as she twirled and dipped gracefully. Dancers came and went following the dictates of their personal tastes and abilities, and Mary delighted in presiding over this ebb and flow.

Marion seized this opportunity to end her visit with Mrs. Wallace. "Wasn't it good of Mrs. Wallace to come, Mother? Did you thank her?" Doing her best to postpone thinking about how she might remove the smudge on her skirt, Edna's daughter smiled charmingly at both women.

"Oh, no thanks necessary," Mrs. Wallace said, pressing Marion's hand. "Your mother brightened many a grey day for us back at the lodge. Miss Jones agrees, I know."

But Miss Jones, intolerant of boredom, had joined Mrs. Strowd at the piano, fascinated by the way her hands moved so knowingly over the keys. From time to time Mrs. Strowd looked up at her, wishing for her old disguise and silently cursing Edna and her finished portrait where it hung on the wall next to the silver dollars.

"I came down here for a reason," Marion said importantly. "Oh, yes. That Frank asked me to give you a message. He said to tell you he got the lid off. He's bringing it over tomorrow. What's he talking about, Mother? What lid?"

"Private business," Edna answered with an enigmatic smile. "Where is he?"

"On the second floor. Painting a shuffleboard in the hallway," Marion answered stiffly. "His sister wants to do my hair, but Mr. Michael would never forgive me if I put myself in the hands of amateurs, good cause or no." Marion touched her golden curls as if the mere mention of Anna Bertini's name might cause them to wilt.

Edna took the portrait of Merle from the wall and, rolling it up said to Miss Jones, "See that Merle gets this, please. And tell her to give Arthur a real run for his money."

Miss Jones laughed. On her way down the hall, she brandished the rolled painting like a cudgel and, joining Mary's group, performed a final shimmy. Laughing, she disappeared through the sparkling beveled-glass doors at the end of the hall.

"She'd fit right in here," Edna said to Mrs. Wallace. "You'd have a good time, too, Wally." Mrs. Wallace kissed Edna's cheek awkwardly before squeezing past the group to head for the door. She looked back but Edna had already disappeared into the sunroom.

"But she's my daughter," Edna said. "Of all the people in the world I should be able to see . . . ."

Diana sprawled on the grass in front of Edna's easel. "Maybe that *should* is the trouble."

Edna looked down at her young friend and curled her upper lip dramatically. "You're too young to be that smart."

Diana grinned. "You're a painter. You work in symbols. What are hers?"

"In relation to me?" The young woman nodded. "She brings frocks, my dear, designer originals I wipe my brushes on." Diana rolled on her back and looked up into the leaves of what she'd come to feel was Edna's oak. August left city dwellers breathless and oppressed and her torrid flat often drove the writer to take refuge with Edna in Tranquil Time's garden.

"Ah, raiments," she said languidly. "Why do we dress? To cover our shame?" She looked up at Edna, inspired. "To protect us. From burning, freezing. To make us beautiful. To disguise our beauty."

Edna sat beside her on the grass. "Go back to shame."

"No," said Diana. "Constellations belong together, form a whole. You can't have shame without protectiveness."

Pensive, Edna touched the pale blue linen wave lapping around her legs. "She gave me this. She's always been so generous," she said, hating the resentment in her voice.

Quietly, Diana picked up this thread. "That's why it was fairly easy to decide to have my tubes tied. I didn't want to have children I suspected I wanted not for their own sakes but to make up for some lack in me."

"I loved her so," Edna said simply. "I shared every joy I had in the world, every poem, every sound, every colour."

"You must have expected something in return."

"I expected her to blossom. To thrive."

"She looks as though she's thriving to me."

"I don't equate fulfillment with being well heeled," Edna retorted.

"I don't either."

Both women glanced in the direction of the circular drive where Marion unloaded rummage from the trunk of her yellow Buick. Edna stared, wanting to see the internal promise she'd seen in the others she'd painted, but something impenetrable prevented her from seeing any more than her daughter's glossy surface. She thought of Mr. Barren. "Do you remember the old gentleman with the remarkably beautiful hands, the one who died recently?"

Diana thought for a minute and then nodded. "Yes, I do remember him. He was your musician without an instrument."

"Yes," said Edna. "For some reason, he was disconnected from his hands."

"Did you ever figure out why?"

"No, and he didn't either. When I asked him about his hands, he said he'd always felt as though they weren't his, as though they should have belonged to someone else." She glanced in the direction of an explosion of shouting. Across the lawn, Miss George shook her cane at an old man wearing a yellow toque and gaping blue bathrobe. Despite several vicious swipes in his direction, he proved too spry for her to land a blow. As Edna watched, the old woman began to torment a woman whose only offense was staring off into the hazy afternoon. "She can't leave people alone," Edna muttered. "And she's worse since becoming a major investor in this place." She touched her copper earrings, sending them swinging back and forth to gently bump her neck.

Diana squinted at her friend, backlit by the sun. "Do you want to hear one of the things I've discovered about mothers and daughters?"

"No," said Edna.

Diana laughed. "Sure you do. I think some daughters are so sensitive to the people who carry them for nine months that they intuit, almost perfectly, whatever it is their mothers yearn to express but don't – for whatever reason. So a mild, introverted woman finds herself with a daughter extroverted beyond belief. A feminist finds herself the mother of a little housewife in the making. And a dedicated bad girl finds she's brought St. Bernadette into the world." The writer paused before adding, "It's as if the daughter picks up, osmotically, on the mother's inability to express whatever is blocked and expresses it automatically, until she does her work and figures out who she is, separate and apart from her mother. It's quite a burden to carry someone else's unexpressed life."

"Did you carry anything around for your mother until you figured yourself out?"

"Her adventurousness, I think. She is still frightened of her own possibilities."

"That doesn't sound so terrible," Edna said.

"Perhaps not for me," Diana answered, rolling onto her stomach and propping her head on her hands.

Edna touched the blonde head. "Maybe that's the nature of life, each generation compensating for the fears and compulsions and triumphs of the previous one." She glanced at the blank paper on her easel. "How would you like a few of the moon's warts to take home with you today? If I remember correctly, I promised you a painting of Lunaria some time ago."

Before dinner, Edna discovered that Frank had left the urn for her in the sunroom and, cradling it, set off down the main hall glad to finally be able to fulfill Elizabeth Schmidt's wish to be scattered. Mrs. O'Shea came out of her office as Edna walked by.

"Mrs. Carver. It's supper time. Don't keep them waiting upstairs." Mystified, she watched Edna walk out of doors and was about to go after her when her telephone rang and the receptionist called her to the phone.

Edna wandered over the grass until she was beyond Tranquil Time's shadow and could feel the sun warm the top of her head. She looked around, unsure of her destination. After months exploring Tranquil Time's garden, she'd concluded it was too tame, too cultivated for Lizzie's final resting place. Lizzie, she knew, yearned as Edna did, for bramble, for secret thickets and thorns, for mystery.

After an hour of walking, Edna followed the sloping road leading into a dusky Rosedale Valley. Where the road straightened at the bottom, she stopped to look up to the Necropolis where it posed, an ancient ruin, at the top of the hill. A thicket hid the fence marking the beginning of the graveyard. She laboured up to it, stumbling to her knees once but managing to prevent the urn's contents from spilling. Out of breath, she collapsed a few feet from the dense shrubbery that marked the cusp of the hilltop. August had been a dry month and the grass pricked her through her light linen dress. She scratched at the parched ground, feebly at first, but after she put the urn between her legs and used both hands, she was able to fashion a shallow grave. A hot wind tugged at the red sash as she emptied the urn's contents into her lap.

Unfolding the red material, she began Elizabeth's eulogy. "Reflection, upon reflection, upon reflection." She smiled at the sky, knowing the moon charmed elsewhere on this hot, early evening. She closed her eyes to imagine its light. The hole she'd dug remained empty until Elizabeth found her way into the underbrush, sailing from Edna's hands into the dark tangle of welcoming vegetation. Her eyes filled as she sensed Elizabeth's pleasure in the place.

After she cried a little, Edna folded the red sash neatly and placed it in the small grave. Covering it over, she said tenderly, "Well, Marion, let's hope this is the end of all the ties that bind."

Sitting on the hillside, Edna enjoyed a growing sense of peace, greeting the dark when it finally came as an old friend. She walked home through its mystery, aware of a constant, ministering presence. At Tranquil Time's iron gates, she looked high into the sky.

With her first glimpse of Edna walking the red-brick path to the house, Mrs. O'Shea rushed down the front steps. She'd been keeping her vigil at the front door for hours, muttering curses and threats as she resisted the urge to call both Marion and the police. She stepped onto the path, the humid night muting her recriminations.

"Mrs. Carver," she cried. "You've given us all quite a scare. I cancelled an admissions appointment because of you. You are never to stay out this late again."

Edna turned from the black sky to smile at the nurse. "You didn't need to worry," she said serenely. "I was only out feeding the moon." She touched her fingers to her lips and tossed the kiss high into the air before allowing Mrs. O'Shea to shepherd her home.